The Phoenix Pick Anthology of
CLASSIC SCIENCE FICTION

The Phoenix Pick Anthology of

Classic Science Fiction

Second Edition

editor

Paul Cook

ISBN: 978-1-61242-301-2

Published by Phoenix Pick
an imprint of Arc Manor
P. O. Box 10339
Rockville, MD 20849-0339
www.ArcManor.com

CONTENTS

THE BIRTH MARK

Nathaniel Hawthorne

NATHANIEL HAWTHORNE (1804-1864), born in Massachusetts, was an early major figure in American literature. He was a member of the New England Renaissance (along with Emerson, Thoreau, and Bronson Alcott) and was a life-long critic in his writings of the Puritan experience in New England. His fictional deacons, doctors, chemists, botanists, mesmerists and inventors usually had a destructive bent (as in "The Birthmark") and their actions often resulted in tragedy. Hawthorne's most enduring masterpiece is *The Scarlet Letter* and his stories and novels form the bedrock of American writing in the 19th century and continue to be popular to this day.

IN the latter part of the last century there lived a man of science, an eminent proficient in every branch of natural philosophy, who not long before our story opens had made experience of a spiritual affinity more attractive than any chemical one. He had left his laboratory to the care of an assistant, cleared his fine countenance from the furnace smoke, washed the stain of acids from his fingers, and persuaded a beautiful woman to become his wife. In those days when the comparatively recent discovery of electricity and other kindred mysteries of Nature seemed to open paths into the region of miracle, it was not unusual for the love of science to rival the love of woman in its depth and absorbing energy. The higher intellect, the imagination, the spirit, and even the heart might all find their congenial aliment in pursuits which, as some of their ardent votaries believed, would ascend from one step of powerful intelligence to another, until the philosopher should lay his hand on the secret of creative force and perhaps make new worlds for himself. We know not whether Aylmer possessed this degree of faith in man's ultimate control over Nature. He had devoted himself, however, too unreservedly to scientific studies ever to be weaned from them by any second passion. His love for his young wife might prove the stronger of the two; but it could only be by intertwining itself with his love of science, and uniting the strength of the latter to his own.

Such a union accordingly took place, and was attended with truly remarkable consequences and a deeply impressive moral. One day, very soon after their marriage, Aylmer sat gazing at his wife with a trouble in his countenance that grew stronger until he spoke.

"Georgiana," said he, "has it never occurred to you that the mark upon your cheek might be removed?"

"No, indeed," said she, smiling; but perceiving the seriousness of his manner, she blushed deeply. "To tell you the truth it has been so often called a charm that I was simple enough to imagine it might be so."

"Ah, upon another face perhaps it might," replied her husband; "but never on yours. No, dearest Georgiana, you came so nearly perfect from the hand of Nature that this slightest possible defect, which we hesitate whether to term a defect or a beauty, shocks me, as being the visible mark of earthly imperfection."

"Shocks you, my husband!" cried Georgiana, deeply hurt; at first reddening with momentary anger, but then bursting into tears. "Then why did you take me from my mother's side? You cannot love what shocks you!"

To explain this conversation it must be mentioned that in the centre of Georgiana's left cheek there was a singular mark, deeply interwoven, as it were, with the texture and substance of her face. In the usual state of her complexion—a healthy though delicate bloom—the mark wore a tint of deeper crimson, which imperfectly defined its shape amid the surrounding rosiness. When she blushed it gradually became more indistinct, and finally vanished amid the triumphant rush of blood that bathed the whole cheek with its brilliant glow. But if any shifting motion caused her to turn pale there was the mark again, a crimson stain upon the snow, in what Aylmer sometimes deemed an almost fearful distinctness. Its shape bore not a little similarity to the human hand, though of the smallest pygmy size. Georgiana's lovers were wont to say that some fairy at her birth hour had laid her tiny hand upon the infant's cheek, and left this impress there in token of the magic endowments that were to give her such sway over all hearts. Many a desperate swain would have risked life for the privilege of pressing his lips to the mysterious hand. It must not be concealed, however, that the impression wrought by this fairy sign manual varied exceedingly, according to the difference of temperament in the beholders. Some fastidious persons—but they were exclusively of her own sex—affirmed that the bloody hand, as they chose to call it, quite destroyed the effect of Georgiana's beauty, and rendered her countenance even hideous. But it would be as reasonable to say that one of those small blue stains which sometimes occur in the purest statuary marble would convert the Eve of Powers to a monster. Masculine observers, if the birthmark did not heighten their admiration, contented themselves with wishing it away, that the world might possess one living specimen of ideal loveliness without the semblance of a flaw. After his marriage—for he thought little or nothing of the matter before—Aylmer discovered that this was the case with himself.

Had she been less beautiful—if Envy's self could have found aught else to sneer at—he might have felt his affection heightened by the prettiness of this mimic hand, now vaguely portrayed, now lost, now stealing forth again and glimmering to and fro with every pulse of emotion that throbbed within her heart; but seeing her otherwise so perfect, he found this one defect grow more and more intolerable with every moment of their united lives. It was the fatal flaw of humanity which Nature, in one shape or another, stamps ineffaceably on all her productions, either to imply that they are temporary and finite, or that their perfection must be wrought by toil and pain. The crimson hand expressed the ineludible gripe in which mortality clutches the highest and purest of earthly mould, degrading them into kindred with the lowest, and even with the very brutes, like whom their visible frames return to dust. In this manner, selecting it as the symbol of his wife's liability to sin, sorrow, decay, and death, Aylmer's sombre imagination was not long in rendering the birthmark a frightful object, causing him more trouble and horror than ever Georgiana's beauty, whether of soul or sense, had given him delight.

At all the seasons which should have been their happiest, he invariably and without intending it, nay, in spite of a purpose to the contrary, reverted to this one disastrous topic. Trifling as it at first appeared, it so connected itself with innumerable trains of thought and modes of feeling that it became the central point of all. With the morning twilight Aylmer opened his eyes upon his wife's face and recognized the symbol of imperfection; and when they sat together at the evening hearth his eyes wandered stealthily to her cheek, and beheld, flickering with the blaze of the wood fire, the spectral hand that wrote mortality where he would fain have worshipped. Georgiana soon learned to shudder at his gaze. It needed but a glance with the peculiar expression that his face often wore to change the roses of her cheek into a deathlike paleness, amid which the crimson hand was brought strongly out, like a bass-relief of ruby on the whitest marble.

Late one night when the lights were growing dim, so as hardly to betray the stain on the poor wife's cheek, she herself, for the first time, voluntarily took up the subject.

"Do you remember, my dear Aylmer," said she, with a feeble attempt at a smile, "have you any recollection of a dream last night about this odious hand?"

"None! None whatever!" replied Aylmer, starting; but then he added, in a dry, cold tone, affected for the sake of concealing the real depth of his emotion, "I might well dream of it; for before I fell asleep it had taken a pretty firm hold of my fancy."

"And you did dream of it?" continued Georgiana, hastily; for she dreaded lest a gush of tears should interrupt what she had to say. "A terrible dream! I wonder that you can forget it. Is it possible to forget this one expression? 'It is in her heart now; we must have it out!' Reflect, my husband; for by all means I would have you recall that dream."

The mind is in a sad state when Sleep, the all-involving, cannot confine her spectres within the dim region of her sway, but suffers them to break forth, affrighting this actual life with secrets that perchance belong to a deeper one. Aylmer now remembered his dream. He had fancied himself with his servant Aminadab, attempting an operation for the removal of the birthmark; but the deeper went the knife, the deeper sank the hand, until at length its tiny grasp appeared to have caught hold of Georgiana's heart; whence, however, her husband was inexorably resolved to cut or wrench it away.

When the dream had shaped itself perfectly in his memory, Aylmer sat in his wife's presence with a guilty feeling. Truth often finds its way to the mind close muffled in robes of sleep, and then speaks with uncompromising directness of matters in regard to which we practise an unconscious self-deception during our waking moments. Until now he had not been aware of the tyrannizing influence acquired by one idea over his mind, and of the lengths which he might find in his heart to go for the sake of giving himself peace.

"Aylmer," resumed Georgiana, solemnly, "I know not what may be the cost to both of us to rid me of this fatal birthmark. Perhaps its removal may cause cureless deformity; or it may be the stain goes as deep as life itself. Again: do we know that there is a possibility, on any terms, of unclasping the firm grip of this little hand which was laid upon me before I came into the world?"

"Dearest Georgiana, I have spent much thought upon the subject," hastily interrupted Aylmer. "I am convinced of the perfect practicability of its removal."

"If there be the remotest possibility of it," continued Georgiana, "let the attempt be made at whatever risk. Danger is nothing to me; for life, while this hateful mark makes me the object of your horror and disgust—life is a burden which I would fling down with joy. Either remove this dreadful hand, or take my wretched life! You have deep science. All the world bears witness of it. You have achieved great wonders. Cannot you remove this little, little mark, which I cover with the tips of two small fingers? Is this beyond your power, for the sake of your own peace, and to save your poor wife from madness?"

"Noblest, dearest, tenderest wife," cried Aylmer, rapturously, "doubt not my power. I have already given this matter the deepest thought—thought which might almost have enlightened me to create a being less perfect than yourself. Georgiana, you have led me deeper than ever into the heart of science. I feel myself fully competent to render this dear cheek as faultless as its fellow; and then, most beloved, what will be my triumph when I shall have corrected what Nature left imperfect in her fairest work! Even Pygmalion, when his sculptured woman assumed life, felt not greater ecstasy than mine will be."

"It is resolved, then," said Georgiana, faintly smiling. "And, Aylmer, spare me not, though you should find the birthmark take refuge in my heart at last."

Her husband tenderly kissed her cheek—her right cheek—not that which bore the impress of the crimson hand.

The next day Aylmer apprised his wife of a plan that he had formed whereby he might have opportunity for the intense thought and constant watchfulness which the proposed operation would require; while Georgiana, likewise, would enjoy the perfect repose essential to its success. They were to seclude themselves in the extensive apartments occupied by Aylmer as a laboratory, and where, during his toilsome youth, he had made discoveries in the elemental powers of Nature that had roused the admiration of all the learned societies in Europe. Seated calmly in this laboratory, the pale philosopher had investigated the secrets of the highest cloud region and of the profoundest mines; he had satisfied himself of the causes that kindled and kept alive the fires of the volcano; and had explained the mystery of fountains, and how it is that they gush forth, some so bright and pure, and others with such rich medicinal virtues, from the dark bosom of the earth. Here, too, at an earlier period, he had studied the wonders of the human frame, and attempted to fathom the very process by which Nature assimilates all her precious influences from earth and air, and from the spiritual world, to create and foster man, her masterpiece. The latter pursuit, however, Aylmer had long laid aside in unwilling recognition of the truth—against which all seekers sooner or later stumble—that our great creative Mother, while she amuses us with apparently working in the broadest sunshine, is yet severely careful to keep her own secrets, and, in spite of her pretended openness, shows us nothing but results. She permits us, indeed, to mar, but seldom to mend, and, like a jealous patentee, on no account to make. Now, however, Aylmer resumed these half-forgotten investigations; not, of course, with such hopes or wishes as first suggested them; but because they involved much physiological truth and lay in the path of his proposed scheme for the treatment of Georgiana.

As he led her over the threshold of the laboratory, Georgiana was cold and tremulous. Aylmer looked cheerfully into her face, with intent to reassure her, but was so startled with the intense glow of the birthmark upon the whiteness of her cheek that he could not restrain a strong convulsive shudder. His wife fainted.

"Aminadab! Aminadab!" shouted Aylmer, stamping violently on the floor.

Forthwith there issued from an inner apartment a man of low stature, but bulky frame, with shaggy hair hanging about his visage, which was grimed with the vapors of the furnace. This personage had been Aylmer's underworker during his whole scientific career, and was admirably fitted for that office by his great mechanical readiness, and the skill with which, while incapable of comprehending a single principle, he executed all the details of his master's experiments. With his vast strength, his shaggy hair, his smoky aspect, and the indescribable earthiness that incrusted him, he seemed to represent man's physical nature; while Aylmer's slender figure, and pale, intellectual face, were no less apt a type of the spiritual element.

"Throw open the door of the boudoir, Aminadab," said Aylmer, "and burn a pastil."

"Yes, master," answered Aminadab, looking intently at the lifeless form of Georgiana; and then he muttered to himself, "If she were my wife, I'd never part with that birthmark."

When Georgiana recovered consciousness she found herself breathing an atmosphere of penetrating fragrance, the gentle potency of which had recalled her from her deathlike faintness. The scene around her looked like enchantment. Aylmer had converted those smoky, dingy, sombre rooms, where he had spent his brightest years in recondite pursuits, into a series of beautiful apartments not unfit to be the secluded abode of a lovely woman. The walls were hung with gorgeous curtains, which imparted the combination of grandeur and grace that no other species of adornment can achieve; and as they fell from the ceiling to the floor, their rich and ponderous folds, concealing all angles and straight lines, appeared to shut in the scene from infinite space. For aught Georgiana knew, it might be a pavilion among the clouds. And Aylmer, excluding the sunshine, which would have interfered with his chemical processes, had supplied its place with perfumed lamps, emitting flames of various hue, but all uniting in a soft, impurpled radiance. He now knelt by his wife's side, watching her earnestly, but without alarm; for he was confident in his science, and felt that he could draw a magic circle round her within which no evil might intrude.

"Where am I? Ah, I remember," said Georgiana, faintly; and she placed her hand over her cheek to hide the terrible mark from her husband's eyes.

"Fear not, dearest!" exclaimed he. "Do not shrink from me! Believe me, Georgiana, I even rejoice in this single imperfection, since it will be such a rapture to remove it."

"Oh, spare me!" sadly replied his wife. "Pray do not look at it again. I never can forget that convulsive shudder."

In order to soothe Georgiana, and, as it were, to release her mind from the burden of actual things, Aylmer now put in practice some of the light and playful secrets which science had taught him among its profounder lore. Airy figures, absolutely bodiless ideas, and forms of unsubstantial beauty came and danced before her, imprinting their momentary footsteps on beams of light. Though she had some indistinct idea of the method of these optical phenomena, still the illusion was almost perfect enough to warrant the belief that her husband possessed sway over the spiritual world. Then again, when she felt a wish to look forth from her seclusion, immediately, as if her thoughts were answered, the procession of external existence flitted across a screen. The scenery and the figures of actual life were perfectly represented, but with that bewitching, yet indescribable difference which always makes a picture, an image, or a shadow so much more attractive than the original. When wearied of this, Aylmer bade her cast her eyes upon a vessel containing a quantity of earth. She did so, with little interest at first; but was soon startled to perceive the germ of a plant shooting upward from the soil. Then came the slender stalk; the leaves gradually unfolded themselves; and amid them was a perfect and lovely flower.

"It is magical!" cried Georgiana. "I dare not touch it."

"Nay, pluck it," answered Aylmer, "pluck it, and inhale its brief perfume while you may. The flower will wither in a few moments and leave nothing save its brown seed vessels; but thence may be perpetuated a race as ephemeral as itself."

But Georgiana had no sooner touched the flower than the whole plant suffered a blight, its leaves turning coal-black as if by the agency of fire.

"There was too powerful a stimulus," said Aylmer, thoughtfully.

To make up for this abortive experiment, he proposed to take her portrait by a scientific process of his own invention. It was to be effected by rays of light striking upon a polished plate of metal. Georgiana assented; but, on looking at the result, was affrighted to find the features of the portrait blurred and indefinable; while the minute figure of a hand appeared where the cheek should have been. Aylmer snatched the metallic plate and threw it into a jar of corrosive acid.

Soon, however, he forgot these mortifying failures. In the intervals of study and chemical experiment he came to her flushed and exhausted, but seemed invigorated by her presence, and spoke in glowing language of the resources of his art. He gave a history of the long dynasty of the alchemists, who spent so many ages in quest of the universal solvent by which the golden principle might be elicited from all things vile and base. Aylmer appeared to believe that, by the plainest scientific logic, it was altogether within the limits of possibility to discover this long-sought medium; "but," he added, "a philosopher who should go deep enough to acquire the power would attain too lofty a wisdom to stoop to the exercise of it." Not less singular were his opinions in regard to the elixir vitae. He more than intimated that it was at his option to concoct a liquid that should prolong life for years, perhaps interminably; but that it would produce a discord in Nature which all the world, and chiefly the quaffer of the immortal nostrum, would find cause to curse.

"Aylmer, are you in earnest?" asked Georgiana, looking at him with amazement and fear. "It is terrible to possess such power, or even to dream of possessing it."

"Oh, do not tremble, my love," said her husband. "I would not wrong either you or myself by working such inharmonious effects upon our lives; but I would have you consider how trifling, in comparison, is the skill requisite to remove this little hand."

At the mention of the birthmark, Georgiana, as usual, shrank as if a redhot iron had touched her cheek.

Again Aylmer applied himself to his labors. She could hear his voice in the distant furnace room giving directions to Aminadab, whose harsh, uncouth, misshapen tones were audible in response, more like the grunt or growl of a brute than human speech. After hours of absence, Aylmer reappeared and proposed that she should now examine his cabinet of chemical products and natural treasures of the earth. Among the former he showed her a small vial, in which, he remarked, was contained a gentle yet most powerful fragrance, capable of impregnating all the breezes that blow across a kingdom. They were of inestimable value, the contents of that little vial; and, as he said so, he threw some of the perfume into the air and filled the room with piercing and invigorating delight.

"And what is this?" asked Georgiana, pointing to a small crystal globe containing a gold-colored liquid. "It is so beautiful to the eye that I could imagine it the elixir of life."

"In one sense it is," replied Aylmer; "or, rather, the elixir of immortality. It is the most precious poison that ever was concocted in this world. By its aid I could apportion the lifetime of any mortal at whom you might point your finger. The strength of the dose would determine whether he were to linger out years, or drop dead in the midst of a breath. No king on his guarded throne could keep his life if I, in my private station, should deem that the welfare of millions justified me in depriving him of it."

"Why do you keep such a terrific drug?" inquired Georgiana in horror.

"Do not mistrust me, dearest," said her husband, smiling; "its virtuous potency is yet greater than its harmful one. But see! Here is a powerful cosmetic. With a few drops of this in a vase of water, freckles may be washed away as easily as the hands are cleansed. A stronger infusion would take the blood out of the cheek, and leave the rosiest beauty a pale ghost."

"Is it with this lotion that you intend to bathe my cheek?" asked Georgiana, anxiously.

"Oh, no," hastily replied her husband; "this is merely superficial. Your case demands a remedy that shall go deeper."

In his interviews with Georgiana, Aylmer generally made minute inquiries as to her sensations and whether the confinement of the rooms and the temperature of the atmosphere agreed with her. These questions had such a particular drift that Georgiana began to conjecture that she was already subjected to certain physical influences, either breathed in with the fragrant air or taken with her food. She fancied likewise, but it might be altogether fancy, that there was a stirring up of her system—a strange, indefinite sensation creeping through her veins, and tingling, half painfully, half pleasurably, at her heart. Still, whenever she dared to look into the mirror, there she beheld herself pale as a white rose and with the crimson birthmark stamped upon her cheek. Not even Aylmer now hated it so much as she.

To dispel the tedium of the hours which her husband found it necessary to devote to the processes of combination and analysis, Georgiana turned over the volumes of his scientific library. In many dark old tomes she met with chapters full of romance and poetry. They were the works of philosophers of the middle ages, such as Albertus Magnus, Cornelius Agrippa, Paracelsus, and the famous friar who created the prophetic Brazen Head. All these antique naturalists stood in advance of their centuries, yet were imbued with some of their credulity, and therefore were believed, and perhaps imagined themselves to have acquired from the investigation of Nature a power above Nature, and from physics a sway over the spiritual world. Hardly less curious and imaginative were the early volumes of the Transactions of the Royal Society, in which the members, knowing little of the limits of natural possibility, were continually recording wonders or proposing methods whereby wonders might be wrought.

But to Georgiana the most engrossing volume was a large folio from her husband's own hand, in which he had recorded every experiment of his scientific career, its original aim, the methods adopted for its development, and its final success or failure, with the circumstances to which either event was attributable. The book, in truth, was both the history and emblem of his ardent, ambitious, imaginative, yet practical and laborious life. He handled physical details as if there were nothing beyond them; yet spiritualized them all, and redeemed himself from materialism by his strong and eager aspiration towards the infinite. In his grasp the veriest clod of earth assumed a soul. Georgiana, as she read, reverenced Aylmer and loved him more profoundly than ever, but with a less entire dependence on his judgment than heretofore. Much as he had accomplished, she could not but observe that his most splendid successes were almost invariably failures, if compared with the ideal at which he aimed. His brightest diamonds were the merest pebbles, and felt to be so by himself, in comparison with the inestimable gems which lay hidden beyond his reach. The volume, rich with achievements that had won renown for its author, was yet as melancholy a record as every mortal hand had penned. It was the sad confession and continual exemplification of the shortcomings of the composite man, the spirit burdened with clay and working in matter, and of the despair that assails the higher nature at finding itself so miserably thwarted by the earthly part. Perhaps every man of genius in whatever sphere might recognize the image of his own experience in Aylmer's journal.

So deeply did these reflections affect Georgiana that she laid her face upon the open volume and burst into tears. In this situation she was found by her husband.

"It is dangerous to read in a sorcerer's books," said he with a smile, though his countenance was uneasy and displeased. "Georgiana, there are pages in that volume which I can scarcely glance over and keep my senses. Take heed lest it prove as detrimental to you."

"It has made me worship you more than ever," said she.

"Ah, wait for this one success," rejoined he, "then worship me if you will. I shall deem myself hardly unworthy of it. But come, I have sought you for the luxury of your voice. Sing to me, dearest."

So she poured out the liquid music of her voice to quench the thirst of his spirit. He then took his leave with a boyish exuberance of gayety, assuring her that her seclusion would endure but a little longer, and that the result was already certain. Scarcely had he departed when Georgiana felt irresistibly impelled to follow him. She had forgotten to inform Aylmer of a symptom which for two or three hours past had begun to excite her attention. It was a sensation in the fatal birthmark, not painful, but which induced a restlessness throughout her system. Hastening after her husband, she intruded for the first time into the laboratory.

The first thing that struck her eye was the furnace, that hot and feverish worker, with the intense glow of its fire, which by the quantities of soot clustered above it seemed to have been burning for ages. There was a distilling apparatus in full operation. Around the room were retorts, tubes, cylinders, crucibles, and other apparatus of chemical research. An electrical machine stood ready for immediate use. The atmosphere felt oppressively close, and was tainted with gaseous odors which had been tormented forth by the processes of science. The severe and homely simplicity of the apartment, with its naked walls and brick pavement, looked strange, accustomed as Georgiana had become to the fantastic elegance of her boudoir. But what chiefly, indeed almost solely, drew her attention, was the aspect of Aylmer himself.

He was pale as death, anxious and absorbed, and hung over the furnace as if it depended upon his utmost watchfulness whether the liquid which it was distilling should be the draught of immortal happiness or misery. How different from the sanguine and joyous mien that he had assumed for Georgiana's encouragement!

"Carefully now, Aminadab; carefully, thou human machine; carefully, thou man of clay!" muttered Aylmer, more to himself than his assistant. "Now, if there be a thought too much or too little, it is all over."

"Ho! Ho!" mumbled Aminadab. "Look, master! Look!"

Aylmer raised his eyes hastily, and at first reddened, then grew paler than ever, on beholding Georgiana. He rushed towards her and seized her arm with a grip that left the print of his fingers upon it.

"Why do you come hither? Have you no trust in your husband?" cried he, impetuously. "Would you throw the blight of that fatal birthmark over my labors? It is not well done. Go, prying woman, go!"

"Nay, Aylmer," said Georgiana with the firmness of which she possessed no stinted endowment, "it is not you that have a right to complain. You mistrust your wife; you have concealed the anxiety with which you watch the development of this experiment. Think not so unworthily of me, my husband. Tell me all the risk we run, and fear not that I shall shrink; for my share in it is far less than your own."

"No, no, Georgiana!" said Aylmer, impatiently; "it must not be."

"I submit," replied she calmly. "And, Aylmer, I shall quaff whatever draught you bring me; but it will be on the same principle that would induce me to take a dose of poison if offered by your hand."

"My noble wife," said Aylmer, deeply moved, "I knew not the height and depth of your nature until now. Nothing shall be concealed. Know, then, that this crimson hand, superficial as it seems, has clutched its grasp into your being with a strength of which I had no previous conception. I have already administered agents powerful enough to do aught except to change your entire physical system. Only one thing remains to be tried. If that fail us we are ruined."

"Why did you hesitate to tell me this?" asked she.

"Because, Georgiana," said Aylmer, in a low voice, "there is danger."

"Danger? There is but one danger—that this horrible stigma shall be left upon my cheek!" cried Georgiana. "Remove it, remove it, whatever be the cost, or we shall both go mad!"

"Heaven knows your words are too true," said Aylmer, sadly. "And now, dearest, return to your boudoir. In a little while all will be tested."

He conducted her back and took leave of her with a solemn tenderness which spoke far more than his words how much was now at stake. After his departure Georgiana became rapt in musings. She considered the character of Aylmer, and did it completer justice than at any previous moment. Her heart exulted, while it trembled, at his honorable love—so pure and lofty that it would accept nothing less than perfection nor miserably make itself contented with an earthlier nature than he had dreamed of. She felt how much more precious was such a sentiment than that meaner kind which would have borne with the imperfection for her sake, and have been guilty of treason to holy love by degrading its perfect idea to the level of the actual; and with her whole spirit she prayed that, for a single moment, she might satisfy his highest and deepest conception. Longer than one moment she well knew it could not be; for his spirit was ever on the march, ever ascending, and each instant required something that was beyond the scope of the instant before.

The sound of her husband's footsteps aroused her. He bore a crystal goblet containing a liquor colorless as water, but bright enough to be the draught of immortality. Aylmer was pale; but it seemed rather the consequence of a highly-wrought state of mind and tension of spirit than of fear or doubt.

"The concoction of the draught has been perfect," said he, in answer to Georgiana's look. "Unless all my science have deceived me, it cannot fail."

"Save on your account, my dearest Aylmer," observed his wife, "I might wish to put off this birthmark of mortality by relinquishing mortality itself in preference to any other mode. Life is but a sad possession to those who have attained precisely the degree of moral advancement at which I stand. Were I weaker and blinder it might be happiness. Were I stronger, it might be endured hopefully. But, being what I find myself, methinks I am of all mortals the most fit to die."

"You are fit for heaven without tasting death!" replied her husband "But why do we speak of dying? The draught cannot fail. Behold its effect upon this plant."

On the window seat there stood a geranium diseased with yellow blotches, which had overspread all its leaves. Aylmer poured a small quantity of the liquid upon the soil in which it grew. In a little time, when the roots of the plant had taken up the moisture, the unsightly blotches began to be extinguished in a living verdure.

"There needed no proof," said Georgiana, quietly. "Give me the goblet. I joyfully stake all upon your word."

"Drink, then, thou lofty creature!" exclaimed Aylmer, with fervid admiration. "There is no taint of imperfection on thy spirit. Thy sensible frame, too, shall soon be all perfect."

She quaffed the liquid and returned the goblet to his hand.

"It is grateful," said she with a placid smile. "Methinks it is like water from a heavenly fountain; for it contains I know not what of unobtrusive fragrance and deliciousness. It allays a feverish thirst that had parched me for many days. Now, dearest, let me sleep. My earthly senses are closing over my spirit like the leaves around the heart of a rose at sunset."

She spoke the last words with a gentle reluctance, as if it required almost more energy than she could command to pronounce the faint and lingering syllables. Scarcely had they loitered through her lips ere she was lost in slumber. Aylmer sat by her side, watching her aspect with the emotions proper to a man the whole value of whose existence was involved in the process now to be tested. Mingled with this mood, however, was the philosophic investigation characteristic of the man of science. Not the minutest symptom escaped him. A heightened flush of the cheek, a slight irregularity of breath, a quiver of the eyelid, a hardly perceptible tremor through the frame—such were the details which, as the moments passed, he wrote down in his folio volume. Intense thought had set its stamp upon every previous page of that volume, but the thoughts of years were all concentrated upon the last.

While thus employed, he failed not to gaze often at the fatal hand, and not without a shudder. Yet once, by a strange and unaccountable impulse he pressed it with his lips. His spirit recoiled, however, in the very act, and Georgiana, out of the midst of her deep sleep, moved uneasily and murmured as if in remonstrance. Again Aylmer resumed his watch. Nor was it without avail. The crimson hand, which at first had been strongly visible upon the marble paleness of Georgiana's cheek, now grew more faintly outlined. She remained not less pale than ever; but the birthmark with every breath that came and went, lost somewhat of its former distinctness. Its presence had been awful; its departure was more awful still. Watch the stain of the rainbow fading out the sky, and you will know how that mysterious symbol passed away.

"By Heaven! It is well-nigh gone!" said Aylmer to himself, in almost irrepressible ecstasy. "I can scarcely trace it now. Success! Success! And now it is like the faintest rose color. The lightest flush of blood across her cheek would overcome it. But she is so pale!"

He drew aside the window curtain and suffered the light of natural day to fall into the room and rest upon her cheek. At the same time he heard a gross, hoarse chuckle, which he had long known as his servant Aminadab's expression of delight.

"Ah, clod! Ah, earthly mass!" cried Aylmer, laughing in a sort of frenzy. "You have served me well! Matter and spirit—earth and heaven—have both done their part in this! Laugh, thing of the senses! You have earned the right to laugh."

These exclamations broke Georgiana's sleep. She slowly unclosed her eyes and gazed into the mirror which her husband had arranged for that purpose. A faint smile flitted over her lips when she recognized how barely perceptible was now that crimson hand which had once blazed forth with such disastrous brilliancy as to scare away all their happiness. But then her eyes sought Aylmer's face with a trouble and anxiety that he could by no means account for.

"My poor Aylmer!" murmured she.

"Poor? Nay, richest, happiest, most favored!" exclaimed he. "My peerless bride, it is successful! You are perfect!"

"My poor Aylmer," she repeated, with a more than human tenderness, "you have aimed loftily; you have done nobly. Do not repent that with so high and pure a feeling, you have rejected the best the earth could offer. Aylmer, dearest Aylmer, I am dying!"

Alas, it was too true! The fatal hand had grappled with the mystery of life, and was the bond by which an angelic spirit kept itself in union with a mortal frame. As the last crimson tint of the birthmark—that sole token of human imperfection—faded from her cheek, the parting breath of the now perfect woman passed into the atmosphere, and her soul, lingering a moment near her husband, took its heavenward flight. Then a hoarse, chuckling laugh was heard again! Thus ever does the gross fatality of earth exult in its invariable triumph over the immortal essence which, in this dim sphere of half development, demands the completeness of a higher state. Yet, had Alymer reached a profounder wisdom, he need not thus have flung away the happiness which would have woven his mortal life of the selfsame texture with the celestial. The momentary circumstance was too strong for him; he failed to look beyond the shadowy scope of Time, and, living once for all in Eternity, to find the perfect Future in the present.

THE FACTS IN THE CASE OF M. VALDEMAR

Edgar Allan Poe

EDGAR ALLAN POE (1809-1849), born in Massachusetts, grew up in Virginia, eventually attending the University of Virginia. After a brief attempt at a military career Poe turned to journalism and writing where he was able to make a living. Though he was alcoholic and probably a chronic depressive (and not ever in the best of health), he was able to became a major figure in the American Romantic movement, writing poetry, short stories, literary criticism, and various kinds of essays which still remain influential. Poe is credited with inventing the short story as well as writing the first American science fiction stories. He also wrote what might be the very first recognizable detective story. His focus was always on the darkly psychological aspects of the human mind and the lengths to which humans, at the edge of madness, can go.

OF course I shall not pretend to consider it any matter for wonder, that the extraordinary case of M. Valdemar has excited discussion. It would have been a miracle had it not—especially under the circumstances. Through the desire of all parties concerned, to keep the affair from the public, at least for the present, or until we had farther opportunities for investigation—through our endeavors to effect this—a garbled or exaggerated account made its way into society, and became the source of many unpleasant misrepresentations; and, very naturally, of a great deal of disbelief.

It is now rendered necessary that I give the facts—as far as I comprehend them myself. They are, succinctly, these:

My attention, for the last three years, had been repeatedly drawn to the subject of Mesmerism; and, about nine months ago, it occurred to me, quite suddenly, that in the series of experiments made hitherto, there had been a very remarkable and most unaccountable omission:—no person had as yet been mesmerized in articulo mortis. It remained to be seen, first, whether, in such condition, there existed in the patient any susceptibility to the magnetic influence; secondly, whether, if any existed, it was impaired or increased by the condition; thirdly, to what extent, or for how long a period, the encroachments of Death might be arrested by the process. There were other points to be ascertained, but these most excited my curiosity—the last in especial, from the immensely important character of its consequences.

In looking around me for some subject by whose means I might test these particulars, I was brought to think of my friend, M. Ernest Valdemar, the well-known compiler of the "Bibliotheca

Forensica," and author (under the nom de plume of Issachar Marx) of the Polish versions of "Wallenstein" and "Gargantua." M. Valdemar, who has resided principally at Harlem, N. Y., since the year 1839, is (or was) particularly noticeable for the extreme parseness of his person—his lower limbs much resembling those of John Randolph; and, also, for the whiteness of his whiskers, in violent contrast to the blackness of his hair—the latter, in consequence, being very generally mistaken for a wig. His temperament was markedly nervous, and rendered him a good subject for mesmeric experiment. On two or three occasions I had put him to sleep with little difficulty, but was disappointed in other results which his peculiar constitution had naturally led me to anticipate. His will was at no period positively, or thoroughly, under my control, and in regard to clairvoyance, I could accomplish with him nothing to be relied upon. I always attributed my failure at these points to the disordered state of his health. For some months previous to my becoming acquainted with him, his physicians had declared him in a confirmed phthisis. It was his custom, indeed, to speak calmly of his approaching dissolution, as of a matter neither to be avoided nor regretted.

When the ideas to which I have alluded first occurred to me, it was of course very natural that I should think of M. Valdemar. I knew the steady philosophy of the man too well to apprehend any scruples from him; and he had no relatives in America who would be likely to interfere. I spoke to him frankly upon the subject; and, to my surprise, his interest seemed vividly excited. I say to my surprise; for, although he had always yielded his person freely to my experiments, he had never before given me any tokens of sympathy with what I did. His disease was of that character which would admit of exact calculation in respect to the epoch of its termination in death; and it was finally arranged between us that he would send for me about twenty-four hours before the period announced by his physicians as that of his decease.

It is now rather more than seven months since I received, from M. Valdemar himself, the subjoined note:

"MY DEAR P______,

"You may as well come now. D______ and F______ are agreed that I cannot hold out beyond to-morrow midnight; and I think they have hit the time very nearly.

"Valdemar."

I received this note within half an hour after it was written, and in fifteen minutes more I was in the dying man's chamber. I had not seen him for ten days, and was appalled by the fearful alteration which the brief interval had wrought in him. His face wore a leaden hue; the eyes were utterly yllabific; and the emaciation was so extreme, that the skin had been broken through by the cheek-bones. His expectoration was excessive. The pulse was barely perceptible. He retained, nevertheless, in a very remarkable manner, both his mental power and a certain degree of physical strength. He spoke with distinctness—took some palliative medicines without aid—and, when I entered the room, was occupied in penciling memoranda in a pocket-book. He was propped up in the bed by pillows. Doctors D______ and F______ were in attendance.

After pressing Valdemar's hand, I took these gentlemen aside, and obtained from them a minute account of the patient's condition. The left lung had been for eighteen months in a semi-osseous or cartilaginous state, and was, of course, entirely useless for all purposes of vitality. The right, in its upper portion, was also partially, if not thoroughly, ossified, while the lower region was merely a mass of purulent tubercles, running one into another. Several extensive perforations existed; and, at one point, permanent adhesion to the ribs had taken place. These appearances in the right lobe were of comparatively recent date. The ossification had proceeded with very unusual rapidity; no sign of it had been discovered a month before, and the adhesion had only been observed during the three previous days. Independently of the phthisis, the patient was suspected of aneurism of the aorta; but on this point the osseous symptoms rendered an exact diagnosis impossible. It was the opinion of both physicians that M.

Valdemar would die about midnight on the morrow. (Sunday.) It was then seven o'clock on Saturday evening.

On quitting the invalid's bed-side to hold conversation with myself, Doctors D______ and F______ had bidden him a final farewell. It had not been their intention to return; but, at my request, they agreed to look in upon the patient about ten the next night.

When they had gone, I spoke freely with M. Valdemar on the subject of his approaching dissolution, as well as, more particularly, of the experiment proposed. He still professed himself quite willing and even anxious to have it made, and urged me to commence it at once. A male and a female nurse were in attendance; but I did not feel myself altogether at liberty to engage in a task of this character with no more reliable witnesses than these people, in case of sudden accident, might prove. I therefore postponed operations until about eight the next night, when the arrival of a medical student, with whom I had some acquaintance, (Mr. Theodore L_____l,) relieved me from further embarrassment. It had been my design, originally, to wait for the physicians; but I was induced to proceed, first, by the urgent entreaties of M. Valdemar, and secondly, by my conviction that I had not a moment to lose, as he was evidently sinking fast.

Mr. L_____l was so kind as to accede to my desire that he would take notes of all that occurred; and it is from his memoranda that what I now have to relate is, for the most part, either condensed or copied verbatim.

It wanted about five minutes of eight when, taking the patient's hand, I begged him to state, as distinctly as he could, to Mr. L_____l, whether he (M. Valdemar,) was entirely willing that I should make the experiment of mesmerizing him in his then condition.

He replied feebly, yet quite audibly, "Yes, I wish to be mesmerized"—adding immediately afterwards, "I fear you have deferred it too long."

While he spoke thus, I commenced the passes which I had already found most effectual in subduing him. He was evidently influenced with the first lateral stroke of my hand across his forehead; but although I exerted all my powers, no farther perceptible effect was induced until some minutes after ten o'clock, when Doctors D______ and F______ called, according to appointment. I explained to them, in a few words, what I designed, and as they opposed no objection, saying that the patient was already in the death agony, I proceeded without hesitation—exchanging, however, the lateral passes for downward ones, and directing my gaze entirely into the right eye of the sufferer.

By this time his pulse was imperceptible and his breathing was stertorious [stertorous], and at intervals of half a minute.

This condition was nearly unaltered for a quarter of an hour. At the expiration of this period, however, a natural although a very deep sigh escaped the bosom of the dying man, and the stertorious [stertorous] breathing ceased—that is to say, its stertoriousness [stertorousness] was no longer apparent; the intervals were undiminished. The patient's extremities were of an icy coldness.

At five minutes before eleven, I perceived unequivocal signs of the mesmeric influence. The glassy roll of the eye was changed for that expression of uneasy inward examination which is never seen except in cases of sleep-waking, and which it is quite impossible to mistake. With a few rapid lateral passes I made the lids quiver, as in incipient sleep, and with a few more I closed them altogether. I was not satisfied, however, with this, but continued the manipulations vigorously, and with the fullest exertion of the will, until I had completely stiffened the limbs of the slumberer, after placing them in a seemingly easy position. The legs were at full length; the arms were nearly so, and reposed on the bed at a moderate distance from the loins. The head was very slightly elevated.

When I had accomplished this, it was fully midnight, and I requested the gentlemen present to examine M. Valdemar's condition. After a few experiments, they admitted him to be in an unusually perfect state of mesmeric trance. The curiosity of both the physicians was greatly excited. Dr. D______ resolved at once to remain with the patient all night, while Dr. F______ took leave with a promise to return at daybreak. Mr. L_____l and the nurses remained.

We left M. Valdemar entirely undisturbed until about three o'clock in the morning, when I approached him and found him in precisely the same condition as when Dr. F______ went away—that is to say, he lay in the same position; the pulse was imperceptible; the breathing was gentle (scarcely noticeable, unless through the application of a mirror to the lips); the eyes were closed naturally; and the limbs were as rigid and as cold as marble. Still, the general appearance was certainly not that of death.

As I approached M. Valdemar I made a kind of half effort to influence his right arm into pursuit of my own, as I passed the latter gently to and fro above his person. In such experiments with this patient, I had never perfectly succeeded before, and assuredly I had little thought of succeeding now; but to my astonishment, his arm very readily, although feebly, followed every direction I assigned it with mine. I determined to hazard a few words of conversation.

"M. Valdemar," I said, "are you asleep?" He made no answer, but I perceived a tremor about the lips, and was thus induced to repeat the question, again and again. At its third repetition, his whole frame was agitated by a very slight shivering; the eye-lids unclosed themselves so far as to display a white line of a ball; the lips moved sluggishly, and from between them, in a barely audible whisper, issued the words:

"Yes;—asleep now. Do not wake me!—let me die so!"

I here felt the limbs and found them as rigid as ever. The right arm, as before, obeyed the direction of my hand. I questioned the sleep-waker again:

"Do you still feel pain in the breast, M. Valdemar?"

The answer now was immediate, but even less audible than before:

"No pain—I am dying."

I did not think it advisable to disturb him farther just then, and nothing more was said or done until the arrival of Dr. F______, who came a little before sunrise, and expressed unbounded astonishment at finding the patient still alive. After feeling the pulse and applying a mirror to the lips, he requested me to speak to the sleep-waker again. I did so, saying:

"M. Valdemar, do you still sleep?"

As before, some minutes elapsed ere a reply was made; and during the interval the dying man seemed to be collecting his energies to speak. At my fourth repetition of the question, he said very faintly, almost inaudibly:

"Yes; still asleep—dying."

It was now the opinion, or rather the wish, of the physicians, that M. Valdemar should be suffered to remain undisturbed in his present apparently tranquil condition, until death should supervene—and this, it was generally agreed, must now take place within a few minutes. I concluded, however, to speak to him once more, and merely repeated my previous question.

While I spoke, there came a marked change over the countenance of the sleep-waker. The eyes rolled themselves slowly open, the pupils disappearing upwardly; the skin generally assumed a cadaverous hue, resembling not so much parchment as white paper; and the circular hectic spots which, hitherto, had been strongly defined in the centre of each cheek, went out at once. I use this expression, because the suddenness of their departure put me in mind of nothing so much as the extinguishment of a candle by a puff of the breath. The upper lip, at the same time, writhed itself away from the teeth, which it had previously covered completely; while the lower jaw fell with an audible jerk, leaving the mouth widely extended, and disclosing in full view the swollen and blackened tongue. I presume that no member of the party then present had been unaccustomed to death-bed horrors; but so hideous beyond conception was the appearance of M. Valdemar at this moment, that there was a general shrinking back from the region of the bed.

I now feel that I have reached a point of this narrative at which every reader will be startled into positive disbelief. It is my business, however, simply to proceed.

There was no longer the faintest sign of vitality in M. Valdemar; and concluding him to be dead, we were consigning him to the charge of the nurses, when a strong vibratory motion was observable in the tongue. This continued for perhaps a minute. At the expiration of this period, there issued from the distended and motionless jaws a voice—such as it would be madness in me to attempt describing. There are, indeed, two or three epithets which might be considered as applicable to it in part; I might say, for example, that the sound was harsh, and broken and hollow; but the hideous whole is indescribable, for the simple reason that no similar sounds have ever jarred upon the ear of humanity. There were two particulars, nevertheless, which I thought then, and still think, might fairly be stated as characteristic of the intonation—as well adapted to convey some idea of its unearthly peculiarity. In the first place, the voice seemed to reach our ears—at least mine—from a vast distance, or from some deep cavern within the earth. In the second place, it impressed me (I fear, indeed, that it will be impossible to make myself comprehended) as gelatinous or glutinous matters impress the sense of touch.

I have spoken both of "sound" and of "voice." I mean to say that the sound was one of distinct—of even wonderfully, thrillingly distinct—yllabification [syllabification]. M. Valdemar spoke—obviously in reply to the question I had propounded to him a few minutes before. I had asked him, it will be remembered, if he still slept. He now said:

"Yes;—no;—I have been sleeping—and now—now—I am dead."

No person present even affected to deny, or attempted to repress, the unutterable, shuddering horror which these few words, thus uttered, were so well calculated to convey. Mr. L_____l (the student) swooned. The nurses immediately left the chamber, and could not be induced to return. My own impressions I would not pretend to render intelligible to the reader. For nearly an hour, we busied ourselves, silently—without the utterance of a word—in endeavors to revive Mr. L_____l. When he came to himself, we addressed ourselves again to an investigation of M. Valdemar's condition.

It remained in all respects as I have last described it, with the exception that the mirror no longer afforded evidence of respiration. An attempt to draw blood from the arm failed. I should mention, too, that this limb was no farther subject to my will. I endeavored in vain to make it follow the direction of my hand. The only real indication, indeed, of the mesmeric influence, was now found in the vibratory movement of the tongue, whenever I addressed M. Valdemar a question. He seemed to be making an effort to reply, but had no longer sufficient volition. To queries put to him by any other person than myself he seemed utterly insensible—although I endeavored to place each member of the company in mesmeric rapport with him. I believe that I have now related all that is necessary to an understanding of the sleep-waker's state at this epoch. Other nurses were procured; and at ten o'clock I left the house in company with the two physicians and Mr. L_____l.

In the afternoon we all called again to see the patient. His condition remained precisely the same. We had now some discussion as to the propriety and feasibility of awakening him; but we had little difficulty in agreeing that no good purpose would be served by so doing. It was evident that, so far, death (or what is usually termed death) had been arrested by the mesmeric process. It seemed clear to us all that to awaken M. Valdemar would be merely to insure his instant, or at least his speedy dissolution.

From this period until the close of last week—an interval of nearly seven months—we continued to make daily calls at M. Valdemar's house, accompanied, now and then, by medical and other friends. All this time the sleeper-waker remained exactly as I have last described him. The nurses' attentions were continual.

It was on Friday last that we finally resolved to make the experiment of awakening, or attempting to awaken him; and it is the (perhaps) unfortunate result of this latter experiment which has given rise to so much discussion in private circles—to so much of what I cannot help thinking unwarranted popular feeling.

For the purpose of relieving M. Valdemar from the mesmeric trance, I made use of the customary passes. These, for a time, were unsuccessful. The first indication of revival was afforded by a partial descent of the iris. It was observed, as especially remarkable, that this lowering of the pupil was accompanied by the profuse out-flowing of a yellowish ichor (from beneath the lids) of a pungent and highly offensive odor.

It was now suggested that I should attempt to influence the patient's arm, as heretofore. I made the attempt and failed. Dr. F______ then intimated a desire to have me put a question. I did so, as follows:

"M. Valdemar, can you explain to us what are your feelings or wishes now?"

There was an instant return of the hectic circles on the cheeks; the tongue quivered, or rather rolled violently in the mouth (although the jaws and lips remained rigid as before); and at length the same hideous voice which I have already described, broke forth:

"For God's sake!—quick!—quick!—put me to sleep—or, quick!—waken me!—quick!—I say to you that I am dead!"

I was thoroughly unnerved, and for an instant remained undecided what to do. At first I made an endeavor to re-compose the patient; but, failing in this through total abeyance of the will, I retraced my steps and as earnestly struggled to awaken him. In this attempt I soon saw that I should be successful—or at least I soon fancied that my success would be complete—and I am sure that all in the room were prepared to see the patient awaken.

For what really occurred, however, it is quite impossible that any human being could have been prepared.

As I rapidly made the mesmeric passes, amid ejaculations of "dead! Dead!" absolutely bursting from the tongue and not from the lips of the sufferer, his whole frame at once—within the space of a single minute, or even less, shrunk—crumbled—absolutely rotted away beneath my hands. Upon the bed, before that whole company, there lay a nearly liquid mass of loathsome—of detestable putrescence.

NOTE:

Griswold was either unaware, or chose not to use, Poe's manuscript correction which made the last sentence end "...of detestable putridity." This change was made in the copy of the Broadway Journal Poe gave to Mrs. Whitman, a copy which Griswold presumably did not see in the preparation of his edition of Poe's works.

THE BELL TOWER

Herman Melville

HERMAN MELVILLE (1819-1891) is best known for his novel, *Moby Dick* (1851), but wrote several stories of a speculative nature, always pitting humankind against natural forces, either through science (as in "The Bell Tower") or sheer arrogance, as in *Moby Dick* or "Benito Cereno". His stories also resemble those of Hawthorne in that they attempted to examine the inexplicable and the limits of human ingenuity.

IN the south of Europe, nigh a once frescoed capital, now with dank mold cankering its bloom, central in a plain, stands what, at distance, seems the black mossed stump of some immeasurable pine, fallen, in forgotten days, with Anak and the Titan.

As all along where the pine tree falls, its dissolution leaves a mossy mound—last-flung shadow of the perished trunk; never lengthening, never lessening; unsubject to the fleet falsities of the sun; shade immutable, and true gauge which cometh by prostration—so westward from what seems the stump, one steadfast spear of lichened ruin veins the plain.

From that treetop, what birded chimes of silver throats had rung. A stone pine, a metallic aviary in its crown: the Bell-Tower, built by the great mechanician, the unblest foundling, Bannadonna.

Like Babel's, its base was laid in a high hour of renovated earth, following the second deluge, when the waters of the Dark Ages had dried up and once more the green appeared. No wonder that, after so long and deep submersion, the jubilant expectation of the race should, as with Noah's sons, soar into Shinar aspiration.

In firm resolve, no man in Europe at that period went beyond Bannadonna. Enriched through commerce with the Levant, the state in which he lived voted to have the noblest Bell-Tower in Italy. His repute assigned him to be architect.

Stone by stone, month by month, the tower rose. Higher, higher, snaillike in pace, but torch or rocket in its pride.

After the masons would depart, the builder, standing alone upon its ever-ascending summit at close of every day, saw that he overtopped still higher walls and trees. He would tarry till a late hour there, wrapped in schemes of other and still loftier piles. Those who of saints' days thronged the spot—hanging to the rude poles of scaffolding like sailors on yards or bees on boughs, unmindful of lime and dust, and falling chips of stone—their homage not the less inspirited him to self-esteem.

At length the holiday of the Tower came. To the sound of viols, the climax-stone slowly rose in air, and, amid the firing of ordnance, was laid by Bannadonna's hands upon the final course. Then mounting it, he stood erect, alone, with folded arms, gazing upon the white summits of blue inland Alps, and whiter crests of bluer Alps offshore—sights invisible from the plain. Invisible, too, from thence was that eye he turned below, when, like the cannon booms, came up to him the people's combustions of applause.

That which stirred them so was seeing with what serenity the builder stood three hundred feet in air, upon an unrailed perch. This none but he durst do. But his periodic standing upon the pile, in each stage of its growth—such discipline had its last result.

Little remained now but the bells. These, in all respects, must correspond with their receptacle.

The minor ones were prosperously cast. A highly enriched one followed, of a singular make, intended for suspension in a manner before unknown. The purpose of this bell, its rotary motion and connection with the clockwork, also executed at the time, will, in the sequel, receive mention.

In the one erection, bell-tower and clock-tower were united, though, before that period, such structures had commonly been built distinct; as the Campanile and Torre del Orologio of St. Mark to this day attest.

But it was upon the great state bell that the founder lavished his more daring skill. In vain did some of the less elated magistrates here caution him, saying that though truly the tower was titanic, yet limit should be set to the dependent weight of its swaying masses. But, undeterred, he prepared his mammoth mold, dented with mythological devices; kindled his fires of balsamic firs; melted his tin and copper, and, throwing in much plate contributed by the public spirit of the nobles, let loose the tide.

The unleashed metals bayed like hounds. The workmen shrunk. Through their fright, fatal harm to the bell was dreaded. Fearless as Shadrach, Bannadonna, rushing through the glow, smote the chief culprit with his ponderous ladle. From the smitten part, a splinter was dashed into the seething mass, and at once was melted in.

Next day a portion of the work was heedfully uncovered. All seemed right. Upon the third morning, with equal satisfaction, it was bared still lower. At length, like some old Theban king, the whole cooled casting was disinterred. All was fair except in one strange spot. But as he suffered no one to attend him in these inspections, he concealed the blemish by some preparation which none knew better to devise.

The casting of such a mass was deemed no small triumph for the caster; one, too, in which the state might not scorn to share. The homicide was overlooked. By the charitable that deed was but imputed to sudden transports of esthetic passion, not to any flagitious quality. A kick from an Arabian charger; not sign of vice, but blood.

His felony remitted by the judge, absolution given him by the priest, what more could even a sickly conscience have desired.

Honoring the tower and its builder with another holiday, the republic witnessed the hoisting of the bells and clockwork amid shows and pomps superior to the former.

Some months of more than usual solitude on Bannadonna's part ensued. It was not unknown that he was engaged upon something for the belfry, intended to complete it and surpass all that had gone before. Most people imagined that the design would involve a casting like the bells. But those who thought they had some further insight would shake their heads, with hints that not for nothing did the mechanician keep so secret. Meantime, his seclusion failed not to invest his work with more or less of that sort of mystery pertaining to the forbidden.

Erelong he had a heavy object hoisted to the belfry, wrapped in a dark sack or cloak—a procedure sometimes had in the case of an elaborate piece of sculpture, or statue, which, being intended to grace the front of a new edifice, the architect does not desire exposed to critical eyes till set up, finished, in its appointed place. Such was the impression now. But, as the object rose, a statuary present observed, or thought he did, that it was not entirely rigid, but was, in a manner, pliant. At last, when the hidden thing had attained its final height, and, obscurely seen from below, seemed almost of itself to step into the belfry, as if with little assistance from the crane, a shrewd old blacksmith present ventured the suspicion that it was but a living man. This surmise was thought a foolish one, while the general interest failed not to augment.

Not without demur from Bannadonna, the chief magistrate of the town, with an associate—both elderly men—followed what seemed the image up the tower. But, arrived at the belfry, they had little recompense. Plausibly entrenching himself behind the conceded mysteries of his art, the mechanician withheld present explanation. The magistrates glanced toward the cloaked object, which, to their surprise, seemed now to have changed its attitude, or else had before been more perplexingly concealed by the violent muffling action of the wind without. It seemed now seated upon some sort of frame, or chair, contained within the domino. They observed that nigh the top, in a sort of square, the web of the cloth, either from accident or design, had its warp partly withdrawn, and the cross threads plucked out here and there, so as to form a sort of woven grating. Whether it were the low wind or no, stealing through the stone latticework, or only their own perturbed imaginations, is uncertain, but they thought they discerned a slight sort of fitful, spring-like motion in the domino. Nothing, however incidental or insignificant, escaped their uneasy eyes. Among other things, they pried out, in a corner, an earthen cup, partly corroded and partly encrusted, and one whispered to the other that this cup was just such a one as might, in mockery, be offered to the lips of some brazen statue, or, perhaps, still worse.

But, being questioned, the mechanician said that the cup was simply used in his founder's business, and described the purpose—in short, a cup to test the condition of metals in fusion. He added that it had got into the belfry by the merest chance.

Again and again they gazed at the domino, as at some suspicious incognito at a Venetian mask. All sorts of vague apprehensions stirred them. They even dreaded lest, when they should descend, the mechanician, though without a flesh-and-blood companion, for all that, would not be left alone.

Affecting some merriment at their disquietude, he begged to relieve them, by extending a coarse sheet of workman's canvas between them and the object.

Meantime he sought to interest them in his other work, nor, now that the domino was out of sight, did they long remain insensible to the artistic wonders lying round them—wonders hitherto beheld but in their unfinished state, because, since hoisting the bells, none but the caster had entered within the belfry. It was one trait of his, that, even in details, he would not let another do what he could, without too great loss of time, accomplish for himself. So, for several preceding weeks, whatever hours were unemployed in his secret design had been devoted to elaborating the figures on the bells.

The clock bell, in particular, now drew attention. Under a patient chisel, the latent beauty of its enrichments, before obscured by the cloudings incident to casting, that beauty in its shyest grace, was now revealed. Round and round the bell, twelve figures of gay girls, garlanded, hand-in-hand, danced in a choral ring the embodied hours.

"Bannadonna," said the chief, "this bell excels all else. No added touch could here improve. Hark!" hearing a sound, "was that the wind?"

"The wind, Excellenza," was the light response. "But the figures, they are not yet without their faults. They need some touches yet. When those are given, and the—block yonder," pointing towards the canvas screen, "when Haman there, as I merrily call him—him? it, I mean—when Haman is fixed on this, his lofty tree, then, gentlemen, will I be most happy to receive you here again."

The equivocal reference to the object caused some return of restlessness. However, on their part, the visitors forbore further allusion to it, unwilling, perhaps, to let the foundling see how easily it lay within his plebeian art to stir the placid dignity of nobles.

"Well, Bannadonna," said the chief, "how long ere you are ready to set the clock going, so that the hour shall be sounded? Our interest in you, not less than in the work itself, makes us anxious to be assured of your success. The people, too—why, they are shouting now. Say the exact hour when you will be ready."

"Tomorrow, Excellenza, if you listen for it—or should you not, all the same—strange music will be heard. The stroke of one shall be the first from yonder bell," pointing to the bell adorned with girls and garlands, "that stroke shall fall there, where the hand of Una clasps Dua's. The stroke of one shall sever that loved clasp. Tomorrow, then, at one o'clock, as struck here, precisely here," advancing and placing his finger upon the clasp, "the poor mechanic will be most happy once more to give you liege audience, in this his littered shop. Farewell till then, illustrious magnificoes, and hark ye for your vassal's stroke."

His still, Vulcanic face hiding its burning brightness like a forge, he moved with ostentatious deference towards the scuttle, as if so far to escort their exit. But the junior magistrate, a kind-hearted man, troubled at what seemed to him a certain sardonical disdain lurking beneath the foundling's humble mien, and in Christian sympathy more distressed at it on his account than on his own, dimly surmising what might be the final fate of such a cynic solitaire, nor perhaps uninfluenced by the general strangeness of surrounding things, this good magistrate had glanced sadly, sideways from the speaker, and thereupon his foreboding eye had started at the expression of the unchanging face of the Hour Una.

"How is this, Bannadonna," he lowly asked, "Una looks unlike her sisters."

"In Christ's name, Bannadonna," impulsively broke in the chief, his attention for the first attracted to the figure by his associate's remark. "Una's face looks just like that of Deborah, the prophetess, as painted by the Florentine, Del Fonca."

"Surely, Bannadonna," lowly resumed the milder magistrate, "you meant the twelve should wear the same jocundly abandoned air. But see, the smile of Una seems but a fatal one. 'Tis different."

While his mild associate was speaking, the chief glanced inquiringly from him to the caster, as if anxious to mark how the discrepancy would be accounted for. As the chief stood, his advanced foot was on the scuttle's curb.

Bannadonna spoke:

"Excellenza, now that, following your keener eye, I glance upon the face of Una, I do, indeed perceive some little variance. But look all round the bell, and you will find no two faces entirely correspond. Because there is a law in art—but the cold wind is rising more; these lattices are but a poor defense. Suffer me, magnificoes, to conduct you at least partly on your way. Those in whose well-being there is a public stake, should be heedfully attended."

"Touching the look of Una, you were saying, Bannadonna, that there was a certain law in art," observed the chief, as the three now descended the stone shaft, "pray, tell me, then—"

"Pardon; another time, Excellenza—the tower is damp."

"Nay, I must rest, and hear it now. Here—here is a wide landing, and through this leeward slit, no wind, but ample light. Tell us of your law, and at large."

"Since, Excellenza, you insist, know that there is a law in art which bars the possibility of duplicates. Some years ago, you may remember, I graved a small seal for your republic, bearing, for its chief device, the head of your own ancestor, its illustrious founder. It becoming necessary, for the customs' use, to have innumerable impressions for bales and boxes, I graved an entire plate, containing one hundred of the seals. Now, though, indeed, my object was to have those hundred heads identical, and though, I dare say, people think them so, yet, upon closely scanning an uncut impression from the plate, no two of those five-score faces, side by side, will be found alike. Gravity is the air of all, but diversified in all. In some, benevolent; in some, ambiguous; in two or three, to a close scrutiny, all but incipiently malign, the variation of less than a hair's breadth in the linear shadings round the mouth sufficing to all this. Now, Excellenza, transmute that general gravity into joyousness, and subject it to twelve of those variations I have described, and tell me, will you not have my hours here, and Una one of them? But I like—"

"Hark! is that—a footfall above?"

"Mortar, Excellenza; sometimes it drops to the belfry floor from the arch where the stonework was left undressed. I must have it seen to. As I was about to say: for one, I like this law forbidding duplicates. It evokes fine personalities. Yes, Excellenza, that strange, and—to you—uncertain smile, and those forelooking eyes of Una, suit Bannadonna very well."

"Hark!—sure we left no soul above?"

"No soul, Excellenza; rest assured, no soul. Again the mortar."

"It fell not while we were there."

"Ah, in your presence, it better knew its place, Excellenza," blandly bowed Bannadonna.

"But Una," said the milder magistrate, "she seemed intently gazing on you; one would have almost sworn that she picked you out from among us three."

"If she did, possibly it might have been her finer apprehension, Excellenza."

"How, Bannadonna? I do not understand you."

"No consequence, no consequence, Excellenza—but the shifted wind is blowing through the slit. Suffer me to escort you on, and then, pardon, but the toiler must to his tools."

"It may be foolish, signor," and the milder magistrate, as, from the third landing, the two now went down unescorted, "but, somehow, our great mechanician moves me strangely. Why, just now, when he so superciliously replied, his walk seemed Sisera's, God's vain foe, in Del Fonca's painting. And that young, sculptured Deborah, too. Aye, and that—"

"Tush, tush, signor!" returned the chief. "A passing whim. Deborah?—Where's Jael, pray?"

"Ah," said the other, as they now stepped upon the sod, "ah, signor, I see you leave your fears behind you with the chill and gloom; but mine, even in this sunny air, remain. Hark!"

It was a sound from just within the tower door, whence they had emerged. Turning, they saw it closed.

"He has slipped down and barred us out," smiled the chief; "but it is his custom."

Proclamation was now made that the next day, at one hour after meridian, the clock would strike, and—thanks to the mechanician's powerful art—with unusual accompaniments. But what those should be, none as yet could say. The announcement was received with cheers.

By the looser sort, who encamped about the tower all night, lights were seen gleaming through the topmost blindwork, only disappearing with the morning sun. Strange sounds, too, were heard, or were thought to be, by those whom anxious watching might not have left mentally undisturbed—sounds, not only of some ringing implement, but also, so they said, half-suppressed screams and plainings, such as might have issued from some ghostly engine overplied.

Slowly the day drew on, part of the concourse chasing the weary time with songs and games, till, at last, the great blurred sun rolled, like a football, against the plain.

At noon, the nobility and principal citizens came from the town in cavalcade, a guard of soldiers, also, with music, the more to honor the occasion.

Only one hour more. Impatience grew. Watches were held in hands of feverish men, who stood, now scrutinizing their small dial-plates, and then, with neck thrown back, gazing toward the belfry as if the eve might foretell that which could only be made sensible to the ear, for, as yet, there was no dial to the tower clock.

The hour hands of a thousand watches now verged within a hair's breadth of the figure 1. A silence, as if the expectations of some Shiloh, pervaded the swarming plain. Suddenly a dull, mangled sound, naught ringing in it, scarcely audible, indeed, to the outer circles of the people—that dull sound dropped heavily from the belfry. At the same moment, each man stared at his neighbor blankly. All watches were upheld. All hour hands were at—had passed—the figure 1. No bell stroke from the tower. The multitude became tumultuous.

Waiting a few moments, the chief magistrate, commanding silence, hailed the belfry to know what thing unforeseen had happened there.

No response.

He hailed again and yet again.

All continued hushed.

By his order, the soldiers burst in the tower door, when, stationing guards to defend it from the now surging mob, the chief, accompanied by his former associate, climbed the winding stairs. Halfway up, they stopped to listen. No sound. Mounting faster, they reached the belfry, but, at the threshold, started at the spectacle disclosed. A spaniel, which, unbeknown to them, had followed them thus far, stood shivering as before some unknown monster in a brake, or, rather, as if it snuffed footsteps leading to some other world.

Bannadonna lay, prostrate and bleeding, at the base of the bell which was adorned with girls and garlands. He lay at the feet of the hour Una, his head coinciding, in a vertical line, with her left hand, clasped by the hour Dua. With downcast face impending over him, like Jael over nailed Sisera in the tent, was the domino; now no more becloaked.

It had limbs, and seemed clad in a scaly mail, lustrous as a dragon-beetle's. It was manacled, and its clubbed arms were uplifted, as if, with its manacles, once more to smite its already smitten victim. One advanced foot of it was inserted beneath the dead body, as if in the act of spurning it.

Uncertainty falls on what now followed.

It were but natural to suppose that the magistrates would, at first, shrink from immediate personal contact with what they saw. At the least, for a time, they would stand in involuntary doubt, it may be, in more or less horrified alarm. Certain it is that an arquebuss was called for from below. And some add that its report, followed by a fierce whiz, as of the sudden snapping of a mainspring, with a steely din, as if a stack of sword blades should be dashed upon a pavement; these blended sounds came ringing to the plain, attracting every eye far upward to the belfry, whence, through the latticework, thin wreaths of smoke were curling.

Some averred that it was the spaniel, gone mad by fear, which was shot. This, others denied. True it was, the spaniel never more was seen; and, probably for some unknown reason, it shared the burial now to be related of the domino. For, whatever the preceding circumstances may have been, the first instinctive panic over, or else all ground of reasonable fear removed, the two magistrates, by themselves, quickly re-hooded the figure in the dropped cloak wherein it had been hoisted. The same night, it was secretly lowered to the ground, smuggled to the beach, pulled far out to sea, and sunk. Nor to any after urgency, even in free convivial hours, would the twain ever disclose the full secrets of the belfry.

From the mystery unavoidably investing it, the popular solution of the foundling's fate involved more or less of supernatural agency. But some few less unscientific minds pretended to find little difficulty in otherwise accounting for it. In the chain of circumstantial inferences drawn, there may or may not have been some absent or defective links. But, as the explanation in question is the only one which tradition has explicitly preserved, in dearth of better, it will here be given. But, in the first place, it is requisite to present the supposition entertained as to the entire motive and mode, with their origin, of the secret design of Bannadonna, the minds above-mentioned assuming to penetrate as well into his soul as into the event. The disclosure will indirectly involve reference to peculiar matters, none of the clearest, beyond the immediate subject.

At that period, no large bell was made to sound otherwise than as at present, by agitation of a tongue within by means of ropes, or percussion from without, either from cumbrous machinery, or stalwart watchmen, armed with heavy hammers, stationed in the belfry or in sentry boxes on the open roof, according as the bell was sheltered or exposed.

It was from observing these exposed bells, with their watchmen, that the foundling, as was opined, derived the first suggestion of his scheme. Perched on a great mast or spire, the human figure, viewed from below, undergoes such a reduction in its apparent size as to obliterate its intelligent features. It evinces no personality. Instead of bespeaking volition, its gestures rather resemble the automatic ones of the arms of a telegraph.

Musing, therefore, upon the purely Punchinello aspect of the human figure thus beheld, it had indirectly occurred to Bannadonna to devise some metallic agent which should strike the hour with its mechanic hand, with even greater precision than the vital one. And, moreover, as the vital watchman on the roof, sallying from his retreat at the given periods, walked to the bell with uplifted mace to smite it, Bannadonna had resolved that his invention should likewise possess the power of locomotion, and, along with that, the appearance, at least, of intelligence and will.

If the conjectures of those who claimed acquaintance with the intent of Bannadonna be thus far correct, no unenterprising spirit could have been his. But they stopped not here; intimating that though, indeed, his design had, in the first place, been prompted by the sight of the watchman, and confined to the devising of a subtle substitute for him, yet, as is not seldom the case with projectors, by insensible gradations proceeding from comparatively pigmy aims to titanic ones, the original scheme had, in its anticipated eventualities, at last attained to an unheard-of degree of daring. He still bent his efforts upon the locomotive figure for the belfry, but only as a partial type of an ulterior creature, a sort of elephantine helot, adapted to further, in a degree scarcely to be imagined, the universal conveniences and glories of humanity; supplying nothing less than a supplement to the Six Days' Work; stocking the earth with a new serf, more useful than the ox, swifter than the dolphin, stronger than the lion, more cunning than the ape, for industry an ant, more fiery than serpents, and yet, in patience, another ass. All excellences of all God-made creatures which served man were here to receive advancement, and then to be combined in one. Talus was to have been the all-accomplished helot's name. Talus, iron slave to Bannadonna, and, through him, to man.

Here, it might well be thought that, were these last conjectures as to the foundling's secrets not erroneous, then must he have been hopelessly infected with the craziest chimeras of his age; far outgoing Albert Magus and Cornelius Agrippa. But the contrary was averred. However marvelous his design, however apparently transcending not alone the bounds of human invention, but those of divine creation, yet the proposed means to be employed were alleged to have been confined within the sober forms of sober reason. It was affirmed that, to a degree of more than skeptic scorn, Bannadonna had been without sympathy for any of the vainglorious irrationalities of his time. For example, he had not concluded, with the visionaries among the metaphysicians, that between the finer mechanic forces and the ruder animal vitality some germ of correspondence might prove discoverable. As little did his scheme partake of the enthusiasm of some natural philosophers, who hoped, by physiological and chemical inductions, to arrive at a knowledge of the source of life, and so qualify themselves to manufacture and improve upon it. Much less had he aught in common with the tribe of alchemists, who sought by a species of incantations to evoke some surprising vitality from the laboratory. Neither had he imagined, with certain sanguine theosophists, that, by faithful adoration of the Highest, unheard-of powers would be vouchsafed to man. A practical materialist, what Bannadonna had aimed at was to have been reached, not by logic, not by crucible, not by conjuration, not by altars, but by plain vise-bench and hammer. In short, to solve nature, to steal into her, to intrigue beyond her, to procure someone else to bind her to his hand—these, one and all, had not been his objects, but, asking no favors from any element or any being, of himself to rival her, outstrip her, and rule her. He stooped to conquer. With him, common sense was theurgy; machinery, miracle; Prometheus, the heroic name for machinist; man, the true God.

Nevertheless, in his initial step, so far as the experimental automaton for the belfry was concerned, he allowed fancy some little play, or, perhaps, what seemed his fancifulness was but his utilitarian ambition collaterally extended. In figure, the creature for the belfry should not be likened after the human pattern, nor any animal one, nor after the ideals, however wild, of ancient fable, but equally in aspect as in organism be an original production—the more terrible to behold, the better.

Such, then, were the suppositions as to the present scheme, and the reserved intent. How, at the very threshold, so unlooked-for a catastrophe overturned all, or rather, what was the conjecture here, is now to be set forth.

It was thought that on the day preceding the fatality, his visitors having left him, Bannadonna had unpacked the belfry image, adjusted it, and placed it in the retreat provided—a sort of sentry box in one corner of the belfry; in short, throughout the night, and for some part of the ensuing morning, he had been engaged in arranging everything connected with the domino: the issuing from the sentry box each sixty minutes; sliding along a grooved way, like a railway; advancing to the clock bell with uplifted manacles; striking it at one of the twelve junctions of the four-and-twenty hands; then wheeling, circling the bell, and retiring to its post, there to bide for another sixty minutes, when the same process was to be repeated; the bell, by a cunning mechanism, meantime turning on its vertical axis, so as to present, to the descending mace, the clasped hands of the next two figures, when it would strike two, three, and so on, to the end. The musical metal in this time bell being so managed in the fusion, by some art perishing with its originator, that each of the clasps of the four-and-twenty hands should give forth its own peculiar resonance when parted.

But on the magic metal, the magic and metallic stranger never struck but that one stroke, drove but that one nail, served but that one clasp, by which Bannadonna clung to his ambitious life. For, after winding up the creature in the sentry box, so that, for the present, skipping the intervening hours, it should not emerge till the hour of one, but should then infallibly emerge, and, after deftly oiling the grooves whereon it was to slide, it was surmised that the mechanician must then have hurried to the bell, to give his final touches to its sculpture. True artist, he here became absorbed, and absorption still further intensified, it may be, by his striving to abate that strange look of Una, which, though, before others, he had treated with such unconcern, might not, in secret, have been without its thorn.

And so, for the interval, he was oblivious of his creature, which, not oblivious of him, and true to its creation, and true to its heedful winding up, left its post precisely at the given moment, along its well-oiled route, slid noiselessly towards its mark, and, aiming at the hand of Una to ring one clangorous note, dully smote the intervening brain of Bannadonna, turned backwards to it, the manacled arms then instantly upspringing to their hovering poise. The falling body clogged the thing's return, so there it stood, still impending over Bannadonna, as if whispering some post-mortem terror. The chisel lay dropped from the hand, but beside the hand; the oil-flask spilled across the iron track.

In his unhappy end, not unmindful of the rare genius of the mechanician, the republic decreed him a stately funeral. It was resolved that the great bell—the one whose casting had been jeopardized through the timidity of the ill-starred workman—should be rung upon the entrance of the bier into the cathedral. The most robust man of the country round was assigned the office of bell ringer.

But as the pallbearers entered the cathedral porch, naught but a broken and disastrous sound, like that of some lone Alpine landslide, fell from the tower upon their ears. And then all was hushed.

Glancing backwards, they saw the groined belfry crashed sideways in. It afterwards appeared that the powerful peasant who had the bell rope in charge, wishing to test at once the full glory of the bell, had swayed down upon the rope with one concentrate jerk. The mass of quaking metal, too ponderous for its frame, and strangely feeble somewhere at its top, loosed from its fastening, tore sideways down, and, tumbling in one sheer fall three hundred feet to the soft sward below, buried itself inverted and half out of sight.

Upon its disinterment, the main fracture was found to have started from a small spot in the ear, which, being scraped, revealed a defect, deceptively minute, in the casting, which defect must subsequently have been pasted over with some unknown compound.

The remolten metal soon reassumed its place in the tower's repaired superstructure. For one year the metallic choir of birds sang musically in its belfry boughwork of sculptured blinds and traceries. But on the first anniversary of the tower's completion—at early dawn, before the concourse had surrounded it—an earthquake came; one loud crash was heard. The stone pine, with all its bower of songsters, lay overthrown upon the plain.

So the blind slave obeyed its blinder lord, but, in obedience, slew him. So the creator was killed by the creature. So the bell was too heavy for the tower. So the bell's main weakness was where man's blood had flawed it. And so pride went before the fall.

THE TALE OF NEGATIVE GRAVITY

Frank R. Stockton

FRANK R. STOCKTON (1834-1902) was born in Philadelphia, Pennsylvania and is better known as an author of popular children's books. He is more famously known for his short story, "The Lady, or the Tiger" (1882). While he wrote four science fiction novels, his best work in the genre is found in his short stories where his whimsy and good humor shines through.

MY wife and I were staying at a small town in northern Italy; and on a certain pleasant afternoon in spring we had taken a walk of six or seven miles to see the sun set behind some low mountains to the west of the town. Most of our walk had been along a hard, smooth highway, and then we turned into a series of narrower roads, sometimes bordered by walls, and sometimes by light fences of reed or cane. Nearing the mountain, to a low spur of which we intended to ascend, we easily scaled a wall about four feet high, and found ourselves upon pasture-land, which led, sometimes by gradual ascents, and sometimes by bits of rough climbing, to the spot we wished to reach. We were afraid we were a little late, and therefore hurried on, running up the grassy hills, and bounding briskly over the rough and rocky places. I carried a knapsack strapped firmly to my shoulders, and under my wife's arm was a large, soft basket of a kind much used by tourists. Her arm was passed through the handles and around the bottom of the basket, which she pressed closely to her side. This was the way she always carried it. The basket contained two bottles of wine, one sweet for my wife, and another a little acid for myself. Sweet wines give me a headache.

When we reached the grassy bluff, well known thereabouts to lovers of sunset views, I stepped immediately to the edge to gaze upon the scene, but my wife sat down to take a sip of wine, for she was very thirsty; and then, leaving her basket, she came to my side. The scene was indeed one of great beauty. Beneath us stretched a wide valley of many shades of green, with a little river running through it, and red-tiled houses here and there. Beyond rose a range of mountains, pink, pale green, and purple where their tips caught the reflection of the setting sun, and of a rich gray-green in shadows. Beyond all was the blue Italian sky, illumined by an especially fine sunset.

My wife and I are Americans, and at the time of this story were middle-aged people and very fond of seeing in each other's company whatever there was of interest or beauty around us. We had a son about twenty-two years old, of whom we were also very fond; but he was not with us, being at that time a student in Germany. Although we had good health, we were not very robust people, and, under ordinary circumstances, not much given to long country tramps. I was of medium size, without much muscular development, while my wife was quite stout, and growing stouter.

The reader may, perhaps, be somewhat surprised that a middle-aged couple, not very strong, or very good walkers, the lady loaded with a basket containing two bottles of wine and a metal drinking-cup, and the gentleman carrying a heavy knapsack, filled with all sorts of odds and ends, strapped to his shoulders, should set off on a seven-mile walk, jump over a wall, run up a hillside, and yet feel in very good trim to enjoy a sunset view. This peculiar state of things I will proceed to explain.

I had been a professional man, but some years before had retired upon a very comfortable income. I had always been very fond of scientific pursuits, and now made these the occupation and pleasure of much of my leisure time. Our home was in a small town; and in a corner of my grounds I built a laboratory, where I carried on my work and my experiments. I had long been anxious to discover the means not only of producing, but of retaining and controlling, a natural force, really the same as centrifugal force, but which I called negative gravity. This name I adopted because it indicated better than any other the action of the force in question, as I produced it. Positive gravity attracts everything toward the centre of the earth. Negative gravity, therefore, would be that power which repels everything from the center of the earth, just as the negative pole of a magnet repels the needle, while the positive pole attracts it. My object was, in fact, to store centrifugal force and to render it constant, controllable, and available for use. The advantages of such a discovery could scarcely be described. In a word, it would lighten the burdens of the world.

I will not touch upon the labors and disappointments of several years. It is enough to say that at last I discovered a method of producing, storing, and controlling negative gravity.

The mechanism of my invention was rather complicated, but the method of operating it was very simple. A strong metallic case, about eight inches long, and half as wide, contained the machinery for producing the force; and this was put into action by means of the pressure of a screw worked from the outside. As soon as this pressure was produced, negative gravity began to be evolved and stored, and the greater the pressure the greater the force. As the screw was moved outward, and the pressure diminished, the force decreased, and when the screw was withdrawn to its fullest extent, the action of negative gravity entirely ceased. Thus this force could be produced or dissipated at will to such degrees as might be desired, and its action, so long as the requisite pressure was maintained, was constant.

When this little apparatus worked to my satisfaction I called my wife into my laboratory and explained to her my invention and its value. She had known that I had been at work with an important object, but I had never told her what it was. I had said that if I succeeded I would tell her all, but if I failed she need not be troubled with the matter at all. Being a very sensible woman, this satisfied her perfectly. Now I explained everything to her—the construction of the machine, and the wonderful uses to which this invention could be applied. I told her that it could diminish, or entirely dissipate, the weight of objects of any kind. A heavily loaded wagon, with two of these instruments fastened to its sides, and each screwed to a proper force, would be so lifted and supported that it would press upon the ground as lightly as an empty cart, and a small horse could draw it with ease. A bale of cotton, with one of these machines attached, could be handled and carried by a boy. A car, with a number of these machines, could be made to rise in the air like a balloon. Everything, in fact, that was heavy could be made light; and as a great part of labor, all over the world, is caused by the attraction of gravitation, so this repellent force, wherever applied, would make weight less and work easier. I told her of many, many ways in which the invention might be used, and would have told her of many more if she had not suddenly burst into tears.

"The world has gained something wonderful," she exclaimed, between her sobs, "but I have lost a husband!"

"What do you mean by that?" I asked, in surprise.

"I haven't minded it so far," she said, "because it gave you something to do, and it pleased you, and it never interfered with our home pleasures and our home life. But now that is all over. You will never be your own master again. It will succeed, I am sure, and you may make a great deal of money, but we don't need money. What we need is the happiness which we have always had until now. Now there will be companies, and patents, and lawsuits, and experiments, and people calling you a humbug, and other people saying they discovered it long ago, and all sorts of persons coming to see you, and you'll be obliged to go to all sorts of places, and you will be an altered man, and we shall never be happy again. Millions of money will not repay us for the happiness we have lost."

These words of my wife struck me with much force. Before I had called her my mind had begun to be filled and perplexed with ideas of what I ought to do now that the great invention was perfected. Until now the matter had not troubled me at all. Sometimes I had gone backward and sometimes forward, but, on the whole, I had always felt encouraged. I had taken great pleasure in the work, but I had never allowed myself to be too much absorbed by it. But now everything was different. I began to feel that it was due to myself and to my fellow-beings that I should properly put this invention before the world. And how should I set about it? What steps should I take? I must make no mistakes. When the matter should become known hundreds of scientific people might set themselves to work; how could I tell but that they might discover other methods of producing the same effect? I must guard myself against a great many things. I must get patents in all parts of the world. Already, as I have said, my mind began to be troubled and perplexed with these things. A turmoil of this sort did not suit my age or disposition. I could not but agree with my wife that the joys of a quiet and contented life were now about to be broken into.

"My dear," said I, "I believe, with you, that the thing will do us more harm than good. If it were not for depriving the world of the invention I would throw the whole thing to the winds. And yet," I added, regretfully, "I had expected a great deal of personal gratification from the use of this invention."

"Now listen," said my wife, eagerly; "don't you think it would be best to do this: use the thing as much as you please for your own amusement and satisfaction, but let the world wait? It has waited a long time, and let it wait a little longer. When we are dead let Herbert have the invention. He will then be old enough to judge for himself whether it will be better to take advantage of it for his own profit, or simply to give it to the public for nothing. It would be cheating him if we were to do the latter, but it would also be doing him a great wrong if we were, at his age, to load him with such a heavy responsibility. Besides, if he took it up, you could not help going into it, too."

I took my wife's advice. I wrote a careful and complete account of the invention, and, sealing it up, I gave it to my lawyers to be handed to my son after my death. If he died first, I would make other arrangements. Then I determined to get all the good and fun out of the thing that was possible without telling any one anything about it. Even Herbert, who was away from home, was not to be told of the invention.

The first thing I did was to buy a strong leathern knapsack, and inside of this I fastened my little machine, with a screw so arranged that it could be worked from the outside. Strapping this firmly to my shoulders, my wife gently turned the screw at the back until the upward tendency of the knapsack began to lift and sustain me. When I felt myself so gently supported and upheld that I seemed to weigh about thirty or forty pounds, I would set out for a walk. The knapsack did not raise me from the ground, but it gave me a very buoyant step. It was no labor at all to walk; it was a delight, an ecstasy. With the strength of a man and the weight of a child, I gayly strode along. The first day I walked half a dozen miles at a very brisk pace, and came back without feeling in the least degree tired. These walks now became one of the greatest joys of my life. When nobody was looking, I would bound over a fence, sometimes just touching it with one hand, and sometimes not touching it at all. I delighted in rough places. I sprang over streams. I jumped and I ran. I felt like Mercury himself.

I now set about making another machine, so that my wife could accompany me in my walks; but when it was finished she positively refused to use it. "I can't wear a knapsack," she said, "and there is no other good way of fastening it to me. Besides, everybody about here knows I am no walker, and it would only set them talking."

I occasionally made use of this second machine, but I will give only one instance of its application. Some repairs were needed to the foundation-walls of my barn, and a two-horse wagon, loaded with building-stone, had been brought into my yard and left there. In the evening, when the men had gone away, I took my two machines and fastened them, with strong chains, one on each side of the loaded wagon. Then, gradually turning the screws, the wagon was so lifted that its weight became very greatly diminished. We had an old donkey which used to belong to Herbert, and which was now occasionally used with a small cart to bring packages from the station. I went into the barn and put the harness on the little fellow, and, bringing him out to the wagon, I attached him to it. In this position he looked very funny with a long pole sticking out in front of him and the great wagon behind him. When all was ready I touched him up; and, to my great delight, he moved off with the two-horse load of stone as easily as if he were drawing his own cart. I led him out into the public road, along which he proceeded without difficulty. He was an opinionated little beast, and sometimes stopped, not liking the peculiar manner in which he was harnessed; but a touch of the switch made him move on, and I soon turned him and brought the wagon back into the yard. This determined the success of my invention in one of its most important uses, and with a satisfied heart I put the donkey into the stable and went into the house.

Our trip to Europe was made a few months after this, and was mainly on our son Herbert's account. He, poor fellow, was in great trouble, and so, therefore, were we. He had become engaged, with our full consent, to a young lady in our town, the daughter of a gentleman whom we esteemed very highly. Herbert was young to be engaged to be married, but as we felt that he would never find a girl to make him so good a wife, we were entirely satisfied, especially as it was agreed on all hands that the marriage was not to take place for some time. It seemed to us that, in marrying Janet Gilbert, Herbert would secure for himself, in the very beginning of his career, the most important element of a happy life. But suddenly, without any reason that seemed to us justifiable, Mr. Gilbert, the only surviving parent of Janet, broke off the match; and he and his daughter soon after left the town for a trip to the West.

This blow nearly broke poor Herbert's heart. He gave up his professional studies and came home to us, and for a time we thought he would be seriously ill. Then we took him to Europe, and after a Continental tour of a month or two we left him, at his own request, in Goettingen, where he thought it would do him good to go to work again. Then we went down to the little town in Italy where my story first finds us. My wife had suffered much in mind and body on her son's account, and for this reason I was anxious that she should take outdoor exercise, and enjoy as much as possible the bracing air of the country. I had brought with me both my little machines. One was still in my knapsack, and the other I had fastened to the inside of an enormous family trunk. As one is obliged to pay for nearly every pound of his baggage on the Continent, this saved me a great deal of money. Everything heavy was packed into this great trunk—books, papers, the bronze, iron, and marble relics we had picked up, and all the articles that usually weigh down a tourist's baggage. I screwed up the negative-gravity apparatus until the trunk could be handled with great ease by an ordinary porter. I could have made it weigh nothing at all, but this, of course, I did not wish to do. The lightness of my baggage, however, had occasioned some comment, and I had overheard remarks which were not altogether complimentary about people travelling around with empty trunks; but this only amused me.

Desirous that my wife should have the advantage of negative gravity while taking our walks, I had removed the machine from the trunk and fastened it inside of the basket, which she could carry under her arm. This assisted her wonderfully. When one arm was tired she put the basket under the other, and thus, with one hand on my arm, she could easily keep up with the free and buoyant steps my knapsack enabled me to take. She did not object to long tramps here, because nobody knew that she was not a walker, and she always carried some wine or other refreshment in the basket, not only because it was pleasant to have it with us, but because it seemed ridiculous to go about carrying an empty basket.

There were English-speaking people stopping at the hotel where we were, but they seemed more fond of driving than walking, and none of them offered to accompany us on our rambles, for which we were very glad. There was one man there, however, who was a great walker. He was an Englishman, a member of an Alpine Club, and generally went about dressed in a knickerbocker suit, with gray woollen stockings covering an enormous pair of calves. One evening this gentleman was talking to me and some others about the ascent of the Matterhorn, and I took occasion to deliver in pretty strong language my opinion upon such exploits. I declared them to be useless, foolhardy, and, if the climber had any one who loved him, wicked.

"Even if the weather should permit a view," I said, "what is that compared to the terrible risk to life? Under certain circumstances," I added (thinking of a kind of waistcoat I had some idea of making, which, set about with little negative-gravity machines, all connected with a conveniently handled screw, would enable the wearer at times to dispense with his weight altogether), "such ascents might be divested of danger, and be quite admissible; but ordinarily they should be frowned upon by the intelligent public."

The Alpine Club man looked at me, especially regarding my somewhat slight figure and thinnish legs.

"It's all very well for you to talk that way," he said, "because it is easy to see that you are not up to that sort of thing."

"In conversations of this kind," I replied, "I never make personal allusions; but since you have chosen to do so, I feel inclined to invite you to walk with me to-morrow to the top of the mountain to the north of this town."

"I'll do it," he said, "at any time you choose to name." And as I left the room soon afterward I heard him laugh.

The next afternoon, about two o'clock, the Alpine Club man and myself set out for the mountain.

"What have you got in your knapsack?" he said.

"A hammer to use if I come across geological specimens, a field-glass, a flask of wine, and some other things."

"I wouldn't carry any weight, if I were you," he said.

"Oh, I don't mind it," I answered, and off we started.

The mountain to which we were bound was about two miles from the town. Its nearest side was steep, and in places almost precipitous, but it sloped away more gradually toward the north, and up that side a road led by devious windings to a village near the summit. It was not a very high mountain, but it would do for an afternoon's climb.

"I suppose you want to go up by the road," said my companion.

"Oh no," I answered, "we won't go so far around as that. There is a path up this side, along which I have seen men driving their goats. I prefer to take that."

"All right, if you say so," he answered, with a smile; "but you'll find it pretty tough."

After a time he remarked:

"I wouldn't walk so fast, if I were you."

"Oh, I like to step along briskly," I said. And briskly on we went.

My wife had screwed up the machine in the knapsack more than usual, and walking seemed scarcely any effort at all. I carried a long alpenstock, and when we reached the mountain and began the ascent, I found that with the help of this and my knapsack I could go uphill at a wonderful rate. My companion had taken the lead, so as to show me how to climb. Making a *detour* over some rocks, I quickly passed him and went ahead. After that it was impossible for him to keep up with me. I ran up steep places, I cut off the windings of the path by lightly clambering over rocks, and even when I followed the beaten track my step was as rapid as if I had been walking on level ground.

"Look here!" shouted the Alpine Club man from below, "you'll kill yourself if you go at that rate! That's no way to climb mountains."

"It's my way!" I cried. And on I skipped.

Twenty minutes after I arrived at the summit my companion joined me, puffing, and wiping his red face with his handkerchief.

"Confound it!" he cried, "I never came up a mountain so fast in my life."

"You need not have hurried," I said, coolly.

"I was afraid something would happen to you," he growled, "and I wanted to stop you. I never saw a person climb in such an utterly absurd way."

"I don't see why you should call it absurd," I said, smiling with an air of superiority. "I arrived here in a perfectly comfortable condition, neither heated nor wearied."

He made no answer, but walked off to a little distance, fanning himself with his hat and growling words which I did not catch. After a time I proposed to descend.

"You must be careful as you go down," he said. "It is much more dangerous to go down steep places than to climb up."

"I am always prudent," I answered, and started in advance. I found the descent of the mountain much more pleasant than the ascent. It was positively exhilarating. I jumped from rocks and bluffs eight and ten feet in height, and touched the ground as gently as if I had stepped down but two feet. I ran down steep paths, and, with the aid of my alpenstock, stopped myself in an instant. I was careful to avoid dangerous places, but the runs and jumps I made were such as no man had ever made before upon that mountain-side. Once only I heard my companion's voice.

"You'll break your—!" he yelled.

"Never fear!" I called back, and soon left him far above.

When I reached the bottom I would have waited for him, but my activity had warmed me up, and as a cool evening breeze was beginning to blow I thought it better not to stop and take cold. Half an hour after my arrival at the hotel I came down to the court, cool, fresh, and dressed for dinner, and just in time to meet the Alpine man as he entered, hot, dusty, and growling.

"Excuse me for not waiting for you," I said; but without stopping to hear my reason, he muttered something about waiting in a place where no one would care to stay, and passed into the house.

There was no doubt that what I had done gratified my pique and tickled my vanity.

"I think now," I said, when I related the matter to my wife, "that he will scarcely say that I am not up to that sort of thing."

"I am not sure," she answered, "that it was exactly fair. He did not know how you were assisted."

"It was fair enough," I said. "He is enabled to climb well by the inherited vigor of his constitution and by his training. He did not tell me what methods of exercise he used to get those great muscles upon his legs. I am enabled to climb by the exercise of my intellect. My method is my business and his method is his business. It is all perfectly fair."

Still she persisted:

"He *thought* that you climbed with your legs, and not with your head."

And now, after this long digression, necessary to explain how a middle-aged couple of slight pedestrian ability, and loaded with a heavy knapsack and basket, should have started out on a rough walk and climb, fourteen miles in all, we will return to ourselves, standing on the little bluff and gazing out upon the sunset view. When the sky began to fade a little we turned from it and prepared to go back to the town.

"Where is the basket?" I said.

"I left it right here," answered my wife. "I unscrewed the machine and it lay perfectly flat."

"Did you afterward take out the bottles?" I asked, seeing them lying on the grass.

"Yes, I believe I did. I had to take out yours in order to get at mine."

"Then," said I, after looking all about the grassy patch on which we stood, "I am afraid you did not entirely unscrew the instrument, and that when the weight of the bottles was removed the basket gently rose into the air."

"It may be so," she said, lugubriously. "The basket was behind me as I drank my wine."

"I believe that is just what has happened," I said. "Look up there! I vow that is our basket!"

I pulled out my field-glass and directed it at a little speck high above our heads. It was the basket floating high in the air. I gave the glass to my wife to look, but she did not want to use it.

"What shall I do?" she cried. "I can't walk home without that basket. It's perfectly dreadful!" And she looked as if she was going to cry.

"Do not distress yourself," I said, although I was a good deal disturbed myself. "We shall get home very well. You shall put your hand on my shoulder, while I put my arm around you. Then you can screw up my machine a good deal higher, and it will support us both. In this way I am sure that we shall get on very well."

We carried out this plan, and managed to walk on with moderate comfort. To be sure, with the knapsack pulling me upward, and the weight of my wife pulling me down, the straps hurt me somewhat, which they had not done before. We did not spring lightly over the wall into the road, but, still clinging to each other, we clambered awkwardly over it. The road for the most part declined gently toward the town, and with moderate ease we made our way along it. But we walked much more slowly than we had done before, and it was quite dark when we reached our hotel. If it had not been for the light inside the court it would have been difficult for us to find it. A travelling-carriage was standing before the entrance, and against the light. It was necessary to pass around it, and my wife went first. I attempted to follow her, but, strange to say, there was nothing under my feet. I stepped vigorously, but only wagged my legs in the air. To my horror I found that I was rising in the air! I soon saw, by the light below me, that I was some fifteen feet from the ground. The carriage drove away, and in the darkness I was not noticed. Of course I knew what had happened. The instrument in my knapsack had been screwed up to such an intensity, in order to support both myself and my wife, that when her weight was removed the force of the negative gravity was sufficient to raise me from the ground. But I was glad to find that when I had risen to the height I have mentioned I did not go up any higher, but hung in the air, about on a level with the second tier of windows of the hotel.

I now began to try to reach the screw in my knapsack in order to reduce the force of the negative gravity; but, do what I would, I could not get my hand to it. The machine in the knapsack had been placed so as to support me in a well-balanced and comfortable way; and in doing this it had been impossible to set the screw so that I could reach it. But in a temporary arrangement of the kind this had not been considered necessary, as my wife always turned the screw for me until sufficient lifting power had been attained. I had intended, as I have said before, to construct a negative-gravity waistcoat, in which the screw should be in front, and entirely under the wearer's control; but this was a thing of the future.

When I found that I could not turn the screw I began to be much alarmed. Here I was, dangling in the air, without any means of reaching the ground. I could not expect my wife to return to look for me, as she would naturally suppose I had stopped to speak to some one. I thought of loosening myself from the knapsack, but this would not do, for I should fall heavily, and either kill myself or break some of my bones. I did not dare to call for assistance, for if any of the simple-minded inhabitants of the town had discovered me floating in the air they would have taken me for a demon, and would probably have shot at me. A moderate breeze was blowing, and it wafted me gently down the street. If it had blown me against a tree I would have seized it, and have endeavored, so to speak, to climb down it; but there were no trees. There was a dim street-lamp here and there, but reflectors above them threw their light upon the pavement, and none up to me. On many accounts I was glad that the night was so dark, for, much as I desired to get down, I wanted no one to see me in my strange position, which, to any one but myself and wife, would be utterly unaccountable. If I could rise as high as the roofs I might get on one of them, and, tearing off an armful of tiles, so load myself that I would be heavy enough to descend. But I did not rise to the eaves of any of the houses. If there had been a telegraph-pole, or anything of the kind that I could have clung to, I would have taken off the knapsack, and would have endeavored to scramble down as well as I could. But there was nothing I could cling to. Even the water-spouts, if I could have reached the face of the houses, were embedded in the walls. At an open window, near which I was slowly blown, I saw two little boys going to bed by the light of a dim candle. I was dreadfully afraid that they would see me and raise an alarm. I actually came so near to the window that I threw out one foot and pushed against the wall with such force that I went nearly across the street. I thought I caught sight of a frightened look on the face of one of the boys; but of this I am not sure, and I heard no cries. I still floated, dangling, down the street. What was to be done? Should I call out? In that case, if I were not shot or stoned, my strange predicament, and the secret of my invention, would be exposed to the world. If I did not do this, I must either let myself drop and be killed or mangled, or hang there and die. When, during the course of the night, the air became more rarefied, I might rise higher and higher, perhaps to an altitude of one or two hundred feet.

It would then be impossible for the people to reach me and get me down, even if they were convinced that I was not a demon. I should then expire, and when the birds of the air had eaten all of me that they could devour, I should forever hang above the unlucky town, a dangling skeleton with a knapsack on its back.

Such thoughts were not reassuring, and I determined that if I could find no means of getting down without assistance, I would call out and run all risks; but so long as I could endure the tension of the straps I would hold out, and hope for a tree or a pole. Perhaps it might rain, and my wet clothes would then become so heavy that I would descend as low as the top of a lamp-post.

As this thought was passing through my mind I saw a spark of light upon the street approaching me. I rightly imagined that it came from a tobacco-pipe, and presently I heard a voice. It was that of the Alpine Club man. Of all people in the world I did not want him to discover me, and I hung as motionless as possible. The man was speaking to another person who was walking with him.

"He is crazy beyond a doubt," said the Alpine man. "Nobody but a maniac could have gone up and down that mountain as he did! He hasn't any muscles, and one need only look at him to know that he couldn't do any climbing in a natural way. It is only the excitement of insanity that gives him strength."

The two now stopped almost under me, and the speaker continued:

"Such things are very common with maniacs. At times they acquire an unnatural strength which is perfectly wonderful. I have seen a little fellow struggle and fight so that four strong men could not hold him."

Then the other person spoke.

"I am afraid what you say is too true," he remarked. "Indeed, I have known it for some time."

At these words my breath almost stopped. It was the voice of Mr. Gilbert, my townsman, and the father of Janet. It must have been he who had arrived in the travelling-carriage. He was acquainted with the Alpine Club man, and they were talking of me. Proper or improper, I listened with all my ears.

"It is a very sad case," Mr. Gilbert continued. "My daughter was engaged to marry his son, but I broke off the match. I could not have her marry the son of a lunatic, and there could be no doubt of his condition. He has been seen—a man of his age, and the head of a family—to load himself up with a heavy knapsack, which there was no earthly necessity for him to carry, and go skipping along the road for miles, vaulting over fences and jumping over rocks and ditches like a young calf or a colt. I myself saw a most heartrending instance of how a kindly man's nature can be changed by the derangement of his intellect. I was at some distance from his house, but I plainly saw him harness a little donkey which he owns to a large two-horse wagon loaded with stone, and beat and lash the poor little beast until it drew the heavy load some distance along the public road. I would have remonstrated with him on this horrible cruelty, but he had the wagon back in his yard before I could reach him."

"Oh, there can be no doubt of his insanity," said the Alpine Club man, "and he oughtn't to be allowed to travel about in this way. Some day he will pitch his wife over a precipice just for the fun of seeing her shoot through the air."

"I am sorry he is here," said Mr. Gilbert, "for it would be very painful to meet him. My daughter and I will retire very soon, and go away as early to-morrow morning as possible, so as to avoid seeing him."

And then they walked back to the hotel.

For a few moments I hung, utterly forgetful of my condition, and absorbed in the consideration of these revelations. One idea now filled my mind. Everything must be explained to Mr. Gilbert, even if it should be necessary to have him called to me, and for me to speak to him from the upper air.

Just then I saw something white approaching me along the road. My eyes had become accustomed to the darkness, and I perceived that it was an upturned face. I recognized the hurried gait, the form; it was my wife. As she came near me, I called her name, and in the same breath entreated her not to scream. It must have been an effort for her to restrain herself, but she did it.

"You must help me to get down," I said, "without anybody seeing us."

"What shall I do?" she whispered.

"Try to catch hold of this string."

Taking a piece of twine from my pocket, I lowered one end to her. But it was too short; she could not reach it. I then tied my handkerchief to it, but still it was not long enough.

"I can get more string, or handkerchiefs," she whispered, hurriedly.

"No," I said; "you could not get them up to me. But, leaning against the hotel wall, on this side, in the corner, just inside of the garden gate, are some fishing-poles. I have seen them there every day. You can easily find them in the dark. Go, please, and bring me one of those."

The hotel was not far away, and in a few minutes my wife returned with a fishing-pole. She stood on tiptoe, and reached it high in air; but all she could do was to strike my feet and legs with it. My most frantic exertions did not enable me to get my hands low enough to touch it.

"Wait a minute," she said; and the rod was withdrawn.

I knew what she was doing. There was a hook and line attached to the pole, and with womanly dexterity she was fastening the hook to the extreme end of the rod. Soon she reached up, and gently struck at my legs. After a few attempts the hook caught in my trousers, a little below my right knee. Then there was a slight pull, a long scratch down my leg, and the hook was stopped by the top of my boot. Then came a steady downward pull, and I felt myself descending. Gently and firmly the rod was drawn down; carefully the lower end was kept free from the ground; and in a few moments my ankle was seized with a vigorous grasp. Then some one seemed to climb up me, my feet touched the ground, an arm was thrown around my neck, the hand of another arm was busy at the back of my knapsack, and I soon stood firmly in the road, entirely divested of negative gravity.

"Oh that I should have forgotten," sobbed my wife, "and that I should have dropped your arms and let you go up into the air! At first I thought that you had stopped below, and it was only a little while ago that the truth flashed upon me. Then I rushed out and began looking up for you. I knew that you had wax matches in your pocket, and hoped that you would keep on striking them, so that you would be seen."

"But I did not wish to be seen," I said, as we hurried to the hotel; "and I can never be sufficiently thankful that it was you who found me and brought me down. Do you know that it is Mr. Gilbert and his daughter who have just arrived? I must see him instantly. I will explain it all to you when I come upstairs."

I took off my knapsack and gave it to my wife, who carried it to our room, while I went to look for Mr. Gilbert. Fortunately I found him just as he was about to go up to his chamber. He took my offered hand, but looked at me sadly and gravely.

"Mr. Gilbert," I said, "I must speak to you in private. Let us step into this room. There is no one here."

"My friend," said Mr. Gilbert, "it will be much better to avoid discussing this subject. It is very painful to both of us, and no good can come from talking of it."

"You cannot now comprehend what it is I want to say to you," I replied. "Come in here, and in a few minutes you will be very glad that you listened to me."

My manner was so earnest and impressive that Mr. Gilbert was constrained to follow me, and we went into a small room called the smoking-room, but in which people seldom smoked, and closed the door. I immediately began my statement. I told my old friend that I had discovered, by means that I need not explain at present, that he had considered me crazy, and that now the most important object of my life was to set myself right in his eyes. I thereupon gave him the whole history of my invention, and explained the reason of the actions that had appeared to him those of a lunatic. I said nothing about the little incident of that evening. That was a mere accident, and I did not care now to speak of it.

Mr. Gilbert listened to me very attentively.

"Your wife is here?" he asked, when I had finished.

"Yes," I said; "and she will corroborate my story in every item, and no one could ever suspect her of being crazy. I will go and bring her to you."

In a few minutes my wife was in the room, had shaken hands with Mr. Gilbert, and had been told of my suspected madness. She turned pale, but smiled.

"He did act like a crazy man," she said, "but I never supposed that anybody would think him one." And tears came into her eyes.

"And now, my dear," said I, "perhaps you will tell Mr. Gilbert how I did all this."

And then she told him the story that I had told.

Mr. Gilbert looked from the one to the other of us with a troubled air.

"Of course I do not doubt either of you, or rather I do not doubt that you believe what you say. All would be right if I could bring myself to credit that such a force as that you speak of can possibly exist."

"That is a matter," said I, "which I can easily prove to you by actual demonstration. If you can wait a short time, until my wife and I have had something to eat—for I am nearly famished, and I am sure she must be—I will set your mind at rest upon that point."

"I will wait here," said Mr. Gilbert, "and smoke a cigar. Don't hurry yourselves. I shall be glad to have some time to think about what you have told me."

When we had finished the dinner, which had been set aside for us, I went upstairs and got my knapsack, and we both joined Mr. Gilbert in the smoking-room. I showed him the little machine, and explained, very briefly, the principle of its construction. I did not give any practical demonstration of its action, because there were people walking about the corridor who might at any moment come into the room; but, looking out of the window, I saw that the night was much clearer. The wind had dissipated the clouds, and the stars were shining brightly.

"If you will come up the street with me," said I to Mr. Gilbert, "I will show you how this thing works."

"That is just what I want to see," he answered.

"I will go with you," said my wife, throwing a shawl over her head. And we started up the street.

When we were outside the little town I found the starlight was quite sufficient for my purpose. The white roadway, the low walls, and objects about us, could easily be distinguished.

"Now," said I to Mr. Gilbert, "I want to put this knapsack on you, and let you see how it feels, and how it will help you to walk." To this he assented with some eagerness, and I strapped it firmly on him. "I will now turn this screw," said I, "until you shall become lighter and lighter."

"Be very careful not to turn it too much," said my wife, earnestly.

"Oh, you may depend on me for that," said I, turning the screw very gradually.

Mr. Gilbert was a stout man, and I was obliged to give the screw a good many turns.

"There seems to be considerable hoist in it," he said, directly. And then I put my arms around him, and found that I could raise him from the ground.

"Are you lifting me?" he exclaimed, in surprise.

"Yes; I did it with ease," I answered.

"Upon—my—word!" ejaculated Mr. Gilbert.

I then gave the screw a half-turn more, and told him to walk and run. He started off, at first slowly, then he made long strides, then he began to run, and then to skip and jump. It had been many years since Mr. Gilbert had skipped and jumped. No one was in sight, and he was free to gambol as much as he pleased. "Could you give it another turn?" said he, bounding up to me. "I want to try that wall." I put on a little more negative gravity, and he vaulted over a five-foot wall with great ease. In an instant he had leaped back into the road, and in two bounds was at my side. "I came down as light as a cat," he said. "There was never anything like it." And away he went up the road, taking steps at least eight feet long, leaving my wife and me laughing heartily at the preternatural agility of our stout friend. In a few minutes he was with us again. "Take it off," he said. "If I wear it any longer I shall want one myself, and then I shall be taken for a crazy man, and perhaps clapped into an asylum."

"Now," said I, as I turned back the screw before unstrapping the knapsack, "do you understand how I took long walks, and leaped and jumped; how I ran uphill and downhill, and how the little donkey drew the loaded wagon?"

"I understand it all," cried he. "I take back all I ever said or thought about you, my friend."

"And Herbert may marry Janet?" cried my wife.

"*May* marry her!" cried Mr. Gilbert. "Indeed, he *shall* marry her, if I have anything to say about it! My poor girl has been drooping ever since I told her it could not be."

My wife rushed at him, but whether she embraced him or only shook his hands I cannot say; for I had the knapsack in one hand and was rubbing my eyes with the other.

"But, my dear fellow," said Mr. Gilbert, directly, "if you still consider it to your interest to keep your invention a secret, I wish you had never made it. No one having a machine like that can help using it, and it is often quite as bad to be considered a maniac as to be one."

"My friend," I cried, with some excitement, "I have made up my mind on this subject. The little machine in this knapsack, which is the only one I now possess, has been a great pleasure to me. But I now know it has also been of the greatest injury indirectly to me and mine, not to mention some direct inconvenience and danger, which I will speak of another time. The secret lies with us three, and we will keep it. But the invention itself is too full of temptation and danger for any of us."

As I said this I held the knapsack with one hand while I quickly turned the screw with the other. In a few moments it was high above my head, while I with difficulty held it down by the straps. "Look!" I cried. And then I released my hold, and the knapsack shot into the air and disappeared into the upper gloom.

I was about to make a remark, but had no chance, for my wife threw herself upon my bosom, sobbing with joy.

"Oh, I am so glad—so glad!" she said. "And you will never make another?"

"Never another!" I answered.

"And now let us hurry in and see Janet," said my wife.

"You don't know how heavy and clumsy I feel," said Mr. Gilbert, striving to keep up with us as we walked back. "If I had worn that thing much longer, I should never have been willing to take it off!"

Janet had retired, but my wife went up to her room.

"I think she has felt it as much as our boy," she said, when she rejoined me. "But I tell you, my dear, I left a very happy girl in that little bedchamber over the garden."

And there were three very happy elderly people talking together until quite late that evening. "I shall write to Herbert to-night," I said, when we separated, "and tell him to meet us all in Geneva. It will do the young man no harm if we interrupt his studies just now."

"You must let me add a postscript to the letter," said Mr. Gilbert, "and I am sure it will require no knapsack with a screw in the back to bring him quickly to us."

And it did not.

There is a wonderful pleasure in tripping over the earth like a winged Mercury, and in feeling one's self relieved of much of that attraction of gravitation which drags us down to earth and gradually makes the movement of our bodies but weariness and labor. But this pleasure is not to be compared, I think, to that given by the buoyancy and lightness of two young and loving hearts, reunited after a separation which they had supposed would last forever.

What became of the basket and the knapsack, or whether they ever met in upper air, I do not know. If they but float away and stay away from ken of mortal man, I shall be satisfied.

And whether or not the world will ever know more of the power of negative gravity depends entirely upon the disposition of my son Herbert, when—after a good many years, I hope—he shall open the packet my lawyers have in keeping.

NOTE:

It would be quite useless for any one to interview my wife on this subject, for she has entirely forgotten how my machine was made. And as for Mr. Gilbert, he never knew.

TO WHOM THIS MAY COME

Edward Bellamy

EDWARD BELLAMY (1850-1898) was born in Massachusetts and was the son and grandson of Baptist ministers. He studied law and worked as a reporter for various newspapers before becoming a novelist. He is remembered for his best-selling *Looking Backward*, 1887, which is considered to be the first Socialist Utopian novel. Bellamy's primary concerns in science fiction are from the perspective of how the average person copes with changes in society that might not be to their benefit. "To Whom This May Come", written in 1889, is an ironic take on a "perfect" society where everyone is telepathic.

IT is now about a year since I took passage at Calcutta in the ship *Adelaide* for New York. We had baffling weather till New Amsterdam Island was sighted, where we took a new point of departure. Three days later, a terrible gale struck us. Four days we flew before it, whither, no one knew, for neither sun, moon, nor stars were at any time visible, and we could take no observation. Toward midnight of the fourth day, the glare of lightning revealed the *Adelaide* in a hopeless position, close in upon a low-lying shore, and driving straight toward it. All around and astern far out to sea was such a maze of rocks and shoals that it was a miracle we had come so far. Presently the ship struck, and almost instantly went to pieces, so great was the violence of the sea. I gave myself up for lost, and was indeed already past the worst of drowning, when I was recalled to consciousness by being thrown with a tremendous shock upon the beach. I had just strength enough to drag myself above the reach of the waves, and then I fell down and knew no more.

When I awoke, the storm was over. The sun, already halfway up the sky, had dried my clothing, and renewed the vigor of my bruised and aching limbs. On sea or shore I saw no vestige of my ship or my companions, of whom I appeared the sole survivor. I was not, however, alone. A group of persons, apparently the inhabitants of the country, stood near, observing me with looks of friendliness which at once freed me from apprehension as to my treatment at their hands. They were a white and handsome people, evidently of a high order of civilization, though I recognized in them the traits of no race with which I was familiar.

Seeing that it was evidently their idea of etiquette to leave it to strangers to open conversation, I addressed them in English, but failed to elicit any response beyond deprecating smiles. I then accosted them successively in the French, German, Italian, Spanish, Dutch, and Portuguese tongues, but with no better results I began to be very much puzzled as to what could possibly be the nationality of a white and evidently civilized race to which not one of the tongues of the great seafaring nations was intelligible. The oddest thing of all was the unbroken silence with which they contemplated my efforts to open communication with them. It was as if they were agreed not to give me a clue to their language by even a whisper; for while they regarded one another with looks of smiling intelligence, they did not once open their lips. But if this behavior suggested that they were amusing themselves at my expense, that presumption was negatived by the unmistakable friendliness and sympathy which their whole bearing expressed.

A most extraordinary conjecture occurred to me. Could it be that these strange people were dumb? Such a freak of nature as an entire race thus afflicted had never indeed been heard of, but who could say what wonders the unexplored vasts of the great Southern Ocean might thus far have hid from human ken? Now, among the scraps of useless information which lumbered my mind was an acquaintance with the deaf-and-dumb alphabet, and forthwith I began to spell out with my fingers some of the phrases I had already uttered to so little effect. My resort to the sign language overcame the last remnant of gravity in the already profusely smiling group. The small boys now rolled on the ground in convulsions of mirth, while the grave and reverend seniors, who had hitherto kept them in check, were fain momentarily to avert their faces, and I could see their bodies shaking with laughter. The greatest clown in the world never received a more flattering tribute to his powers to amuse than had been called forth by mine to make myself understood. Naturally, however, I was not flattered, but on the contrary entirely discomfited. Angry I could not well be, for the deprecating manner in which all, excepting of course the boys, yielded to their perception of the ridiculous, and the distress they showed at their failure in self-control, made me seem the aggressor. It was as if they were very sorry for me, and ready to put themselves wholly at my service, if I would only refrain from reducing them to a state of disability by being so exquisitely absurd. Certainly this evidently amiable race had a very embarrassing way of receiving strangers.

Just at this moment, when my bewilderment was fast verging on exasperation, relief came. The circle opened, and a little elderly man, who had evidently come in haste, confronted me, and, bowing very politely, addressed me in English. His voice was the most pitiable abortion of a voice I had ever heard. While having all the defects in articulation of a child's who is just beginning to talk, it was not even a child's in strength of tone, being in fact a mere alternation of squeaks and whispers inaudible a rod away. With some difficulty I was, however, able to follow him pretty nearly.

"As the official interpreter," he said, "I extend you a cordial welcome to these islands. I was sent for as soon as you were discovered, but being at some distance, I was unable to arrive until this moment. I regret this, as my presence would have saved you embarrassment. My countrymen desire me to intercede with you to pardon the wholly involuntary and uncontrollable mirth provoked by your attempts to communicate with them. You see, they understood you perfectly well, but could not answer you."

"Merciful heavens!" I exclaimed, horrified to find my surmise correct; "can it be that they are all thus afflicted? Is it possible that you are the only man among them who has the power of speech?"

Again it appeared that, quite unintentionally, I had said something excruciatingly funny; for at my speech there arose a sound of gentle laughter from the group, now augmented to quite an assemblage, which drowned the splashing of the waves on the beach at our feet. Even the interpreter smiled.

"Do they think it so amusing to be dumb?" I asked.

"They find it very amusing," replied the interpreter, "that their inability to speak should be regarded by any one as an affliction; for it is by the voluntary disuse of the organs of articulation that they have lost the power of speech, and, as a consequence, the ability even to understand speech."

"But," said I, somewhat puzzled by this statement, "didn't you just tell me that they understood me, though they could not reply, and are they not laughing now at what I just said?"

"It is you they understood, not your words," answered the interpreter. "Our speech now is gibberish to them, as unintelligible in itself as the growling of animals; but they know what we are saying, because they know our thoughts. You must know that these are the islands of the mind-readers."

Such were the circumstances of my introduction to this extraordinary people. The official interpreter being charged by virtue of his office with the first entertainment of shipwrecked members of the talking nations, I became his guest, and passed a number of days under his roof before going out to any considerable extent among the people. My first impression had been the somewhat oppressive one that the power to read the thoughts of others could be possessed only by beings of a superior order to man. It was the first effort of the interpreter to disabuse me of this notion. It appeared from his account that the experience of the mind-readers was a case simply of a slight acceleration, from special causes, of the course of universal human evolution, which in time was destined to lead to the disuse of speech and the substitution of direct mental vision on the part of all races. This rapid evolution of these islanders was accounted for by their peculiar origin and circumstances.

Some three centuries before Christ, one of the Parthian kings of Persia, of the dynasty of the Arsacid, undertook a persecution of the soothsayers and magicians in his realms. These people were credited with supernatural powers by popular prejudice, but in fact were merely persons of special gifts in the way of hypnotizing, mind-reading, thought transference, and such arts, which they exercised for their own gain.

Too much in awe of the soothsayers to do them outright violence, the king resolved to banish them, and to this end put them, with their families, on ships and sent them to Ceylon. When, however, the fleet was in the neighborhood of that island, a great storm scattered it, and one of the ships, after being driven for many days before the tempest, was wrecked upon one of an archipelago of uninhabited islands far to the south, where the survivors settled. Naturally, the posterity of the parents possessed of such peculiar gifts had developed extraordinary psychical powers.

Having set before them the end of evolving a new and advanced order of humanity, they had aided the development of these powers by a rigid system of stirpiculture. The result was that, after a few centuries, mind-reading became so general that language fell into disuse as a means of communicating ideas. For many generations the power of speech still remained voluntary, but gradually the vocal organs had become atrophied, and for several hundred years the power of articulation had been wholly lost. Infants for a few months after birth did, indeed, still emit inarticulate cries, but at an age when in less advanced races these cries began to be articulate, the children of the mind-readers developed the power of direct vision, and ceased to attempt to use the voice.

The fact that the existence of the mind-readers had never been found out by the rest of the world was explained by two considerations. In the first place, the group of islands was small, and occupied a corner of the Indian Ocean quite out of the ordinary track of ships. In the second place, the approach to the islands was rendered so desperately perilous by terrible currents, and the maze of outlying rocks and shoals, that it was next to impossible for any ship to touch their shores save as a wreck. No ship at least had ever done so in the two thousand years since the mind-readers' own arrival, and the *Adelaide* had made the one hundred and twenty-third such wreck.

Apart from motives of humanity, the mind-readers made strenuous efforts to rescue shipwrecked persons, for from them alone, through the interpreters, could they obtain information of the outside world. Little enough this proved when, as often happened, the sole survivor of the shipwreck was some ignorant sailor, who had no news to communicate beyond the latest varieties of forecastle blasphemy. My hosts gratefully assured me that, as a person of some little education, they considered me a veritable godsend. No less a task was mine than to relate to them the history of the world for the past two centuries, and often did I wish, for their sakes, that I had made a more exact study of it.

It is solely for the purpose of communicating with shipwrecked strangers of the talking nations that the office of the interpreters exists. When, as from time to time happens, a child is born with some powers of articulation, he is set apart, and trained to talk in the interpreters' college. Of course the partial atrophy of the vocal organs, from which even the best interpreters suffer, renders many of the sounds of language impossible for them. None, for instance, can pronounce v, f, or s; and as to the sound represented by th, it is five generations since the last interpreter lived who could utter it. But for the occasional inter-marriage of shipwrecked strangers with the island-ers, it is probable that the supply of interpreters would have long ere this quite failed.

I imagine that the very unpleasant sensations which followed the realization that I was among people who, while inscrutable to me, knew my every thought, were very much what anyone would have experienced in the same case. They were very comparable to the panic which accidental nudity causes a person among races whose custom it is to conceal the figure with drapery. I wanted to run away and hide myself. If I analyzed my feeling, it did not seem to arise so much from the consciousness of any particularly heinous secrets, as from the knowledge of a swarm of fatuous, ill-natured, and unseemly thoughts and half thoughts concerning those around me, and concerning myself, which it was insufferable that any person should peruse in however benevolent a spirit. But while my chagrin and distress on this account were at first intense, they were also very short-lived, for almost immediately I discovered that the very knowledge that my mind was overlooked by others operated to check thoughts that might be painful to them, and that, too, without more effort of the will than a kindly person exerts to check the utterance of disagreeable remarks. As very few lessons in the elements of courtesy cures a decent person of inconsiderate speaking, so a brief experience among the mind-readers went far in my case to check inconsiderate thinking. It must not be supposed, however, that courtesy among the mind-readers prevents them from thinking pointedly and freely concerning one another upon serious occasions, any more than the finest courtesy among the talking races restrains them from speaking to one another with entire plainness when it desirable to do so. Indeed, among the mind-readers, politeness never can extend to the point of insincerity, as among talking nations, seeing that it is always one another's real and inmost thought that they read. I may fitly mention here, though it was not till later that I fully understood why it must necessarily be so, that one need feel far less chagrin at the complete revelation of his weaknesses to a mind-reader than at the slightest betrayal of them to one of another race. For the very reason that the mind-reader reads all your thoughts, particular thoughts are judged with reference to the general tenor of thought. Your characteristic and habitual frame of mind is what he takes account of. No one need fear being misjudged by a mind-reader on account of sentiments or emotions which are not representative of the real character or general attitude. Justice may, indeed, be said to be a necessary consequence of mind-reading.

As regards the interpreter himself, the instinct of courtesy was not long needed to check wanton or offensive thoughts. In all my life before, I had been very slow to form friendships, but before I had been three days in the company of this stranger of a strange race, I had become enthusiastically devoted to him. It was impossible not to be. The peculiar joy of friendship is the sense of being understood by our friend as we are not by others, and yet of being loved in spite of the understanding. Now here was one whose every word testified to a knowledge of my secret thoughts and motives which the oldest and nearest of my former friends had never, and could never, have approximated. Had such a knowledge bred in him contempt of me, I should neither have blamed him nor been at all surprised. Judge, then, whether the cordial friendliness which he showed was likely to leave me indifferent.

Imagine my incredulity when he informed me that our friendship was not based upon more than ordinary mutual suitability of temperaments. The faculty of mind-reading, he explained, brought minds so close together, and so heightened sympathy, that the lowest order of friendship between mind-readers implied a mutual delight such as only rare friends enjoyed among other races. He assured me that later on, when I came to know others of his race, I should find, by the far greater intensity of sympathy and affection I should conceive for some of them, how true this saying was.

It may be inquired how, on beginning to mingle with the mind-readers in general, I managed to communicate with them, seeing that, while they could read my thoughts, they could not, like the interpreter, respond to them by speech. I must here explain that, while these people have no use for a spoken language, a written language is needful for purposes of record. They consequently all know how to write. Do they, then, write Persian? Luckily for me, no. It appears that, for a long period after mind-reading was fully developed, not only was spoken language disused, but also written, no records whatever having been kept during this period. The delight of the people in the newly found power of direct mind-to-mind vision, whereby pictures of the total mental state were communicated, instead of the imperfect descriptions of single thoughts which words at best could give, induced an invincible distaste for the laborious impotence of language.

When, however, the first intellectual intoxication had, after several generations, somewhat sobered down, it was recognized that records of the past were desirable, and that the despised medium of words was needful to preserve it. Persian had meanwhile been wholly forgotten. In order to avoid the prodigious task of inventing a complete new language, the institution of the interpreters was now set up, with the idea of acquiring through them a knowledge of some of the languages of the outside world from the mariners wrecked on the islands.

Owing to the fact that most of the castaway ships were English, a better knowledge of that tongue was acquired than of any other, and it was adopted as the written language of the people. As a rule, my acquaintances wrote slowly and laboriously, and yet the fact that they knew exactly what was in my mind rendered their responses so apt that, in my conversations with the slowest speller of them all, the interchange of thought was as rapid and incomparably more accurate and satisfactory than the fastest talkers attain to.

It was but a very short time after I had begun to extend my acquaintance among the mind-readers before I discovered how truly the interpreter had told me that I should find others to whom, on account of greater natural congeniality, I should become more strongly attached than I had been to him. This was in no wise, however, because I loved him less, but them more. I would fain write particularly of some of these beloved friends, comrades of my heart, from whom I first learned the undreamed-of possibilities of human friendship, and how ravishing the satisfactions of sympathy may be. Who, among those who may read this, has not known that sense of a gulf fixed between soul and soul which mocks love. I, who has not felt that loneliness which oppresses the heart that loves it best! Think no longer that this gulf is eternally fixed, or is any necessity of human nature. It has no existence for the race of our fellow-men which I describe, and by that fact we may be assured that eventually it will be bridged also for us. Like the touch of shoulder to shoulder, like the clasping of hands, is the contact of their minds and their sensation of sympathy.

I say that I would fain speak more particularly of some of my friends, but waning strength forbids, and moreover, now that I think of it, another consideration would render any comparison of their characters rather confusing than instructive to a reader. This is the fact that, in common with the rest of the mind-readers, they had no names. Everyone had, indeed, an arbitrary sign for his designation in records, but it has no sound value. A register of these names is kept, so they can at any time be ascertained, but it is very common to meet persons who have forgotten titles which are used solely for biographical and official purposes. For social intercourse names are of course superfluous, for these people accost one another merely by a mental act of attention, and refer to third persons by transferring their mental pictures—something as dumb persons might by means of photographs. Something so, I say, for in the pictures of one another's personalities which the mind-readers conceive, the physical aspect, as might be expected with people who directly contemplate each other's minds and hearts, is a subordinate element.

I have already told how my first qualms of morbid self-consciousness at knowing that my mind was an open book to all around me disappeared as I learned that the very completeness of the disclosure of my thoughts and motives was a guarantee that I would be judged with a fairness and a sympathy such as even self-judgment cannot pretend to, affected as that is by so many subtle reactions. The assurance of being so judged by every one might well seem an inestimable privilege to one accustomed to a world in which not even the tenderest love is any pledge of comprehension, and yet I soon discovered that open-mindedness had a still greater profit than this. How shall I describe the delightful exhilaration of moral health and cleanness, the breezy oxygenated mental condition, which resulted from the consciousness that I had absolutely nothing concealed! Truly I may say that I enjoyed myself. I think surely that no one needs to have had my marvelous experience to sympathize with this portion of it. Are we not all ready to agree that this having a curtained chamber where we may go to grovel, out of the sight of our fellows, troubled only by a vague apprehension that God may look over the top, is the most demoralizing incident in the human condition? It is the existence within the soul of this secure refuge of lies which has always been the despair of the saint and the exultation of the knave. It is the foul cellar which taints the whole house above, be it never so fine.

What stronger testimony could there be to the instinctive consciousness that concealment is debauching, and openness our only cure, than the world-old conviction of the virtue of confession for the soul, and that the uttermost exposing of one's worst and foulest is the first step toward moral health? The wickedest man, if he could but somehow attain to writhe himself inside out as to his soul, so that its full sickness could be seen, would feel ready for a new life. Nevertheless, owing to the utter impotence of the words to convey mental conditions in their totality, or to give other than mere distortions of them, confession is, we must needs admit, but a mockery of that longing for self-revelation to which it testifies. But think what health and soundness there must be for souls among a people who see in every face a conscience which, unlike their own, they cannot sophisticate, who confess one another with a glance, and shrive with a smile! Ah, friends, let me now predict, though ages may elapse before the slow event shall justify me, that in no way will the mutual vision of minds, when at last it shall be perfected, so enhance the blessedness of mankind as by rending the veil of self, and leaving no spot of darkness in the mind for lies to hide in. Then shall the soul no longer be a coal smoking among ashes, but a star in a crystal sphere.

From what I have said of the delights which friendship among the mind-readers derives from the perfection of the mental rapport, it may be imagined how intoxicating must be the experience when one of the friends is a woman, and the subtle attractions and correspondences of sex touch with passion the intellectual sympathy. With my first venturing into society I had begun, to their extreme amusement, to fall in love with the women right and left. In the perfect frankness which is the condition of all intercourse among this people, these adorable women told me that what I felt was only friendship, which was a very good thing, but wholly different from love, as I should well know if I were beloved. It was difficult to believe that the melting emotions which I had experienced in their company were the result merely of the friendly and kindly attitude of their minds toward mine; but when I found that I was affected in the same way by every gracious woman I met, I had to make up my mind that they must be right about it, and that I should have to adapt myself to a world in which, friendship being a passion, love must needs be nothing less than rapture.

The homely proverb, "Every Jack has his Gill," may, I suppose, be taken to mean that for all men there are certain women expressly suited by mental and moral as well as by physical constitution. It is a thought painful, rather than cheering, that this may be the truth, so altogether do the chances preponderate against the ability of these elect ones to recognize each other even if they meet, seeing that speech is so inadequate and so misleading a medium of self-revelation. But among the mind-readers, the search for one's ideal mate is a quest reasonably sure of being crowned with success, and no one dreams of wedding unless it be; for so to do, they consider, would be to throw away the choicest blessing of life, and not alone to wrong themselves and their unfound mates, but likewise those whom they themselves and those undiscovered mates might wed. Therefore, passionate pilgrims, they go from isle to isle till they find each other, and, as the population of the islands is but small, the pilgrimage is not often long.

When I met her first we were in company, and I was struck by the sudden stir and the looks and smiling interest with which all around turned and regarded us, the women with moistened eyes. They had read her thought when she saw me, but this I did not know, neither what was the custom in these matters, till afterward. But I knew, from the moment she first fixed her eyes on me, and I felt her mind brooding upon mine, how truly I had been told by those other women that the feeling with which they had inspired me was not love.

With people who become acquainted at a glance, and old friends in an hour, wooing is naturally not a long process. Indeed, it may be said that between lovers among mind-readers there is no wooing, but merely recognition. The day after we met, she became mine.

Perhaps I cannot better illustrate how subordinate the merely physical element is in the impression which mind-readers form of their friends than by mentioning an incident that occurred some months after our union. This was my discovery, wholly by accident, that my love, in whose society I had almost constantly been, had not the least idea what was the color of my eyes, or whether my hair and complexion were light or dark. Of course, as soon as I asked her the question, she read the answer in my mind, but she admitted that she had previously had no distinct impression on those points. On the other hand, if in the blackest midnight I should come to her, she would not need to ask who the comer was. It is by the mind, not the eye, that these people know one another. It is really only in their relations to soulless and inanimate things that they need eyes at all.

It must not be supposed that their disregard of one another's bodily aspect grows out of any ascetic sentiment. It is merely a necessary consequence of their power of directly apprehending mind, that whenever mind is closely associated with matter the latter is comparatively neglected on account of the greater interest of the former, suffering as lesser things always do when placed in immediate contrast with greater. Art is with them confined to the inanimate, the human form having, for the reason mentioned, ceased to inspire the artist. It will be naturally and quite correctly inferred that among such a race physical beauty is not the important factor in human fortune and felicity that it elsewhere is. The absolute openness of their minds and hearts to one another makes their happiness far more dependent on the moral and mental qualities of their companions than upon their physical. A genial temperament, a wide-grasping, godlike intellect, a poet soul, are incomparably more fascinating to them than the most dazzling combination conceivable of mere bodily graces.

A woman of mind and heart has no more need of beauty to win love in these islands than a beauty elsewhere of mind or heart. I should mention here, perhaps, that this race, which makes so little account of physical beauty, is itself a singularly handsome one. This is owing doubtless in part to the absolute compatibility of temperaments in all the marriages, and partly also to the reaction upon the body of a state of ideal mental and moral health and placidity.

Not being myself a mind-reader, the fact that my love was rarely beautiful in form and face had doubtless no little part in attracting my devotion. This, of course, she knew, as she knew all my thoughts, and, knowing my limitations, tolerated and forgave the element of sensuousness in my passion. But if it must have seemed to her so little worthy in comparison with the high spiritual communion which her race know as love, to me it became, by virtue of her almost superhuman relation to me, an ecstasy more ravishing surely than any lover of my race tasted before. The ache at the heart of the intensest love is the impotence of words to make it perfectly understood to its object. But my passion was without this pang, for my heart was absolutely open to her. I loved. Lovers may imagine, but I cannot describe, the ecstatic thrill of communion into which this consciousness transformed every tender emotion. As I considered what mutual love must be where both parties are mind-readers, I realized the high communion which my sweet companion had sacrificed for me.

She might indeed comprehend her lover and his love for her, but the higher satisfaction of knowing that she was comprehended by him and her love understood, she had foregone. For that I should ever attain the power of mind-reading was out of the question, the faculty never having been developed in a single lifetime.

Why my inability should move my dear companion to such depths of pity I was not able fully to understand until I learned that mind-reading is chiefly held desirable, not for the knowledge of others which it gives its possessors, but for the self-knowledge which is its reflex effect. Of all they see in the minds of others, that which concerns them most is the reflection of themselves, the photographs of their own characters. The most obvious consequence of the self-knowledge thus forced upon them is to render them alike incapable of self-conceit or self-depreciation. Everyone must needs always think of himself as he is, being no more able to do otherwise than is a man in a hall of mirrors to cherish delusions as to his personal appearance.

But self-knowledge means to the mind-readers much more than this—nothing less, indeed, than a shifting of the sense of identity. When a man sees himself in a mirror, he is compelled to distinguish between the bodily self he sees and his real self, which is within and unseen. When in turn the mind-reader comes to see the mental and moral self-reflected in other minds as in mirrors, the same thing happens. He is compelled to distinguish between this mental and moral self which has been made objective to him, and can be contemplated by him as impartially as if it were another's, from the inner ego which still remains subjective, unseen, and indefinable. In this inner ego the mind-readers recognize the essential identity and being, the noumenal self, the core of the soul, and the true hiding of its eternal life, to which the mind as well as the body is but the garment of a day.

The effect of such a philosophy as this—which, indeed, with the mind-readers is rather an instinctive consciousness than a philosophy—must obviously be to impart a sense of wonderful superiority to the vicissitudes of this earthly state, and a singular serenity in the midst of the haps and mishaps which threaten or befall the personality. They did indeed appear to me, as I never dreamed men could attain to be, lords of themselves.

It was because I might not hope to attain this enfranchisement from the false ego of the apparent self, without which life seemed to her race scarcely worth living, that my love so pitied me.

But I must hasten on, leaving a thousand things unsaid, to relate the lamentable catastrophe to which it is owing that, instead of being still a resident of those blessed islands, in the full enjoyment of that intimate and ravishing companionship which by contrast would forever dim the pleasures of all other human society, I recall the bright picture as a memory under other skies.

Among a people who are compelled by the very constitution of their minds to put themselves in the places of others, the sympathy which is the inevitable consequence of perfect comprehension renders envy, hatred, and uncharitableness impossible. But of course there are people less genially constituted than others, and these are necessarily the objects of a certain distaste on the part of associates. Now, owing to the unhindered impact of minds upon one another, the anguish of persons so regarded, despite the tenderest consideration of those about them, is so great that they beg the grace of exile, that, being out of the way, people may think less frequently upon them. There are numerous small islets, scarcely more than rocks, lying to the north of the archipelago, and on these the unfortunates are permitted to live. Only one lives on each islet, as they cannot endure each other even as well as the more happily constituted can endure them. From time to time supplies of food are taken to them, and of course, any time they wish to take the risk, they are permitted to return to society.

Now, as I have said, the fact which, even more than their out-of-the-way location, makes the islands of the mind-readers unapproachable, is the violence with which the great Antarctic current, owing probably to some configuration of the ocean bed, together with the innumerable rocks and shoals, flows through and about the archipelago.

Ships making the islands from the southward are caught by this current and drawn among the rocks, to their almost certain destruction; while, owing to the violence with which the current sets to the north, it is not possible to approach at all from that direction, or at least it has never been accomplished. Indeed, so powerful are the currents that even the boats which cross the narrow straits between the main islands and the islets of the unfortunate, to carry the latter their supplies, are ferried over by cables, not trusting to oar or sail.

The brother of my love had charge of one of the boats engaged in this transportation, and, being desirous of visiting the islets, I accepted an invitation to accompany him on one of his trips. I know nothing of how the accident happened, but in the fiercest part of the current of one of the straits we parted from the cable and were swept out to sea. There was no question of stemming the boiling current, our utmost endeavors barely sufficing to avoid being dashed to pieces on the rocks. From the first, there was no hope of our winning back to the land, and so swiftly did we drift that by noon—the accident having befallen in the morning—the islands, which are low-lying, had sunk beneath the southwestern horizon.

Among these mind-readers, distance is not an insuperable obstacle to the transfer of thought. My companion was in communication with our friends, and from time to time conveyed to me messages of anguish from my dear love; for, being well aware of the nature of the currents and the unapproachableness of the islands, those we had left behind, as well as we ourselves, knew well we should see each other's faces no more. For five days we continued to drift to the northwest, in no danger of starvation, owing to our lading of provisions, but constrained to unintermitting watch and ward by the roughness of the weather. On the fifth day my companion died from exposure and exhaustion. He died very quietly—indeed, with great appearance of relief. The life of the mind-readers while yet they are in the body is so largely spiritual that the idea of an existence wholly so, which seems vague and chill to us, suggests to them a state only slightly more refined than they already know on earth.

After that I suppose I must have fallen into an unconscious state, from which I roused to find myself on an American ship bound for New York, surrounded by people whose only means of communicating with one another is to keep up while together a constant clatter of hissing, guttural, and explosive noises, eked out by all manner of facial contortions and bodily gestures. I frequently find myself staring open-mouthed at those who address me, too much struck by their grotesque appearance to bethink myself of replying.

I find that I shall not live out the voyage, and I do not care to. From my experience of the people on the ship, I can judge how I should fare on land amid the stunning Babel of a nation of talkers. And my friends,—God bless them! how lonely I should feel in their very presence! Nay, what satisfaction or consolation, what but bitter mockery, could I ever more find in such human sympathy and companionship as suffice others and once sufficed me,—I who have seen and known what I have seen and known! Ah, yes, doubtless it is far better I should die; but the knowledge of the things that I have seen I feel should not perish with me. For hope's sake, men should not miss the glimpse of the higher, sun-bathed reaches of the upward path they plod. So thinking, I have written out some account of my wonderful experience, though briefer far, by reason of my weakness, than fits the greatness of the matter. The captain seems an honest, well-meaning man, and to him I shall confide the narrative, charging him, on touching shore, to see it safely in the hands of someone who will bring it to the world's ear.

NOTE:

The extent of my own connection with the foregoing document is sufficiently indicated by the author himself in the final paragraph.—E.B

IN THE YEAR 2889

Jules Verne

JULES VERNE (1828-1905), French playwright and novelist, only began writing science fiction in order to make a consistent living. His friend and publisher, Jules Hetzel, commissioned Verne to serialize travel stories in Hetzel's magazines. These stories were given the overall title, *Voyages Extraordinaires*, and became instant bestsellers. Verne is better known universally for his novels, but he also wrote a number of short stories in both the science fiction and fantasy field. Verne lived to see H.G. Wells begin his career, and like Wells, Verne never claimed to be the father of science fiction.

[**Redactor's note**: "In the Year 2889" was first published in the Forum, February,1889; p. 262. It was published in France the next year. Although published under the name of Jules Verne, it is now believed to be chiefly if not entirely the work of Jules' son, Michel Verne. In any event, many of the topics in the article echo Verne's ideas.]

LITTLE though they seem to think of it, the people of this twenty-ninth century live continually in fairyland. Surfeited as they are with marvels, they are indifferent in presence of each new marvel. To them all seems natural. Could they but duly appreciate the refinements of civilization in our day; could they but compare the present with the past, and so better comprehend the advance we have made! How much fairer they would find our modern towns, with populations amounting sometimes to 10,000,000 souls; their streets 300 feet wide, their houses 1000 feet in height; with a temperature the same in all seasons; with their lines of aërial locomotion crossing the sky in every direction! If they would but picture to themselves the state of things that once existed, when through muddy streets rumbling boxes on wheels, drawn by horses—yes, by horses!—were the only means of conveyance. Think of the railroads of the olden time, and you will be able to appreciate the pneumatic tubes through which to-day one travels at the rate of 1000 miles an hour. Would not our contemporaries prize the telephone and the telephote more highly if they had not forgotten the telegraph?

Singularly enough, all these transformations rest upon principles which were perfectly familiar to our remote ancestors, but which they disregarded. Heat, for instance, is as ancient as man himself; electricity was known 3000 years ago, and steam 1100 years ago. Nay, so early as ten centuries ago it was known that the differences between the several chemical and physical forces depend on the mode of vibration of the etheric particles, which is for each specifically different. When at last the kinship of all these forces was discovered, it is simply astounding that 500 years should still have to elapse before men could analyze and describe the several modes of vibration that constitute these differences. Above all, it is singular that the mode of reproducing these forces directly from one another, and of reproducing one without the others, should have remained undiscovered till less than a hundred years ago. Nevertheless, such was the course of events, for it was not till the year 2792 that the famous Oswald Nier made this great discovery.

Truly was he a great benefactor of the human race. His admirable discovery led to many another. Hence is sprung a pleiad of inventors, its brightest star being our great Joseph Jackson. To Jackson we are indebted for those wonderful instruments the new accumulators. Some of these absorb and condense the living force contained in the sun's rays; others, the electricity stored in our globe; others again, the energy coming from whatever source, as a waterfall, a stream, the winds, etc. He, too, it was that invented the transformer, a more wonderful contrivance still, which takes the living force from the accumulator, and, on the simple pressure of a button, gives it back to space in whatever form may be desired, whether as heat, light, electricity, or mechanical force, after having first obtained from it the work required. From the day when these two instruments were contrived is to be dated the era of true progress. They have put into the hands of man a power that is almost infinite. As for their applications, they are numberless. Mitigating the rigors of winter, by giving back to the atmosphere the surplus heat stored up during the summer, they have revolutionized agriculture. By supplying motive power for aërial navigation, they have given to commerce a mighty impetus. To them we are indebted for the continuous production of electricity without batteries or dynamos, of light without combustion or incandescence, and for an unfailing supply of mechanical energy for all the needs of industry.

Yes, all these wonders have been wrought by the accumulator and the transformer. And can we not to them also trace, indirectly, this latest wonder of all, the great "Earth Chronicle" building in 25^{3d} Avenue, which was dedicated the other day? If George Washington Smith, the founder of the Manhattan "Chronicle", should come back to life to-day, what would he think were he to be told that this palace of marble and gold belongs to his remote descendant, Fritz Napoleon Smith, who, after thirty generations have come and gone, is owner of the same newspaper which his ancestor established!

For George Washington Smith's newspaper has lived generation after generation, now passing out of the family, anon coming back to it. When, 200 years ago, the political center of the United States was transferred from Washington to Centropolis, the newspaper followed the government and assumed the name of Earth Chronicle. Unfortunately, it was unable to maintain itself at the high level of its name. Pressed on all sides by rival journals of a more modern type, it was continually in danger of collapse. Twenty years ago its subscription list contained but a few hundred thousand names, and then Mr. Fritz Napoleon Smith bought it for a mere trifle, and originated telephonic journalism.

Every one is familiar with Fritz Napoleon Smith's system—a system made possible by the enormous development of telephony during the last hundred years. Instead of being printed, the Earth Chronicle is every morning spoken to subscribers, who, in interesting conversations with reporters, statesmen, and scientists, learn the news of the day. Furthermore, each subscriber owns a phonograph, and to this instrument he leaves the task of gathering the news whenever he happens not to be in a mood to listen directly himself. As for purchasers of single copies, they can at a very trifling cost learn all that is in the paper of the day at any of the innumerable phonographs set up nearly everywhere.

Fritz Napoleon Smith's innovation galvanized the old newspaper. In the course of a few years the number of subscribers grew to be 80,000,000, and Smith's wealth went on growing, till now it reaches the almost unimaginable figure of $10,000,000,000. This lucky hit has enabled him to erect his new building, a vast edifice with four façades each 3,250 feet in length, over which proudly floats the hundred-starred flag of the Union. Thanks to the same lucky hit, he is to-day king of newspaperdom; indeed, he would be king of all the Americans, too, if Americans could ever accept a king. You do not believe it? Well, then, look at the plenipotentiaries of all nations and our own ministers themselves crowding about his door, entreating his counsels, begging for his approbation, imploring the aid of his all-powerful organ. Reckon up the number of scientists and artists that he supports, of inventors that he has under his pay.

Yes, a king is he. And in truth his is a royalty full of burdens. His labors are incessant, and there is no doubt at all that in earlier times any man would have succumbed under the overpowering stress of the toil which Mr. Smith has to perform. Very fortunately for him, thanks to the progress of hygiene, which, abating all the old sources of unhealthfulness, has lifted the mean of human life from 37 up to 52 years, men have stronger constitutions now than heretofore. The discovery of nutritive air is still in the future, but in the meantime men today consume food that is compounded and prepared according to scientific principles, and they breathe an atmosphere freed from the micro-organisms that formerly used to swarm in it; hence they live longer than their forefathers and know nothing of the innumerable diseases of olden times.

Nevertheless, and notwithstanding these considerations, Fritz Napoleon Smith's mode of life may well astonish one. His iron constitution is taxed to the utmost by the heavy strain that is put upon it. Vain the attempt to estimate the amount of labor he undergoes; an example alone can give an idea of it. Let us then go about with him for one day as he attends to his multifarious concernments. What day? That matters little; it is the same every day. Let us then take at random September 25th of this present year 2889.

This morning Mr. Fritz Napoleon Smith awoke in very bad humor. His wife having left for France eight days ago, he was feeling disconsolate. Incredible though it seems, in all the ten years since their marriage, this is the first time that Mrs. Edith Smith, the professional beauty, has been so long absent from home; two or three days usually suffice for her frequent trips to Europe. The first thing that Mr. Smith does is to connect his phonotelephote, the wires of which communicate with his Paris mansion. The telephote! Here is another of the great triumphs of science in our time. The transmission of speech is an old story; the transmission of images by means of sensitive mirrors connected by wires is a thing but of yesterday. A valuable invention indeed, and Mr. Smith this morning was not niggard of blessings for the inventor, when by its aid he was able distinctly to see his wife notwithstanding the distance that separated him from her. Mrs. Smith, weary after the ball or the visit to the theater the preceding night, is still abed, though it is near noontide at Paris.

She is asleep, her head sunk in the lace-covered pillows. What? She stirs? Her lips move. She is dreaming perhaps? Yes, dreaming. She is talking, pronouncing a name his name—Fritz! The delightful vision gave a happier turn to Mr. Smith's thoughts. And now, at the call of imperative duty, light-hearted he springs from his bed and enters his mechanical dresser.

Two minutes later the machine deposited him all dressed at the threshold of his office. The round of journalistic work was now begun. First he enters the hall of the novel-writers, a vast apartment crowned with an enormous transparent cupola. In one corner is a telephone, through which a hundred Earth Chronicle littérateurs in turn recount to the public in daily installments a hundred novels. Addressing one of these authors who was waiting his turn, "Capital! Capital! my dear fellow," said he, "your last story. The scene where the village maid discusses interesting philosophical problems with her lover shows your very acute power of observation. Never have the ways of country folk been better portrayed. Keep on, my dear Archibald, keep on! Since yesterday, thanks to you, there is a gain of 5000 subscribers."

"Mr. John Last," he began again, turning to a new arrival, "I am not so well pleased with your work. Your story is not a picture of life; it lacks the elements of truth. And why? Simply because you run straight on to the end; because you do not analyze. Your heroes do this thing or that from this or that motive, which you assign without ever a thought of dissecting their mental and moral natures. Our feelings, you must remember, are far more complex than all that. In real life every act is the resultant of a hundred thoughts that come and go, and these you must study, each by itself, if you would create a living character. 'But,' you will say, 'in order to note these fleeting thoughts one must know them, must be able to follow them in their capricious meanderings.' Why, any child can do that, as you know. You have simply to make use of hypnotism, electrical or human, which gives one a two-fold being, setting free the witness-personality so that it may see, understand, and remember the reasons which determine the personality that acts. Just study yourself as you live from day to day, my dear Last. Imitate your associate whom I was complimenting a moment ago. Let yourself be hypnotized. What's that? You have tried it already? Not sufficiently, then, not sufficiently!"

Mr. Smith continues his round and enters the reporters' hall. Here 1500 reporters, in their respective places, facing an equal number of telephones, are communicating to the subscribers the news of the world as gathered during the night. The organization of this matchless service has often been described. Besides his telephone, each reporter, as the reader is aware, has in front of him a set of commutators, which enable him to communicate with any desired telephotic line. Thus the subscribers not only hear the news but see the occurrences. When an incident is described that is already past, photographs of its main features are transmitted with the narrative. And there is no confusion withal. The reporters' items, just like the different stories and all the other component parts of the journal, are classified automatically according to an ingenious system, and reach the hearer in due succession. Furthermore, the hearers are free to listen only to what specially concerns them. They may at pleasure give attention to one editor and refuse it to another.

Mr. Smith next addresses one of the ten reporters in the astronomical department—a department still in the embryonic stage, but which will yet play an important part in journalism.

"Well, Cash, what's the news?"

"We have phototelegrams from Mercury, Venus, and Mars."

"Are those from Mars of any interest?"

"Yes, indeed. There is a revolution in the Central Empire."

"And what of Jupiter?" asked Mr. Smith.

"Nothing as yet. We cannot quite understand their signals. Perhaps ours do not reach them."

"That's bad," exclaimed Mr. Smith, as he hurried away, not in the best of humor, toward the hall of the scientific editors.

With their heads bent down over their electric computers, thirty scientific men were absorbed in transcendental calculations. The coming of Mr. Smith was like the falling of a bomb among them.

"Well, gentlemen, what is this I hear? No answer from Jupiter? Is it always to be thus? Come, Cooley, you have been at work now twenty years on this problem, and yet—"

"True enough," replied the man addressed. "Our science of optics is still very defective, and though our mile-and-three-quarter telescopes."

"Listen to that, Peer," broke in Mr. Smith, turning to a second scientist. "Optical science defective! Optical science is your specialty. But," he continued, again addressing William Cooley, "failing with Jupiter, are we getting any results from the moon?"

"The case is no better there."

"This time you do not lay the blame on the science of optics. The moon is immeasurably less distant than Mars, yet with Mars our communication is fully established. I presume you will not say that you lack telescopes?"

"Telescopes? O no, the trouble here is about inhabitants!"

"That's it," added Peer.

"So, then, the moon is positively uninhabited?" asked Mr. Smith.

"At least," answered Cooley, "on the face which she presents to us. As for the opposite side, who knows?"

"Ah, the opposite side! You think, then," remarked Mr. Smith, musingly, "that if one could but—"

"Could what?"

"Why, turn the moon about-face."

"Ah, there's something in that," cried the two men at once. And indeed, so confident was their air, they seemed to have no doubt as to the possibility of success in such an undertaking.

"Meanwhile," asked Mr. Smith, after a moment's silence, "have you no news of interest to-day'?"

"Indeed we have," answered Cooley. "The elements of Olympus are definitively settled. That great planet gravitates beyond Neptune at the mean distance of 11,400,799,642 miles from the sun, and to traverse its vast orbit takes 1311 years, 294 days, 12 hours, 43 minutes, 9 seconds."

"Why didn't you tell me that sooner?" cried Mr. Smith. "Now inform the reporters of this straightaway. You know how eager is the curiosity of the public with regard to these astronomical questions. That news must go into to-day's issue."

Then, the two men bowing to him, Mr. Smith passed into the next hall, an enormous gallery upward of 3200 feet in length, devoted to atmospheric advertising. Every one has noticed those enormous advertisements reflected from the clouds, so large that they may be seen by the populations of whole cities or even of entire countries. This, too, is one of Mr. Fritz Napoleon Smith's ideas, and in the Earth

Chronicle building a thousand projectors are constantly engaged in displaying upon the clouds these mammoth advertisements.

When Mr. Smith to-day entered the sky-advertising department, he found the operators sitting with folded arms at their motionless projectors, and inquired as to the cause of their inaction. In response, the man addressed simply pointed to the sky, which was of a pure blue. "Yes," muttered Mr. Smith, "a cloudless sky! That's too bad, but what's to be done? Shall we produce rain? That we might do, but is it of any use? What we need is clouds, not rain. Go," said he, addressing the head engineer, "go see Mr. Samuel Mark, of the meteorological division of the scientific department, and tell him for me to go to work in earnest on the question of artificial clouds. It will never do for us to be always thus at the mercy of cloudless skies!"

Mr. Smith's daily tour through the several departments of his newspaper is now finished. Next, from the advertisement hall he passes to the reception chamber, where the ambassadors accredited to the American government are awaiting him, desirous of having a word of counsel or advice from the all-powerful editor. A discussion was going on when he entered. "Your Excellency will pardon me," the French Ambassador was saying to the Russian, "but I see nothing in the map of Europe that requires change. 'The North for the Slavs?' Why, yes, of course; but the South for the Matins. Our common frontier, the Rhine, it seems to me, serves very well. Besides, my government, as you must know, will firmly oppose every movement, not only against Paris, our capital, or our two great prefectures, Rome and Madrid, but also against the kingdom of Jerusalem, the dominion of Saint Peter, of which France means to be the trusty defender."

"Well said!" exclaimed Mr. Smith. "How is it," he asked, turning to the Russian ambassador, "that you Russians are not content with your vast empire, the most extensive in the world, stretching from the banks of the Rhine to the Celestial Mountains and the Kara-Korum, whose shores are washed by the Frozen Ocean, the Atlantic, the Mediterranean, and the Indian Ocean? Then, what is the use of threats? Is war possible in view of modern inventions-asphyxiating shells capable of being projected a distance of 60 miles, an electric spark of 90 miles, that can at one stroke annihilate a battalion; to say nothing of the plague, the cholera, the yellow fever, that the belligerents might spread among their antagonists mutually, and which would in a few days destroy the greatest armies?"

"True," answered the Russian; "but can we do all that we wish? As for us Russians, pressed on our eastern frontier by the Chinese, we must at any cost put forth our strength for an effort toward the west."

"O, is that all? In that case," said Mr. Smith, "the thing can be arranged. I will speak to the Secretary of State about it. The attention of the Chinese government shall be called to the matter. This is not the first time that the Chinese have bothered us."

"Under these conditions, of course—" And the Russian ambassador declared himself satisfied.

"Ah, Sir John, what can I do for you?" asked Mr. Smith as he turned to the representative of the people of Great Britain, who till now had remained silent.

"A great deal," was the reply. "If the Earth Chronicle would but open a campaign on our behalf—"

"And for what object?"

"Simply for the annulment of the Act of Congress annexing to the United States the British islands."

Though, by a just turn-about of things here below, Great Britain has become a colony of the United States, the English are not yet reconciled to the situation. At regular intervals they are ever addressing to the American government vain complaints.

"A campaign against the annexation that has been an accomplished fact for 150 years!" exclaimed Mr. Smith. "How can your people suppose that I would do anything so unpatriotic?"

"We at home think that your people must now be sated. The Monroe doctrine is fully applied; the whole of America belongs to the Americans. What more do you want? Besides, we will pay for what we ask."

"Indeed!" answered Mr. Smith, without manifesting the slightest irritation. "Well, you English will ever be the same. No, no, Sir John, do not count on me for help. Give up our fairest province, Britain? Why not ask France generously to renounce possession of Africa, that magnificent colony the complete conquest of which cost her the labor of 800 years? You will be well received!"

"You decline! All is over then!" murmured the British agent sadly. "The United Kingdom falls to the share of the Americans; the Indies to that of—"

"The Russians," said Mr. Smith, completing the sentence.

"Australia—"

"Has an independent government."

"Then nothing at all remains for us!" sighed Sir John, downcast.

"Nothing?" asked Mr. Smith, laughing. "Well, now, there's Gibraltar!"

With this sally, the audience ended. The clock was striking twelve, the hour of breakfast. Mr. Smith returns to his chamber. Where the bed stood in the morning a table all spread comes up through the floor. For Mr. Smith, being above all a practical man; has reduced the problem of existence to its simplest terms. For him, instead of the endless suites of apartments of the olden time, one room fitted with ingenious mechanical contrivances is enough. Here he sleeps, takes his meals, in short, lives.

He seats himself. In the mirror of the phonotelephote is seen the same chamber at Paris which appeared in it this morning. A table furnished forth is likewise in readiness here, for notwithstanding the difference of hours, Mr. Smith and his wife have arranged to take their meals simultaneously. It is delightful thus to take breakfast tête-a-tête with one who is 3000 miles or so away. Just now, Mrs. Smith's chamber has no occupant.

"She is late! Woman's punctuality! Progress everywhere except there!" muttered Mr. Smith as he turned the tap for the first dish. For like all wealthy folk in our day, Mr. Smith has done away with the domestic kitchen and is a subscriber to the Grand Alimentation Company, which sends through a great network of tubes to subscribers' residences all sorts of dishes, as a varied assortment is always in readiness. A subscription costs money, to be sure, but the cuisine is of the best, and the system has this advantage, that it, does away with the pestering race of the cordons-bleus. Mr. Smith received and ate, all alone, the hors-d'oeuvre, entrées, rôti and legumes that constituted the repast. He was just finishing the dessert when Mrs. Smith appeared in the mirror of the telephote.

"Why, where have you been?" asked Mr. Smith through the telephone.

"What! You are already at the dessert? Then I am late," she exclaimed, with a winsome naïveté. "Where have I been, you ask? Why, at my dress-maker's. The hats are just lovely this season! I suppose I forgot to note the time, and so am a little late."

"Yes, a little," growled Mr. Smith; "so little that I have already quite finished breakfast. Excuse me if I leave you now, but I must be going."

"O certainly, my dear; good-by till evening."

Smith stepped into his air-coach, which was in waiting for him at a window. "Where do you wish to go, sir?" inquired the coachman.

"Let me see; I have three hours," Mr. Smith mused. "Jack, take me to my accumulator works at Niagara."

For Mr. Smith has obtained a lease of the great falls of Niagara. For ages the energy developed by the falls went unutilized. Smith, applying Jackson's invention, now collects this energy, and lets or sells it. His visit to the works took more time than he had anticipated. It was four o'clock when he returned home, just in time for the daily audience which he grants to callers.

One readily understands how a man situated as Smith is must be beset with requests of all kinds. Now it is an inventor needing capital; again it is some visionary who comes to advocate a brilliant scheme which must surely yield millions of profit. A choice has to be made between these projects, rejecting the worthless, examining the questionable ones, accepting the meritorious. To this work Mr. Smith devotes every day two full hours.

The callers were fewer to-day than usual—only twelve of them. Of these, eight had only impracticable schemes to propose. In fact, one of them wanted to revive painting, an art fallen into desuetude owing to the progress made in color-photography. Another, a physician, boasted that he had discovered a cure for nasal catarrh! These impracticables were dismissed in short order. Of the four projects favorably received, the first was that of a young man whose broad forehead betokened his intellectual power.

"Sir, I am a chemist," he began, "and as such I come to you."

"Well!"

"Once the elementary bodies," said the young chemist, "were held to be sixty-two in number; a hundred years ago they were reduced to ten; now only three remain irresolvable, as you are aware."

"Yes, yes."

"Well, sir, these also I will show to be composite. In a few months, a few weeks, I shall have succeeded in solving the problem. Indeed, it may take only a few days."

"And then?"

"Then, sir, I shall simply have determined the absolute. All I want is money enough to carry my research to a successful issue."

"Very well," said Mr. Smith. "And what will be the practical outcome of your discovery?"

"The practical outcome? Why, that we shall be able to produce easily all bodies whatever—stone, wood, metal, fibers—"

"And flesh and blood?" queried Mr. Smith, interrupting him. "Do you pretend that you expect to manufacture a human being out and out?"

"Why not?"

Mr. Smith advanced $100,000 to the young chemist, and engaged his services for the Earth Chronicle laboratory.

The second of the four successful applicants, starting from experiments made so long ago as the nineteenth century and again and again repeated, had conceived the idea of removing an entire city all at once from one place to another. His special project had to do with the city of Granton, situated, as everybody knows, some fifteen miles inland. He proposes to transport the city on rails and to change it into a watering-place. The profit, of course, would be enormous. Mr. Smith, captivated by the scheme, bought a half-interest in it.

"As you are aware, sir," began applicant No. 3, "by the aid of our solar and terrestrial accumulators and transformers, we are able to make all the seasons the same. I propose to do something better still. Transform into heat a portion of the surplus energy at our disposal; send this heat to the poles; then the polar regions, relieved of their snow-cap, will become a vast territory available for man's use. What think you of the scheme?"

"Leave your plans with me, and come back in a week. I will have them examined in the meantime."

Finally, the fourth announced the early solution of a weighty scientific problem. Every one will remember the bold experiment made a hundred years ago by Dr. Nathaniel Faithburn. The doctor, being a firm believer in human hibernation—in other words, in the possibility of our suspending our vital functions and of calling them into action again after a time—resolved to subject the theory to a practical test. To this end, having first made his last will and pointed out the proper method of awakening him; having also directed that his sleep was to continue a hundred years to a day from the date of his apparent death, he unhesitatingly put the theory to the proof in his own person.

Reduced to the condition of a mummy, Dr. Faithburn was coffined and laid in a tomb. Time went on. September 25th, 2889, being the day set for his resurrection, it was proposed to Mr. Smith that he should permit the second part of the experiment to be performed at his residence this evening.

"Agreed. Be here at ten o'clock," answered Mr. Smith; and with that the day's audience was closed.

Left to himself, feeling tired, he lay down on an extension chair. Then, touching a knob, he established communication with the Central Concert Hall, whence our greatest maestros send out to subscribers their delightful successions of accords determined by recondite algebraic formulas. Night was approaching. Entranced by the harmony, forgetful of the hour, Smith did not notice that it was growing dark. It was quite dark when he was aroused by the sound of a door opening. "Who is there?" he asked, touching a commutator.

Suddenly, in consequence of the vibrations produced, the air became luminous.

"Ah! you, Doctor?"

"Yes," was the reply. "How are you?"

"I am feeling well."

"Good! Let me see your tongue. All right! Your pulse. Regular! And your appetite?"

"Only passably good."

"Yes, the stomach. There's the rub. You are over-worked. If your stomach is out of repair, it must be mended. That requires study. We must think about it."

"In the meantime," said Mr. Smith, "you will dine with me."

As in the morning, the table rose out of the floor. Again, as in the morning, the potage, rôti, ragoûts, and legumes were supplied through the food-pipes. Toward the close of the meal, phonotelephotic communication was made with Paris. Smith saw his wife, seated alone at the dinner-table, looking anything but pleased at her loneliness.

"Pardon me, my dear, for having left you alone," he said through the telephone. "I was with Dr. Wilkins."

"Ah, the good doctor!" remarked Mrs. Smith, her countenance lighting up.

"Yes. But, pray, when are you coming home?"

"This evening."

"Very well. Do you come by tube or by air-train?"

"Oh, by tube."

"Yes; and at what hour will you arrive?"

"About eleven, I suppose."

"Eleven by Centropolis time, you mean?"

"Yes."

"Good-by, then, for a little while," said Mr. Smith as he severed communication with Paris.

Dinner over, Dr. Wilkins wished to depart. "I shall expect you at ten," said Mr Smith. "To-day, it seems, is the day for the return to life of the famous Dr. Faithburn. You did not think of it, I suppose. The awakening is to take place here in my house. You must come and see. I shall depend on your being here."

"I will come back," answered Dr. Wilkins.

Left alone, Mr. Smith busied himself with examining his accounts—a task of vast magnitude, having to do with transactions which involve a daily expenditure of upward of $800,000. Fortunately, indeed, the stupendous progress of mechanic art in modern times makes it comparatively easy. Thanks to the Piano Electro-Reckoner, the most complex calculations can be made in a few seconds. In two hours Mr. Smith completed his task. Just in time. Scarcely had he turned over the last page when Dr. Wilkins arrived. After him came the body of Dr. Faithburn, escorted by a numerous company of men of science. They commenced work at once. The casket being laid down in the middle of the room, the telephote was got in readiness. The outer world, already notified, was anxiously expectant, for the whole world could be eye-witnesses of the performance, a reporter meanwhile, like the chorus in the ancient drama, explaining it all viva voce through the telephone.

"They are opening the casket," he explained. "Now they are taking Faithburn out of it—a veritable mummy, yellow, hard, and dry. Strike the body and it resounds like a block of wood. They are now applying heat; now electricity. No result. These experiments are suspended for a moment while Dr. Wilkins makes an examination of the body. Dr. Wilkins, rising, declares the man to be dead. 'Dead!' exclaims every one present. 'Yes,' answers Dr. Wilkins, 'dead!' 'And how long has he been dead?' Dr. Wilkins makes another examination. 'A hundred years,' he replies."

The case stood just as the reporter said. Faithburn was dead, quite certainly dead! "Here is a method that needs improvement," remarked Mr. Smith to Dr. Wilkins, as the scientific committee on hibernation bore the casket out. "So much for that experiment. But if poor Faithburn is dead, at least he is sleeping," he continued. "I wish I could get some sleep. I am tired out, Doctor, quite tired out! Do you not think that a bath would refresh me?"

"Certainly. But you must wrap yourself up well before you go out into the hall-way. You must not expose yourself to cold."

"Hall-way? Why, Doctor, as you well know, everything is done by machinery here. It is not for me to go to the bath; the bath will come to me. Just look!" and he pressed a button. After a few seconds a faint rumbling was heard, which grew louder and louder. Suddenly the door opened, and the tub appeared.

Such, for this year of grace 2889, is the history of one day in the life of the editor of the Earth Chronicle. And the history of that one day is the history of 365 days every year, except leap-years, and then of 366 days—for as yet no means has been found of increasing the length of the terrestrial year.

IN THE YEAR TEN THOUSAND

William Harben

WILLIAM N. HARBEN (1858-1919), born in Dalton, Georgia, became one of America's most popular authors around the turn of the century. Though Harben wrote mostly mainstream novels in a sentimentalist vein, he did manage to write several science fiction stories and one science fiction novel, *Land of the Changing Sun*, which appeared in 1894. Though heavily influenced by Jules Verne and Arthur Conan Doyle, Harben was able to develop a writing style that captured the speech rhythms of his day which made his characters come alive in a manner not found among his peers, within the science fiction field or without. Harben's fluid story-telling is all too apparent in "In the Year Ten-Thousand" where we find a doting father telling his son what early humans used to be like.

A.D. 10,000.

An old man, more than six hundred years of age, was walking with a boy through a great museum. The people who were moving around them had beautiful forms, and faces which were indescribably refined and spiritual.

"Father," said the boy, "you promised to tell me to-day about the Dark Ages. I like to hear how men lived and thought long ago."

"It is no easy task to make you understand the past," was the reply. "It is hard to realize that man could have been so ignorant as he was eight thousand years ago, but come with me; I will show you something."

He led the boy to a cabinet containing a few time-worn books bound in solid gold.

"You have never seen a book," he said, taking out a large volume and carefully placing it on a silk cushion on a table. "There are only a few in the leading museums of the world. Time was when there were as many books on earth as inhabitants."

"I cannot understand," said the boy with a look of perplexity on his intellectual face. "I cannot see what people could have wanted with them; they are not attractive; they seem to be useless."

The old man smiled. "When I was your age, the subject was too deep for me; but as I grew older and made a close study of the history of the past, the use of books gradually became plain to me. We know that in the year 2000 they were read by the best minds. To make you understand this, I shall first have to explain that eight thousand years ago human beings communicated their thoughts to one another by making sounds with their tongues, and not by mind-reading, as you and I do. To understand me, you have simply to read my thoughts as well as your education will permit; but primitive man knew nothing about thought-intercourse, so he invented speech. Humanity then was divided up in various races, and each race had a separate language. As certain sounds conveyed definite ideas, so did signs and letters; and later, to facilitate the exchange of thought, writing and printing were invented. This book was printed."

The boy leaned forward and examined the pages closely; his young brow clouded. "I cannot understand," he said, "it seems so useless."

The old man put his delicate fingers on the page. "A line of these words may have conveyed a valuable thought to a reader long ago," he said, reflectively. "In fact, this book purports to be a history of the world up to the year 2000. Here are some pictures," he continued, turning the worn leaves carefully. "This is George Washington; this a pope of a church called the Roman Catholic; this is a man named Gladstone, who was a great political leader in England. Pictures then, as you see, were very crude. We have preserved some of the oil paintings made in those days. Art was in its cradle. In producing a painting of an object, the early artists mixed colored paints and spread them according to taste on stretched canvas or on the walls or windows of buildings. You know that our artists simply throw light and darkness into space in the necessary variations, and the effect is all that could be desired in the way of imitating nature. See that landscape in the alcove before you. The foliage of the trees, the grass, the flowers, the stretch of water, have every appearance of life because the light which produces them is alive."

The boy looked at the scene admiringly for a few minutes, then bent again over the book. Presently he recoiled from the pictures, a strange look of disgust struggling in his tender features.

"These men have awful faces," he said. "They are so unlike people living now. The man you call a pope looks like an animal. They all have huge mouths and frightfully heavy jaws. Surely men could not have looked like that."

"Yes," the old man replied, gently. "There is no doubt that human beings then bore a nearer resemblance to the lower animals than we now do. In the sculpture and portraits of all ages we can trace a gradual refinement in the appearances of men. The features "of the human race to-day are more ideal. Thought has always given form and expression to faces. In those dark days the thoughts of men were not refined. Human beings died of starvation and lack of attention in cities where there were people so wealthy that they could not use their fortunes. And they were so nearly related to the lower animals that they believed in war. George Washington was for several centuries reverenced by millions of people as a great and good man; and yet under his leadership thousands of human beings lost their lives in battle."

The boy's susceptible face turned white.

"Do you mean that he encouraged men to kill one another?" he asked, bending more closely over the book.

"Yes, but we cannot blame him; he thought he was right. Millions of his countrymen applauded him. A greater warrior than he was a man named Napoleon Bonaparte. Washington fought under the belief that he was doing his country a service in defending it against enemies, but everything in history goes to prove that Bonaparte waged war to gratify a personal ambition to distinguish himself as a hero. Wild animals of the lowest orders were courageous, and would fight one another till they died; and yet the most refined of the human race, eight or nine thousand years ago, prided themselves on the same ferocity of nature. Women, the gentlest half of humanity, honored men more for bold achievements in shedding blood than for any other quality. But murder was not only committed in wars; men in private life killed one another; fathers and mothers were now and then so depraved as to put their own children to death; and the highest tribunals of the world executed murderers without dreaming that it was wrong, erroneously believing that to kill was the only way to prevent killing."

"Did no one in those days realize that it was horrible?" asked the youth.

"Yes," answered the father, "as far back as ten thousand years ago there was a humble man, it is said, who was called Jesus Christ. He went from place to place, telling every one he met that the world would be better if men would love one another as themselves."

"What kind of man was he?" asked the boy, with kindling eyes.

"He was a spiritual genius," was the earnest reply, "and the greatest that has ever lived."

"Did he prevent them from killing one another?" asked the youth, with a tender upward glance.

"No, for he himself was killed by men who were too barbarous to understand him. But long after his death his words were remembered. People were not civilized enough to put his teachings into practice, but they were able to see that he was right."

"After he was killed, did the people not do as he had told them?" asked the youth, after a pause of several minutes.

"It seems not," was the reply. "They said no human being could live as he had directed. And when he had been dead for several centuries, people began to say that he was the Son of God who had come to earth to show men how to live. Some even believed that he was God himself."

"Did they believe that he was a person like ourselves?"

The old man reflected for a few minutes, then, looking into the boy's eager face, he answered: "That subject will be hard for you to understand. I will try to make it plain. To the unformed minds of early humanity there could be nothing without a personal creator. As man could build a house with his own hands, and was superior to his work, so he argued that some unknown being, greater than all visible things, had made the universe. They called that being by different names according to the language they spoke. In English the word used was 'God.'"

"They believed that somebody had made the universe!" said the boy, "how very strange!"

"No, not somebody as you comprehend it," replied the father gently, "but some vague, infinite being who punished the evil and rewarded the good. Men could form no idea of a creator that did not in some way resemble themselves; and as they could subdue their enemies through fear and by the infliction of pain, so did they believe that God would punish those who did not please him. Some people long ago believed that God's punishment was inflicted after death for eternity. The numerous beliefs about the personality and laws of the creator caused more bloodshed in the gloomy days of the past than anything else. Religion was the foundation of many of the most horrible wars. People committed thousands of crimes in the name of the God of the universe. Men and women were burned alive because they would not believe certain creeds, and yet they adhered to convictions equally as preposterous; but you will learn all these things later in life. That picture before you was the last queen of England, called Victoria."

"I hoped that the women would not have such repulsive features as the men," said the boy, looking critically at the picture, "but this face makes me shudder. Why do they all look so coarse and brutal?"

"People living when this queen reigned had the most degrading habit that ever blackened the history of mankind."

"What was that?" asked the youth.

"The consumption of flesh. They believed that animals, fowls, and fish were created to be eaten."

"Is it possible?" The boy shuddered convulsively, and turned away from the book. "I understand now why their faces repel me so. I do not like to think that we have descended from such people."

"They knew no better," said the father. "As they gradually became more refined they learned to burn the meat over flames and to cook it in heated vessels to change its appearance. The places where animals were killed and sold were withdrawn to retired places. Mankind was slowly turning from the habit, but they did not know it. As early as 2050 learned men, calling themselves vegetarians, proved conclusively that the consumption of such food was cruel and barbarous, and that it retarded refinement and mental growth. However, it was not till about 2300 that the vegetarian movement became of marked importance. The most highly educated classes in all lands adopted vegetarianism, and only the uneducated continued to kill and eat animals. The vegetarians tried for years to enact laws prohibiting the consumption of flesh, but opposition was very strong. In America in 2320 a colony was formed consisting of about three hundred thousand vegetarians. They purchased large tracts of land in what was known as the Indian Territory, and there made their homes, determined to prove by example the efficacy of their tenets. Within the first year the colony had doubled its number: people joined it from all parts of the globe. In the year 4000 it was a country of its own, and was the wonder of the world. The brightest minds were born there. The greatest discoveries and inventions were made by its inhabitants. In 4030 Gillette discovered the process of manufacturing crystal. Up to that time people had built their houses of natural stone, inflammable wood, and metals; but the new material, being fireproof and beautiful in its various colors, was used for all building purposes. In 4050 Holloway found the submerged succession of mountain chains across the Atlantic Ocean, and intended to construct a bridge on their summits; but the vast improvement in air ships rendered his plans impracticable.

"In 4051 John Saunders discovered and put into practice thought-telegraphy. This discovery was the signal for the introduction in schools and colleges of the science of mind-reading, and by the year 5000 so great had been the progress in that branch of knowledge that words were spoken only among the lowest of the uneducated. In no age of the world's history has there been such an important discovery. It civilized the world. Its early promoters did not dream of the vast good mind-reading would accomplish. Slowly it killed evil. Societies for the prevention of evil thought were organized in all lands. Children were born pure of mind and grew up in purity. Crime was choked out of existence. If a man had an evil thought, it was read in his heart, and he was not allowed to keep it. Men at first shunned evil for fear of detection, and then grew to love purity.

"In the year 6021 all countries of the world, having then a common language, and being drawn together in brotherly love by constant exchange of thought, agreed to call themselves a union without ruler or rulers. It was the greatest event in the history of the world. Certain sensitive mind students in Germany, who had for years been trying to communicate with other planets through the channel of thought, declared that, owing to the terrestrial unanimity of purpose in that direction, they had received mental impressions from other worlds, and that thorough interplanetary intercourse was a future possibility.

"Important inventions were made as the mind of humanity grew more elevated. Thornton discovered the plan to heat the earth's surface from its internal fire, and this discovery made journeys to the wonderful ice-bound countries situated at the North and the South Poles easy of accomplishment. At the North Pole, in the extensive concave lands, was found a peculiar race of men. Their sun was the great perpetually boiling lake of lava which bubbled from the centre of the earth in the bottom of their bowl-shaped world. And a strange religion was theirs! They believed that the earth was a monster on whose hide they had to live for a mortal lifetime, and that to the good was given the power after death to walk over the icy waste to their god, whose starry eyes they could see twinkling in space, and that the evil were condemned to feed the fire in the stomach of the monster as long as it lived. They told beautiful stories about the creation of their world, and held that if they lived too near the hot, dazzling mouth of evil, they would become blinded to the soft, forgiving eyes of the god of space. Hence they suffered the extreme cold of the lands near the frozen seas, believing that the physical ordeal prepared them for the icy journey to immortal rest after death. But there were those who hungered after the balmy atmosphere and the wonderful fruits and flowers that grew in the lowlands, and they lived there in indolence and so-called sin."

The old man and his son left the museum and walked into a wonderful park. Flowers of the most beautiful kinds and of sweetest fragrance grew on all sides. They came to a tall tower, four thousand feet in height, built of manufactured crystal. Something, like a great white bird, a thousand feet long, flew across the sky and settled down on the tower's summit.

"This was one of the most wonderful inventions of the Seventieth century," said the old man. "The early inhabitants of the earth could not have dreamed that it would be possible to go around it in twenty-four hours. In fact, there was a time when they were not able to go around it at all. Scientists were astonished when a man called Malburn, a great inventor, announced that, at a height of four thousand feet, he could disconnect an air ship from the laws of gravitation, and cause it to stand still in space till the earth had turned over. Fancy what must have been that immortal genius' feelings when he stood in space and saw the earth for the first time whirling beneath him!"

They walked on for some distance across the park till they came to a great instrument made to magnify the music in light. Here they paused and seated themselves.

"It will soon be night," said the old man. "The tones are those of bleeding sunset. I came here last evening to listen to the musical struggle between the light of dying day and that of the coming stars. The sunlight had been playing a powerful solo; but the gentle chorus of the stars, led by the moon, was inexplicably touching. Light is the voice of immortality; it speaks in all things."

An hour passed. It was growing dark.

"Tell me what immortality is," said the boy. "What does life lead to?"

"We do not know," replied the old man. "If we knew we would be infinite. Immortality is increasing happiness for all time; it is—"

A meteor shot across the sky. There was a burst of musical laughter among the singing stars. The old man bent over the boy's face and kissed it. "Immortality," said he—"immortality must be love immortal."

THE DAMNED THING

Ambrose Bierce

AMBROSE BIERCE (1842-1914) was a prolific writer and journalist, composing stories of the eerie and ironic. He traveled widely and in 1914 disappeared in Mexico, presumably on the trail of a story regarding one of Mexico's many revolutions. Bierce wrote some of the first and best stories about the Civil War (*In the Midst of Life*, 1892) as well as a biting satire of human nature, called *Devil's Dictionary*, in 1911 which was very much in the traditional satiric mode of both Swift and Twain. Like Hawthorne and Poe, Bierce wrote stories that attempted to get at the psychological workings of the individual under extraordinary, even unworldly circumstances, even as they approached death, as in "Occurrence at Owl Creek Bridge". Bierce wrote about robots, invisible creatures, men escaping into other dimensions—all typical subjects of science fiction. "The Damned Thing" is anecdotally credited as being the inspiration to the movie, Predator.

◆❖◆

CHAPTER ONE

One Does Not Always Eat What is on the Table

BY the light of a tallow candle which had been placed on one end of a rough table a man was reading something written in a book. It was an old account book, greatly worn; and the writing was not, apparently, very legible, for the man sometimes held the page close to the flame of the candle to get a stronger light on it. The shadow of the book would then throw into obscurity a half of the rooms, darkening a number of faces and figures; for besides the reader, eight other men were present. Seven of them sat against the rough log walls, silent, motionless, and the room being small, not very far from the table. By extending an arm any one of them could have touched the eighth man, who lay on the table, face upward, partly covered by a sheet, his arms at his sides. He was dead.

The man with the book was not reading aloud, and no one spoke; all seemed to be waiting for something to occur; the dead man only was without expectation. From the bland darkness outside came in, through the aperture that served for a window, all the ever unfamiliar noises of night in the wilderness—the long nameless note of a distant coyote; the drone of great blundering beetles, and all that mysterious chorus of small sounds that seem always to have been but half heard when they have suddenly ceased, as if conscious of an indiscretion. But nothing of all this was noted in that company; its members were not overmuch addicted to idle interest in matters of no practical importance; that was obvious in every line of their rugged faces—obvious even in the dim light of the single candle. They were evidently men of the vicinity—farmers and woodsmen.

The person reading was a trifle different; one would have said of him that he was of the world, worldly, albeit there was that in his attire which attested a certain fellowship with the organisms of his environment. His coat would hardly have passed muster in San Francisco; his foot-gear was not of urban origin, and the hat that lay by him on the floor (he was the only one uncovered) was such that if one had considered it as an article of mere personal adornment he would have missed its meaning. In countenance the man was rather prepossessing, with just a hint of sternness; though that he may have assumed or cultivated, as appropriate to one in authority. For he was a coroner. It was by virtue of his office that he had possession of the book in which he was reading; it had been found among the dead man's effects—in his cabin, where the inquest was now taking place.

When the coroner had finished reading he put the book into his breast pocket. At that moment the door was pushed open and a young man entered. He, clearly, was not of mountain birth and breeding: he was clad as those who dwell in cities. His clothing was dusty, however, as from travel. He had, in fact, been riding hard to attend the inquest.

The coroner nodded; no one else greeted him.

"We have waited for you," said the coroner. "It is necessary to have done with this business to-night."

The young man smiled. "I am sorry to have kept you," he said. "I went away, not to evade your summons, but to post to my newspaper an account of what I suppose I am called back to relate."

The coroner smiled.

"The account that you posted to your newspaper," he said, "differs, probably, from that which you will give here under oath."

"That," replied the other, rather hotly and with a visible flush, "is as you please. I used manifold paper and have a copy of what I sent. It was not written as news, for it is incredible, but as fiction. It may go as part of my testimony under oath."

"But you say it is incredible."

"That is nothing to you, sir, if I also swear that it is true."

The coroner was silent for a time, his eyes upon the floor.

The men about the sides of the cabin talked in whispers, but seldom withdrew their gaze from the face of the corpse. Presently the coroner lifted his eyes and said: "We will resume the inquest."

The men removed their hats. The witness was sworn.

"What is your name?" the coroner asked.

"William Harker."

"Age?"

"Twenty-seven."

"You knew the deceased, Hugh Morgan?"

"Yes."

"You were with him when he died?"

"Near him."

"How did that happen—your presence, I mean?"

"I was visiting him at this place to shoot and fish. A part of my purpose, however, was to study him and his odd, solitary way of life. He seemed a good model for a character in fiction. I sometimes write stories."

"I sometimes read them."

"Thank you."

"Stories in general—not yours."

Some of the jurors laughed. Against a sombre background humour shows high lights. Soldiers in the intervals of battle laugh easily, and a jest in the death chamber conquers by surprise.

"Relate the circumstances of this man's death," said the coroner. "You may use any notes or memoranda that you please."

The witness understood. Pulling a manuscript from his breast pocket he held it near the candle and turning the leaves until he found the passage that he wanted began to read.

CHAPTER TWO

What May Happen in a Field of Wild Oats

"...The sun had hardly risen when we left the house. We were looking for quail, each with a shotgun, but we had only one dog. Morgan said that our best ground was beyond a certain ridge that he pointed out, and we crossed it by a trail through the chaparral. On the other side was comparatively level ground, thickly covered with wild oats. As we emerged from the chaparral Morgan was but a few yards in advance. Suddenly we heard, at a little distance to our right and partly in front, a noise as of some animal thrashing about in the bushes, which we could see were violently agitated.

"'We've started a deer,' I said. 'I wish we had brought a rifle.'

"Morgan, who had stopped and was intently watching the agitated chaparral, said nothing, but had cocked both barrels of his gun and was holding it in readiness to aim. I thought him a trifle excited, which surprised me, for he had a reputation for exceptional coolness, even in moments of sudden and imminent peril.

"'Oh, come,' I said. 'You are not going to fill up a deer with quailshot, are you?'

"Still he did not reply; but catching sight of his face as he turned it slightly toward me I was struck by the intensity of his look. Then I understood that we had serious business in hand, and my first conjecture was that we had 'jumped' a grizzly. I advanced to Morgan's side, cocking my piece as I moved.

"The bushes were now quiet and the sounds had ceased, but Morgan was as attentive to the place as before.

"'What is it? What the devil is it?' I asked.

"'That Damned Thing!' he replied, without turning his head. His voice was husky and unnatural. He trembled visibly.

"I was about to speak further, when I observed the wild oats near the place of the disturbance moving in the most inexplicable way. I can hardly describe it. It seemed as if stirred by a streak of wind, which not only bent it, but pressed it down—crushed it so that it did not rise; and this movement was slowly prolonging itself directly toward us.

"Nothing that I had ever seen had affected me so strangely as this unfamiliar and unaccountable phenomenon, yet I am unable to recall any sense of fear. I remember—and tell it here because, singularly enough, I recollected it then—that once in looking carelessly out of an open window I momentarily mistook a small tree close at hand for one of a group of larger trees at a little distance away. It looked the same size as the others, but being more distinctly and sharply defined in mass and detail seemed out of harmony with them. It was a mere falsification of the law of aerial perspective, but it startled, almost terrified me. We so rely upon the orderly operation of familiar natural laws that any seeming suspension of them is noted as a menace to our safety, as warning of unthinkable calamity. So now the apparent causeless movement of the herbage and the slow, undeviating approach of the line of disturbance were distinctly disquieting. My companion appeared actually frightened, and I could hardly credit my senses when I saw him suddenly throw his gun to his shoulder and fire both barrels at the agitated grain! Before the smoke had cleared away I heard a loud savage cry—a scream like that of a wild animal—and flinging his gun upon the ground Morgan sprang away and ran swiftly from the spot. At the same instant I was thrown violently to the ground by the impact of something unseen in the smoke—some soft, heavy substance that seemed thrown against me with great force.

"Before I could get upon my feet and recover my gun, which seemed to have been struck from my hands, I heard Morgan crying out as if in mortal agony, and mingling with his cries were such hoarse, savage sounds as one hears from fighting dogs. Inexpressibly terrified, I struggled to my feet and looked in the direction of Morgan's retreat; and may Heaven in mercy spare me from another sight like that! At a distance of less than thirty yards was my friend, down upon one knee, his head thrown back at a frightful angle, hatless, his long hair in disorder and his whole body in violent movement from side to side, backward and forward. His right arm was lifted and seemed to lack the hand—at least, I could see none. The other arm was invisible. At times, as my memory now reports this extraordinary scene, I could discern but a part of his body; it was as if he had been partly blotted out—I cannot otherwise express it—then a shifting of his position would bring it all into view again.

"All this must have occurred within a few seconds, yet in that time Morgan assumed all the postures of a determined wrestler vanquished by superior weight and strength. I saw nothing but him and not always distinctly. During the entire incident his shouts and curses were heard, as if through an enveloping uproar of such sounds of rage and fury as I had never heard from the throat of man or brute!

"For a moment only I stood irresolute, then throwing down my gun I ran forward to my friend's assistance. I had a vague belief that he was suffering from a fit, or some form of convulsion. Before I could reach his side he was down and quiet. All sounds had ceased, but with a feeling of such terror as even these awful events had not inspired I now saw again the mysterious movement of the wild oats, prolonging itself from the trampled area about the prostrate man toward the edge of a wood. It was only when it had reached the wood that I was able to withdraw my eyes and look at my companion. He was dead."

CHAPTER THREE A Man Though Naked May be in Rags

The coroner rose from his seat and stood beside the dead man. Lifting an edge of the sheet he pulled it away, exposing the entire body, altogether naked and showing in the candle—light a clay-like yellow. It had, however, broad maculations of bluish black, obviously caused by extravasated blood from contusions. The chest and sides looked as if they had been beaten with a bludgeon. There were dreadful lacerations; the skin was torn in strips and shreds.

The coroner moved round to the end of the table and undid a silk handkerchief which had been passed under the chin and knotted on the top of the head. When the handkerchief was drawn away it exposed what had been the throat. Some of the jurors who had risen to get a better view repented their curiosity and turned away their faces. Witness Harker went to the open window and leaned out across the sill, faint and sick. Dropping the handkerchief upon the dead man's neck the coroner stepped to an angle of the room and from a pile of clothing produced one garment after another, each of which he held up a moment for inspection. All were torn, and stiff with blood. The jurors did not make a closer inspection. They seemed rather uninterested. They had, in truth, seen all this before; the only thing that was new to them being Harker's testimony.

"Gentlemen," the coroner said, "we have no more evidence, I think. Your duty has been already explained to you; if there is nothing you wish to ask you may go outside and consider your verdict."

The foreman rose—a tall, bearded man of sixty, coarsely clad.

"I shall like to ask one question, Mr. Coroner," he said. "What asylum did this yer last witness escape from?"

"Mr. Harker," said the coroner gravely and tranquilly, "from what asylum did you last escape?"

Harker flushed crimson again, but said nothing, and the seven jurors rose and solemnly filed out of the cabin.

"If you have done insulting me, sir," said Harker, as soon as he and the officer were left alone with the dead man, "I suppose I am at liberty to go?"

"Yes."

Harker started to leave, but paused, with his hand on the door latch. The habit of his profession was strong in him—stronger than his sense of personal dignity. He turned about and said:

"The book you have there—I recognize it as Morgan's diary. You seemed greatly interested in it; you read in it while I was testifying. May I see it? The public would like—"

"The book will cut no figure in this matter," replied the official, slipping it into his coat pocket; "all the entries in it were made before the writer's death."

As Harker passed out of the house the jury re-entered and stood about the table, on which the now covered corpse showed under the sheet with sharp definition. The foreman seated himself near the candle, produced from his breast pocket a pencil and scrap of paper and wrote rather laboriously the following verdict, which with various degrees of effort all signed:

"We, the jury, do find that the remains come to their death at the hands of a mountain lion, but some of us thinks, all the same, they had fits."

CHAPTER FOUR

An Explanation From the Tomb

In the diary of the late Hugh Morgan are certain interesting entries having, possibly, a scientific value as suggestions. At the inquest upon his body the book was not put in evidence; possibly the coroner thought it not worth while to confuse the jury. The date of the first of the entries mentioned cannot be ascertained; the upper part of the leaf is torn away; the part of the entry remaining follows:

"...would run in a half-circle, keeping his head turned always toward the centre, and again he would stand still, barking furiously. At last he ran away into the brush as fast as he could go. I thought at first that he had gone mad, but on returning to the house found no other alteration in his manner than what was obviously due to fear of punishment.

"Can a dog see with his nose? Do odours impress some cerebral centre with images of the thing that emitted them?....

"Sept. 2.—Looking at the stars last night as they rose above the crest of the ridge east of the house, I observed them successively disappear—from left to right. Each was eclipsed but an instant, and only a few at a time, but along the entire length of the ridge all that were within a degree or two of the crest were blotted out. It was as if something had passed along between me and them; but I could not see it, and the stars were not thick enough to define its outline. Ugh! don't like this."

Several weeks' entries are missing, three leaves being torn from the book.

"Sept. 27.—It has been about here again—I find evidences of its presence every day. I watched again all last night in the same cover, gun in hand, double-charged with buckshot. In the morning the fresh footprints were there, as before. Yet I would have sworn that I did not sleep—indeed, I hardly sleep at all. It is terrible, insupportable! If these amazing experiences are real I shall go mad; if they are fanciful I am mad already.

"Oct. 3.—I shall not go—it shall not drive me away. No, this is my house, my land. God hates a coward....

"Oct. 5.—I can stand it no longer; I have invited Harker to pass a few weeks with me—he has a level head. I can judge from his manner if he thinks me mad.

"Oct. 7.—I have the solution of the mystery; it came to me last night—suddenly, as by revelation. How simple—how terribly simple!

"There are sounds we cannot hear. At either end of the scale are notes that stir no chord of that imperfect instrument, the human ear. They are too high or too grave. I have observed a flock of blackbirds occupying an entire tree-top—the tops of several trees—and all in full song. Suddenly—in a moment—at absolutely the same instant—all spring into the air and fly away. How? They could not all see one another—whole tree-tops intervened. At no point could a leader have been visible to all. There must have been a signal of warning or command, high and shrill above the din, but by me unheard. I have observed, too, the same simultaneous flight when all were silent, among not only blackbirds, but other birds—quail, for example, widely separated by bushes—even on opposite sides of a hill.

"It is known to seamen that a school of whales basking or sporting on the surface of the ocean, miles apart, with the convexity of the earth between, will sometimes dive at the same instant—all gone out of sight in a moment. The signal has been sounded—too grave for the ear of the sailor at the masthead and his comrades on the deck—who nevertheless feel its vibrations in the ship as the stones of a cathedral are stirred by the bass of the organ.

"As with sounds, so with colours. At each end of the solar spectrum the chemist can detect the presence of what are known as 'actinic' rays. They represent colours—integral colours in the composition of light—which we are unable to discern. The human eye is an imperfect instrument; its range is but a few octaves of the real 'chromatic scale.' I am not mad; there are colours that we cannot see.

"And, God help me! the Damned Thing is of such a colour!"

THE RAY OF DISPLACEMENT

Harriet Elizabeth Prescott Spofford

HARRIET ELIZABETH PRESCOTT SPOFFORD (1835-1921) wrote successfully in a number of genres, mostly Gothic fantasy and the supernatural, her influences being Nathaniel Hawthorne and Robert Louis Stevenson. Most of her fiction is located in rural New England and deals, in a realist fashion, with people and places she would have known personally. But by the time she turned sixty, the world had changed dramatically, with Thomas Edison cranking out one invention after another and Madame Curie discovering elements no one thought possible. "The Ray of Displacement" was written with this new spirit of discovery, haunted, as it is, with Spofford's usual mood of Gothic dread.

"We should have to reach the Infinite to arrive at the Impossible."

IT would interest none but students should I recite the circumstances of the discovery. Prosecuting my usual researches, I seemed rather to have stumbled on this tremendous thing than to have evolved it from formulæ.

Of course, you already know that all molecules, all atoms, are separated from each other by spaces perhaps as great, when compared relatively, as those which separate the members of the stellar universe. And when by my Y-ray I could so far increase these spaces that I could pass one solid body through another, owing to the differing situation of their atoms, I felt no disembodied spirit had wider, freer range than I. Until my discovery was made public my power over the material universe was practically unlimited.

Le Sage's theory concerning ultra-mundane corpuscles was rejected because corpuscles could not pass through solids. But here were corpuscles passing through solids. As I proceeded, I found that at the displacement of one one-billionth of a centimeter the object capable of passing through another was still visible, owing to the refraction of the air, and had the power of communicating its polarization; and that at two one-billionths the object became invisible, but that at either displacement the subject, if a person, could see into the present plane; and all movement and direction were voluntary. I further found my Y-ray could so polarize a substance that its touch in turn temporarily polarized anything with which it came in contact, a negative current moving atoms to the left, and a positive to the right of the present plane.

My first experience with this new principle would have made a less determined man drop the affair. Brant had been by way of dropping into my office and laboratory when in town. As I afterwards recalled, he showed a signal interest in certain toxicological experiments. "Man alive!" I had said to him once, "let those crystals alone! A single one of them will send you where you never see the sun!" I was uncertain if he brushed one off the slab. He did not return for some months. His wife, as I heard afterwards, had a long and baffling illness in the meantime, divorcing him on her recovery; and he had remained out of sight, at last leaving his native place for the great city. He had come in now, plausibly to ask my opinion of a stone—a diamond of unusual size and water.

I put the stone on a glass shelf in the next room while looking for the slide. You can imagine my sensation when that diamond, with something like a flash of shadow, so intense and swift it was, burst into a hundred rays of blackness and subsided—a pile of carbon! I had forgotten that the shelf happened to be negatively polarized, consequently everything it touched sharing its polarization, and that in pursuing my experiment I had polarized myself also, but with the opposite current; thus the atoms of my fingers passing through the spaces of the atoms of the stone already polarized, separated them negatively so far that they suffered disintegration and returned to the normal. "Good heavens! What has happened!" I cried before I thought. In a moment he was in the rear room and bending with me over the carbon. "Well," he said straightening himself directly, "you gave me a pretty fright. I thought for a moment that was my diamond."

"But it is!" I whispered.

"Pshaw!" he exclaimed roughly. "What do you take me for? Come, come, I'm not here for tricks. That's enough damned legerdemain. Where's my diamond?"

With less dismay and more presence of mind I should have edged along to my batteries, depolarized myself, placed in vacuum the tiny shelf of glass and applied my Y-ray; and with, I knew not what, of convulsion and flame the atoms might have slipped into place. But, instead, I stood gasping. He turned and surveyed me; the low order of his intelligence could receive but one impression.

"Look here," he said, "you will give me back my stone! Now! Or I will have an officer here!"

My mind was flying like the current through my coils. How could I restore the carbon to its original, as I must, if at all, without touching it, and how could I gain time without betraying my secret? "You are very short," I said. "What would you do with your officer?"

"Give you up! Give you up, appear against you, and let you have a sentence of twenty years behind bars."

"Hard words, Mr. Brant. You could say I had your property. I could deny it. Would your word outweigh mine? But return to the office in five minutes—if it is a possible thing you shall—"

"And leave you to make off with my jewel! Not by a long shot! I'm a bad man to deal with, and I'll have my stone or—"

"Go for your officer," said I.

His eye, sharp as a dagger's point, fell an instant. How could he trust me? I might escape with my booty. Throwing open the window to call, I might pinion him from behind, powerful as he was. But before he could gainsay, I had taken half a dozen steps backward, reaching my batteries.

"Give your alarm," I said. I put out my hand, lifting my lever, turned the current into my coils, and blazed up my Y-ray for half a heart-beat, succeeding in that brief time in reversing and in receiving the current that so far changed matters that the thing I touched would remain normal, although I was left still so far subjected to the ray of the less displacement that I ought, when the thrill had subsided, to be able to step through the wall as easily as if no wall were there. "Do you see what I have here?" I most unwisely exclaimed. "In one second I could annihilate you—" I had no time for more, or even to make sure I was correct, before, keeping one eye on me, he had called the officer.

"Look here," he said again, turning on me. "I know enough to see you have something new there, some of your damned inventions. Come, give me my diamond, and if it is worth while I'll find the capital, go halves, and drop this matter."

"Not to save your life!" I cried.

"You know me, officer," he said, as the blue coat came running in. "I give this man into custody for theft."

"It is a mistake, officer," I said. "But you will do your duty."

"Take him to the central station," said Mr. Brant, "and have him searched. He has a jewel of mine on his person."

"Yer annar's sure it's not on the primmises?" asked the officer.

"He has had no time—"

"Sure, if it's quick he do be he's as like to toss it in a corner—"

I stretched out my hand to a knob that silenced the humming among my wires, and at the same time sent up a thread of white fire whose instant rush and subsidence hinted of terrible power behind. The last divisible particle of radium—their eyeballs throbbed for a week.

"Search," I said. "But be careful about shocks. I don't want murder here, too."

Apparently they also were of that mind. For, recovering their sight, they threw my coat over my shoulders and marched me between them to the station, where I was searched, and, as it was already late, locked into a cell for the night.

I could not waste strength on the matter. I was waiting for the dead middle of the night. Then I should put things to proof.

I confess it was a time of intense breathlessness while waiting for silence and slumber to seal the world. Then I called upon my soul, and I stepped boldly forward and walked through that stone wall as if it had been air.

Of course, at my present displacement I was perfectly visible, and I slipped behind this and that projection, and into that alley, till sure of safety. There I made haste to my quarters, took the shelf holding the carbon, and at once subjected it to the necessary treatment. I was unprepared for the result. One instant the room seemed full of a blinding white flame, an intolerable heat, which shut my eyes and singed my hair and blistered my face.

"It is the atmosphere of a fire-dissolving planet," I thought. And then there was darkness and a strange odor.

I fumbled and stumbled about till I could let in the fresh air; and presently I saw the dim light of the street lamp. Then I turned on my own lights—and there was the quartz slab with a curious fusing of its edges, and in the center, flashing, palpitating, lay the diamond, all fire and whiteness. I wonder if it were not considerably larger; but it was hot as if just fallen from Syra Vega; it contracted slightly after subjection to dephlogistic gases.

It was near morning when, having found Brant's address, I passed into his house and his room, and took my bearings. I found his waistcoat, left the diamond in one of its pockets, and returned. It would not do to remain away, visible or invisible. I must be vindicated, cleared of the charge, set right before the world by Brant's appearing and confessing his mistake on finding the diamond in his pocket.

Judge Brant did nothing of the kind. Having visited me in my cell and in vain renewed his request to share in the invention which the habit of his mind convinced him must be of importance, he appeared against me. And the upshot of the business was that I went to prison for the term of years he had threatened.

I asked for another interview with him; but was refused, unless on the terms already declined. My lawyer, with the prison chaplain, went to him, but to no purpose. At last I went myself, as I had gone before, begging him not to ruin the work of my life. He regarded me as a bad dream, and I could not undeceive him without betraying my secret. I returned to my cell and again waited. For to escape was only to prevent possible vindication. If Mary had lived—but I was alone in the world.

The chaplain arranged with my landlord to take a sum of money I had, and to keep my rooms and apparatus intact till the expiration of my sentence. And then I put on the shameful and degrading prison garb and submitted to my fate.

It was a black fate. On the edge of the greatest triumph over matter that had ever been achieved, on the verge of announcing the actuality of the Fourth Dimension of Space, and of defining and declaring its laws, I was a convict laborer at a prison bench.

One day Judge Brant, visiting a client under sentence of death, in relation to his fee, made pretext to look me up, and stopped at my bench. "And how do you like it as far as you've gone?" he said.

"So that I go no farther," I replied. "And unless you become accessory to my taking off, you will acknowledge you found the stone in your pocket—"

"Not yet, not yet," he said, with an unctuous laugh. "It was a keen jest you played. Regard this as a jest in return. But when you are ready, I am ready."

The thing was hopeless. That night I bade good-bye to the life that had plunged me from the pinnacle of light to the depths of hell.

When again conscious I lay on a cot in the prison hospital. My attempt had been unsuccessful. St. Angel sat beside me. It was here, practically, he came into my life—alas! that I came into his.

In the long nights of darkness and failing faintness, when horror had me by the throat, he was beside me, and his warm, human touch was all that held me while I hung over the abyss. When I swooned off again his hand, his voice, his bending face recalled me. "Why not let me go, and then an end?" I sighed.

"To save you from a great sin," he replied. And I clung to his hand with the animal instinct of living.

I was well, and in my cell, when he said. "You claim to be an honest man—"

"And yet?"

"You were about taking that which did not belong to you."

"I hardly understand"

"Can you restore life once taken?"

"Oh, life! That worthless thing!"

"Lent for a purpose."

"For torture!"

"If by yourself you could breathe breath into any pinch of feathers and toss it off your hand a creature—but, as it is, life is a trust. And you, a man of parts, of power, hold it only to return with usury."

"And stripped of the power of gathering usury! Robbed of the work about to revolutionize the world!"

"The world moves on wide waves. Another man will presently have reached your discovery."

As if that were a thing to be glad of! I learned afterwards that St. Angel had given up the sweetness of life for the sake of his enemy. He had gone to prison, and himself worn the stripes, rather than the woman he loved should know her husband was the criminal. Perhaps he did not reconcile this with his love of inviolate truth. But St. Angel had never felt so much regard for his own soul as for the service of others. Self-forgetfulness was the dominant of all his nature.

"Tell me," he said, sitting with me, "about your work."

A whim of trustfulness seized me. I drew an outline, but paused at the look of pity on his face. He felt there was but one conclusion to draw—that I was a madman.

"Very well," I said, "you shall see." And I walked through the wall before his amazed eyes, and walked back again.

For a moment speechless, "You have hypnotic power," then he said. "You made me think I saw it."

"You did see it. I can go free any day I choose."

"And you do not?"

"I must be vindicated." And I told exactly what had taken place with Brant and his diamond. "Perhaps that vindication will never come," I said at last. "The offended amour propre, and the hope of gain, hindered in the beginning. Now he will find it impossible."

"That is too monstrous to believe!" said St. Angel. "But since you can, why not spend an hour or two at night with your work?"

"In these clothes! How long before I should be brought back? The first wayfarer—oh, you see!"

St. Angel thought a while. "You are my size," he said then. "We will exchange clothes. I will remain here. In three hours return, that you may get your sleep. It is fortunate the prison should be in the same town."

Night after night then I was in my old rooms, the shutters up, lost in my dreams and my researches, arriving at great ends.

Night after night I reappeared on the moment, and St. Angel went his way.

I had now found that molecular displacement can be had in various directions. Going further, I saw that gravity acts on bodies whose molecules are on the same plane, and one of the possible results of the application of the Y-ray was the suspension of the laws of gravity. This possibly accounted for an almost inappreciable buoyancy and the power of directing one's course. My last studies showed that a substance thus treated has the degenerative power of attracting the molecules of any norm into its new orbit—a disastrous possibility. A chair might disappear into a table previously treated by a Y-ray. In fact, the outlook was to infinity. The change so slight—the result so astonishing! The subject might go into molecular interstices as far removed, to all essential purpose, as if billions of miles away in interstellar space. Nothing was changed, nothing disrupted; but the thing had stepped aside to let the world go by. The secrets of the world were mine. The criminal was at my mercy. The lover had no reserves from me. And as for my enemy, the Lord had delivered him into my hand. I could leave him only a puzzle for the dissectors. I could make him, although yet alive, a conscious ghost to stand or wander in his altered shape through years of nightmare alone and lost. What wonders of energy would follow this ray of displacement. What withdrawal of malignant growth and deteriorating tissue was to come. "To what heights of succor for humanity the surgeon can rise with it!" said St. Angel, as, full of my enthusiasm, I dilated on the marvel.

"He can work miracles!" I exclaimed. "He can heal the sick, walk on the deep, perhaps—who knows—raise the dead!"

I was at the height of my endeavor when St. Angel brought me my pardon. He had so stated my case to the Governor, so spoken of my interrupted career, and of my prison conduct, that the pardon had been given. I refused to accept it. "I accept," I said, "nothing but vindication, if I stay here till the day of judgment!"

"But there is no provision for you now," he urged. "Officially you no longer exist."

"Here I am," I said, "and here I stay."

"At any rate," he continued, "come out with me now and see the Governor, and see the world and the daylight outdoors, and be a man among men a while!"

With the stipulation that I should return, I put on a man's clothes again and went out the gates.

It was with a thrill of exultation that, exhibiting the affairs in my room to St. Angel, finally I felt the vibrating impulse that told me I had received the ray of the larger displacement. In a moment I should be viewless as the air.

"Where are you?" said St. Angel, turning this way and that. "What has become of you?"

"Seeing is believing," I said. "Sometimes not seeing is the naked truth."

"Oh, but this is uncanny!" he exclaimed. "A voice out of empty air."

"Not so empty! But place your hand under the second coil. Have no fear. You hear me now," I said. "I am in perhaps the Fourth Dimension. I am invisible to any one not there—to all the world, except, presently, yourself. For now you, you also, pass into the unseen. Tell me what you feel."

"Nothing," he said. "A vibration—a suspicion of one. No, a blow, a sense of coming collapse, so instant it has passed."

"Now," I said, "there is no one on earth with eyes to see you but myself!"

"That seems impossible."

"Did you see me? But now you do. We are on the same plane. Look in that glass. There is the reflection of the room, of the window, the chair. Do you see me? Yourself?"

"Powers of the earth and air, but this is ghastly!" said St. Angel.

"It is the working of natural law. Now we will see the world, ourselves unseen."

"An unfair advantage."

"Perhaps. But there are things to accomplish to-day." What things I never dreamed; or I had stayed on the threshold.

I wanted St. Angel to know the manner of man this Brant was. We went out, and arrested our steps only inside Brant's office.

"This door is always blowing open!" said the clerk, and he returned to a woman standing in a suppliant attitude. "The Judge has gone to the races," he said, "and he's left word that Tuesday morning your goods'll be put out of the house if you don't pay up!" The woman went her way weeping.

Leaving, we mounted a car; we would go to the races ourselves. I doubt if St. Angel had ever seen anything of the sort. I observed him quietly slip a dime into the conductor's pocket—he felt that even the invisible, like John Gilpin, carried a right. "This opens a way for the right hand undreamed of the left," he said to me later.

It was not long before we found Judge Brant, evidently in an anxious frame, his expanse of countenance white with excitement. He had been plunging heavily, as I learned, and had big money staked, not upon the favorite but upon Hannan, the black mare. "That man would hardly put up so much on less than a certainty," I thought. Winding our way unseen among the grooms and horses, I found what I suspected—a plan to pocket the favorite. "But I know a game worth two of that," I said. I took a couple of small smooth pebbles, previously prepared, from the chamois bag into which I had put them with some others and an aluminum wafer treated for the larger displacement, and slipped one securely under the favorite's saddle-girth.

When he warmed to his work he should be, for perhaps half an hour, at the one-billionth point, before the virtue expired, and capable of passing through every obstacle as he was directed.

"Hark you, Danny," then I whispered in the jockey's ear.

"Who are you? What—I—I—don't—" looking about with terror.

"It's no ghost," I whispered hurriedly. "Keep your nerve. I am flesh and blood—alive as you. But I have the property which for half an hour I give you—a new discovery. And knowing Bub and Whittler's game, it's up to you to knock 'em out. Now, remember, when they try the pocket ride straight through them!"

Other things kept my attention; and when the crucial moment came I had some excited heart-beats. And so had Judge Brant. It was in the instant when Danny, having held the favorite well in hand for the first stretch, Hannan and Darter in the lead and the field following, was about calling on her speed, that suddenly Bub and Whittler drew their horses' heads a trifle more closely together, in such wise that it was impossible to pass on either side, and a horse could no more shoot ahead than if a stone wall stood there. "Remember, Danny!" I shouted, making a trumpet of my hands. "Ride straight through!"

And Danny did. He pulled himself together, and set his teeth as if it were a compact with powers of evil, and rode straight through without turning a hair, or disturbing either horse or rider. Once more the Y-ray was triumphant.

But about Judge Brant the air was blue. It would take a very round sum of money to recoup the losses of those few moments. I disliked to have St. Angel hear him; but it was all in the day's work.

The day had not been to Judge Brant's mind, as at last he bent his steps to the club. As he went it occurred to me to try upon him the larger ray of displacement, and I slipped down the back of his collar the wafer I had ready. He would not at once feel its action, but in the warmth either of walking or dining, its properties should be lively for nearly an hour. I had curiosity to see if the current worked not only through all substances, but through all sorts and conditions.

"I should prefer a better pursuit," said St. Angel, as we reached the street. "Is there not something ignoble in it?"

"In another case. Here it is necessary to hound the criminal, to see the man entirely. A game not to be played too often, for there is work to be done before establishing the counteracting currents that may ensure reserves and privacies to people. To-night let us go to the club with Judge Brant, and then I will back to my cell."

As you may suppose, Brant was a man neither of imagination nor humor. As you have seen, he was hard and cruel, priding himself on being a good hater, which in his contention meant indulgence of a preternaturally vindictive temper when prudence allowed. With more cunning than ability, he had achieved some success in his profession, and he secured admission to a good club, recently crowning his efforts, when most of the influential members were absent, by getting himself made one of its governors.

It would be impossible to find a greater contrast to this wretch than in St. Angel—a man of delicate imagination and pure fancy, tender to the child on the street, the fly on the wall; all his atmosphere that of kindness. Gently born, but too finely bred, his physical resistance was so slight that his immunity lay in not being attacked. His clean, fair skin, his brilliant eyes, spoke of health, but the fragility of frame did not speak of strength. Yet St. Angel's life was the active principle of good; his neighborhood was purification.

I was revolving these things while we followed Judge Brant, when I saw him pause in an agitated manner, like one startled out of sleep. A quick shiver ran over his strong frame; he turned red and pale, then with a shrug went on. The displacement had occurred. He was now on the plane of invisibility, and we must have a care ourselves.

Wholly unconscious of any change, the man pursued his way. The street was as usual. There was the boy who always waited for him with the extra but to-night was oblivious; and failing to get his attention the Judge walked on. A shower that had been threatening began to fall, the sprinkle becoming a downpour, with umbrellas spread and people hurrying. The Judge hailed a car; but the motorman was as blind as the newsboy. The shower stopped as suddenly as it had begun, but he went on some paces before perceiving that he was perfectly dry, for as he shut and shook his umbrella not a drop fell, and as he took off his hat and looked at it, not an atom of moisture was to be found there. Evidently bewildered, and looking about shamefacedly, I fancied I could hear him saying, with his usual oaths, "I must be deucedly overwrought, or this is some blue devilment."

As the Judge took his accustomed seat in the warm and brilliantly lighted room, and picking up the evening paper, looked over the columns, the familiar every-day affair quieting his nerves so that he could have persuaded himself he had been half asleep as he walked, he was startled by the voice, not four feet away, of one of the old officers who made the Kings County their resort. Something had ruffled the doughty hero. "By the Lord Harry, sir," he was saying in unmodulated tones, "I should like to know what this club is coming to when you can spring on it the election of such a man as this Brant! Judge? What's he Judge of? Beat his wife, too, didn't he? The governors used to be gentlemen!"

"But you know, General," said his vis-à-vis, "I think no more of him than you do; but when a man lives at the Club—"

"Lives here!" burst in the other angrily. "He hasn't anywhere else to live! Is there a decent house in town open to him? Well, thank goodness, I've somewhere else to go before he comes in! The sight of him gives me a fit of the gout!" And the General stumped out stormily.

"Old boy seems upset!" said some one not far away. "But he's right. It was sheer impudence in the fellow to put up his name."

I could see Brant grow white and gray with anger, as surprised and outraged, wondering what it meant—if the General intended insult—if Scarsdale—but no, apparently they had not seen him. The contemptuous words rankled; the sweat stood on his forehead.

Had not the moment been serious, there were a thousand tricks to play. But the potency of the polarization was subsiding and in a short time the normal molecular plane would be re-established. It was there that I made my mistake. I should not have allowed him to depolarize so soon. I should have kept him bewildered and foodless till famished and weak. Instead, as ion by ion the effect of the ray decreased, his shape grew vague and misty, and then one and another man there rubbed his eyes, for Judge Brant was sitting in his chair and a waiter was hastening towards him.

It had all happened in a few minutes. Plainly the Judge understood nothing of the circumstances. He was dazed, but he must put the best face on it; and he ordered his dinner and a pony of brandy, eating like a hungry animal.

He rose, after a time, refreshed, invigorated, and all himself. Choosing a cigar, he went into another room, seeking a choice lounging place, where for a while he could enjoy his ease and wonder if anything worse than a bad dream had befallen. As for the General's explosion, it did not signify; he was conscious of such opinion; he was overliving it; he would be expelling the old cock yet for conduct unbecoming a gentleman.

Meanwhile, St. Angel, tiring of the affair, and weary, had gone into this room, and in an arm-chair by the hearth was awaiting me—the intrusive quality of my observations not at all to his mind. He had eaten nothing all day, and was somewhat faint. He had closed his eyes, and perhaps fallen into a light doze when he must have been waked by the impact of Brant's powerful frame, as the latter took what seemed to him the empty seat. I expected to see Brant at once flung across the rug by St. Angel's natural effort in rising. Instead, Brant sank into the chair as into down pillows.

I rushed, as quickly as I could, to seize and throw him off, "Through him! Pass through him! Come out! Come to me!" I cried. And people to-day remember that voice out of the air, in the Kings County Club.

It seemed to me that I heard a sound, a sob, a whisper, as if one cried with a struggling sigh, "Impossible!" And with that a strange trembling convulsed Judge Brant's great frame, he lifted his hands, he thrust out his feet, his head fell forward, he groaned gurglingly, shudder after shudder shook him as if every muscle quivered with agony or effort, the big veins started out as if every pulse were a red-hot iron. He was wrestling with something, he knew not what, something as antipathetic to him as white is to black; every nerve was concentrated in rebellion, every fiber struggled to break the spell.

The whole affair was that of a dozen heart-beats—the attempt of the opposing molecules each to draw the other into its own orbit. The stronger physical force, the greater aggregation of atoms was prevailing. Thrust upward for an instant, Brant fell back into his chair exhausted, the purple color fading till his face shone fair as a girl's, sweet and smiling as a child's, white as the face of a risen spirit—Brant's!

Astounded, I seized his shoulder and whirled him about. There was no one else in the chair. I looked in every direction. There was no St. Angel to be seen. There was but one conclusion to draw—the molecules of Brant's stronger material frame had drawn into their own plane the molecules of St. Angel's.

I rushed from the place, careless if seen or unseen, howling in rage and misery. I sought my laboratory, and in a fiend's fury depolarized myself, and I demolished every instrument, every formula, every vestige of my work. I was singed and scorched and burned, but I welcomed any pain. And I went back to prison, admitted by the officials who hardly knew what else to do. I would stay there, I thought, all my days. God grant they should be few! It would be seen that a life of imprisonment and torture were too little punishment for the ruin I had wrought.

It was after a sleepless night, of which every moment seemed madness, that, the door of my cell opening, I saw St. Angel. St. Angel? God have mercy on me, no, it was Judge Brant I saw!

He came forward, with both hands extended, a grave, imploring look on his face. "I have come," he said, a singular sweet overtone in his voice that I had never heard before, yet which echoed like music in my memory, "to make you all the reparation in my power. I will go with you at once before the Governor, and acknowledge that I have found the diamond. I can never hope to atone for what you have suffered. But as long as I live, all that I have, all that I am, is yours!"

There was a look of absolute sweetness on his face that for a dizzy moment made me half distraught. "We will go together," he said. "I have to stop on the way and tell a woman whose mortgage comes due to-day that I have made a different disposition; and, do you know," he added brightly, after an instant's hesitation, "I think I shall help her pay it!" and he laughed gayly at the jest involved.

"Will you say that you have known my innocence all these years?" I said sternly.

"Is not that," he replied, with a touching and persuasive quality of tone, "a trifle too much? Do you think this determination has been reached without a struggle? If you are set right before the world, is not something due to—Brant?"

"If I did not know who and what you are," I said, "I should think the soul of St. Angel had possession of you!"

The man looked at me dreamily. "Strange!" he murmured. "I seem to have heard something like that before. However," as if he shook off a perplexing train of thought, "all that is of no consequence. It is not who you are, but what you do. Come, my friend, don't deny me, don't let the good minute slip. Surely the undoing of the evil of a lifetime, the turning of that force to righteousness, is work outweighing all a prison chaplain's—"

My God, what had the intrusion of my incapable hands upon forbidden mysteries done!

"Come," he said. "We will go together. We will carry light into dark places—there are many waiting—"

"St. Angel!" I cried, with a loud voice, "are you here?"

And again the smile of infinite sweetness illuminated the face even as the sun shines up from the depths of a stagnant pool.

THE EMPIRE OF THE ANTS

H. G. Wells

H. G. WELLS (1866-1946) is considered to be the "father of science fiction" but he actually considered himself to be a social critic. Besides science fiction (for which he is mostly known today) he wrote mainstream fiction as well as books and essays on science, history, and politics. His most famous non-fiction book is his *Outline of History* (1920). Though his science fiction was solidly based on the science of the day, nearly everything he wrote in the science fiction field had an element of satire to it. *War of the Worlds* (1898), for example, is as much of a criticism of colonialism as Joseph Conrad's story, "Heart of Darkness". Certainly "The Empire of the Ants" can be seen as a kind of reverse colonialism—as well as being a rather stunning prediction of something that actually happened with 26 Tanzanian queen African honey bees being accidentally released in Brazil in 1957.

CHAPTER ONE

WHEN Captain Gerilleau received instructions to take his new gunboat, the *Benjamin Constant*, to Badama on the Batemo arm of the Guaramadema and there assist the inhabitants against a plague of ants, he suspected the authorities of mockery. His promotion had been romantic and irregular, the affections of a prominent Brazilian lady and the captain's liquid eyes had played a part in the process, and the *Diario* and *O Futuro* had been lamentably disrespectful in their comments. He felt he was to give further occasion for disrespect.

He was a Creole, his conceptions of etiquette and discipline were pure-blooded Portuguese, and it was only to Holroyd, the Lancashire engineer who had come over with the boat, and as an exercise in the use of English—his "th" sounds were very uncertain—that he opened his heart.

"It is in effect," he said, "to make me absurd! What can a man do against ants? Dey come, dey go."

"They say," said Holroyd, "that these don't go. That chap you said was a Sambo—"

"Zambo;—it is a sort of mixture of blood."

"Sambo. He said the people are going!"

The captain smoked fretfully for a time. "Dese tings 'ave to happen," he said at last. "What is it? Plagues of ants and suchlike as God wills. Dere was a plague in Trinidad—the little ants that carry leaves. All der orange-trees, all der mangoes! What does it matter? Sometimes ant armies come into your houses—fighting ants; a different sort. You go and they clean the house. Then you come back again;—the house is clean, like new! No cockroaches, no fleas, no jiggers in the floor."

"That Sambo chap," said Holroyd, "says these are a different sort of ant."

The captain shrugged his shoulders, fumed, and gave his attention to a cigarette.

Afterwards he reopened the subject. "My dear 'Olroyd, what am I to do about dese infernal ants?"

The captain reflected. "It is ridiculous," he said. But in the afternoon he put on his full uniform and went ashore, and jars and boxes came back to the ship and subsequently he did. And Holroyd sat on deck in the evening coolness and smoked profoundly and marvelled at Brazil. They were six days up the Amazon, some hundreds of miles from the ocean, and east and west of him there was a horizon like the sea, and to the south nothing but a sand-bank island with some tufts of scrub. The water was always running like a sluice, thick with dirt, animated with crocodiles and hovering birds, and fed by some inexhaustible source of tree trunks; and the waste of it, the headlong waste of it, filled his soul. The town of Alemquer, with its meagre church, its thatched sheds for houses, its discoloured ruins of ampler days, seemed a little thing lost in this wilderness of Nature, a sixpence dropped on Sahara. He was a young man, this was his first sight of the tropics, he came straight from England, where Nature is hedged, ditched, and drained, into the perfection of submission, and he had suddenly discovered the insignificance of man. For six days they had been steaming up from the sea by unfrequented channels; and man had been as rare as a rare butterfly. One saw one day a canoe, another day a distant station, the next no men at all. He began to perceive that man is indeed a rare animal, having but a precarious hold upon this land.

He perceived it more clearly as the days passed, and he made his devious way to the Batemo, in the company of this remarkable commander, who ruled over one big gun, and was forbidden to waste his ammunition. Holroyd was learning Spanish industriously, but he wa still in the present tense and substantive stage of speech, and the only other person who had any words of English was a negro stoker, who had them all wrong. The second in command was a Portuguese, da Cunha, who spoke French, but it was a different sort of French from the French Holroyd had learnt in Southport, and their intercourse was confined to politenesses and simple propositions about the weather. And the weather, like everything else in this amazing new world, the weather had no human aspect, and was hot by night and hot by day, and the air steam, even the wind was hot steam, smelling of vegetation in decay: and the alligators and the strange birds, the flies of many sorts and sizes, the beetles, the ants, the snakes and monkeys seemed to wonder what man was doing in an atmosphere that had no gladness in its sunshine and no coolness in its night. To wear clothing was intolerable, but to cast it aside was to scorch by day, and expose an ampler area to the mosquitoes by night; to go on deck by day was to be blinded by glare and to stay below was to suffocate. And in the daytime came certain flies, extremely clever and noxious about one's wrist and ankle. Captain Gerilleau, who was Holroyd's sole distraction from these physical distresses, developed into a formidable bore, telling the simple story of his heart's affections day by day, a string of anonymous women, as if he was telling beads. Sometimes he suggested sport, and they shot at alligators, and at rare intervals they came to human aggregations in the waste of trees, and stayed for a day or so, and drank and sat about, and, one night, danced with Creole girls, who found Holroyd's poor elements of Spanish, without either past tense or future, amply sufficient for their purposes. But these were mere luminous chinks in the long grey passage of the streaming river, up which the throbbing engines beat. A certain liberal heathen deity, in the shape of a demi-john, held seductive court aft, and, it is probable, forward.

But Gerilleau learnt things about the ants, more things and more, at this stopping-place and that, and became interested in his mission.

"Dey are a new sort of ant," he said. "We have got to be—what do you call it? entomologie? Big. Five centimetres! Some bigger! It is ridiculous. We are like the monkeys—-sent to pick insects...But dey are eating up the country."

He burst out indignantly. "Suppose—suddenly, there are complications with Europe. Here am I—soon we shall be above the Rio Negro—and my gun, useless!"

He nursed his knee and mused.

"Dose people who were dere at de dancing place, dey 'ave come down. Dey 'ave lost all they got. De ants come to deir house one afternoon. Everyone run out. You know when de ants come one must—everyone runs out and they go over the house. If you stayed they'd eat you. See? Well, presently dey go back; dey say, 'The ants 'ave gone.'... De ants *'aven't* gone. Dey try to go in—de son, 'e goes in. De ants fight."

"Swarm over him?"

"Bite 'im. Presently he comes out again—screaming and running. He runs past them to the river. See? He gets into de water and drowns de ants—yes." Gerilleau paused, brought his liquid eyes close to Holroyd's face, tapped Holroyd's knee with his knuckle. "That night he dies, just as if he was stung by a snake."

"Poisoned—by the ants?"

"Who knows?" Gerilleau shrugged his shoulders. "Perhaps they bit him badly.... When I joined dis service I joined to fight men. Dese things, dese ants, dey come and go. It is no business for men."

After that he talked frequently of the ants to Holroyd, and whenever they chanced to drift against any speck of humanity in that waste of water and sunshine and distant trees, Holroyd's improving knowledge of the language enabled him to recognise the ascendant word *Saüba*, more and more completely dominating the whole.

He perceived the ants were becoming interesting, and the nearer he drew to them the more interesting they became. Gerilleau abandoned his old themes almost suddenly, and the Portuguese lieutenant became a conversational figure; he knew something about the leaf cutting ant, and expanded his knowledge. Gerilleau sometimes rendered what he had to tell to Holroyd. He told of the little workers that swarm and fight, and the big workers that command and rule, and how these latter always crawled to the neck and how their bites drew blood. He told how they cut leaves and made fungus beds, and how their nests in Caracas are sometimes a hundred yards across. Two days the three men spent disputing whether ants have eyes. The discussion grew dangerously heated on the second afternoon, and Holroyd saved the situation by going ashore in a boat to catch ants and see. He captured various specimens and returned, and some had eyes and some hadn't. Also, they argued, do ants bite or sting?

"Dese ants," said Gerilleau, after collecting information at a rancho, "have big eyes. They don't run about blind—not as most ants do. No! Dey get in corners and watch what you do."

"And they sting?" asked Holroyd.

"Yes. Dey sting. Dere is poison in the sting." He meditated. "I do not see what men can do against ants. Dey come and go."

"But these don't go."

"They will," said Gerilleau.

Past Tamandu there is a long low coast of eighty miles without any population, and then one comes to the confluence of the main river and the Batemo arm like a great lake, and then the forest came nearer, came at last intimately near. The character of the channel changes, snags abound, and the *Benjamin Constant* moored by a cable that night, under the very shadow of dark trees. For the first time for many days came a spell of coolness, and Holroyd and Gerilleau sat late, smoking cigars and enjoying this delicious sensation. Gerilleau's mind was full of ants and what they could do. He decided to sleep at last, and lay down on a mattress on deck, a man hopelessly perplexed, his last words, when he already seemed asleep, were to ask, with a flourish of despair, "What can one do with ants?.... De whole thing is absurd."

Holroyd was left to scratch his bitten wrists, and meditate alone.

He sat on the bulwark and listened to the little changes in Gerilleau's breathing until he was fast asleep, and then the ripple and lap of the stream took his mind, and brought back that sense of immensity that had been growing upon him since first he had left Para and come up the river. The monitor showed but one small light, and there was first a little talking forward and then stillness. His eyes went from the dim black outlines of the middle works of the gunboat towards the bank, to the black overwhelming mysteries of forest, lit now and then by a fire-fly, and never still from the murmur of alien and mysterious activities....

It was the inhuman immensity of this land that astonished and oppressed him. He knew the skies were empty of men, the stars were specks in an incredible vastness of space; he knew the ocean was enormous and untamable, but in England he had come to think of the land as man's. In England it is indeed man's, the wild things live by sufferance, grow on lease, everywhere the roads, the fences, and absolute security runs. In an atlas, too, the land is man's, and all coloured to show his claim to it—in vivid contrast to the universal independent blueness of the sea. He had taken it for granted that a day would come when everywhere about the earth, plough and culture, light tramways and good roads, an ordered security, would prevail. But now, he doubted.

This forest was interminable, it had an air of being invincible, and Man seemed at best an infrequent precarious intruder. One travelled for miles, amidst the still, silent struggle of giant trees, of strangulating creepers, of assertive flowers, everywhere the alligator, the turtle, and endless varieties of birds and insects seemed at home, dwelt irreplaceably—but man, man at most held a footing upon resentful clearings, fought weeds, fought beasts and insects for the barest foothold, fell a prey to snake and beast, insect and fever, and was presently carried away. In many places down the river he had been manifestly driven back, this deserted creek or that preserved the name of a *casa*, and here and there ruinous white walls and a shattered tower enforced the lesson. The puma, the jaguar, were more the masters here....

Who were the real masters?

In a few miles of this forest there must be more ants than there are men in the whole world! This seemed to Holroyd a perfectly new idea. In a few thousand years men had emerged from barbarism to a stage of civilization that made them feel lords of the future and masters of the earth! But what was to prevent the ants evolving also? Such ants as one knew lived in little communities of a few thousand individuals, made no concerted efforts against the greater world. But they had a language, they had an intelligence! Why should things stop at that any more than men had stopped at the barbaric stage? Suppose presently the ants began to store knowledge, just as men had done by means of books and records, use weapons, form great empires, sustain a planned and organised war?

Things came back to him that Gerilleau had gathered about these ants they were approaching. They used a poison like the poison of snakes. They obeyed greater leaders even as the leaf-cutting ants do. They were carnivorous, and where they came they stayed....

The forest was very still. The water lapped incessantly against the side. About the lantern overhead there eddied a noiseless whirl of phantom moths.

Gerilleau stirred in the darkness and sighed. "What can one *do?*" he murmured, and turned over and was still again.

Holroyd was roused from meditations that were becoming sinister by the hum of a mosquito.

CHAPTER TWO

The next morning Holroyd learnt they were within forty kilometres of Badama, and his interest in the banks intensified. He came up whenever an opportunity offered to examine his surroundings. He could see no signs of human occupation whatever, save for a weedy ruin of a house and the green-stained facade of the long-deserted monastery at Mojû, with a forest tree growing out of a vacant window space, and great creepers netted across its vacant portals. Several flights of strange yellow butterflies with semi-transparent wings crossed the river that morning, and many alighted on the monitor and were killed by the men. It was towards afternoon that they came upon the derelict *cuberta*.

She did not at first appear to be derelict; both her sails were set and hanging slack in the afternoon calm, and there was the figure of a man sitting on the fore planking beside the shipped sweeps. Another man appeared to be sleeping face downwards on the sort of longitudinal bridge these big canoes have in the waist. But it was presently apparent, from the sway of her rudder and the way she drifted into the course of the gunboat, that something was out of order with her. Gerilleau surveyed her through a field-glass, and became interested in the queer darkness of the face of the sitting man, a red-faced man he seemed, without a nose—crouching he was rather than sitting, and the longer the captain looked the less he liked to look at him, and the less able he was to take his glasses away.

But he did so at last, and went a little way to call up Holroyd. Then he went back to hail the cuberta. He ailed her again, and so she drove past him. *Santa Rosa* stood out clearly as her name.

As she came by and into the wake of the monitor, she pitched a little, and suddenly the figure of the crouching man collapsed as though all its joints had given way. His hat fell off, his head was not nice to look at, and his body flopped lax and rolled out of sight behind the bulwarks.

"Caramba!" cried Gerilleau, and resorted to Holroyd forthwith.

Holroyd was half-way up the companion. "Did you see dat?" said the captain.

"Dead!" said Holroyd. "Yes. You'd better send a boat aboard. There's something wrong."

"Did you—by any chance—see his face?"

"What was it like?"

"It was—ugh!—I have no words." And the captain suddenly turned his back on Holroyd and became an active and strident commander.

The gunboat came about, steamed parallel to the erratic course of the canoe, and dropped the boat with Lieutenant da Cunha and three sailors to board her. Then the curiosity of the captain made him draw up almost alongside as the lieutenant got aboard, so that the whole of the *Santa Rosa*, deck and hold, was visible to Holroyd.

He saw now clearly that the sole crew of the vessel was these two dead men, and though he could not see their faces, he saw by their outstretched hands, which were all of ragged flesh, that they had been subjected to some strange exceptional process of decay. For a moment his attention concentrated on those two enigmatical bundles of dirty clothes and laxly flung limbs, and then his eyes went forward to discover the open hold piled high with trunks and cases, and aft, to where the little cabin gaped inexplicably empty. Then he became aware that the planks of the middle decking were dotted with moving black specks.

His attention was riveted by these specks. They were all walking in directions radiating from the fallen man in a manner—the image came unsought to his mind—like the crowd dispersing from a bull-fight.

He became aware of Gerilleau beside him. "Capo," he said, "have you your glasses? Can you focus as closely as those planks there?"

Gerilleau made an effort, grunted, and handed him the glasses.

There followed a moment of scrutiny. "It's ants," said the Englishman, and handed the focused field-glass back to Gerilleau.

His impression of them was of a crowd of large black ants, very like ordinary ants except for their size, and for the fact that some of the larger of them bore a sort of clothing of grey. But at the time his inspection was too brief for particulars. The head of Lieutenant da Cunha appeared over the side of the cuberta, and a brief colloquy ensued.

"You must go aboard," said Gerilleau.

The lieutenant objected that the boat was full of ants.

"You have your boots," said Gerilleau.

The lieutenant changed the subject. "How did these en die?" he asked.

Captain Gerilleau embarked upon speculations that Holroyd could not follow, and the two men disputed with a certain increasing vehemence. Holroyd took up the field-glass and resumed his scrutiny, first of the ants and then of the dead man amidships.

He has described these ants to me very particularly.

He says they were as large as any ants he has ever seen, black and moving with a steady deliberation very different from the mechanical fussiness of the common ant. About one in twenty was much larger than its fellows, and with an exceptionally large head. These reminded him at once of the master workers who are said to rule over the leaf-cutter ants; like them they seemed to be directing and co-ordinating the general movements. They tilted their bodies back in a manner altogether singular as if they made some use of the fore feet. And he had a curious fancy that he was too far off to verify, that most of these ants of both kinds were wearing accoutrements, had things strapped about their bodies by bright white bands like white metal threads....

He put down the glasses abruptly, realising that the question of discipline between the captain and his subordinate had become acute.

"It is your duty," said the captain, "to go aboard. It is my instructions."

The lieutenant seemed on the verge of refusing. The head of one of the mulatto sailors appeared beside him.

"I believe these men were killed by the ants," said Holroyd abruptly in English.

The captain burst into a rage. He made no answer to Holroyd. "I have commanded you to go aboard," he screamed to his subordinate in Portuguese. "If you do not go aboard forthwith it is mutiny—rank mutiny. Mutiny and cowardice! Where is the courage that should animate us? I will have you in irons, I will have you shot like a dog." He began a torrent of abuse and curses, he danced to and fro. He shook his fists, he behaved as if beside himself with rage, and the lieutenant, white and still, stood looking at him. The crew appeared forward, with amazed faces.

Suddenly, in a pause of this outbreak, the lieutenant came to some heroic decision, saluted, drew himself together and clambered upon the deck of the cuberta.

"Ah!" said Gerilleau, and his mouth shut like a trap. Holroyd saw the ants retreating before da Cunha's boots. The Portuguese walked slowly to the fallen man, stooped down, hesitated, clutched his coat and turned him over. A black swarm of ants rushed out of the clothes, and da Cunha stepped back very quickly and trod two or three times on the deck.

Holroyd put up the glasses. He saw the scattered ants about the invader's feet, and doing what he had never seen ants doing before. They had nothing of the blind movements of the common ant; they were looking at him—as a rallying crowd of men might look at some gigantic monster that had dispersed it.

"How did he die?" the captain shouted.

Holroyd understood the Portuguese to say the body was too much eaten to tell.

"What is there forward?" asked Gerilleau.

The lieutenant walked a few paces, and began his answer in Portuguese. He stopped abruptly and beat off something from his leg. He made some peculiar steps as if he was trying to stamp on something invisible, and went quickly towards the side. Then he controlled himself, turned about, walked deliberately forward to the hold, clambered up to the fore decking, from which the sweeps are worked, stooped for a time over the second man, groaned audibly, and made his way back and aft to the cabin, moving very rigidly. He turned and began a conversation with his captain, cold and respectful in tone on either side, contrasting vividly with the wrath and insult of a few moments before. Holroyd gathered only fragments of its purport.

He reverted to the field-glass, and was surprised to find the ants had vanished from all the exposed surfaces of the deck. He turned towards the shadows beneath the decking, and it seemed to him they were full of watching eyes.

The cuberta, it was agreed; was derelict, but too full of ants to put men aboard to sit and sleep: it must be towed. The lieutenant went forward to take in and adjust the cable, and the men in the boat stood up to be ready to help him. Holroyd's glasses searched the canoe.

He became more and more impressed by the fact that a great if minute and furtive activity was going on. He perceived that a number of gigantic ants—they seemed nearly a couple of inches in length—carrying oddly-shaped burthens for which he could imagine no use—were moving in rushes from one point of obscurity to another. They did not move in columns across the exposed places, but in open, spaced-out lines, oddly suggestive of the rushes of modern infantry advancing under fire. A number were taking cover under the dead man's clothes, and a perfect swarm was gathering along the side over which da Cunha must presently go.

He did not see them actually rush for the lieutenant as he returned, but he has no doubt they did make a concerted rush. Suddenly the lieutenant was shouting and cursing and beating at his legs. "I'm stung!" he shouted, with a face of hate and accusation towards Gerilleau.

Then he vanished over the side, dropped into his boat, and plunged at once into the water. Holroyd heard the splash.

The three men in the boat pulled him out and brought him aboard, and that night he died.

CHAPTER THREE

Holroyd and the captain came out of the cabin in which the swollen and contorted body of the lieutenant lay and stood together at the stern of the monitor, staring at the sinister vessel they trailed behind them. It was a close, dark night that had only phantom flickerings of sheet lightning to illuminate it. The cuberta, a vague black triangle, rocked about in the steamer's wake, her sails bobbing and flapping, and the black smoke from the funnels, spark-lit ever and again, streamed over her swaying masts.

Gerilleau's mind was inclined to run on the unkind things the lieutenant had said in the heat of his last fever.

"He says I murdered 'im," he protested. "It is simply absurd. Someone *'ad* to go aboard. Are we to run away from these confounded ants whenever they show up?"

Holroyd said nothing. He was thinking of a disciplined rush of little black shapes across bare sunlit planking.

"It was his place to go," harped Gerilleau. "He died in the execution of his duty. What has he to complain of? Murdered!.... But the poor fellow was—what is it?—demented. He was not in his right mind. The poison swelled him…um."

They came to a long silence.

"We will sink that canoe—burn it."

"And then?"

The inquiry irritated Gerilleau. His shoulders went up, his hands flew out at right angles from his body. "What is one to *do?*" he said, his voice going up to an angry squeak.

"Anyhow," he broke out vindictively, "every ant in dat cuberta!—I will burn dem alive!"

Holroyd was not moved to conversation. A distant ululation of howling monkeys filled the sultry night with foreboding sounds, and as the gunboat drew near the black mysterious banks this was reinforced by a depressing clamour of frogs.

"What is one to *do?*" the captain repeated after a vast interval, and suddenly becoming active and savage and blasphemous, decided to burn the *Santa Rosa* without further delay. Everyone aboard was pleased by that idea, everyone helped with zest; they pulled in the cable, cut it, and dropped the boat and fired her with tow and kerosene, and soon the cuberta was crackling and flaring merrily amidst the immensities of the tropical night. Holroyd watched the mounting yellow flare against the blackness, and the livid flashes of sheet lightning that came and went above the forest summits, throwing them into momentary silhouette, and his stoker stood behind him watching also.

The stoker was stirred to the depths of his linguistics. "*Saüba* go pop, pop," he said, "Wahaw" and laughed richly.

But Holroyd was thinking that these little creatures on the decked canoe had also eyes and brains.

The whole thing impressed him as incredibly foolish and wrong, but—what was one to *do?* This question came back enormously reinforced on the morrow, when at last the gunboat reached Badama.

This place, with its leaf-thatch-covered houses and sheds, its creeper-invaded sugar-mill, its little jetty of timber and canes, was very still in the morning heat, and showed never a sign of living men. Whatever ants there were at that distance were too small to see.

"All the people have gone," said Gerilleau, "but we will do one thing anyhow. We will 'oot and vissel."

So Holroyd hooted and whistled.

Then the captain fell into a doubting fit of the worst kind. "Dere is one thing we can do," he said presently,.

"What's that?" said Holroyd.

"'Oot and vissel again."

So they did.

The captain walked his deck and gesticulated to himself. He seemed to have many things on his mind. Fragments of speeches came from his lips. He appeared to be addressing some imaginary public tribunal either in Spanish or Portuguese. Holroyd's improving ear detected something about ammunition. He came out of these preoccupations suddenly into English. "My dear 'Olroyd!" he cried, and broke off with "But what *can* one do?"

They took the boat and the field-glasses, and went close in to examine the place. They made out a number of big ants, whose still postures had a certain effect of watching them, dotted about the edge of the rude embarkation jetty. Gerilleau tried ineffectual pistol shots at these. Holroyd thinks he distinguished curious earthworks running between the nearer houses, that may have been the work of the insect conquerors of those human habitations. The explorers pulled past the jetty, and became aware of a human skeleton wearing a loin cloth, and very bright and clean and shining, lying beyond. They came to a pause regarding this...

"I 'ave all dose lives to consider," said Gerilleau suddenly.

Holroyd turned and stared at the captain, nappetiz slowly that he referred to the nappetizing mixture of races that constituted his crew.

"To send a landing party—it is impossible—impossible. They will be poisoned, they will swell, they will swell up and abuse me and die. It is totally impossible.... If we land, I must land alone, alone, in thick boots and with my life in my hand. Perhaps I should live. Or again—I might not land. I do not know. I do not know."

Holroyd thought he did, but he said nothing.

"De whole thing," said Gerilleau suddenly, "'as been got up to make me ridiculous. De whole thing!"

They paddled about and regarded the clean white skeleton from various points of view, and then they returned to the gunboat. Then Gerilleau's indecisions became terrible. Steam was got up, and in the afternoon the monitor went on up the river with an air of going to ask somebody something, and by sunset came back again and anchored. A thunderstorm gathered and broke furiously, and then the night became beautifully cool and quiet and everyone slept on deck. Except Gerilleau, who tossed about and muttered. In the dawn he awakened Holroyd.

"Lord!" said Holroyd, "what now?"

"I have decided," said the captain.

"What—to land?" said Holroyd, sitting up brightly.

"No!" said the captain, and was for a time very reserved. "I have decided," he repeated, and Holroyd manifested symptoms of impatience.

"Well—yes," said the captain, "*I shall fire de big gun!*"

And he did! Heaven knows what the ants thought of it, but he did. He fired it twice with great sternness and ceremony. All the crew had wadding in their ears, and there was an effect of going into action about the whole affair, and first they hit and wrecked the old sugar-mill, and then they smashed the abandoned store behind the jetty. And then Gerilleau experienced the inevitable reaction.

"It is no good," he said to Holroyd; "no good at all. No sort of bally good. We must go back—for instructions. Dere will be de *devil* of a row about dis ammunition—oh! De devil of a row! You don't know, 'Olroyd...."

He stood regarding the world in infinite perplexity for a space.

"But what else was there to *do?*" he cried.

In the afternoon the monitor started down stream again, and in the evening a landing party took the body of the lieutenant and buried it on the bank upon which the new ants have so far not appeared....

CHAPTER FOUR

I heard this story in a fragmentary state from Holroyd not three weeks ago.

These new ants have got into his brain, and he has come back to England with the idea, as he says, of "exciting people" about them "before it is too late." He says they threaten British Guiana, which cannot be much over a trifle of a thousand miles from their present sphere of activity, and that the Colonial Office ought to get to work upon them at once. He declaims with great passion: "These are intelligent ants. Just think what that means!"

There can be no doubt they are a serious pest, and that the Brazilian Government is well advised in offering a prize of five hundred pounds for some effectual method of extirpation. It is certain too that since they first appeared in the hills beyond Badama, about three years ago, they have achieved extraordinary conquests. The whole of the south bank of the Batemo River, for nearly sixty miles, they have in their effectual occupation; they have driven men out completely, occupied plantations and settlements, and boarded and captured at least one ship. It is even said they have in some inexplicable way bridged the very considerable Capuarana arm and pushed many miles towards the Amazon itself. There can be little doubt that they are far more reasonable and with a far better social organisation than any previously known ant species; instead of being in dispersed societies they are organised into what is in effect a single nation; but their peculiar and immediate formidableness lies not so much in this as in the intelligent use they make of poison against their larger enemies. It would seem this poison of theirs is closely akin to snake poison, and it is highly probable they actually manufacture it, and that the larger individuals among them carry the needle-like crystals of it in their attacks upon men.

Of course it is extremely difficult to get any detailed information about these new competitors for the sovereignty of the globe. No eyewitnesses of their activity, except for such glimpses as Holroyd's, have survived the encounter. The most extraordinary legends of their prowess and capacity are in circulation in the region of the Upper Amazon, and grow daily as the steady advance of the invader stimulates men's imaginations through their fears. These strange little creatures are credited not only with the use of implements and a knowledge of fire and metals and with organised feats of engineering that stagger our northern minds unused as we are to such feats as that of the Saübas of Rio de Janeiro, who in 1841 drove a tunnel under the Parahyba where it is as wide as the Thames at London Bridge—but with an organized and detailed method of record and communication analogous to our books. So far their action has been a steady progressive settlement, involving the flight or slaughter of every human being in the new areas they invade. They are increasing rapidly in numbers, and Holroyd at least is firmly convinced that they will finally dispossess man over the whole of tropical South America.

And why should they stop at tropical South America?

Well, there they are, anyhow. By 1911 or thereabouts, if they go on as they are going, they ought to strike the Capuarana Extension Railway, and force themselves upon the attention of the European capitalist.

By 1920 they will be half-way down the Amazon. I fix 1950 or '60 at the latest for the discovery of Europe.

FINIS

Frank Lillie Pollock

Little is known about **FRANK LILLIE POLLOCK** (1876-1957), but he managed to write several science fiction stories around the turn of the 20th century. He wrote "The Crimson Blight" in 1905 and "The World Wrecker" in 1908. "Finis" was published in the June 1906 issue of Argosy, an early "pulp" magazine published by Frank Munsey that was instrumental in bringing not only science fiction to the public, but adventure fiction as well. One Munsey magazine would, in 1912, serialize *Tarzan of the Apes* by Edgar Rice Burroughs, thus initiating the "pulp" era officially. Frank L. Pollock's writings were very much part of this early history of the pulps.

"I'M getting tired," complained Davis, lounging in the window of the Physics Building, "and sleepy. It's after eleven o'clock. This makes the fourth night I've sat up to see your new star, and it'll be the last. Why, the thing was billed to appear three weeks ago."

"Are you tired, Miss Wardour?" asked Eastwood, and the girl glanced up with a quick flush and a negative murmur.

Eastwood made the reflection anew that she certainly was painfully shy. She was almost as plain as she was shy, though her hair had an unusual beauty of its own, fine as silk and colored like palest flame.

Probably she had brains; Eastwood had seen her reading some extremely "deep" books, but she seemed to have no amusements, few interests. She worked daily at the Art Students' League, and boarded where he did, and he had thus come to ask her with the Davises to watch for the new star from the laboratory windows on the Heights.

"Do you really think that it's worth while to wait any longer, professor?" inquired Mrs. Davis, concealing a yawn.

Eastwood was somewhat annoyed by the continued failure of the star to show itself and he hated to be called "professor," being only an assistant professor of physics.

"I don't know," he answered somewhat curtly. "This is the twelfth night that I have waited for it. Of course, it would have been a mathematical miracle if astronomers should have solved such a problem exactly, though they've been figuring on it for a quarter of a century."

The new Physics Building of Columbia University was about twelve stories high. The physics laboratory occupied the ninth and tenth floors, with the astronomical rooms above it, an arrangement which would have been impossible before the invention of the oil vibration cushion, which practically isolated the instrument rooms from the earth.

Eastwood had arranged a small telescope at the window, and below them spread the illuminated map of Greater New York, sending up a faintly musical roar. Ali the streets were crowded, as they had been every night since the fifth of the month, when the great new star, or sun, was expected to come into view.

Some error had been made in the calculations, though, as Eastwood said, astronomers had been figuring on them for twenty-five years.

It was, in fact, nearly forty years since Professor Adolphe Bernier first announced his theory of a limited universe at the International Congress of Sciences in Paris, where it was counted as little more than a masterpiece of imagination.

Professor Bernier did not believe that the universe was infinite. Somewhere, he argued, the universe must have a center, which is the pivot for its revolution.

The moon revolves around the earth, the planetary system revolves about the sun, the solar system revolves about one of the fixed stars, and this whole system in its turn undoubtedly revolves around some more distant point. But this sort of progression must definitely stop somewhere.

Somewhere there must be a central sun, a vast incandescent body which does not move at all. And as a sun is always larger and hotter than its satellites, therefore the body at the center of the universe must be of an immensity and temperature beyond anything known or imagined.

It was objected that this hypothetical body should then be large enough to be visible from the earth, and Professor Bernier replied that some day it undoubtedly would be visible. Its light had simply not yet had time to reach the earth.

The passage of light from the nearest of the fixed stars is a matter of three years, and there must be many stars so distant that their rays have not yet reached us. The great central sun must be so inconceivably remote that perhaps hundreds, perhaps thousands of years would elapse before its light should burst upon the solar system.

All this was contemptuously classed as "newspaper science" till the extraordinary mathematical revival a little after the middle of the twentieth century afforded the means of verifying it.

Following the new theorems discovered by Professor Burnside, of Princeton, and elaborated by Dr. Taneka, of Tokyo, astronomers succeeded in calculating the arc of the sun's movements through space, and its ratio to the orbit of its satellites. With this as a basis, it was possible to follow the widening circles, the consecutive systems of the heavenly bodies and their rotations.

The theory of Professor Bernier was justified. It was demonstrated that there really was a gigantic mass of incandescent matter, which, whether the central point of the universe or not, appeared to be without motion.

The weight and distance of this new sun were approximately calculated, and, the speed of light being known, it was an easy matter to reckon when its rays would reach the earth.

It was then estimated that the approaching rays would arrive at the earth in twenty-six years, and that was twenty-six years ago. Three weeks had passed since the date when the new heavenly body was expected to become visible, and it had not yet appeared.

Popular interest had risen to a high pitch, stimulated by innumerable newspaper and magazine articles, and the streets were nightly thronged with excited crowds armed with opera-glasses and star maps, while at every corner a telescope man had planted his tripod instrument at a nickel a look.

Similar scenes were taking place in every civilized city on the globe.

It was generally supposed that the new luminary would appear in size about midway between Venus and the moon. Better informed persons expected something like the sun, and a syndicate of capitalists quietly leased large areas on the coast of Greenland in anticipation of a great rise in temperature and a northward movement in population.

Even the business situation was appreciably affected by the public uncertainty and excitement. There was a decline in stocks, and a minor religious sect boldly prophesied the end of the world.

"I've had enough of this," said Davis, looking at his watch again. "Are you ready to go, Grace? By the way, isn't it getting warmer?"

It had been a sharp February day, but the temperature was certainly rising. Water was dripping from the roofs, and from the icicles that fringed the window ledges, as if a warm wave had suddenly arrived.

"What's that light?" suddenly asked Alice Wardour, who was lingering by the open window.

"It must be moonrise," said Eastwood, though the illumination of the horizon was almost like daybreak.

Davis abandoned his intention of leaving, and they watched the east grow pale and flushed till at last a brilliant white disc heaved itself above the horizon.

It resembled the full moon, but as if trebled in luster, and the streets grew almost as light as by day.

"Good heavens, that must be the new star, after all!" said Davis in an awed voice.

"No, it's only the moon. This is the hour and minute for her rising," answered Eastwood, who had grasped the cause of the phenomenon. "But the new sun must have appeared on the other side of the earth. Its light is what makes the moon so brilliant. It will rise here just as the sun does, no telling how soon. It must be brighter than was expected—and maybe hotter," he added with a vague uneasiness.

"Isn't it getting very warm in here?" said Mrs. Davis, loosening her jacket. "Couldn't you turn off some of the steam heat?"

Eastwood turned it all off, for, in spite of the open window, the room was really growing uncomfortably close. But the warmth appeared to come from without; it was like a warm spring evening, and the icicles were breaking loose from the cornices.

For half an hour they leaned from the windows with but desultory conversation, and below them the streets were black with people and whitened with upturned faces. The brilliant moon rose higher, and the mildness of the night sensibly increased.

It was after midnight when Eastwood first noticed the reddish flush tinging the clouds low in the east, and he pointed it out to his companions.

"That must be it at last," he exclaimed, with a thrill of vibrating excitement at what he was going to see, a cosmic event unprecedented in intensity.

The brightness waxed rapidly.

"By Jove, see it redden!" Davis ejaculated. "It's getting lighter than day—and hot! Whew!"

The whole eastern sky glowed with a deepening pink that extended half round the horizon. Sparrows chirped from the roofs, and it looked as if the disc of the unknown star might at any moment be expected to lift above the Atlantic, but it delayed long.

The heavens continued to burn with myriad hues, gathering at last to a fiery furnace glow on the skyline.

Mrs. Davis suddenly screamed. An American flag blowing freely from its staff on the roof of the tall building had all at once burst into flame.

Low in the east lay a long streak of intense fire which broadened as they squinted with watering eyes. It was as if the edge of the world had been heated to whiteness.

The brilliant moon faded to a feathery white film in the glare. There was a confused outcry from the observatory overhead, and a crash of something being broken, and as the strange new sunlight fell through the window the onlookers leaped back as if a blast furnace had been opened before them.

The glass cracked and fell inward. Something like the sun, but magnified fifty times in size and hotness, was rising out of the sea. An iron instrument-table by the window began to smoke with an acrid smell of varnish.

"What the devil is this, Eastwood?" shouted Davis accusingly.

From the streets rose a sudden, enormous wail of fright and pain, the outcry of a million throats at once, and the roar of a stampede followed. The pavements were choked with struggling, panic-stricken people in the fierce glare, and above the din arose the clanging rush of fire engines and trucks.

Smoke began to rise from several points below Central Park, and two or three church chimes pealed crazily.

The observers from overhead came running down the stairs with a thunderous trampling, for the elevator man had deserted his post.

"Here, we've got to get out of this," shouted Davis, seizing his wife by the arm and hustling her toward the door. "This place'll be on fire directly."

"Hold on. You can't go down into that crush on the street," Eastwood cried, trying to prevent him.

But Davis broke away and raced down the stairs, half carrying his terrified wife. Eastwood got his back against the door in time to prevent Alice from following them.

"There's nothing in this building that will burn, Miss Wardour," he said as calmly as he could. "We had better stay here for the present. It would be sure death to get involved in that stampede below. Just listen to it."

The crowds on the street seemed to sway to and fro in contending waves, and the cries, curses, and screams came up in a savage chorus.

The heat was already almost blistering to the skin, though they carefully avoided the direct rays, and instruments of glass in the laboratory cracked loudly one by one.

A vast cloud of dark smoke began to rise from the harbor, where the shipping must have caught fire, and something exploded with a terrific report. A few minutes later half a dozen fires broke out in the lower part of the city, rolling up volumes of smoke that faded to a thin mist in the dazzling light.

The great new sun was now fully above the horizon, and the whole east seemed ablaze. The stampede in the streets had quieted all at once, for the survivors had taken refuge in the nearest houses, and the pavements were black with motionless forms of men and women.

"I'll do whatever you say," said Alice, who was deadly pale, but remarkably collected. Even at that moment Eastwood was struck by the splendor of her ethereally brilliant hair that burned like pale flame above her pallid face. "But we can't stay here, can we?"

"No," replied Eastwood, trying to collect his faculties in the face of this catastrophic revolution of nature. "We'd better go to the basement, I think."

In the basement were deep vaults used for the storage of delicate instruments, and these would afford shelter for a time at least. It occurred to him as he spoke that perhaps temporary safety was the best that any living thing on earth could hope for.

But he led the way down the well staircase. They had gone down six or seven flights when a gloom seemed to grow upon the air, with a welcome relief.

It seemed almost cool, and the sky had clouded heavily, with the appearance of polished and heated silver.

A deep but distant roaring arose and grew from the southeast, and they stopped on the second landing to look from the window.

A vast black mass seemed to fill the space between sea and sky, and it was sweeping toward the city, probably from the harbor, Eastwood thought, at a speed that made it visibly grow as they watched it.

"A cyclone—and a waterspout!" muttered Eastwood, appalled.

He might have foreseen it from the sudden, excessive evaporation and the heating of the air. The gigantic black pillar drove toward them swaying and reeling, and a gale came with it, and a wall of impenetrable mist behind.

As Eastwood watched its progress he saw its cloudy bulk illumined momentarily by a dozen lightning-like flashes, and a moment later, above its roar, came the tremendous detonations of heavy cannon.

The forts and the warships were firing shells to break the waterspout, but the shots seemed to produce no effect. It was the city's last and useless attempt at resistance. A moment later forts and ships alike must have been engulfed.

"Hurry! This building will collapse!" Eastwood shouted.

They rushed down another flight, and heard the crash with which the monster broke over the city. A deluge of water, like the emptying of a reservoir, thundered upon the street, and the water was steaming hot as it fell.

There was a rending crash of falling walls, and in another instant the Physics Building seemed to be twisted around by a powerful hand. The walls blew out, and the whole structure sank in a chaotic mass.

But the tough steel frame was practically unwreckable, and, in fact, the upper portion was simply bent down upon the lower stories, peeling off most of the shell of masonry and stucco.

Eastwood was stunned as he was hurled to the floor, but when he came to himself he was still upon the landing, which was tilted at an alarming angle. A tangled mass of steel rods and beams hung a yard over his head, and a huge steel girder had plunged down perpendicularly from above, smashing everything in its way.

Wreckage choked the well of the staircase, a mass of plaster, bricks, and shattered furniture surrounded him, and he could look out in almost every direction through the rent iron skeleton.

A yard away Alice was sitting up, mechanically wiping the mud and water from her face, and apparently uninjured. Tepid water was pouring through the interstices of the wreck in torrents, though it did not appear to be raining.

A steady, powerful gale had followed the whirlwind, and it brought a little coolness with it. Eastwood inquired perfunctorily of Alice if she were hurt, without being able to feel any degree of interest in the matter. His faculty of sympathy seemed paralyzed.

"I don't know. I thought—I thought that we were all dead!" the girl murmured in a sort of daze. "What was it? Is it all over?"

"I think it's only beginning," Eastwood answered dully.

The gale had brought up more clouds and the skies were thickly overcast, but shining white-hot. Presently the rain came down in almost scalding floods and as it fell upon the hissing streets it steamed again into the air.

In three minutes all the world was choked with hot vapor, and from the roar and splash the streets seemed to be running rivers.

The downpour seemed too violent to endure, and after an hour it did cease, while the city reeked with mist. Through the whirling fog Eastwood caught glimpses of ruined buildings, vast heaps of débris, all the wreckage of the greatest city of the twentieth century.

Then the torrents fell again, like a cataract, as if the waters of the earth were shuttlecocking between sea and heaven. With a jarring tremor of the ground a landslide went down into the Hudson.

The atmosphere was like a vapor bath, choking and sickening. The physical agony of respiration aroused Alice from a sort of stupor, and she cried out pitifully that she would die.

The strong wind drove the hot spray and steam through the shattered building till it seemed impossible that human lungs could extract life from the semi-liquid that had replaced the air, but the two lived.

After hours of this parboiling the rain slackened, and, as the clouds parted, Eastwood caught a glimpse of a familiar form halfway up the heavens. It was the sun, the old sun, looking small and watery.

But the intense heat and brightness told that the enormous body still blazed behind the clouds. The rain seemed to have ceased definitely, and the hard, shining whiteness of the sky grew rapidly hotter.

The heat of the air increased to an oven-like degree; the mists were dissipated, the clouds licked up, and the earth seemed to dry itself almost immediately. The heat from the two suns beat down simultaneously till it became a monstrous terror, unendurable.

An odor of smoke began to permeate the air; there was a dazzling shimmer over the streets, and great clouds of mist arose from the bay, but these appeared to evaporate before they could darken the sky.

The piled wreck of the building sheltered the two refugees from the direct rays of the new sun, now almost overhead, but not from the penetrating heat of the air. But the body will endure almost anything, short of tearing asunder, for a time at least; it is the finer mechanism of the nerves that suffers most.

Alice lay face down among the bricks, gasping and moaning. The blood hammered in Eastwood's brain, and the strangest mirages flickered before his eyes.

Alternately he lapsed into heavy stupors, and awoke to the agony of the day. In his lucid moments he reflected that this could not last long, and tried to remember what degree of heat would cause death.

Within an hour after the drenching rains he was feverishly thirsty, and the skin felt as if peeling from his whole body.

This fever and horror lasted until he forgot that he had ever known another state; but at last the west reddened, and the flaming sun went down. It left the familiar planet high in the heavens, and there was no darkness until the usual hour, though there was a slight lowering of the temperature.

But when night did come it brought life-giving coolness, and though the heat was still intense it seemed temperate by comparison. More than all, the kindly darkness seemed to set a limit to the cataclysmic disorders of the day.

"Ouf! This is heavenly!" said Eastwood, drawing long breaths and feeling mind and body revived in the gloom.

"It won't last long," replied Alice, and her voice sounded extraordinarily calm through the darkness. "The heat will come again when the new sun rises in a few hours."

"We might find some better place in the meanwhile—a deep cellar; or we might get into the subway," Eastwood suggested.

"It would be no use. Don't you understand? I have been thinking it all out. After this, the new sun will always shine, and we could not endure it even another day. The wave of heat is passing round the world as it revolves, and in a few hours the whole earth will be a burnt-up ball. Very likely we are the only people left alive in New York, or perhaps in America."

She seemed to have taken the intellectual initiative, and spoke with an assumption of authority that amazed him.

"But there must be others," said Eastwood, after thinking for a moment. "Other people have found sheltered places, or miners, or men underground."

"They would have been drowned by the rain. At any rate, there will be none left alive by tomorrow night."

"Think of it," she went dreamily, "for a thousand years this wave of fire has been rushing toward us, while life has been going on so happily in the world, so unconscious that the world was doomed all the time. And now this is the end of life."

"I don't know," Eastwood said slowly. "It may be the end of human life, but there must be some forms that will survive—some micro-organisms perhaps capable of resisting high temperatures, if nothing higher. The seed of life will be left at any rate, and that is everything. Evolution will begin over again, producing new types to suit the changed conditions. I only wish I could see what creatures will be here in a few thousand years.

"But I can't realize it at all—this thing!" he cried passionately, after a pause. "Is it real? Or have we all gone mad? It seems too much like a bad dream."

The rain crashed down again as he spoke, and the earth steamed, though not with the dense reek of the day. For hours the waters roared and splashed against the earth in hot billows till the streets were foaming yellow rivers, dammed by the wreck of fallen buildings.

There was a continual rumble as earth and rock slid into the East River, and at last the Brooklyn Bridge collapsed with a thunderous crash and splash that made all Manhattan vibrate. A gigantic billow like a tidal wave swept up the river from its fall.

The downpour slackened and ceased soon after the moon began to shed an obscured but brilliant light through the clouds.

Presently the east commenced to grow luminous, and this time there could be no doubt as to what was coming.

Alice crept closer to the man as the gray light rose upon the watery air.

"Kiss me!" she whispered suddenly, throwing her arms around his neck. He could feel her trembling. "Say you love me; hold me in your arms. There is only an hour."

"Don't be afraid. Try to face it bravely," stammered Eastwood.

"I don't fear it—not death. But I have never lived. I have always been timid and wretched and afraid—afraid to speak—and I've almost wished for suffering and misery or anything rather than to be stupid and dumb and dead, the way I've always been.

"I've never dared to tell anyone what I was, what I wanted. I've been afraid all my life, but I'm not afraid now. I have never lived; I have never been happy; and now we must die together!"

It seemed to Eastwood the cry of the perishing world. He held her in his arms and kissed her wet, tremulous face that was strained to his.

The twilight was gone before they knew it. The sky was blue already, with crimson flakes mounting to the zenith, and the heat was growing once more intense.

"This is the end, Alice," said Eastwood, and his voice trembled.

She looked at him, her eyes shining with an unearthly softness and brilliancy, and turned her face to the east.

There, in crimson and orange, flamed the last dawn that human eyes would ever see.

THE MACHINE STOPS

E. M. Forster

E. M. FORSTER (1879-1970), was a British novelist and writer of short stories and often examined problems in modern society relating to wealth, class, and culture. He is best known for the novels, *A Room With a View* (1908), *Howard's End* (1910) and *A Passage to India* (1924). "The Machine Stops" is actually an anti-Wells satire of a time in the future where people have become so dependent upon technology that they are barbaric without it.

CHAPTER ONE

The Air-Ship

IMAGINE, if you can, a small room, hexagonal in shape, like the cell of a bee. It is lighted neither by window nor by lamp, yet it is filled with a soft radiance. There are no apertures for ventilation, yet the air is fresh. There are no musical instruments, and yet, at the moment that my meditation opens, this room is throbbing with melodious sounds. An armchair is in the centre, by its side a reading desk that is all the furniture. And in the armchair there sits a swaddled lump of flesh—a woman, about five feet high, with a face as white as a fungus. It is to her that the little room belongs.

An electric bell rang.

The woman touched a switch and the music was silent.

"I suppose I must see who it is", she thought, and set her chair in motion. The chair, like the music, was worked by machinery and it rolled her to the other side of the room where the bell still rang importunately.

"Who is it?" she called. Her voice was irritable, for she had been interrupted often since the music began. She knew several thousand people, in certain directions human intercourse had advanced enormously.

But when she listened into the receiver, her white face wrinkled into smiles, and she said:

"Very well. Let us talk, I will isolate myself. I do not expect anything important will happen for the next five minutes, for I can give you fully five minutes, Kuno. Then I must deliver my lecture on 'Music during the Australian Period.'"

She touched the isolation knob, so that no one else could speak to her. Then she touched the lighting apparatus, and the little room was plunged into darkness.

"Be quick!" She called, her irritation returning. "Be quick, Kuno; here I am in the dark wasting my time."

But it was fully fifteen seconds before the round plate that she held in her hands began to glow. A faint blue light shot across it, darkening to purple, and presently she could see the image of her son, who lived on the other side of the earth, and he could see her.

"Kuno, how slow you are."

He smiled gravely.

"I really believe you enjoy dawdling."

"I have called you before, mother, but you were always busy or isolated. I have something particular to say."

"What is it, dearest boy? Be quick. Why could you not send it by pneumatic post?"

"Because I prefer saying such a thing. I want—"

"Well?"

"I want you to come and see me."

Vashti watched his face in the blue plate.

"But I can see you!" she exclaimed. "What more do you want?"

"I want to see you not through the Machine," said Kuno. "I want to speak to you not through the wearisome Machine."

"Oh, hush!" said his mother, vaguely shocked. "You mustn't say anything against the Machine."

"Why not?"

"One mustn't."

"You talk as if a god had made the Machine," cried the other.

"I believe that you pray to it when you are unhappy. Men made it, do not forget that. Great men, but men. The Machine is much, but it is not everything. I see something like you in this plate, but I do not see you. I hear something like you through this telephone, but I do not hear you. That is why I want you to come. Pay me a visit, so that we can meet face to face, and talk about the hopes that are in my mind."

She replied that she could scarcely spare the time for a visit.

"The air-ship barely takes two days to fly between me and you."

"I dislike air-ships."

"Why?"

"I dislike seeing the horrible brown earth, and the sea, and the stars when it is dark. I get no ideas in an air-ship."

"I do not get them anywhere else."

"What kind of ideas can the air give you?"

He paused for an instant. "Do you not know four big stars that form an oblong, and three stars close together in the middle of the oblong, and hanging from these stars, three other stars?"

"No, I do not. I dislike the stars. But did they give you an idea? How interesting; tell me."

"I had an idea that they were like a man."

"I do not understand."

"The four big stars are the man's shoulders and his knees. The three stars in the middle are like the belts that men wore once, and the three stars hanging are like a sword."

"A sword?"

"Men carried swords about with them, to kill animals and other men."

"It does not strike me as a very good idea, but it is certainly original. When did it come to you first?"

"In the air-ship—" He broke off, and she fancied that he looked sad. She could not be sure, for the Machine did not transmit nuances of expression. It only gave a general idea of people—an idea that was good enough for all practical purposes, Vashti thought. The imponderable bloom, declared by a discredited philosophy to be the actual essence of intercourse, was rightly ignored by the Machine, just as the imponderable bloom of the grape was ignored by the manufacturers of artificial fruit. Something "good enough" had long since been accepted by our race.

"The truth is," he continued, "that I want to see these stars again. They are curious stars. I want to see them not from the air-ship, but from the surface of the earth, as our ancestors did, thousands of years ago. I want to visit the surface of the earth."

She was shocked again.

"Mother, you must come, if only to explain to me what is the harm of visiting the surface of the earth."

"No harm," she replied, controlling herself. "But no advantage. The surface of the earth is only dust and mud, no advantage. The surface of the earth is only dust and mud, no life remains on it, and you would need a respirator, or the cold of the outer air would kill you. One dies immediately in the outer air."

"I know; of course I shall take all precautions."

"And besides—"

"Well?"

She considered, and chose her words with care. Her son had a queer temper, and she wished to dissuade him from the expedition.

"It is contrary to the spirit of the age," she asserted.

"Do you mean by that, contrary to the Machine?"

"In a sense, but—"

His image is the blue plate faded.

"Kuno!"

He had isolated himself.

For a moment Vashti felt lonely.

Then she generated the light, and the sight of her room, flooded with radiance and studded with electric buttons, revived her. There were buttons and switches everywhere—buttons to call for food for music, for clothing. There was the hot-bath button, by pressure of which a basin of (imitation) marble rose out of the floor, filled to the brim with a warm deodorized liquid. There was the cold bath button. There was the button that produced literature. and there were of course the buttons by which she communicated with her friends. The room, though it contained nothing, was in touch with all that she cared for in the world.

Vashanti's next move was to turn off the isolation switch, and all the accumulations of the last three minutes burst upon her. The room was filled with the noise of bells, and speaking-tubes. What was the new food like? Could she recommend it? Has she had any ideas lately? Might one tell her one's own ideas? Would she make an engagement to visit the public nurseries at an early date?—say this month.

To most of these questions she replied with irritation—a growing quality in that accelerated age. She said that the new food was horrible. That she could not visit the public nurseries through press of engagements. That she had no ideas of her own but had just been told one—that four stars and three in the middle were like a man: she doubted there was much in it. Then she switched off her correspondents, for it was time to deliver her lecture on Australian music.

The clumsy system of public gatherings had been long since abandoned; neither Vashti nor her audience stirred from their rooms. Seated in her armchair she spoke, while they in their armchairs heard her, fairly well, and saw her, fairly well. She opened with a humorous account of music in the pre Mongolian epoch, and went on to describe the great outburst of song that followed the Chinese conquest. Remote and primæval as were the methods of I-San-So and the Brisbane school, she yet felt (she said) that study of them might repay the musicians of today: they had freshness; they had, above all, ideas. Her lecture, which lasted ten minutes, was well received, and at its conclusion she and many of her audience listened to a lecture on the sea; there were ideas to be got from the sea; the speaker had donned a respirator and visited it lately. Then she fed, talked to many friends, had a bath, talked again, and summoned her bed.

The bed was not to her liking. It was too large, and she had a feeling for a small bed. Complaint was useless, for beds were of the same dimension all over the world, and to have had an alternative size would have involved vast alterations in the Machine. Vashti isolated herself—it was necessary, for neither day nor night existed under the ground—and reviewed all that had happened since she had summoned the bed last. Ideas? Scarcely any. Events—was Kuno's invitation an event?

By her side, on the little reading-desk, was a survival from the ages of litter—one book. This was the Book of the Machine. In it were instructions against every possible contingency. If she was hot or cold or dyspeptic or at a loss for a word, she went to the book, and it told her which button to press. The Central Committee published it. In accordance with a growing habit, it was richly bound.

Sitting up in the bed, she took it reverently in her hands. She glanced round the glowing room as if some one might be watching her. Then, half ashamed, half joyful, she murmured "O Machine!" and raised the volume to her lips. Thrice she kissed it, thrice inclined her head, thrice she felt the delirium of acquiescence. Her ritual performed, she turned to page 1367, which gave the times of the departure of the air-ships from the island in the southern hemisphere, under whose soil she lived, to the island in the northern hemisphere, whereunder lived her son.

She thought, "I have not the time."

She made the room dark and slept; she awoke and made the room light; she ate and exchanged ideas with her friends, and listened to music and attended lectures; she made the room dark and slept. Above her, beneath her, and around her, the Machine hummed eternally; she did not notice the noise, for she had been born with it in her ears. The earth, carrying her, hummed as it sped through silence, turning her now to the invisible sun, now to the invisible stars. She awoke and made the room light.

"Kuno!"

"I will not talk to you." he answered, "until you come."

"Have you been on the surface of the earth since we spoke last?"

His image faded.

Again she consulted the book. She became very nervous and lay back in her chair palpitating. Think of her as without teeth or hair. Presently she directed the chair to the wall, and pressed an unfamiliar button. The wall swung apart slowly. Through the opening she saw a tunnel that curved slightly, so that its goal was not visible. Should she go to see her son, here was the beginning of the journey.

Of course she knew all about the communication system. There was nothing mysterious in it. She would summon a car and it would fly with her down the tunnel until it reached the lift that communicated with the air-ship station: the system had been in use for many, many years, long before the universal establishment of the Machine. And of course she had studied the civilization that had immediately preceded her own—the civilization that had mistaken the functions of the system, and had used it for bringing people to things, instead of for bringing things to people. Those funny old days, when men went for change of air instead of changing the air in their rooms! And yet—she was frightened of the tunnel: she had not seen it since her last child was born. It curved—but not quite as she remembered; it was brilliant—but not quite as brilliant as a lecturer had suggested. Vashti was seized with the terrors of direct experience. She shrank back into the room, and the wall closed up again.

"Kuno," she said, "I cannot come to see you. I am not well."

Immediately an enormous apparatus fell on to her out of the ceiling, a thermometer was automatically laid upon her heart. She lay powerless. Cool pads soothed her forehead. Kuno had telegraphed to her doctor.

So the human passions still blundered up and down in the Machine. Vashti drank the medicine that the doctor projected into her mouth, and the machinery retired into the ceiling. The voice of Kuno was heard asking how she felt.

"Better." Then with irritation: "But why do you not come to me instead?"

"Because I cannot leave this place."

"Why?"

"Because, any moment, something tremendous many happen."

"Have you been on the surface of the earth yet?"

"Not yet."

"Then what is it?"

"I will not tell you through the Machine."

She resumed her life.

But she thought of Kuno as a baby, his birth, his removal to the public nurseries, her own visit to him there, his visits to her—visits which stopped when the Machine had assigned him a room on the other side of the earth. "Parents, duties of," said the book of the Machine, "cease at the moment of birth. P.422327483." True, but there was something special about Kuno—indeed there had been something special about all her children—and, after all, she must brave the journey if he desired it. And "something tremendous might happen". What did that mean? The nonsense of a youthful man, no doubt, but she must go. Again she pressed the unfamiliar button, again the wall swung back, and she saw the tunnel that curves out of sight. Clasping the Book, she rose, tottered on to the platform, and summoned the car. Her room closed behind her: the journey to the northern hemisphere had begun.

Of course it was perfectly easy. The car approached and in it she found armchairs exactly like her own. When she signaled, it stopped, and she tottered into the lift. One other passenger was in the lift, the first fellow creature she had seen face to face for months. Few travelled in these days, for, thanks to the advance of science, the earth was exactly alike all over. Rapid intercourse, from which the previous civilization had hoped so much, had ended by defeating itself. What was the good of going to Peking when it was just like Shrewsbury? Why return to Shrewsbury when it would all be like Peking? Men seldom moved their bodies; all unrest was concentrated in the soul.

The air-ship service was a relic form the former age. It was kept up, because it was easier to keep it up than to stop it or to diminish it, but it now far exceeded the wants of the population. Vessel after vessel would rise form the vomitories of Rye or of Christchurch (I use the antique names), would sail into the crowded sky, and would draw up at the wharves of the south—empty. so nicely adjusted was the system, so independent of meteorology, that the sky, whether calm or cloudy, resembled a vast kaleidoscope whereon the same patterns periodically recurred. The ship on which Vashti sailed started now at sunset, now at dawn. But always, as it passed above Rheas, it would neighbour the ship that served between Helsingfors and the Brazils, and, every third time it surmounted the Alps, the fleet of Palermo would cross its track behind. Night and day, wind and storm, tide and earthquake, impeded man no longer. He had harnessed Leviathan. All the old literature, with its praise of Nature, and its fear of Nature, rang false as the prattle of a child.

Yet as Vashti saw the vast flank of the ship, stained with exposure to the outer air, her horror of direct experience returned. It was not quite like the air-ship in the cinematophote. For one thing it smelt—not strongly or unpleasantly, but it did smell, and with her eyes shut she should have known that a new thing was close to her. Then she had to walk to it from the lift, had to submit to glances form the other passengers. The man in front dropped his Book—no great matter, but it disquieted them all. In the rooms, if the Book was dropped, the floor raised it mechanically, but the gangway to the air-ship was not so prepared, and the sacred volume lay motionless. They stopped—the thing was unforeseen—and the man, instead of picking up his property, felt the muscles of his arm to see how they had failed him. Then some one actually said with direct utterance: "We shall be late"—and they trooped on board, Vashti treading on the pages as she did so.

Inside, her anxiety increased. The arrangements were old—fashioned and rough. There was even a female attendant, to whom she would have to announce her wants during the voyage. Of course a revolving platform ran the length of the boat, but she was expected to walk from it to her cabin. Some cabins were better than others, and she did not get the best. She thought the attendant had been unfair, and spasms of rage shook her. The glass valves had closed, she could not go back. She saw, at the end of the vestibule, the lift in which she had ascended going quietly up and down, empty. Beneath those corridors of shining tiles were rooms, tier below tier, reaching far into the earth, and in each room there sat a human being, eating, or sleeping, or producing ideas. And buried deep in the hive was her own room. Vashti was afraid.

"O Machine!" she murmured, and caressed her Book, and was comforted.

Then the sides of the vestibule seemed to melt together, as do the passages that we see in dreams, the lift vanished, the Book that had been dropped slid to the left and vanished, polished tiles rushed by like a stream of water, there was a slight jar, and the air-ship, issuing from its tunnel, soared above the waters of a tropical ocean.

It was night. For a moment she saw the coast of Sumatra edged by the phosphorescence of waves, and crowned by lighthouses, still sending forth their disregarded beams. These also vanished, and only the stars distracted her. They were not motionless, but swayed to and fro above her head, thronging out of one sky-light into another, as if the universe and not the air-ship was careening. And, as often happens on clear nights, they seemed now to be in perspective, now on a plane; now piled tier beyond tier into the infinite heavens, now concealing infinity, a roof limiting for ever the visions of men. In either case they seemed intolerable. "Are we to travel in the dark?" called the passengers angrily, and the attendant, who had been careless, generated the light, and pulled down the blinds of pliable metal. When the air-ships had been built, the desire to look direct at things still lingered in the world. Hence the extraordinary number of skylights and windows, and the proportionate discomfort to those who were civilized and refined. Even in Vashti's cabin one star peeped through a flaw in the blind, and after a few hours uneasy slumber, she was disturbed by an unfamiliar glow, which was the dawn.

Quick as the ship had sped westwards, the earth had rolled eastwards quicker still, and had dragged back Vashti and her companions towards the sun. Science could prolong the night, but only for a little, and those high hopes of neutralizing the earth's diurnal revolution had passed, together with hopes that were possibly higher. To "keep pace with the sun," or even to outstrip it, had been the aim of the civilization preceding this. Racing aeroplanes had been built for the purpose, capable of enormous speed, and steered by the greatest intellects of the epoch. Round the globe they went, round and round, westward, westward, round and round, amidst humanity's applause. In vain. The globe went eastward quicker still, horrible accidents occurred, and the Committee of the Machine, at the time rising into prominence, declared the pursuit illegal, unmechanical, and punishable by Homelessness.

Of Homelessness more will be said later.

Doubtless the Committee was right. Yet the attempt to "defeat the sun" aroused the last common interest that our race experienced about the heavenly bodies, or indeed about anything. It was the last time that men were compacted by thinking of a power outside the world. The sun had conquered, yet it was the end of his spiritual dominion. Dawn, midday, twilight, the zodiacal path, touched neither men's lives not their hearts, and science retreated into the ground, to concentrate herself upon problems that she was certain of solving.

So when Vashti found her cabin invaded by a rosy finger of light, she was annoyed, and tried to adjust the blind. But the blind flew up altogether, and she saw through the skylight small pink clouds, swaying against a background of blue, and as the sun crept higher, its radiance entered direct, brimming down the wall, like a golden sea. It rose and fell with the air-ship's motion, just as waves rise and fall, but it advanced steadily, as a tide advances. Unless she was careful, it would strike her face. A spasm of horror shook her and she rang for the attendant. The attendant too was horrified, but she could do nothing; it was not her place to mend the blind. She could only suggest that the lady should change her cabin, which she accordingly prepared to do.

People were almost exactly alike all over the world, but the attendant of the air-ship, perhaps owing to her exceptional duties, had grown a little out of the common. She had often to address passengers with direct speech, and this had given her a certain roughness and originality of manner. When Vashti served away from the sunbeams with a cry, she behaved barbarically—she put out her hand to steady her.

"How dare you!" exclaimed the passenger. "You forget yourself!"

The woman was confused, and apologized for not having let her fall. People never touched one another. The custom had become obsolete, owing to the Machine.

"Where are we now?" asked Vashti haughtily.

"We are over Asia," said the attendant, anxious to be polite.

"Asia?"

"You must excuse my common way of speaking. I have got into the habit of calling places over which I pass by their unmechanical names."

"Oh, I remember Asia. The Mongols came from it."

"Beneath us, in the open air, stood a city that was once called Simla."

"Have you ever heard of the Mongols and of the Brisbane school?"

"No."

"Brisbane also stood in the open air."

"Those mountains to the right—let me show you them." She pushed back a metal blind. The main chain of the Himalayas was revealed. "They were once called the Roof of the World, those mountains."

"You must remember that, before the dawn of civilization, they seemed to be an impenetrable wall that touched the stars. It was supposed that no one but the gods could exist above their summits. How we have advanced, thanks to the Machine!"

"How we have advanced, thanks to the Machine!" said Vashti.

"How we have advanced, thanks to the Machine!" echoed the passenger who had dropped his Book the night before, and who was standing in the passage.

"And that white stuff in the cracks?—what is it?"

"I have forgotten its name."

"Cover the window, please. These mountains give me no ideas."

The northern aspect of the Himalayas was in deep shadow: on the Indian slope the sun had just prevailed. The forests had been destroyed during the literature epoch for the purpose of making newspaper-pulp, but the snows were awakening to their morning glory, and clouds still hung on the breasts of Kinchinjunga. In the plain were seen the ruins of cities, with diminished rivers creeping by their walls, and by the sides of these were sometimes the signs of vomitories, marking the cities of to day. Over the whole prospect air-ships rushed, crossing the inter-crossing with incredible aplomb, and rising nonchalantly when they desired to escape the perturbations of the lower atmosphere and to traverse the Roof of the World.

"We have indeed advance, thanks to the Machine," repeated the attendant, and hid the Himalayas behind a metal blind.

The day dragged wearily forward. The passengers sat each in his cabin, avoiding one another with an almost physical repulsion and longing to be once more under the surface of the earth. There were eight or ten of them, mostly young males, sent out from the public nurseries to inhabit the rooms of those who had died in various parts of the earth. The man who had dropped his Book was on the homeward journey. He had been sent to Sumatra for the purpose of propagating the race. Vashti alone was travelling by her private will.

At midday she took a second glance at the earth. The air-ship was crossing another range of mountains, but she could see little, owing to clouds. Masses of black rock hovered below her, and merged indistinctly into grey. Their shapes were fantastic; one of them resembled a prostrate man.

"No ideas here," murmured Vashti, and hid the Caucasus behind a metal blind.

In the evening she looked again. They were crossing a golden sea, in which lay many small islands and one peninsula. She repeated, "No ideas here," and hid Greece behind a metal blind.

CHAPTER TWO

The Mending Apparatus

By a vestibule, by a lift, by a tubular railway, by a platform, by a sliding door—by reversing all the steps of her departure did Vashti arrive at her son's room, which exactly resembled her own. She might well declare that the visit was superfluous. The buttons, the knobs, the reading-desk with the Book, the temperature, the atmosphere, the illumination—all were exactly the same. And if Kuno himself, flesh of her flesh, stood close beside her at last, what profit was there in that? She was too well-bred to shake him by the hand.

Averting her eyes, she spoke as follows:

"Here I am. I have had the most terrible journey and greatly retarded the development of my soul. It is not worth it, Kuno, it is not worth it. My time is too precious. The sunlight almost touched me, and I have met with the rudest people. I can only stop a few minutes. Say what you want to say, and then I must return."

"I have been threatened with Homelessness," said Kuno.

She looked at him now.

"I have been threatened with Homelessness, and I could not tell you such a thing through the Machine."

Homelessness means death. The victim is exposed to the air, which kills him.

"I have been outside since I spoke to you last. The tremendous thing has happened, and they have discovered me."

"But why shouldn't you go outside?" she exclaimed, "It is perfectly legal, perfectly mechanical, to visit the surface of the earth. I have lately been to a lecture on the sea; there is no objection to that; one simply summons a respirator and gets an Egression-permit. It is not the kind of thing that spiritually minded people do, and I begged you not to do it, but there is no legal objection to it."

"I did not get an Egression-permit."

"Then how did you get out?"

"I found out a way of my own."

The phrase conveyed no meaning to her, and he had to repeat it.

"A way of your own?" she whispered. "But that would be wrong."

"Why?"

The question shocked her beyond measure.

"You are beginning to worship the Machine," he said coldly.

"You think it irreligious of me to have found out a way of my own. It was just what the Committee thought, when they threatened me with Homelessness."

At this she grew angry. "I worship nothing!" she cried. "I am most advanced. I don't think you irreligious, for there is no such thing as religion left. All the fear and the superstition that existed once have been destroyed by the Machine. I only meant that to find out a way of your own was—Besides, there is no new way out."

"So it is always supposed."

"Except through the vomitories, for which one must have an Egression-permit, it is impossible to get out. The Book says so."

"Well, the Book's wrong, for I have been out on my feet."

For Kuno was possessed of a certain physical strength.

By these days it was a demerit to be muscular. Each infant was examined at birth, and all who promised undue strength were destroyed. Humanitarians may protest, but it would have been no true kindness to let an athlete live; he would never have been happy in that state of life to which the Machine had called him; he would have yearned for trees to climb, rivers to bathe in, meadows and hills against which he might measure his body. Man must be adapted to his surroundings, must he not? In the dawn of the world our weakly must be exposed on Mount Taygetus, in its twilight our strong will suffer euthanasia, that the Machine may progress, that the Machine may progress, that the Machine may progress eternally.

"You know that we have lost the sense of space. We say "space is annihilated", but we have annihilated not space, but the sense thereof. We have lost a part of ourselves. I determined to recover it, and I began by walking up and down the platform of the railway outside my room. Up and down, until I was tired, and so did recapture the meaning of "Near" and "Far". "Near" is a place to which I can get quickly on my feet, not a place to which the train or the air-ship will take me quickly. "Far" is a place to which I cannot get quickly on my feet; the vomitory is "far", though I could be there in thirty-eight seconds by summoning the train. Man is the measure. That was my first lesson. Man's feet are the measure for distance, his hands are the measure for ownership, his body is the measure for all that is lovable and desirable and strong. Then I went further: it was then that I called to you for the first time, and you would not come.

"This city, as you know, is built deep beneath the surface of the earth, with only the vomitories protruding. Having paced the platform outside my own room, I took the lift to the next platform and paced that also, and so with each in turn, until I came to the topmost, above which begins the earth. All the platforms were exactly alike, and all that I gained by visiting them was to develop my sense of space and my muscles. I think I should have been content with this—it is not a little thing—but as I walked and brooded, it occurred to me that our cities had been built in the days when men still breathed the outer air, and that there had been ventilation shafts for the workmen. I could think of nothing but these ventilation shafts. Had they been destroyed by all the food-tubes and medicine-tubes and music-tubes that the Machine has evolved lately? Or did traces of them remain? One thing was certain. If I came upon them anywhere, it would be in the railway-tunnels of the topmost storey. Everywhere else, all space was accounted for.

"I am telling my story quickly, but don't think that I was not a coward or that your answers never depressed me. It is not the proper thing, it is not mechanical, it is not decent to walk along a railway-tunnel. I did not fear that I might tread upon a live rail and be killed. I feared something far more intangible—doing what was not contemplated by the Machine. Then I said to myself, "Man is the measure", and I went, and after many visits I found an opening.

"The tunnels, of course, were lighted. Everything is light, artificial light; darkness is the exception. So when I saw a black gap in the tiles, I knew that it was an exception, and rejoiced. I put in my arm—I could put in no more at first—and waved it round and round in ecstasy. I loosened another tile, and put in my head, and shouted into the darkness: "I am coming, I shall do it yet," and my voice reverberated down endless passages. I seemed to hear the spirits of those dead workmen who had returned each evening to the starlight and to their wives, and all the generations who had lived in the open air called back to me, "You will do it yet, you are coming,"

He paused, and, absurd as he was, his last words moved her.

For Kuno had lately asked to be a father, and his request had been refused by the Committee. His was not a type that the Machine desired to hand on.

"Then a train passed. It brushed by me, but I thrust my head and arms into the hole. I had done enough for one day, so I crawled back to the platform, went down in the lift, and summoned my bed. Ah what dreams! And again I called you, and again you refused."

She shook her head and said:

"Don't. Don't talk of these terrible things. You make me miserable. You are throwing civilization away."

"But I had got back the sense of space and a man cannot rest then. I determined to get in at the hole and climb the shaft. And so I exercised my arms. Day after day I went through ridiculous movements, until my flesh ached, and I could hang by my hands and hold the pillow of my bed outstretched for many minutes. Then I summoned a respirator, and started.

"It was easy at first. The mortar had somehow rotted, and I soon pushed some more tiles in, and clambered after them into the darkness, and the spirits of the dead comforted me. I don't know what I mean by that. I just say what I felt. I felt, for the first time, that a protest had been lodged against corruption, and that even as the dead were comforting me, so I was comforting the unborn. I felt that humanity existed, and that it existed without clothes. How can I possibly explain this? It was naked, humanity seemed naked, and all these tubes and buttons and machineries neither came into the world with us, nor will they follow us out, nor do they matter supremely while we are here. Had I been strong, I would have torn off every garment I had, and gone out into the outer air unswaddled. But this is not for me, nor perhaps for my generation. I climbed with my respirator and my hygienic clothes and my dietetic tabloids! Better thus than not at all.

"There was a ladder, made of some primæval metal. The light from the railway fell upon its lowest rungs, and I saw that it led straight upwards out of the rubble at the bottom of the shaft. Perhaps our ancestors ran up and down it a dozen times daily, in their building. As I climbed, the rough edges cut through my gloves so that my hands bled. The light helped me for a little, and then came darkness and, worse still, silence which pierced my ears like a sword. The Machine hums! Did you know that? Its hum penetrates our blood, and may even guide our thoughts. Who knows! I was getting beyond its power. Then I thought: "This silence means that I am doing wrong." But I heard voices in the silence, and again they strengthened me." He laughed. "I had need of them. The next moment I cracked my head against something."

She sighed.

"I had reached one of those pneumatic stoppers that defend us from the outer air. You may have noticed them no the air-ship. Pitch dark, my feet on the rungs of an invisible ladder, my hands cut; I cannot explain how I lived through this part, but the voices till comforted me, and I felt for fastenings. The stopper, I suppose, was about eight feet across. I passed my hand over it as far as I could reach. It was perfectly smooth. I felt it almost to the centre. Not quite to the centre, for my arm was too short. Then the voice said: "Jump. It is worth it. There may be a handle in the centre, and you may catch hold of it and so come to us your own way. And if there is no handle, so that you may fall and are dashed to pieces—it is till worth it: you will still come to us your own way." So I jumped. There was a handle, and—"

He paused. Tears gathered in his mother's eyes. She knew that he was fated. If he did not die today he would die tomorrow. There was not room for such a person in the world. And with her pity disgust mingled. She was ashamed at having borne such a son, she who had always been so respectable and so full of ideas. Was he really the little boy to whom she had taught the use of his stops and buttons, and to whom she had given his first lessons in the Book? The very hair that disfigured his lip showed that he was reverting to some savage type. On atavism the Machine can have no mercy.

"There was a handle, and I did catch it. I hung tranced over the darkness and heard the hum of these workings as the last whisper in a dying dream. All the things I had cared about and all the people I had spoken to through tubes appeared infinitely little. Meanwhile the handle revolved. My weight had set something in motion and I span slowly, and then—

"I cannot describe it. I was lying with my face to the sunshine. Blood poured from my nose and ears and I heard a tremendous roaring. The stopper, with me clinging to it, had simply been blown out of the earth, and the air that we make down here was escaping through the vent into the air above. It burst up like a fountain. I crawled back to it—for the upper air hurts—and, as it were, I took great sips from the edge. My respirator had flown goodness knows here, my clothes were torn. I just lay with my lips close to the hole, and I sipped until the bleeding stopped. You can imagine nothing so curious. This hollow in the grass—I will speak of it in a minute,—the sun shining into it, not brilliantly but through marbled clouds,—the peace, the nonchalance, the sense of space, and, brushing my cheek, the roaring fountain of our artificial air! Soon I spied my respirator, bobbing up and down in the current high above my head, and higher still were many air-ships. But no one ever looks out of air-ships, and in any case they could not have picked me up. There I was, stranded. The sun shone a little way down the shaft, and revealed the topmost rung of the ladder, but it was hopeless trying to reach it. I should either have been tossed up again by the escape, or else have fallen in, and died. I could only lie on the grass, sipping and sipping, and from time to time glancing around me.

"I knew that I was in Wessex, for I had taken care to go to a lecture on the subject before starting. Wessex lies above the room in which we are talking now. It was once an important state. Its kings held all the southern coast form the Andredswald to Cornwall, while the Wansdyke protected them on the north, running over the high ground. The lecturer was only concerned with the rise of Wessex, so I do not know how long it remained an international power, nor would the knowledge have assisted me. To tell the truth I could do nothing but laugh, during this part. There was I, with a pneumatic stopper by my side and a respirator bobbing over my head, imprisoned, all three of us, in a grass-grown hollow that was edged with fern."

Then he grew grave again.

"Lucky for me that it was a hollow. For the air began to fall back into it and to fill it as water fills a bowl. I could crawl about. Presently

I stood. I breathed a mixture, in which the air that hurts predominated whenever I tried to climb the sides. This was not so bad. I had not lost my tabloids and remained ridiculously cheerful, and as for the Machine, I forgot about it altogether. My one aim now was to get to the top, where the ferns were, and to view whatever objects lay beyond.

"I rushed the slope. The new air was still too bitter for me and I came rolling back, after a momentary vision of something grey. The sun grew very feeble, and I remembered that he was in Scorpio—I had been to a lecture on that too. If the sun is in Scorpio, and you are in Wessex, it means that you must be as quick as you can, or it will get too dark. (This is the first bit of useful information I have ever got from a lecture, and I expect it will be the last.) It made me try frantically to breathe the new air, and to advance as far as I dared out of my pond. The hollow filled so slowly. At times I thought that the fountain played with less vigour. My respirator seemed to dance nearer the earth; the roar was decreasing."

He broke off.

"I don't think this is interesting you. The rest will interest you even less. There are no ideas in it, and I wish that I had not troubled you to come. We are too different, mother."

She told him to continue.

"It was evening before I climbed the bank. The sun had very nearly slipped out of the sky by this time, and I could not get a good view. You, who have just crossed the Roof of the World, will not want to hear an account of the little hills that I saw—low colourless hills. But to me they were living and the turf that covered them was a skin, under which their muscles rippled, and I felt that those hills had called with incalculable force to men in the past, and that men had loved them. Now they sleep—perhaps for ever. They commune with humanity in dreams. Happy the man, happy the woman, who awakes the hills of Wessex. For though they sleep, they will never die."

His voice rose passionately.

"Cannot you see, cannot all you lecturers see, that it is we that are dying, and that down here the only thing that really lives in the Machine? We created the Machine, to do our will, but we cannot make it do our will now. It was robbed us of the sense of space and of the sense of touch, it has blurred every human relation and narrowed down love to a carnal act, it has paralysed our bodies and our wills, and now it compels us to worship it. The Machine develops—but not on our lies. The Machine proceeds—but not to our goal. We only exist as the blood corpuscles that course through its arteries, and if it could work without us, it would let us die. Oh, I have no remedy—or, at least, only one—to tell men again and again that I have seen the hills of Wessex as Ælfrid saw them when he overthrew the Danes.

"So the sun set. I forgot to mention that a belt of mist lay between my hill and other hills, and that it was the colour of pearl."

He broke off for the second time.

"Go on," said his mother wearily.

He shook his head.

"Go on. Nothing that you say can distress me now. I am hardened."

"I had meant to tell you the rest, but I cannot: I know that I cannot: good-bye."

Vashti stood irresolute. All her nerves were tingling with his blasphemies. But she was also inquisitive.

"This is unfair," she complained. "You have called me across the world to hear your story, and hear it I will. Tell me—as briefly as possible, for this is a disastrous waste of time—tell me how you returned to civilization."

"Oh—that!" he said, starting. "You would like to hear about civilization. Certainly. Had I got to where my respirator fell down?"

"No—but I understand everything now. You put on your respirator, and managed to walk along the surface of the earth to a vomitory, and there your conduct was reported to the Central Committee."

"By no means."

He passed his hand over his forehead, as if dispelling some strong impression. Then, resuming his narrative, he warmed to it again.

"My respirator fell about sunset. I had mentioned that the fountain seemed feebler, had I not?"

"Yes."

"About sunset, it let the respirator fall. As I said, I had entirely forgotten about the Machine, and I paid no great attention at the time, being occupied with other things. I had my pool of air, into which I could dip when the outer keenness became intolerable, and which would possibly remain for days, provided that no wind sprang up to disperse it. Not until it was too late did I realize what the stoppage of the escape implied. You see—the gap in the tunnel had been mended; the Mending Apparatus; the Mending Apparatus, was after me.

"One other warning I had, but I neglected it. The sky at night was clearer than it had been in the day, and the moon, which was about half the sky behind the sun, shone into the dell at moments quite brightly. I was in my usual place—on the boundary between the two atmospheres—when I thought I saw something dark move across the bottom of the dell, and vanish into the shaft. In my folly, I ran down. I bent over and listened, and I thought I heard a faint scraping noise in the depths.

"At this—but it was too late—I took alarm. I determined to put on my respirator and to walk right out of the dell. But my respirator had gone. I knew exactly where it had fallen—between the stopper and the aperture—and I could even feel the mark that it had made in the turf. It had gone, and I realized that something evil was at work, and I had better escape to the other air, and, if I must die, die running towards the cloud that had been the colour of a pearl. I never started. Out of the shaft—it is too horrible. A worm, a long white worm, had crawled out of the shaft and gliding over the moonlit grass.

"I screamed. I did everything that I should not have done, I stamped upon the creature instead of flying from it, and it at once curled round the ankle. Then we fought. The worm let me run all over the dell, but edged up my leg as I ran. "Help!" I cried. (That part is too awful. It belongs to the part that you will never know.) "Help!" I cried. (Why cannot we suffer in silence?) "Help!" I cried. When my feet were wound together, I fell, I was dragged away from the dear ferns and the living hills, and past the great metal stopper (I can tell you this part), and I thought it might save me again if I caught hold of the handle. It also was enwrapped, it also. Oh, the whole dell was full of the things. They were searching it in all directions, they were denuding it, and the white snouts of others peeped out of the hole, ready if needed. Everything that could be moved they brought—brushwood, bundles of fern, everything, and down we all went intertwined into hell. The last things that I saw, ere the stopper closed after us, were certain stars, and I felt that a man of my sort lived in the sky. For I did fight, I fought till the very end, and it was only my head hitting against the ladder that quieted me. I woke up in this room. The worms had vanished. I was surrounded by artificial air, artificial light, artificial peace, and my friends were calling to me down speaking-tubes to know whether I had come across any new ideas lately."

Here his story ended. Discussion of it was impossible, and Vashti turned to go.

"It will end in Homelessness," she said quietly.

"I wish it would," retorted Kuno.

"The Machine has been most merciful."

"I prefer the mercy of God."

"By that superstitious phrase, do you mean that you could live in the outer air?"

"Yes."

"Have you ever seen, round the vomitories, the bones of those who were extruded after the Great Rebellion?"

"Yes."

"Have you ever seen, round the vomitories, the bones of those who were extruded after the Great Rebellion?"

"Yes."

"They were left where they perished for our edification. A few crawled away, but they perished, too—who can doubt it? And so with the Homeless of our own day. The surface of the earth supports life no longer."

"Indeed."

"Ferns and a little grass may survive, but all higher forms have perished. Has any air-ship detected them?"

"No."

"Has any lecturer dealt with them?"

"No."

"Then why this obstinacy?"

"Because I have seen them," he exploded.

"Seen what?"

"Because I have seen her in the twilight—because she came to my help when I called—because she, too, was entangled by the worms, and, luckier than I, was killed by one of them piercing her throat."

He was mad. Vashti departed, nor, in the troubles that followed, did she ever see his face again.

CHAPTER THREE

The Homeless

During the years that followed Kuno's escapade, two important developments took place in the Machine. On the surface they were revolutionary, but in either case men's minds had been prepared beforehand, and they did but express tendencies that were latent already.

The first of these was the abolition of respirator.

Advanced thinkers, like Vashti, had always held it foolish to visit the surface of the earth. Air-ships might be necessary, but what was the good of going out for mere curiosity and crawling along for a mile or two in a terrestrial motor? The habit was vulgar and perhaps faintly improper: it was unproductive of ideas, and had no connection with the habits that really mattered. So respirators were abolished, and with them, of course, the terrestrial motors, and except for a few lecturers, who complained that they were debarred access to their subject—matter, the development was accepted quietly. Those who still wanted to know what the earth was like had after all only to listen to some gramophone, or to look into some cinematophote. And even the lecturers acquiesced when they found that a lecture on the sea was none the less stimulating when compiled out of other lectures that had already been delivered on the same subject. "Beware of first—hand ideas!" exclaimed one of the most advanced of them. "First-hand ideas do not really exist. They are but the physical impressions produced by live and fear, and on this gross foundation who could erect a philosophy? Let your ideas be second-hand, and if possible tenth-hand, for then they will be far removed from that disturbing element—direct observation. Do not learn anything about this subject of mine—the French Revolution. Learn instead what I think that Enicharmon thought Urizen thought Gutch thought Ho-Yung thought Chi-Bo-Sing thought LafcadioHearn thought Carlyle thought Mirabeau said about the French Revolution. Through the medium of these ten great minds, the blood that was shed at Paris and the windows that were broken at Versailles will be clarified to an idea which you may employ most profitably in your daily lives. But be sure that the intermediates are many and varied, for in history one authority exists to counteract another. Urizen must counteract the scepticism of Ho-Yung and Enicharmon, I must myself counteract the impetuosity of Gutch. You who listen to me are in a better position to judge about the French Revolution than I am. Your descendants will be even in a better position than you, for they will learn what you think I think, and yet another intermediate will be added to the chain. And in time"—his voice rose—"there will come a generation that had got beyond facts, beyond impressions, a generation absolutely colourless, a generation seraphically free from taint of personality, which will see the French Revolution not as it happened, nor as they would like it to have happened, but as it would have happened, had it taken place in the days of the Machine."

Tremendous applause greeted this lecture, which did but voice a feeling already latent in the minds of men—a feeling that terrestrial facts must be ignored, and that the abolition of respirators was a positive gain. It was even suggested that air-ships should be abolished too. This was not done, because air-ships had somehow worked themselves into the Machine's system. But year by year they were used less, and mentioned less by thoughtful men.

The second great development was the re-establishment of religion.

This, too, had been voiced in the celebrated lecture. No one could mistake the reverent tone in which the peroration had concluded, and it awakened a responsive echo in the heart of each. Those who had long worshipped silently, now began to talk. They described the strange feeling of peace that came over them when they handled the Book of the Machine, the pleasure that it was to repeat certain numerals out of it, however little meaning those numerals conveyed to the outward ear, the ecstasy of touching a button, however unimportant, or of ringing an electric bell, however superfluously.

"The Machine," they exclaimed, "feeds us and clothes us and houses us; through it we speak to one another, through it we see one another, in it we have our being. The Machine is the friend of ideas and the enemy of superstition: the Machine is omnipotent, eternal; blessed is the Machine." And before long this allocution was printed on the first page of the Book, and in subsequent editions the ritual swelled into a complicated system of praise and prayer. The word "religion" was sedulously avoided, and in theory the Machine was still the creation and the implement of man. but in practice all, save a few retrogrades, worshipped it as divine. Nor was it worshipped in unity. One believer would be chiefly impressed by the blue optic plates, through which he saw other believers; another by the mending apparatus, which sinful Kuno had compared to worms; another by the lifts, another by the Book. And each would pray to this or to that, and ask it to intercede for him with the Machine as a whole. Persecution—that also was present. It did not break out, for reasons that will be set forward shortly. But it was latent, and all who did not accept the minimum known as "undenominational Mechanism" lived in danger of Homelessness, which means death, as we know.

To attribute these two great developments to the Central Committee, is to take a very narrow view of civilization. The Central Committee announced the developments, it is true, but they were no more the cause of them than were the kings of the imperialistic period the cause of war. Rather did they yield to some invincible pressure, which came no one knew whither, and which, when gratified, was succeeded by some new pressure equally invincible. To such a state of affairs it is convenient to give the name of progress. No one confessed the Machine was out of hand. Year by year it was served with increased efficiency and decreased intelligence. The better a man knew his own duties upon it, the less he understood the duties of his neighbour, and in all the world there was not one who understood the monster as a whole. Those master brains had perished. They had left full directions, it is true, and their successors had each of them mastered a portion of those directions. But Humanity, in its desire for comfort, had over-reached itself. It had exploited the riches of nature too far. Quietly and complacently, it was sinking into decadence, and progress had come to mean the progress of the Machine.

As for Vashti, her life went peacefully forward until the final disaster. She made her room dark and slept; she awoke and made the room light. She lectured and attended lectures. She exchanged ideas with her innumerable friends and believed she was growing more spiritual. At times a friend was granted Euthanasia, and left his or her room for the homelessness that is beyond all human conception. Vashti did not much mind. After an unsuccessful lecture, she would sometimes ask for Euthanasia herself. But the death-rate was not permitted to exceed the birth-rate, and the Machine had hitherto refused it to her.

The troubles began quietly, long before she was conscious of them.

One day she was astonished at receiving a message from her son. They never communicated, having nothing in common, and she had only heard indirectly that he was still alive, and had been transferred from the northern hemisphere, where he had behaved so mischievously, to the southern—indeed, to a room not far from her own.

"Does he want me to visit him?" she thought. "Never again, never. And I have not the time."

No, it was madness of another kind.

He refused to visualize his face upon the blue plate, and speaking out of the darkness with solemnity said:

"The Machine stops."

"What do you say?"

"The Machine is stopping, I know it, I know the signs."

She burst into a peal of laughter. He heard her and was angry, and they spoke no more.

"Can you imagine anything more absurd?" she cried to a friend. "A man who was my son believes that the Machine is stopping. It would be impious if it was not mad."

"The Machine is stopping?" her friend replied. "What does that mean? The phrase conveys nothing to me."

"Nor to me."

"He does not refer, I suppose, to the trouble there has been lately with the music?"

"Oh no, of course not. Let us talk about music."

"Have you complained to the authorities?"

"Yes, and they say it wants mending, and referred me to the Committee of the Mending Apparatus. I complained of those curious gasping sighs that disfigure the symphonies of the Brisbane school. They sound like some one in pain. The Committee of the Mending Apparatus say that it shall be remedied shortly."

Obscurely worried, she resumed her life. For one thing, the defect in the music irritated her. For another thing, she could not forget

Kuno"s speech. If he had known that the music was out of repair—he could not know it, for he detested music—if he had known that it was wrong, "the Machine stops" was exactly the venomous sort of remark he would have made. Of course he had made it at a venture, but the coincidence annoyed her, and she spoke with some petulance to the Committee of the Mending Apparatus.

They replied, as before, that the defect would be set right shortly.

"Shortly! At once!" she retorted. "Why should I be worried by imperfect music? Things are always put right at once. If you do not mend it at once, I shall complain to the Central Committee."

"No personal complaints are received by the Central Committee," the Committee of the Mending Apparatus replied.

"Through whom am I to make my complaint, then?"

"Through us."

"I complain then."

"Your complaint shall be forwarded in its turn."

"Have others complained?"

This question was unmechanical, and the Committee of the Mending Apparatus refused to answer it.

"It is too bad!" she exclaimed to another of her friends.

"There never was such an unfortunate woman as myself. I can never be sure of my music now. It gets worse and worse each time I summon it."

"What is it?"

"I do not know whether it is inside my head, or inside the wall."

"Complain, in either case."

"I have complained, and my complaint will be forwarded in its turn to the Central Committee."

Time passed, and they resented the defects no longer. The defects had not been remedied, but the human tissues in that latter day had become so subservient, that they readily adapted themselves to every caprice of the Machine. The sigh at the crises of the Brisbane symphony no longer irritated Vashti; she accepted it as part of the melody. The jarring noise, whether in the head or in the wall, was no longer resented by her friend. And so with the mouldy artificial fruit, so with the bath water that began to stink, so with the defective rhymes that the poetry machine had taken to emit. all were bitterly complained of at first, and then acquiesced in and forgotten. Things went from bad to worse unchallenged.

It was otherwise with the failure of the sleeping apparatus. That was a more serious stoppage. There came a day when over the whole world—in Sumatra, in Wessex, in the innumerable cities of Courland and Brazil—the beds, when summoned by their tired owners, failed to appear. It may seem a ludicrous matter, but from it we may date the collapse of humanity. The Committee responsible for the failure was assailed by complainants, whom it referred, as usual, to the Committee of the Mending Apparatus, who in its turn assured them that their complaints would be forwarded to the Central Committee. But the discontent grew, for mankind was not yet sufficiently adaptable to do without sleeping.

"Some one is meddling with the Machine—" they began.

"Some one is trying to make himself king, to reintroduce the personal element."

"Punish that man with Homelessness."

"To the rescue! Avenge the Machine! Avenge the Machine!"

"War! Kill the man!"

But the Committee of the Mending Apparatus now came forward, and allayed the panic with well-chosen words. It confessed that the Mending Apparatus was itself in need of repair.

The effect of this frank confession was admirable.

"Of course," said a famous lecturer—he of the French Revolution, who gilded each new decay with splendour—"of course we shall not press our complaints now. The Mending Apparatus has treated us so well in the past that we all sympathize with it, and will wait patiently for its recovery. In its own good time it will resume its duties. Meanwhile let us do without our beds, our tabloids, our other little wants. Such, I feel sure, would be the wish of the Machine."

Thousands of miles away his audience applauded. The Machine still linked them. Under the seas, beneath the roots of the mountains, ran the wires through which they saw and heard, the enormous eyes and ears that were their heritage, and the hum of many workings clothed their thoughts in one garment of subserviency. Only the old and the sick remained ungrateful, for it was rumoured that Euthanasia, too, was out of order, and that pain had reappeared among men.

It became difficult to read. A blight entered the atmosphere and dulled its luminosity. At times Vashti could scarcely see across her room. The air, too, was foul. Loud were the complaints, impotent the remedies, heroic the tone of the lecturer as he cried: "Courage! courage! What matter so long as the Machine goes on? To it the darkness and the light are one." And though things improved again after a time, the old brilliancy was never recaptured, and humanity never recovered from its entrance into twilight. There was an hysterical talk of "measures," of "provisional dictatorship," and the inhabitants of Sumatra were asked to familiarize themselves with the workings of the central power station, the said power station being situated in France. But for the most part panic reigned, and men spent their strength praying to their Books, tangible proofs of the Machine's omnipotence. There were gradations of terror—at times came rumours of hope—the Mending Apparatus was almost mended—the enemies of the Machine had been got under—new "nerve-centres" were evolving which would do the work even more magnificently than before. But there came a day when, without the slightest warning, without any previous hint of feebleness, the entire communication-system broke down, all over the world, and the world, as they understood it, ended.

Vashti was lecturing at the time and her earlier remarks had been punctuated with applause. As she proceeded the audience became silent, and at the conclusion there was no sound. Somewhat displeased, she called to a friend who was a specialist in sympathy. No sound: doubtless the friend was sleeping. And so with the next friend whom she tried to summon, and so with the next, until she remembered Kuno's cryptic remark, "The Machine stops".

The phrase still conveyed nothing. If Eternity was stopping it would of course be set going shortly.

For example, there was still a little light and air—the atmosphere had improved a few hours previously. There was still the Book, and while there was the Book there was security.

Then she broke down, for with the cessation of activity came an unexpected terror—silence.

She had never known silence, and the coming of it nearly killed her—it did kill many thousands of people outright. Ever since her birth she had been surrounded by the steady hum. It was to the ear what artificial air was to the lungs, and agonizing pains shot across her head. And scarcely knowing what she did, she stumbled forward and pressed the unfamiliar button, the one that opened the door of her cell.

Now the door of the cell worked on a simple hinge of its own. It was not connected with the central power station, dying far away in France. It opened, rousing immoderate hopes in Vashti, for she thought that the Machine had been mended. It opened, and she saw the dim tunnel that curved far away towards freedom. One look, and then she shrank back. For the tunnel was full of people—she was almost the last in that city to have taken alarm.

People at any time repelled her, and these were nightmares from her worst dreams. People were crawling about, people were screaming, whimpering, gasping for breath, touching each other, vanishing in the dark, and ever and anon being pushed off the platform on to the live rail. Some were fighting round the electric bells, trying to summon trains which could not be summoned. Others were yelling for Euthanasia or for respirators, or blaspheming the Machine. Others stood at the doors of their cells fearing, like herself, either to stop in them or to leave them. And behind all the uproar was silence—the silence which is the voice of the earth and of the generations who have gone.

No—it was worse than solitude. She closed the door again and sat down to wait for the end. The disintegration went on, accompanied by horrible cracks and rumbling. The valves that restrained the Medical Apparatus must have weakened, for it ruptured and hung hideously from the ceiling. The floor heaved and fell and flung her from the chair. A tube oozed towards her serpent fashion. And at last the final horror approached—light began to ebb, and she knew that civilization's long day was closing.

She whirled around, praying to be saved from this, at any rate, kissing the Book, pressing button after button. The uproar outside was increasing, and even penetrated the wall. Slowly the brilliancy of her cell was dimmed, the reflections faded from the metal switches. Now she could not see the reading-stand, now not the Book, though she held it in her hand. Light followed the flight of sound, air was following light, and the original void returned to the cavern from which it has so long been excluded. Vashti continued to whirl, like the devotees of an earlier religion, screaming, praying, striking at the buttons with bleeding hands.

It was thus that she opened her prison and escaped—escaped in the spirit: at least so it seems to me, ere my meditation closes. That she escapes in the body—I cannot perceive that. She struck, by chance, the switch that released the door, and the rush of foul air on her skin, the loud throbbing whispers in her ears, told her that she was facing the tunnel again, and that tremendous platform on which she had seen men fighting. They were not fighting now. Only the whispers remained, and the little whimpering groans. They were dying by hundreds out in the dark.

She burst into tears.

Tears answered her.

They wept for humanity, those two, not for themselves. They could not bear that this should be the end. Ere silence was completed their hearts were opened, and they knew what had been important on the earth. Man, the flower of all flesh, the noblest of all creatures visible, man who had once made god in his image, and had mirrored his strength on the constellations, beautiful naked man was dying, strangled in the garments that he had woven. Century after century had he toiled, and here was his reward. Truly the garment had seemed heavenly at first, shot with colours of culture, sewn with the threads of self-denial. And heavenly it had been so long as man could shed it at will and live by the essence that is his soul, and the essence, equally divine, that is his body. The sin against the body—it was for that they wept in chief; the centuries of wrong against the muscles and the nerves, and those five portals by which we can alone apprehend—glozing it over with talk of evolution, until the body was white pap, the home of ideas as colourless, last sloshy stirrings of a spirit that had grasped the stars.

"Where are you?" she sobbed.

His voice in the darkness said, "Here."

Is there any hope, Kuno?"

"None for us."

"Where are you?"

She crawled over the bodies of the dead. His blood spurted over her hands.

"Quicker," he gasped, "I am dying—but we touch, we talk, not through the Machine."

He kissed her.

"We have come back to our own. We die, but we have recaptured life, as it was in Wessex, when Ælfrid overthrew the Danes. We know what they know outside, they who dwelt in the cloud that is the colour of a pearl."

"But Kuno, is it true? Are there still men on the surface of the earth? Is this—tunnel, this poisoned darkness—really not the end?"

He replied:

"I have seen them, spoken to them, loved them. They are hiding in the midst and the ferns until our civilization stops. Today they are the Homeless—tomorrow—"

"Oh, tomorrow—some fool will start the Machine again, tomorrow."

"Never," said Kuno, "never. Humanity has learnt its lesson."

As he spoke, the whole city was broken like a honeycomb. An air-ship had sailed in through the vomitory into a ruined wharf. It crashed downwards, exploding as it went, rending gallery after gallery with its wings of steel. For a moment they saw the nations of the dead, and, before they joined them, scraps of the untainted sky.

AS EASY AS A.B.C

Rudyard Kipling

RUDYARD KIPLING (1865-1936) was born a British subject in Bombay, India and became one of the most popular writers of his day. Besides writing scores of poems, dozens of short stories and several novels (including stories and novels for children), Kipling also penned true science fiction as well as tales of the supernatural. Though much of his writing casts colonialism and Empire in a romantic light, many of his stories, particularly his science fiction, are actually biting satires. One such story is "As Easy as A.B.C.", a very pointed satire about people who wield extraordinary powers

The A.B.C., that semi-elected, semi-nominated body of a few score persons, controls the Planet. Transportation is Civilisation, our motto runs. Theoretically we do what we please, so long as we do not interfere with the traffic and all it implies. Practically, the A.B.C. confirms or annuls all international arrangements, and, to judge from its last report, finds our tolerant, humorous, lazy little Planet only too ready to shift the whole burden of public administration on its shoulders.

"With the Night Mail"

ISN'T it almost time that our Planet took some interest in the proceedings of the Aerial Board of Control? One knows that easy communications nowadays, and lack of privacy in the past, have killed all curiosity among mankind, but as the Board's Official Reporter I am bound to tell my tale.

At 9.30 A.M., August 26, A.D. 2065, the Board, sitting in London, was informed by De Forest that the District of Northern Illinois had riotously cut itself out of all systems and would remain disconnected till the Board should take over and administer it direct.

Every Northern Illinois freight and passenger tower was, he reported, out of action; all District mai.0n, local, and guiding lights had been extinguished; all General Communications were dumb, and through traffic had been diverted. No reason had been given, but he gathered unofficially from the Mayor of Chicago that the District complained of "crowd-making and invasion of privacy."

As a matter of fact, it is of no importance whether Northern Illinois stay in or out of planetary circuit; as a matter of policy, any complaint of invasion of privacy needs immediate investigation, lest worse follow.

By 9.45 A.M. De Forest, Dragomiroff (Russia), Takahira (Japan), and Pirolo (Italy) were empowered to visit Illinois and "to take such steps as might be necessary for the resumption of traffic and all that that implies." By 10 A.M. the Hall was empty, and the four Members and I were aboard what Pirolo insisted on calling "my leetle godchild"—that is to say, the new Victor Pirolo. Our Planet prefers to know Victor Pirolo as a gentle, grey-haired enthusiast who spends his time near Foggia, inventing or creating new breeds of Spanish-Italian olive-trees; but there is another side to his nature—the manufacture of quaint inventions, of which the Victor Pirolo is perhaps, not the least surprising. She and a few score sister-craft of the same type embody his latest ideas. But she is not comfortable. An A.B.C. boat does not take the air with the level-keeled lift of a liner, but shoots up rocket-fashion like the "aeroplane" of our ancestors, and makes her height at top-speed from the first. That is why I found myself sitting suddenly on the large lap of Eustace Arnott, who commands the A.B.C. Fleet. One knows vaguely that there is such a thing as a Fleet somewhere on the Planet, and that, theoretically, it exists for the purposes of what used to be known as "war." Only a week before, while visiting a glacier sanatorium behind Gothaven, I had seen some squadrons making false auroras far to the north while they manoeuvred round the Pole; but, naturally, it had never occurred to me that the things could be used in earnest.

Said Arnott to De Forest as I staggered to a seat on the chart-room divan: "We're tremendously grateful to 'em in Illinois. We've never had a chance of exercising all the Fleet together. I've turned in a General Call, and I expect we'll have at least two hundred keels aloft this evening."

"Well aloft?" De Forest asked.

"Of course, sir. Out of sight till they're called for."

Arnott laughed as he lolled over the transparent chart-table where the map of the summer-blue Atlantic slid along, degree by degree, in exact answer to our progress. Our dial already showed 320 m.p.h. and we were two thousand feet above the uppermost traffic lines.

"Now, where is this Illinois District of yours?" said Dragomiroff. "One travels so much, one sees so little. Oh, I remember! It is in North America."

De Forest, whose business it is to know the out districts, told us that it lay at the foot of Lake Michigan, on a road to nowhere in particular, was about half an hour's run from end to end, and, except in one corner, as flat as the sea. Like most flat countries nowadays, it was heavily guarded against invasion of privacy by forced timber—fifty-foot spruce and tamarack, grown in five years. The population was close on two millions, largely migratory between Florida and California, with a backbone of small farms (they call a thousand acres a farm in Illinois) whose owners come into Chicago for amusements and society during the winter. They were, he said noticeably kind, quiet folk, but a little exacting, as all flat countries must be, in their notions of privacy. There had, for instance, been no printed news-sheet in Illinois for twenty-seven years. Chicago argued that engines for printed news sooner or later developed into engines for invasion of privacy, which in turn might bring the old terror of Crowds and blackmail back to the Planet. So news-sheets were not.

"And that's Illinois," De Forest concluded. "You see, in the Old Days, she was in the fore-front of what they used to call 'progress,' and Chicago—"

"Chicago?" said Takahira. "That's the little place where there is Salati's Statue of the Nigger in Flames. A fine bit of old work."

"When did you see it?" asked De Forest quickly. "They only unveil it once a year."

"I know. At Thanksgiving. It was then," said Takahira, with a shudder. "And they sang MacDonough's Song, too."

"Whew!" De Forest whistled. "I did not know that! I wish you'd told me before. MacDonough's Song may have had its uses when it was composed, but it was an infernal legacy for any man to leave behind."

"It's protective instinct, my dear fellows," said Pirolo, rolling a cigarette. "The Planet, she has had her dose of popular government. She suffers from inherited agoraphobia. She has no—ah—use for crowds."

Dragomiroff leaned forward to give him a light. "Certainly," said the white-bearded Russian, "the Planet has taken all precautions against crowds for the past hundred years. What is our total population today? Six hundred million, we hope; five hundred, we think; but—but if next year's census shows more than four hundred and fifty, I myself will eat all the extra little babies. We have cut the birth-rate out—right out! For a long time we have said to Almighty God, 'Thank You, Sir, but we do not much like Your game of life, so we will not play.'"

"Anyhow," said Arnott defiantly, "men live a century apiece on the average now."

"Oh, that is quite well! I am rich—you are rich—we are all rich and happy because we are so few and we live so long. Only I think Almighty God He will remember what the Planet was like in the time of Crowds and the Plague. Perhaps He will send us nerves. Eh, Pirolo?"

The Italian blinked into space. "Perhaps," he said, "He has sent them already. Anyhow, you cannot argue with the Planet. She does not forget the Old Days, and—what can you do?"

"For sure we can't remake the world." De Forest glanced at the map flowing smoothly across the table from west to east. "We ought to be over our ground by nine to-night. There won't be much sleep afterwards."

On which hint we dispersed, and I slept till Takahira waked me for dinner. Our ancestors thought nine hours' sleep ample for their little lives. We, living thirty years longer, feel ourselves defrauded with less than eleven out of the twenty-four.

By ten o'clock we were over Lake Michigan. The west shore was lightless, except for a dull ground-glare at Chicago, and a single traffic-directing light—its leading beam pointing north—at Waukegan on our starboard bow. None of the Lake villages gave any sign of life; and inland, westward, so far as we could see, blackness lay unbroken on the level earth. We swooped down and skimmed low across the dark, throwing calls county by county. Now and again we picked up the faint glimmer of a house-light, or heard the rasp and rend of a cultivator being played across the fields, but Northern Illinois as a whole was one inky, apparently uninhabited, waste of high, forced woods. Only our illuminated map, with its little pointer switching from county to county, as we wheeled and twisted, gave us any idea of our position. Our calls, urgent, pleading, coaxing or commanding, through the General Communicator brought no answer. Illinois strictly maintained her own privacy in the timber which she grew for that purpose.

"Oh, this is absurd!" said De Forest. "We're like an owl trying to work a wheat-field. Is this Bureau Creek? Let's land, Arnott, and get hold of some one."

We brushed over a belt of forced woodland—fifteen-year-old maple sixty feet high—grounded on a private meadow-dock, none too big, where we moored to our own grapnels, and hurried out through the warm dark night towards a light in a verandah. As we neared the garden gate I could have sworn we had stepped knee-deep in quicksand, for we could scarcely drag our feet against the prickling currents that clogged them. After five paces we stopped, wiping our foreheads, as hopelessly stuck on dry smooth turf as so many cows in a bog.

"Pest!" cried Pirolo angrily. "We are ground-circuited. And it is my own system of ground-circuits too! I know the pull."

"Good evening," said a girl's voice from the verandah. "Oh, I'm sorry! We've locked up. Wait a minute."

We heard the click of a switch, and almost fell forward as the currents round our knees were withdrawn.

The girl laughed, and laid aside her knitting. An old-fashioned Controller stood at her elbow, which she reversed from time to time, and we could hear the snort and clank of the obedient cultivator half a mile away, behind the guardian woods.

"Come in and sit down," she said. "I'm only playing a plough. Dad's gone to Chicago to—Ah! Then it was your call I heard just now!"

She had caught sight of Arnott's Board uniform, leaped to the switch, and turned it full on.

We were checked, gasping, waist-deep in current this time, three yards from the verandah.

"We only want to know what's the matter with Illinois," said De Forest placidly.

"Then hadn't you better go to Chicago and find out ?" she answered. "There's nothing wrong here. We own ourselves."

"How can we go anywhere if you won't loose us?" De Forest went on, while Arnott scowled. Admirals of Fleets are still quite human when their dignity is touched.

"Stop a minute—you don't know how funny you look!" She put her hands on her hips and laughed mercilessly.

"Don't worry about that," said Arnott, and whistled. A voice answered from the Victor Pirolo in the meadow.

"Only a single-fuse ground-circuit!" Arnott called. "Sort it out gently, please."

We heard the ping of a breaking lamp; a fuse blew out somewhere in the verandah roof, frightening a nest full of birds. The groud-circuit was open. We stooped and rubbed our tingling ankles.

"How rude—how very rude of you!" the maiden cried.

"Sorry, but we haven't time to look funny," said Arnott. "We've got to go to Chicago; and if I were you, young lady, I'd go into the cellars for the next two hours, and take mother with me."

Off he strode, with us at his heels, muttering indignantly, till the humour of the thing struck and doubled him up with laughter at the foot of the gangway ladder.

"The Board hasn't shown what you might call a fat spark on this occasion," said De Forest, wiping his eyes. "I hope I didn't look as big a fool as you did, Arnott! Hullo! What on earth is that? Dad coming home from Chicago?"

There was a rattle and a rush, and a five-plough cultivator, blades in air like so many teeth, trundled itself at us round the edge of the timber, fuming and sparking furiously.

"Jump!" said Arnott, as we hurled ourselves through the none-too-wide door. "Never mind about shutting it. Up!"

The Victor Pirolo lifted like a bubble, and the vicious machine shot just underneath us, clawing high as it passed.

"There's a nice little spit-kitten for you!" said Arnott, dusting his knees. "We ask her a civil question. First she circuits us and then she plays a cultivator at us!"

"And then we fly," said Dragomirof. "If I were forty years more young, I would go back and kiss her. Ho! Ho!"

"I," said Pirolo, "would smack her! My pet ship has been chased by a dirty plough; a—how do you say?—agricultural implement."

"Oh, that is Illinois all over," said De Forest. "They don't content themselves with talking about privacy. They arrange to have it. And now, where's your alleged fleet, Arnott? We must assert ourselves against this wench."

Arnott pointed to the black heavens. "Waiting on—up there," said he. "Shall I give them the whole installation, sir?"

"Oh, I don't think the young lady is quite worth that," said De Forest. "Get over Chicago, and perhaps we'll see something."

In a few minutes we were hanging at two thousand feet over an oblong block of incandescence in the centre of the little town.

"That looks like the old City Hall. Yes, there's Salati's Statue in front of it," said Takahira.

"But what on earth are they doing to the place? I thought they used it for a market nowadays! Drop a little, please."

We could hear the sputter and crackle of road-surfacing machines—the cheap Western type which fuse stone and rubbish into lava-like ribbed glass for their rough country roads. Three or four surfacers worked on each side of a square of ruins. The brick and stone wreckage crumbled, slid forward, and presently spread out into white-hot pools of sticky slag, which the levelling-rods smoothed more or less flat. Already a third of the big block had been so treated, and was cooling to dull red before our astonished eyes.

"It is the Old Market," said De Forest. "Well, there's nothing to prevent Illinois from making a road through a market. It doesn't interfere with traffic, that I can see."

"Hsh!" said Arnott, gripping me by the shoulder. "Listen! They're s0inging. Why on the earth are they singing?"

We dropped again till we could see the black fringe of people at the edge of that glowing square.

At first they only roared against the roar of the surfacers and levellers. Then the words came up clearly—the words of the Forbidden Song that all men knew, and none let pass their lips—poor Pat MacDonough's Song, made in the days of the Crowds and the Plague—every silly word of it loaded to sparking-point with the Planet's inherited memories of horror, panic, fear and cruelty. And Chicago—innocent, contented little Chicago—was singing it aloud to the infernal tune that carried riot, pestilence and lunacy round our Planet a few generations ago!

"Once there was The People—Terror gave it birth;
Once there was The People, and it made a hell of earth!"
(Then the stamp and pause):
"Earth arose and crushed it. Listen, oh, ye slain!
Once there was The People—it shall never be again!"

The evelers thrust in savagely against the ruins as the song renewed itself again, again and again, louder than the crash of the melting walls.

De Forest frowned.

"I don't like that," he said. "They've broken back to the Old Days! They'll be killing somebody soon. I think we'd better divert 'em, Arnott."

"Ay, ay, sir." Arnott's hand went to his cap, and we heard the hull of the Victor Pirolo ring to the command: "Lamps! Both watches stand by! Lamps! Lamps! Lamps!"

"Keep still!" Takahira whispered to me. "Blinkers, please, quartermaster."

"It's all right—all right!" said Pirolo from behind, and to my horror slipped over my head some sort of rubber helmet that locked with a snap. I could feel thick colloid bosses before my eyes, but I stood in absolute darkness.

"To save the sight," he explained, and pushed me on to the chart-room divan. "You will see in a minute."

As he spoke I became aware of a thin thread of almost intolerable light, let down from heaven at an immense distance—one vertical hairs breadth of frozen lightning.

"Those are our flanking ships," said Arnott at my elbow. "That one is over Galena. Look south—that other one's over Keithburg. Vincennes is behind us, and north yonder is Winthrop Woods. The Fleet's in position, sir"—this to De Forest. "As soon as you give the word."

"Ah no! No!" cried Dragomiroff at my side. I could feel the old man tremble. "I do not know all that you can do, but be kind! I ask you to be a little kind to them below! This is horrible horrible!"

"When a Woman kills a Chicken,
Dynasties and Empires sicken,"

Takahira quoted. "It is too late to be gentle now.

"Then take off my helmet! Take off my helmet!" Dragomiroff began hysterically.

Pirolo must have put his arm round him.

"Hush," he said, "I am here. It is all right, Ivan, my dear fellow."

"I'll just send our little girl in Bureau County a warning," said Arnott. "She don't deserve it, but we'll allow her a minute or two to take mamma to the cellar."

In the utter hush that followed the growling spark after Arnott had linked up his Service Communicator with the invisible Fleet, we heard MacDonough's Song from the city beneath us grow fainter as we rose to position. Then I clapped my hand before my mask lenses, for it was as though the floor of Heaven had been riddled and all the inconceivable blaze of suns in the making was poured through the manholes.

"You needn't count," said Arnott. I had had no thought of such a thing. "There are two hundred and fifty keels up there, five miles apart. Full power, please, for another twelve seconds."

The firmament, as far as eye could reach, stood on pillars of white fire. One fell on the glowing square at Chicago, and turned it black.

"Oh! Oh! Oh! Can men be allowed to do such things?" Dragomiroff cried, and fell across our knees.

"Glass of water, please," said Takahira to a helmeted shape that leaped forward. "He is a little faint."

The lights switched off, and the darkness stunned like an avalanche. We could hear Dragomiroff's teeth on the glass edge.

Pirolo was comforting him.

"All right, all ra-ight," he repeated. "Come and lie down. Come below and take off your mask. I give you my word, old friend, it is all right. They are my siege-lights. Little Victor Pirolo's leetle lights. You know me! I do not hurt people."

"Pardon!" Dragomiroff moaned. "I have never seen Death. I have never seen the Board take action. Shall we go down and burn them alive, or is that already done?"

"Oh, hush," said Pirolo, and I think he rocked him in his arms.

"Do we repeat, sir?" Arnott asked De Forest.

"Give 'em a minute's break," De Forest replied. "They may need it."

We waited a minute, and then MacDonough's Song, broken but defiant, rose from undefeated Chicago.

"They seem fond of that tune," said De Forest. "I should let 'em have it, Arnott."

"Very good, sir," said Arnott, and felt his way to the Communicator keys.

No lights broke forth, but the hollow of the skies made herself the mouth for one note that touched the raw fibre of the brain. Men hear such sounds in delirium, advancing like tides from horizons beyond the ruled foreshores of space.

"That's our pitch-pipe," said Arnott. "We may be a bit ragged. I've never conducted two hundred and fifty performers before." He pulled out the couplers, and struck a full chord on the Service Communicators.

The beams of light leaped down again, and danced, solemnly and awfully, a stilt-dance, sweeping thirty or forty miles left and right at each stiff-legged kick, while the darkness delivered itself—there is no scale to measure against that utterance—of the tune to which they kept time. Certain notes—one learnt to expect them with terror—cut through one's marrow, but, after three minutes, thought and emotion passed in indescribable agony.

We saw, we heard, but I think we were in some sort swooning. The two hundred and fifty beams shifted, re-formed, straddled and split, narrowed, widened, rippled in ribbons, broke into a thousand white-hot parallel lines, melted and revolved in interwoven rings like old-fashioned engine-turning, flung up to the zenith, made as if to descend and renew the torment, halted at the last instant, twizzled insanely round the horizon, and vanished, to bring back for the hundredth time darkness more shattering than their instantly renewed light over all Illinois. Then the tune and lights ceased together, and we heard one single devastating wail that shook all the horizon as a rubbed wet finger shakes the rim of a bowl.

"Ah, that is my new siren," said Pirolo. "You can break an iceberg in half, if you find the proper pitch. They will whistle by squadrons now. It is the wind through pierced shutters in the bows."

I had collapsed beside Dragomiroff, broken and snivelling feebly, because I had been delivered before my time to all the terrors of Judgment Day, and the Archangels of the Resurrection were hailing me naked across the Universe to the sound of the music of the spheres.

Then I saw De Forest smacking Arnott's helmet with his open hand. The wailing died down in a long shriek as a black shadow swooped past us, and returned to her place above the lower clouds.

"I hate to interrupt a specialist when he's enjoying himself," said De Forest. "But, as a matter of fact, all Illinois has been asking us to stop for these last fifteen seconds."

"What a pity." Arnott slipped off his mask. "I wanted you to hear us really hum. Our lower C can lift street-paving."

"It is Hell—Hell!" cried Dragomiroff, and sobbed aloud.

Arnott looked away as he answered: "It's a few thousand volts ahead of the old shoot-'em-and-sink-'em game, but I should scarcely call it that. What shall I tell the Fleet, sir?"

"Tell 'em we're very pleased and impressed. I don't think they need wait on any longer. There isn't a spark left down there." De Forest pointed. "They'll be deaf and blind."

"Oh, I think not, sir. The demonstration lasted less than ten minutes."

"Marvellous!" Takahira sighed. "I should have said it was half a night. Now, shall we go down and pick up the pieces?"

"But first a small drink," said Pirolo. "The Board must not arrive weeping at its own works."

"I am an old fool—an old fool!" Dragomiroff began piteously. "I did not know what would happen. It is all new to me. We reason with them in Little Russia."

Chicago North landing-tower was unlighted, and Arnott worked his ship into the clips by her own lights. As soon as these broke out we heard groanings of horror and appeal from many people below.

All right," shouted Arnott into the darkness. We aren't beginning again!" We descended by the stairs, to find ourselves knee deep in a grovelling crowd, some crying that they were blind, others beseeching us not to make any more noises, but the greater part writhing face downward, their hands or their caps before their eyes.

It was Pirolo who came to our rescue. He climbed the side of a surfacing-machine, and there, gesticulating as though they could see, made oration to those afflicted people of Illinois.

"You stchewpids!" he began. "There is nothing to fuss for. Of course, your eyes will smart and be red to-morrow. You will look as if you and your wives had drunk too much, but in a little while you will see again as well as before. I tell you this, and I—I am Pirolo. Victor Pirolo!"

The crowd with one accord shuddered, for many legends attach to Victor Pirolo of Foggia, deep in the secrets of God.

"Pirolo?" An unsteady voice lifted itself. "Then tell us was there anything except light in those lights of yours just now?"

The question was repeated from every corner of the darkness.

Pirolo laughed.

"No!" he thundered. (Why have small men such large voices) "I give you my word and the Board's word that there was nothing except light—just light! You stchewpids! Your birth-rate is too low already as it is. Some day I must invent something to send it up, but send it down—never!"

"Is that true?—We thought—somebody said—"

One could feel the tension relax all round.

"You too big fools," Pirolo cried. "You could have sent us a call and we would have told you."

"Send you a call!" a deep voice shouted. "I wish you had been at our end of the wire."

"I'm glad I wasn't," said De Forest. "It was bad enough from behind the lamps. Never mind! It's over now. Is there any one here I can talk business with? I'm De Forest—for the Board."

"You might begin with me, for one—I'm Mayor," the bass voice replied.

A big man rose unsteadily from the street, and staggered towards us where we sat on the broad turf-edging, in front of the garden fences.

"I ought to be the first on my feet. Am I?" said he.

"Yes," said De Forest, and steadied him as he dropped down beside us.

"Hello, Andy. Is that you?" a voice called.

"Excuse me," said the Mayor; "that sounds like my Chief of Police, Bluthner!"

"Bluthner it is; and here's Mulligan and Keefe—on their feet."

"Bring 'em up please, Blut. We're supposed to be the Four in charge of this hamlet. What we says, goes. And, De Forest, what do you say?"

"Nothing—yet," De Forest answered, as we made room for the panting, reeling men. "You've cut out of system. Well?"

"Tell the steward to send down drinks, please," Arnott whispered to an orderly at his side.

"Good!" said the Mayor, smacking his dry lips. "Now I suppose we can take it, De Forest, that henceforward the Board will administer us direct?"

"Not if the Board can avoid it," De Forest laughed. "The A.B.C. is responsible for the planetary traffic only."

"And all that that implies." The big Four who ran Chicago chanted their Magna Charta like children at school.

"Well, get on," said De Forest wearily. "What is your silly trouble anyway?"

"Too much dam' Democracy," said the Mayor, laying his hand on De Forest's knee.

"So? I thought Illinois had had her dose of that."

"She has. That's why. But, what did you do with our prisoners last night?"

"Locked 'em in the water-tower to prevent the women killing 'em," the Chief of Police replied. I'm too blind to move just yet, but—"

"Arnott, send some of your people, please, and fetch 'em along," said De Forest.

"They're triple-circuited," the Mayor called. "You'll have to blow out three fuses." He turned to De Forest, his large outline just visible in the paling darkness. "I hate to throw any more work on the Board. I'm an administrator myself, but we've had a little fuss with our Serviles. What? In a big city there's bound to be a few men and women who can't live without listening to themselves, and who prefer drinking out of pipes they don't own both ends of. They inhabit flats and hotels all the year round. They say it saves 'em trouble. Anyway, it gives 'em more time to make trouble for their neighbours. We call 'em Serviles locally. And they are apt to be tuberculous."

"Just so!" said the man called Mulligan. "Transportation is Civilisation. Democracy is Disease. I've proved it by the blood-test, every time."

"Mulligan's our Health Officer, and a one-idea man," said the Mayor, laughing. "But it's true that most Serviles haven't much control.

They will talk; and when people take to talking as a business, anything may arrive—mayn't it, De Forest?"

"Anything—except the facts of the case," said De Forest, laughing.

"I'll give you those in a minute," said the Mayor. "Our Serviles got to talking—first in their houses and then on the streets, telling men and women how to manage their own affairs. (You can't teach a Servile not to finger his neighbour's soul.) That's invasion of privacy, of course, but in Chicago we'll suffer anything sooner than make crowds. Nobody took much notice, and so I let 'em alone. My fault! I was warned there would be trouble, but there hasn't been a crowd or murder in Illinois for nineteen years."

"Twenty-two," said his Chief of Police.

"Likely. Anyway, we'd forgot such things. So, from talking in the houses and on the streets, our Serviles go to calling a meeting at the Old Market yonder." He nodded across the square where the wrecked buildings heaved up grey in the dawn-glimmer behind the square-cased statue of The Negro in Flames. "There's nothing to prevent anyone calling meetings except that it's against human nature to stand in a crowd, besides being bad for the health. I ought to have known by the way our men and women attended that first meeting that trouble was brewing. There were as many as a thousand in the market-place, touching each other. Touching! Then the Serviles turned in all tongue-switches and talked, and we—"

"What did they talk about?" said Takahira.

"First, how badly things were managed in the city. That pleased us Four—we were on the platform—because we hoped to catch one or two good men for City work. You know how rare executive capacity is. Even if we didn't it's—it's refreshing to find any one interested enough in our job to damn our eyes. You don't know what it means to work, year in, year out, without a spark of difference with a living soul."

"Oh, don't we!" said De Forest. "There are times on the Board when we'd give our positions if any one would kick us out and take hold of things themselves."

"But they won't," said the Mayor ruefully. "I assure you, sir, we Four have done things in Chicago, in the hope of rousing people, that would have discredited Nero. But what do they say? 'Very good, Andy. Have it your own way. Anything's better than a crowd. I'll go back to my land.' You can't do anything with folk who can go where they please, and don't want anything on God's earth except their own way. There isn't a kick or a kicker left on the Planet."

"Then I suppose that little shed yonder fell down by itself?" said De Forest. We could see the bare and still smoking ruins, and hear the slag-pools crackle as they hardened and set.

"Oh, that's only amusement. Tell you later. As I was saying, our Serviles held the meeting, and pretty soon we had to ground—circuit the platform to save 'em from being killed. And that didn't make our people any more pacific."

"How d'you mean?" I ventured to ask.

"If you've ever been ground—circuited," said the Mayor, "you'll know it don't improve any man's temper to be held up straining against nothing. No, sir! Eight or nine hundred folk kept pawing and buzzing like flies in treacle for two hours, while a pack of perfectly safe Serviles invades their mental and spiritual privacy, may be amusing to watch, but they are not pleasant to handle afterwards."

Pirolo chuckled.

"Our folk own themselves. They were of opinion things were going too far and too fiery. I warned the Serviles; but they're born house-dwellers. Unless a fact hits 'em on the head, they cannot see it. Would you believe me, they went on to talk of what they called "popular government"? They did! They wanted us to go back to the old Voodoo-business of voting with papers and wooden boxes, and word-drunk people and printed formulas, and news-sheets! They said they practised it among themselves about what they'd have to eat in their flats and hotels. Yes, sir! They stood up behind Bluthner's doubled ground-circuits, and they said that, in this present year of grace, to self-owning men and women, on that very spot! Then they finished"—he lowered his voice cautiously—"by talking about 'The People.' And then Bluthner he had to sit up all night in charge of the circuits because he couldn't trust his men to keep 'em shut."

"It was trying 'em too high," the Chief of Police broke in. "But we couldn't hold the crowd ground-circuited for ever. I gathered in all the Serviles on charge of crowd-making, and put 'em in the water-tower, and then I let things cut loose. I had to! The District lit like a sparked gas-tank!"

"The news was out over seven degrees of country," the Mayor continued; "and when once it's a question of invasion of privacy, goodbye to right and reason in Illinois! They began turning out traffic-lights and locking up landing-towers on Thursday night. Friday, they stopped all traffic and asked for the Board to take over. Then they wanted to clean Chicago off the side of the Lake and rebuild elsewhere—just for a souvenir of 'The People' that the Serviles talked about. I suggested that they should slag the Old Market where the meeting was held, while I turned in a call to you all on the Board. That kept'em quiet till you came along. And—and now you can take hold of the situation."

"Any chance of their quieting down?" De Forest asked.

"You can try," said the Mayor.

De Forest raised his voice in the face of the reviving crowd that had edged in towards us. Day was come.

"Don't you think this business can be arranged?" he began. But there was a roar of angry voices:

"We've finished with Crowds! We aren't going back to the Old Days! Take us over! Take the Serviles away! Administer direct or we'll kill 'em! Down with The People!"

An attempt was made to begin MacDonough's Song. It got no further than the first line, for the Victor Pirolo sent down a warning drone on one stopped horn. A wrecked side-wall of the Old Market tottered and fell inwards on the slag-pools. None spoke or moved till the last of the dust had settled down again, turning the steel case of Salati's Statue ashy grey.

"You see you'll just have to take us over", the Mayor whispered.

De Forest shrugged his shoulders.

"You talk as if executive capacity could be snatched out of the air like so much horse-power. Can't you manage yourselves on any terms?" he said.

"We can, if you say so. It will only cost those few lives to begin with."

The Mayor pointed across the square, where Arnott's men guided a stumbling group of ten or twelve men and women to the lake front and halted them under the Statue.

"Now I think," said Takahira under his breath, "there will be trouble."

The mass in front of us growled like beasts.

At that moment the sun rose clear, and revealed the blinking assembly to itself. As soon as it realised that it was a crowd we saw the shiver of horror and mutual repulsion shoot across it precisely as the steely flaws shot across the lake outside. Nothing was said, and, being half blind, of course it moved slowly. Yet in less than fifteen minutes most of that vast multitude—three thousand at the lowest count—melted away like frost on south eaves. The remnant stretched themselves on the grass, where a crowd feels and looks less like a crowd.

"These mean business," the Mayor whispered to Takahira. "There are a goodish few women there who've borne children. I don't like it."

The morning draught off the lake stirred the trees round us with promise of a hot day; the sun reflected itself dazzlingly on the canister-shaped covering of Salati's Statue; cocks crew in the gardens, and we could hear gate-latches clicking in the distance as people stumblingly resought their homes.

"I'm afraid there won't be any morning deliveries," said De Forest. "We rather upset things in the country last night."

"That makes no odds," the Mayor returned. "We're all provisioned for six months. We take no chances. Nor, when you come to think of it, does anyone else. It must be three-quarters of a generation since any house or city faced a food shortage. Yet is there house or city on the Planet today that has not half a year's provisions laid in? We are like the shipwrecked seamen in the old books, who, having once nearly starved to death, ever afterwards hide away bits of food and biscuit. Truly we trust no Crowds, nor system based on Crowds!"

De Forest waited till the last footstep had died away. Meantime the prisoners at the base of the Statue shuffled, posed and fidgeted, with the shamelessness of quite little children. None of them were more than six feet high, and many of them were as grey-haired as the ravaged, harassed heads of old pictures. They huddled together in actual touch, while the crowd, spaced at large intervals, looked at them with congested eyes.

Suddenly a man among them began to talk. The Mayor had not in the least exaggerated. It appeared that our Planet lay sunk in slavery beneath the heel of the Aerial Board of Control. The orator urged us to arise in our might, burst our prison doors and break our fetters (all his metaphors, by the way, were of the most medieval).

Next he demanded that every matter of daily life, including most of the physical functions, should be submitted for decision at any time of the week, month, or year to, I gathered, anybody who happened to be passing by or residing within a certain radius, and that everybody should forthwith abandon his concerns to settle the matter, first by crowd-making, next by talking to the crowds made, and lastly by describing crosses on pieces of paper, which rubbish should later be counted with certain mystic ceremonies and oaths. Out of this amazing play, he assured us, would automatically arise a higher, nobler, and kinder world, based—he demonstrated this with the awful lucidity of the insane—based on the sanctity of the Crowd and the villainy of the single person. In conclusion, he called loudly upon God to testify to his personal merits and integrity. When the flow ceased, I turned bewildered to Takahira, who was nodding solemnly.

"Quite correct," said he "It is all in the old books. He has left nothing out, not even the war-talk."

"But I don't see how this stuff can upset a child, much less a district," I replied.

"Ah, you are too young," said Dragomiroff. "For another thing, you are not a mamma. Please look at the mammas."

Ten or fifteen women who remained had separated themselves from the silent men, and were drawing in towards the prisoners. It reminded one of the stealthy encircling, before the rush in at the quarry, of wolves round musk oxen in the North. The prisoners saw, and drew together more closely. The Mayor covered his face with his hands for an instant. De Forest, bareheaded, stepped forward between the prisoners and the slowly, stiffly moving line.

"That's all very interesting," he said to the dry-lipped orator. "But the point seems that you've been making crowds and invading privacy."

A woman stepped forward, and would have spoken, but there was a quick assenting murmur from the men, who realised that De Forest was trying to pull the situation down to ground-line.

"Yes! Yes!" they cried. "We cut out because they made crowds and invaded privacy! Stick to that! Keep on that switch! Lift the Serviles out of this! The Board's in charge! Hsh!"

"Yes, the Board's in charge," said De Forest.

"I'll take formal evidence of crowd-making if you like, but the Members of the Board can testify to it. Will that do?"

The women had closed in another pace, with hands that clenched and unclenched at their sides.

"Good! Good enough!" the men cried. "We're content. Only take them away quickly."

"Come along up!" said De Forest to the captives. "Breakfast is quite ready."

It appeared, however, that they did not wish to go. They intended to remain in Chicago and make crowds. They pointed out that De Forest's proposal was gross invasion of privacy.

"My dear fellow," said Pirolo to the most voluble of the leaders, "you hurry, or your crowd that can't be wrong will kill you!"

"But that would be murder," answered the believer in crowds; and there was a roar of laughter from all sides that seemed to show the crisis had broken.

A woman stepped forward from the line of women, laughing, I protest, as merrily as any of the company. One hand, of course, shaded her eyes, the other was at her throat.

"Oh, they needn't be afraid of being killed!" she called.

"Not in the least," said De Forest. "But don't you think that, now the Board's in charge, you might go home while we get these people away?"

"I shall be home long before that. It—it has been rather a trying day."

She stood up to her full height, dwarfing even De Forest's six-foot-eight, and smiled, with eyes closed against the fierce light.

"Yes, rather," said De Forest. "I'm afraid you feel the glare a little. We'll have the ship down."

He motioned to the Pirolo to drop between us and the sun, and at the same time to loop-circuit the prisoners, who were a trifle unsteady. We saw them stiffen to the current where they stood. The woman's voice went on, sweet and deep and unshaken:

"I don't suppose you men realise how much this—this sort of thing means to a woman. I've borne three. We women don't want our children given to Crowds. It must be an inherited instinct. Crowds make trouble. They bring back the Old Days. Hate, fear, blackmail, publicity, 'The People'—That! That! That!" She pointed to the Statue, and the crowd growled once more.

"Yes, if they are allowed to go on," said De Forest. "But this little affair—"

"It means so much to us women that this—this little affair should never happen again. Of course, never's a big word, but one feels so strongly that it is important to stop crowds at the very beginning. Those creatures"—she pointed with her left hand at the prisoners swaying like seaweed in a tide way as the circuit pulled them—"those people have friends and wives and children in the city and elsewhere. One doesn't want anything done to them, you know. It's terrible to force a human being out of fifty or sixty years of good life. I'm only forty myself. I know. But, at the same time, one feels that an example should be made, because no price is too heavy to pay if—if these people and all that they imply can be put an end to. Do you quite understand or would you be kind enough to tell your men to take the casing off the Statue? It's worth looking at."

"I understand perfectly. But I don't think anybody here wants to see the Statue on an empty stomach. Excuse me one moment." De Forest called up to the ship, "A flying loop ready on the port side, if you please." Then to the woman he said with some crispness, "You might leave us a little discretion in the matter."

"Oh, of course. Thank you for being so patient. I know my arguments are silly, but—" She half turned away and went on in a changed voice, "Perhaps this will help you to decide."

She threw out her right arm with a knife in it. Before the blade could be returned to her throat or her bosom it was twitched from her grip, sparked as it flew out of the shadow of the ship above, and fell flashing in the sunshine at the foot of the Statue fifty yards away. The outflung arm was arrested, rigid as a bar for an instant, till the releasing circuit permitted her to bring it slowly to her side. The other women shrank back silent among the men.

Pirolo rubbed his hands, and Takahira nodded.

"That was clever of you, De Forest," said he.

"What a glorious pose!" Dragomiroff murmured, for the frightened woman was on the edge of tears.

"Why did you stop me? I would have done it!" she cried.

"I have no doubt you would," said De Forest. "But we can't waste a life like yours on these people. I hope the arrest didn't sprain your wrist; it's so hard to regulate a flying loop. But I think you are quite right about those persons' women and children. We'll take them all away with us if you promise not to do anything stupid to yourself."

"I promise—I promise." She controlled herself with an effort. "But it is so important to us women. We know what it means; and I thought if you saw I was in earnest—"

"I saw you were, and you've gained your point. I shall take all your Serviles away with me at once. The Mayor will make lists of their friends and families in the city and the district, and he'll ship them after us this afternoon."

"Sure," said the Mayor, rising to his feet. "Keefe, if you can see, hadn't you better finish levelling off the Old Market? It don't look sightly the way it is now, and we shan't use it for crowds any more."

"I think you had better wipe out that Statue as well, Mr. Mayor," said De Forest. "I don't question its merits as a work of art, but I believe it's a shade morbid."

"Certainly, sir. Oh, Keefe! Slag the Nigger before you go on to fuse the Market. I'll get to the Communicators and tell the District tha the Board is in charge. Are you making any special appointments, sir?"

"None. We haven't men to waste on these backwoods. Carry on as before, but under the Board. Arnott, run your Serviles aboard, please. Ground ship and pass them through the bilge-doors. We'll wait till we've finished with this work of art."

The prisoners trailed past him, talking fluently, but unable to gesticulate in the drag of the current. Then the surfacers rolled up, two on each side of the Statue. With one accord the spectators looked elsewhere, but there was no need. Keefe turned on full power, and the thing simply melted within its case. All I saw was a surge of white-hot metal pouring over the plinth, a glimpse of Salati's inscription, "To the Eternal Memory of the Justice of the People," ere the stone base itself cracked and powdered into finest lime. The crowd cheered.

"Thank you," said De Forest; "but we want our breakfasts, and I expect you do too. Good-bye, Mr. Mayor! Delighted to see you at any time, but I hope I shan't have to, officially, for the next thirty years. Good-bye, madam. Yes. We're all given to nerves nowadays. I suffer from them myself. Good-bye, gentlemen all! You're under the tyrannous heel of the Board from this moment, but if ever you feel like breaking your fetters you've only to let us know. This is no treat to us. Good luck!"

We embarked amid shouts, and did not check our lift till they had dwindled into whispers. Then De Forest flung himself on the chart room divan and mopped his forehead.

"I don't mind men," he panted, "but women are the devil!"

"Still the devil," said Pirolo cheerfully. "That one would have suicided."

"I know it. That was why I signalled for the flying loop to be clapped on her. I owe you an apology for that, Arnott. I hadn't time to catch your eye, and you were busy with our caitiffs. By the way, who actually answered my signal? It was a smart piece of work."

"Ilroy," said Arnott; "but he overloaded the wave. It may be pretty gallery-work to knock a knife out of a lady's hand, but didn't you notice how she rubbed 'em? He scorched her fingers. Slovenly, I call it."

"Far be it from me to interfere with Fleet discipline, but don't be too hard on the boy. If that woman had killed herself they would have killed every Servile and everything related to a Servile throughout the district by nightfall."

"That was what she was playing for," Takahira said. "And with our Fleet gone we could have done nothing to hold them."

"I may be ass enough to walk into a ground-circuit," said Arnott, "but I don't dismiss my Fleet till I'm reasonably sure that trouble is over. They're in position still, and I intend to keep 'em there till the Serviles are shipped out of the district. That last little crowd meant murder, my friends."

"Nerves! All nerves!" said Pirolo. "You cannot argue with agoraphobia."

"And it is not as if they had seen much dead—or is it?" said Takahira.

"In all my ninety years I have never seen death." Dragomiroff spoke as one who would excuse himself. "Perhaps that was why—last night—"

Then it came out as we sat over breakfast, that, with the exception of Arnott and Pirolo, none of us had ever seen a corpse, or knew in what manner the spirit passes.

"We're a nice lot to flap about governing the Planet," De Forest laughed. "I confess, now it's all over, that my main fear was I mightn't be able to pull it off without losing a life."

"I thought of that too," said Arnott; "but there's no death reported, and I've inquired everywhere. What are we supposed to do with our passengers? I've fed 'em."

"We're between two switches," De Forest drawled. "If we drop them in any place that isn't under the Board, the natives will make their presence an excuse for cutting out, same as Illinois did, and forcing the Board to take over. If we drop them in any place under the Board's control they'll be killed as soon as our backs are turned."

"If you say so," said Pirolo thoughtfully, "I can guarantee that they will become extinct in process of time, quite happily. What is their birth-rate now?"

"Go down and ask 'em," said De Forest.

"I think they might become nervous and tear me to bits," the philosopher of Foggia replied.

"Not really? Well?"

"Open the bilge-doors," said Takahira with a downward jerk of the thumb.

"Scarcely—after all the trouble we've taken to save 'em," said De Forest.

"Try London," Arnott suggested. "You could turn Satan himself loose there, and they'd only ask him to dinner."

"Good man! You've given me an idea. Vincent! Oh, Vincent!" He threw the General Communicator open so that we could all hear, and in a few minutes the chartroom filled with the rich, fruity voice of Leopold Vincent, who has purveyed all London her choicest amusements for the last thirty years. We answered with expectant grins, as though we were actually in the stalls of, say, the Combination on a first night.

"We've picked up something in your line," De Forest began.

"That's good, dear man. if it's old enough. There's nothing to beat the old things for business purposes. Have you seen London, Chatham, and Dover at Earl's Court? No? I thought I missed you there. Im-mense! I've had the real steam locomotive engines built from the old designs and the iron rails cast specially by hand. Cloth cushions in the carriages, too! Im-mense! And paper railway tickets. And Polly Milton."

"Polly Milton back again!" said Arnott rapturously. "Book me two stalls for to-morrow night. What's she singing now, bless her?"

"The old songs. Nothing comes up to the old touch. Listen to this, dear men." Vincent carolled with flourishes:

> Oh, cruel lamps of London,
> If tears your light could drown,
> Your victims' eyes would weep them,
> Oh, lights of London Town!

"Then they weep."

"You see?" Pirolo waved his hands at us. "The old world always weeped when it saw crowds together. It did not know why, but it weeped. We know why, but we do not weep, except when we pay to be made to by fat, wicked old Vincent."

"Old, yourself!" Vincent laughed. "I'm a public benefactor, I keep the world soft and united."

"And I'm De Forest of the Board," said De Forest acidly, "trying to get a little business done. As I was saying, I've picked up a few people in Chicago."

"I cut out. Chicago is—"

"Do listen! They're perfectly unique."

"Do they build houses of baked mud blocks while you wait—eh? That's an old contact."

"They're an untouched primitive community, with all the old ideas."

"Sewing-machines and maypole-dances? Cooking on coal-gas stoves, lighting pipes with matches, and driving horses? Gerolstein tried that last year. An absolute blow-out!"

De Forest plugged him wrathfully, and poured out the story of our doings for the last twenty-four hours on the top-note.

"And they do it all in public," he concluded. "You can't stop 'em. The more public, the better they are pleased. They'll talk for hours—like you! Now you can come in again!"

"Do you really mean they know how to vote?" said Vincent. "Can they act it?"

"Act? It's their life to 'em! And you never saw such faces! Scarred like volcanoes. Envy, hatred, and malice in plain sight. Wonderfully flexible voices. They weep, too."

"Aloud? In public?"

"I guarantee. Not a spark of shame or reticence in the entire installation. It's the chance of your career."

"D'you say you've brought their voting props along—those papers and ballot—box things?"

"No, confound you! I'm not a luggage-lifter. Apply direct to the Mayor of Chicago. He'll forward you everything. Well?"

"Wait a minute. Did Chicago want to kill 'em? That 'ud look well on the Communicators."

"Yes! They were only rescued with difficulty from a howling mob—if you know what that is."

"But I don't," answered the Great Vincent simply.

"Well then, they'll tell you themselves. They can make speeches hours long."

"How many are there?"

"By the time we ship 'em all over they'll be perhaps a hundred, counting children. An old world in miniature. Can't you see it?"

"M-yes; but I've got to pay for it if it's a blow-out, dear man."

"They can sing the old war songs in the streets. They can get word-drunk, and make crowds, and invade privacy in the genuine old-fashioned way; and they'll do the voting trick as often as you ask 'em a question."

"Too good!" said Vincent.

"You unbelieving Jew! I've got a dozen head aboard here. I'll put you through direct. Sample 'em yourself."

He lifted the switch and we listened. Our passengers on the lower deck at once, but not less than five at a time, explained themselves to Vincent. They had been taken from the bosom of their families, stripped of their possessions, given food without finger-bowls, and cast into captivity in a noisome dungeon.

"But look here," said Arnott aghast; "they're saying what isn't true. My lower deck isn't noisome, and I saw to the finger-bowls myself."

"My people talk like that sometimes in Little Russia," said Dragomiroff. "We reason with them. We never kill. No!"

"But it's not true," Arnott insisted. "What can you do with people who don't tell facts? They're mad!"

"Hsh!" said Pirolo, his hand to his ear. "It is such a little time since all the Planet told lies."

We heard Vincent silkily sympathetic. Would they, he asked, repeat their assertions in public—before a vast public? Only let Vincent give them a chance, and the Planet, they vowed, should ring with their wrongs. Their aim in life—two women and a man explained it together—was to reform the world. Oddly enough, this also had been Vincent's life-dream. He offered them an arena in which to explain, and by their living example to raise the Planet to loftier levels. He was eloquent on the moral uplift of a simple, old-world life presented in its entirety to a deboshed civilisation.

Could they—would they—for three months certain, devote themselves under his auspices, as missionaries, to the elevation of mankind at a place called Earl's Court, which he said, with some truth, was one of the intellectual centres of the Planet? They thanked him, and demanded (we could hear his chuckle of delight) time to discuss and to vote on the matter. The vote, solemnly managed by counting heads—one head, one vote—was favourable. His offer, therefore, was accepted, and they moved a vote of thanks to him in two speeches—one by what they called the "proposer" and the other by the "seconder."

Vincent threw over to us, his voice shaking with gratitude:

"I've got 'em! Did you hear those speeches? That's Nature, dear men. Art can't teach that. And they voted as easily as lying. I've never had a troupe of natural liars before. Bless you, dear men! Remember, you're on my free lists for ever, anywhere—all of you. Oh, Gerolstein will be sick—sick!"

"Then you think they'll do?" said De Forest.

"Do? The Little Village'll go crazy! I'll knock up a series of old—world plays for 'em. Their voices will make you laugh and cry. My God, dear men, where do you suppose they picked up all their misery from, on this sweet earth? I'll have a pageant of the world's beginnings, and Mosenthal shall do the music. I'll—"

"Go and knock up a village for 'em by to-night. We'll meet you at No. 15 West Landing Tower," said De Forest. "Remember the rest will be coming along to-morrow."

"Let 'em all come!" said Vincent. "You don't know how hard it is nowadays even for me, to find something that really gets under the public's damned iridium-plated hide. But I've got it at last. Good-bye!"

"Well," said De Forest when we had finished laughing, "if any one understood corruption in London I might have played off Vincent against Gerolstein, and sold my captives at enormous prices. As it is, I shall have to be their legal adviser to-night when the contracts are signed. And they won't exactly press any commission on me, either."

"Meantime," said Takahira, "we cannot, of course, confine members of Leopold Vincent's last-engaged company. Chairs for the ladies, please, Arnott."

"Then I go to bed," said De Forest. "I can't face any more women!" And he vanished.

When our passengers were released and given another meal (finger-bowls came first this time) they told us what they thought of us and the Board; and, like Vincent, we all marvelled how they had contrived to extract and secrete so much bitter poison and unrest out of the good life God gives us. They raged, they stormed, they palpitated, flushed and exhausted their poor, torn nerves, panted themselves into silence, and renewed the senseless, shameless attacks.

"But can't you understand," said Pirolo pathetically to a shrieking woman, "that if we'd left you in Chicago you'd have been killed?"

"No, we shouldn't. You were bound to save us from being murdered."

"Then we should have had to kill a lot of other people."

"That doesn't matter. We were preaching the Truth. You can't stop us. We shall go on preaching in London; and then you'll see!"

"You can see now," said Pirolo, and opened a lower shutter.

We were closing on the Little Village, with her three Million people spread out at ease inside her ring of girdling Main-Traffic lights—those eight fixed beams at Chatham, Tonbridge, Redhill, Dorking, Woking, St. Albans, Chipping Ongar, and Southend.

Leopold Vincent's new company looked, with small pale faces, at the silence, the size, and the separated houses.

Then some began to weep aloud, shamelessly—always without shame.

MACDONOUGH'S SONG

Whether the State can loose and bind
  In Heaven as well as on Earth:
If it be wiser to kill mankind
  Before or after the birth—
These are matters of high concern
  Where State-kept school men are;
But Holy State (we have lived to learn)
  Endeth in Holy War.

Whether The People be led by the Lord,
  Or lured by the loudest throat:
If it be quicker to die by the sword
  Or cheaper to die by vote—
These are the things we have dealt with once,
  (And they will not rise from their grave)
For Holy People, however it runs,
  Endeth in wholly Slave.

Whatsoever, for any cause,
  Seeketh to take or give,
Power above or beyond the Laws,
  Suffer it not to live!
Holy State or Holy King—
  Or Holy People's Will—
Have no truck with the senseless thing.
  Order the guns and kill!

Saying—after—me:—

Once there was The People—Terror gave it birth;
Once there was The People and it made a Hell of Earth.
Earth arose and crushed it. Listen, O ye slain!
Once There was The People—it shall never be again!

◆❖◆

THE RED ONE

Jack London

JACK LONDON (1876-1916) was an American writer in the naturalism tradition, writing extensively about Man's relationship to Nature as well as Man's relation to his own animal nature. He was practically self-taught and studied all of the sciences and philosophies of his day and was one of the few writers of the time to make a living publishing commercial fiction. He wrote nearly 20 stories of recognizable science fiction and two novels, *Before Adam* (1906) and *The Iron Heel* (1907). He is known for one of the greatest of American short stories, "To Build a Fire" and his masterpiece, *The Call of the Wild.*

THERE it was! The abrupt liberation of sound! As he timed it with his watch, Bassett likened it to the trump of an archangel. Walls of cities, he meditated, might well fall down before so vast and compelling a summons. For the thousandth time vainly he tried to analyse the tone-quality of that enormous peal that dominated the land far into the strong-holds of the surrounding tribes. The mountain gorge which was its source rang to the rising tide of it until it brimmed over and flooded earth and sky and air. With the wantonness of a sick man's fancy, he likened it to the mighty cry of some Titan of the Elder World vexed with misery or wrath. Higher and higher it arose, challenging and demanding in such profounds of volume that it seemed intended for ears beyond the narrow confines of the solar system. There was in it, too, the clamour of protest in that there were no ears to hear and comprehend its utterance.

—Such the sick man's fancy. Still he strove to analyse the sound. Sonorous as thunder was it, mellow as a golden bell, thin and sweet as a thrummed taut cord of silver—no; it was none of these, nor a blend of these. There were no words nor semblances in his vocabulary and experience with which to describe the totality of that sound.

Time passed. Minutes merged into quarters of hours, and quarters of hours into half-hours, and still the sound persisted, ever changing from its initial vocal impulse yet never receiving fresh impulse—fading, dimming, dying as enormously as it had sprung into being. It became a confusion of troubled mutterings and babblings and colossal whisperings. Slowly it withdrew, sob by sob, into whatever great bosom had birthed it, until it whimpered deadly whispers of wrath and as equally seductive whispers of delight, striving still to be heard, to convey some cosmic secret, some understanding of infinite import and value. It dwindled to a ghost of sound that had lost its menace and promise, and became a thing that pulsed on in the sick man's consciousness for minutes after it had ceased. When he could hear it no longer, Bassett glanced at his watch. An hour had elapsed ere that archangel's trump had subsided into tonal nothingness.

Was this, then, HIS dark tower?—Bassett pondered, remembering his Browning and gazing at his skeleton-like and fever-wasted hands. And the fancy made him smile—of Childe Roland bearing a slug-horn to his lips with an arm as feeble as his was. Was it months, or years, he asked himself, since he first heard that mysterious call on the beach at Ringmanu? To save himself he could not tell. The long sickness had been most long. In conscious count of time he knew of months, many of them; but he had no way of estimating the long intervals of delirium and stupor. And how fared Captain Bateman of the blackbirder NARI? he wondered; and had Captain Bateman's drunken mate died of delirium tremens yet?

From which vain speculations, Bassett turned idly to review all that had occurred since that day on the beach of Ringmanu when he first heard the sound and plunged into the jungle after it. Sagawa had protested. He could see him yet, his queer little monkeyish face eloquent with fear, his back burdened with specimen cases, in his hands Bassett's butterfly net and naturalist's shot-gun, as he quavered, in Beche-de-mer English: "Me fella too much fright along bush. Bad fella boy, too much stop'm along bush."

Bassett smiled sadly at the recollection. The little New Hanover boy had been frightened, but had proved faithful, following him without hesitancy into the bush in the quest after the source of the wonderful sound. No fire-hollowed tree-trunk, that, throbbing war through the jungle depths, had been Bassett's conclusion. Erroneous had been his next conclusion, namely, that the source or cause could not be more distant than an hour's walk, and that he would easily be back by mid-afternoon to be picked up by the NARI'S whale-boat.

"That big fella noise no good, all the same devil-devil," Sagawa had adjudged. And Sagawa had been right. Had he not had his head hacked off within the day? Bassett shuddered. Without doubt Sagawa had been eaten as well by the "bad fella boys too much" that stopped along the bush. He could see him, as he had last seen him, stripped of the shot-gun and all the naturalist's gear of his master, lying on the narrow trail where he had been decapitated barely the moment before. Yes, within a minute the thing had happened. Within a minute, looking back, Bassett had seen him trudging patiently along under his burdens. Then Bassett's own trouble had come upon him. He looked at the cruelly healed stumps of the first and second fingers of his left hand, then rubbed them softly into the indentation in the back of his skull. Quick as had been the flash of the long handled tomahawk, he had been quick enough to duck away his head and partially to deflect the stroke with his up-flung hand. Two fingers and a hasty scalp-wound had been the price he paid for his life. With one barrel of his ten—gauge shot-gun he had blown the life out of the bushman who had so nearly got him; with the other barrel he had peppered the bushmen bending over Sagawa, and had the pleasure of knowing that the major portion of the charge had gone into the one who leaped away with Sagawa's head. Everything had occurred in a flash. Only himself, the slain bushman, and what remained of Sagawa, were in the narrow, wild-pig run of a path. From the dark jungle on either side came no rustle of movement or sound of life. And he had suffered distinct and dreadful shock. For the first time in his life he had killed a human being, and he knew nausea as he contemplated the mess of his handiwork.

Then had begun the chase. He retreated up the pig-run before his hunters, who were between him and the beach. How many there were, he could not guess. There might have been one, or a hundred, for aught he saw of them. That some of them took to the trees and travelled along through the jungle roof he was certain; but at the most he never glimpsed more than an occasional flitting of shadows. No bowstrings twanged that he could hear; but every little while, whence discharged he knew not, tiny arrows whispered past him or struck tree-boles and fluttered to the ground beside him. They were bone-tipped and feather shafted, and the feathers, torn from the breasts of humming-birds, iridesced like jewels.

Once—and now, after the long lapse of time, he chuckled gleefully at the recollection—he had detected a shadow above him that came to instant rest as he turned his gaze upward. He could make out nothing, but, deciding to chance it, had fired at it a heavy charge of number five shot. Squalling like an infuriated cat, the shadow crashed down through tree-ferns and orchids and thudded upon the earth at his feet, and, still squalling its rage and pain, had sunk its human teeth into the ankle of his stout tramping boot. He, on the other hand, was not idle, and with his free foot had done what reduced the squalling to silence. So inured to savagery has Bassett since become, that he chuckled again with the glee of the recollection.

What a night had followed! Small wonder that he had accumulated such a virulence and variety of fevers, he thought, as he recalled that sleepless night of torment, when the throb of his wounds was as nothing compared with the myriad stings of the mosquitoes. There had been no escaping them, and he had not dared to light a fire. They had literally pumped his body full of poison, so that, with the coming of day, eyes swollen almost shut, he had stumbled blindly on, not caring much when his head should be hacked off and his carcass started on the way of Sagawa's to the cooking fire. Twenty-four hours had made a wreck of him—of mind as well as body. He had scarcely retained his wits at all, so maddened was he by the tremendous inoculation of poison he had received. Several times he fired his shot-gun with effect into the shadows that dogged him. Stinging day insects and gnats added to his torment, while his bloody wounds attracted hosts of loathsome flies that clung sluggishly to his flesh and had to be brushed off and crushed off.

Once, in that day, he heard again the wonderful sound, seemingly more distant, but rising imperiously above the nearer war-drums in the bush. Right there was where he had made his mistake. Thinking that he had passed beyond it and that, therefore, it was between him and the beach of Ringmanu, he had worked back toward it when in reality he was penetrating deeper and deeper into the mysterious heart of the unexplored island. That night, crawling in among the twisted roots of a banyan tree, he had slept from exhaustion while the mosquitoes had had their will of him.

Followed days and nights that were vague as nightmares in his memory. One clear vision he remembered was of suddenly finding himself in the midst of a bush village and watching the old men and children fleeing into the jungle. All had fled but one. From close at hand and above him, a whimpering as of some animal in pain and terror had startled him. And looking up he had seen her—a girl, or young woman rather, suspended by one arm in the cooking sun. Perhaps for days she had so hung. Her swollen, protruding tongue spoke as much. Still alive, she gazed at him with eyes of terror. Past help, he decided, as he noted the swellings of her legs which advertised that the joints had been crushed and the great bones broken. He resolved to shoot her, and there the vision terminated. He could not remember whether he had or not, any more than could he remember how he chanced to be in that village, or how he succeeded in getting away from it.

Many pictures, unrelated, came and went in Bassett's mind as he reviewed that period of his terrible wanderings. He remembered invading another village of a dozen houses and driving all before him with his shot-gun save, for one old man, too feeble to flee, who spat at him and whined and snarled as he dug open a ground-oven and from amid the hot stones dragged forth a roasted pig that steamed its essence deliciously through its green-leaf wrappings. It was at this place that a wantonness of savagery had seized upon him. Having feasted, ready to depart with a hind-quarter of the pig in his hand, he deliberately fired the grass thatch of a house with his burning glass.

But seared deepest of all in Bassett's brain, was the dank and noisome jungle. It actually stank with evil, and it was always twilight. Rarely did a shaft of sunlight penetrate its matted roof a hundred feet overhead. And beneath that roof was an aerial ooze of vegetation, a monstrous, parasitic dripping of decadent life—forms that rooted in death and lived on death. And through all this he drifted, ever pursued by the flitting shadows of the anthropophagi, themselves ghosts of evil that dared not face him in battle but that knew that, soon or late, they would feed on him. Bassett remembered that at the time, in lucid moments, he had likened himself to a wounded bull pursued by plains' coyotes too cowardly to battle with him for the meat of him, yet certain of the inevitable end of him when they would be full gorged. As the bull's horns and stamping hoofs kept off the coyotes, so his shot—gun kept off these Solomon Islanders, these twilight shades of bushmen of the island of Guadalcanal.

Came the day of the grass lands. Abruptly, as if cloven by the sword of God in the hand of God, the jungle terminated. The edge of it, perpendicular and as black as the infamy of it, was a hundred feet up and down. And, beginning at the edge of it, grew the grass—sweet, soft, tender, pasture grass that would have delighted the eyes and beasts of any husbandman and that extended, on and on, for leagues and leagues of velvet verdure, to the backbone of the great island, the towering mountain range flung up by some ancient earth-cataclysm, serrated and gullied but not yet erased by the erosive tropic rains. But the grass! He had crawled into it a dozen yards, buried his face in it, smelled it, and broken down in a fit of involuntary weeping.

And, while he wept, the wonderful sound had pealed forth—if by PEAL, he had often thought since, an adequate description could be given of the enunciation of so vast a sound melting sweet. Sweet it was, as no sound ever heard. Vast it was, of so mighty a resonance that it might have proceeded from some brazen-throated monster. And yet it called to him across that leagues-wide savannah, and was like a benediction to his long-suffering, pain racked spirit.

He remembered how he lay there in the grass, wet-cheeked but no longer sobbing, listening to the sound and wondering that he had been able to hear it on the beach of Ringmanu. Some freak of air pressures and air currents, he reflected, had made it possible for the sound to carry so far. Such conditions might not happen again in a thousand days or ten thousand days, but the one day it had happened had been the day he landed from the NARI for several hours' collecting. Especially had he been in quest of the famed jungle butterfly, a foot across from wing-tip to wing-tip, as velvet-dusky of lack of colour as was the gloom of the roof, of such lofty arboreal habits that it resorted only to the jungle roof and could be brought down only by a dose of shot. It was for this purpose that Sagawa had carried the ten-gauge shot-gun.

Two days and nights he had spent crawling across that belt of grass land. He had suffered much, but pursuit had ceased at the jungle—edge. And he would have died of thirst had not a heavy thunderstorm revived him on the second day.

And then had come Balatta. In the first shade, where the savannah yielded to the dense mountain jungle, he had collapsed to die. At first she had squealed with delight at sight of his helplessness, and was for beating his brain out with a stout forest branch. Perhaps it was his very utter helplessness that had appealed to her, and perhaps it was her human curiosity that made her refrain. At any rate, she had refrained, for he opened his eyes again under the impending blow, and saw her studying him intently. What especially struck her about him were his blue eyes and white skin. Coolly she had squatted on her hams, spat on his arm, and with her finger-tips scrubbed away the dirt of days and nights of muck and jungle that sullied the pristine whiteness of his skin.

And everything about her had struck him especially, although there was nothing conventional about her at all. He laughed weakly at the recollection, for she had been as innocent of garb as Eve before the fig-leaf adventure. Squat and lean at the same time, asymmetrically limbed, string-muscled as if with lengths of cordage, dirt-caked from infancy save for casual showers, she was as unbeautiful a prototype of woman as he, with a scientist's eye, had ever gazed upon. Her breasts advertised at the one time her maturity and youth; and, if by nothing else, her sex was advertised by the one article of finery with which she was adorned, namely a pig's tail, thrust though a hole in her left ear-lobe. So lately had the tail been severed, that its raw end still oozed blood that dried upon her shoulder like so much candle-droppings. And her face! A twisted and wizened complex of apish features, perforated by upturned, sky-open, Mongolian nostrils, by a mouth that sagged from a huge upper-lip and faded precipitately into a retreating chin, by peering querulous eyes that blinked as blink the eyes of denizens of monkey-cages.

Not even the water she brought him in a forest-leaf, and the ancient and half-putrid chunk of roast pig, could redeem in the slightest the grotesque hideousness of her. When he had eaten weakly for a space, he closed his eyes in order not to see her, although again and again she poked them open to peer at the blue of them. Then had come the sound. Nearer, much nearer, he knew it to be; and he knew equally well, despite the weary way he had come, that it was still many hours distant. The effect of it on her had been startling. She cringed under it, with averted face, moaning and chattering with fear. But after it had lived its full life of an hour, he closed his eyes and fell asleep with Balatta brushing the flies from him.

When he awoke it was night, and she was gone. But he was aware of renewed strength, and, by then too thoroughly inoculated by the mosquito poison to suffer further inflammation, he closed his eyes and slept an unbroken stretch till sun-up. A little later Balatta had returned, bringing with her a half-dozen women who, unbeautiful as they were, were patently not so unbeautiful as she. She evidenced by her conduct that she considered him her find, her property, and the pride she took in showing him off would have been ludicrous had his situation not been so desperate.

Later, after what had been to him a terrible journey of miles, when he collapsed in front of the devil-devil house in the shadow of the breadfruit tree, she had shown very lively ideas on the matter of retaining possession of him. Ngurn, whom Bassett was to know afterward as the devil-devil doctor, priest, or medicine man of the village, had wanted his head. Others of the grinning and chattering monkey-men, all as stark of clothes and bestial of appearance as Balatta, had wanted his body for the roasting oven. At that time he had not understood their language, if by LANGUAGE might be dignified the uncouth sounds they made to represent ideas. But Bassett had thoroughly understood the matter of debate, especially when the men pressed and prodded and felt of the flesh of him as if he were so much commodity in a butcher's stall.

Balatta had been losing the debate rapidly, when the accident happened. One of the men, curiously examining Bassett's shot-gun, managed to cock and pull a trigger. The recoil of the butt into the pit of the man's stomach had not been the most sanguinary result, for the charge of shot, at a distance of a yard, had blown the head of one of the debaters into nothingness.

Even Balatta joined the others in flight, and, ere they returned, his senses already reeling from the oncoming fever-attack, Bassett had regained possession of the gun. Whereupon, although his teeth chattered with the ague and his swimming eyes could scarcely see, he held on to his fading consciousness until he could intimidate the bushmen with the simple magics of compass, watch, burning glass, and matches. At the last, with due emphasis, of solemnity and awfulness, he had killed a young pig with his shot-gun and promptly fainted.

Bassett flexed his arm-muscles in quest of what possible strength might reside in such weakness, and dragged himself slowly and totteringly to his feet. He was shockingly emaciated; yet, during the various convalescences of the many months of his long sickness, he had never regained quite the same degree of strength as this time. What he feared was another relapse such as he had already frequently experienced. Without drugs, without even quinine, he had managed so far to live through a combination of the most pernicious and most malignant of malarial and black-water fevers. But could he continue to endure? Such was his everlasting query. For, like the genuine scientist he was, he would not be content to die until he had solved the secret of the sound.

Supported by a staff, he staggered the few steps to the devil-devil house where death and Ngurn reigned in gloom. Almost as infamously dark and evil-stinking as the jungle was the devil-devil house—in Bassett's opinion. Yet therein was usually to be found his favourite crony and gossip, Ngurn, always willing for a yarn or a discussion, the while he sat in the ashes of death and in a slow smoke shrewdly revolved curing human heads suspended from the rafters. For, through the months' interval of consciousness of his long sickness, Bassett had mastered the psychological simplicities and lingual difficulties of the language of the tribe of Ngurn and Balatta and Vngngn—the latter the addle-headed young chief who was ruled by Ngurn, and who, whispered intrigue had it, was the son of Ngurn.

"Will the Red One speak to-day?" Bassett asked, by this time so accustomed to the old man's gruesome occupation as to take even an interest in the progress of the smoke-curing.

With the eye of an expert Ngurn examined the particular head he was at work upon.

"It will be ten days before I can say 'finish,'" he said. "Never has any man fixed heads like these."

Bassett smiled inwardly at the old fellow's reluctance to talk with him of the Red One. It had always been so. Never, by any chance, had Ngurn or any other member of the weird tribe divulged the slightest hint of any physical characteristic of the Red One. Physical the Red One must be, to emit the wonderful sound, and though it was called the Red One, Bassett could not be sure that red represented the colour of it. Red enough were the deeds and powers of it, from what abstract clues he had gleaned. Not alone, had

Ngurn informed him, was the Red One more bestial powerful than the neighbour tribal gods, ever athirst for the red blood of living human sacrifices, but the neighbour gods themselves were sacrificed and tormented before him. He was the god of a dozen allied villages similar to this one, which was the central and commanding village of the federation. By virtue of the Red One many alien villages had been devastated and even wiped out, the prisoners sacrificed to the Red One. This was true to-day, and it extended back into old history carried down by word of mouth through the generations. When he, Ngurn, had been a young man, the tribes beyond the grass lands had made a war raid. In the counter raid, Ngurn and his fighting folk had made many prisoners. Of children alone over five score living had been bled white before the Red One, and many, many more men and women.

The Thunderer was another of Ngurn's names for the mysterious deity. Also at times was he called The Loud Shouter, The God—Voiced, The Bird-Throated, The One with the Throat Sweet as the Throat of the Honey-Bird, The Sun Singer, and The Star-Born.

Why The Star-Born? In vain Bassett interrogated Ngurn. According to that old devil-devil doctor, the Red One had always been, just where he was at present, for ever singing and thundering his will over men. But Ngurn's father, wrapped in decaying grass-matting and hanging even then over their heads among the smoky rafters of the devil-devil house, had held otherwise. That departed wise one had believed that the Red One came from out of the starry night, else why—so his argument had run—had the old and forgotten ones passed his name down as the Star-Born? Bassett could not but recognize something cogent in such argument. But Ngurn affirmed the long years of his long life, wherein he had gazed upon many starry nights, yet never had he found a star on grass land or in jungle depth—and he had looked for them. True, he had beheld shooting stars (this in reply to Bassett's contention); but likewise had he beheld the phosphorescence of fungoid growths and rotten meat and fireflies on dark nights, and the flames of wood—fires and of blazing candle-nuts; yet what were flame and blaze and glow when they had flamed and blazed and glowed? Answer: memories, memories only, of things which had ceased to be, like memories of matings accomplished, of feasts forgotten, of desires that were the ghosts of desires, flaring, flaming, burning, yet unrealized in achievement of easement and satisfaction. Where was the appetite of yesterday? the roasted flesh of the wild pig the hunter's arrow failed to slay? the maid, unwed and dead ere the young man knew her?

A memory was not a star, was Ngurn's contention. How could a memory be a star? Further, after all his long life he still observed the starry night-sky unaltered. Never had he noted the absence of a single star from its accustomed place. Besides, stars were fire, and the Red One was not fire—which last involuntary betrayal told Bassett nothing.

"Will the Red One speak to-morrow?" he queried.

Ngurn shrugged his shoulders as who should say.

"And the day after?—and the day after that?" Bassett persisted.

"I would like to have the curing of your head," Ngurn changed the subject. "It is different from any other head. No devil-devil has a head like it. Besides, I would cure it well. I would take months and months. The moons would come and the moons would go, and the smoke would be very slow, and I should myself gather the materials for the curing smoke. The skin would not wrinkle. It would be as smooth as your skin now."

He stood up, and from the dim rafters, grimed with the smoking of countless heads, where day was no more than a gloom, took down a matting-wrapped parcel and began to open it.

"It is a head like yours," he said, "but it is poorly cured."

Bassett had pricked up his ears at the suggestion that it was a white man's head; for he had long since come to accept that these jungle-dwellers, in the midmost centre of the great island, had never had intercourse with white men. Certainly he had found them without the almost universal beche-de-mer English of the west South Pacific. Nor had they knowledge of tobacco, nor of gunpowder. Their few precious knives, made from lengths of hoop-iron, and their few and more precious tomahawks from cheap trade hatchets, he had surmised they had captured in war from the bushmen of the jungle beyond the grass lands, and that they, in turn, had similarly gained them from the salt-water men who fringed the coral beaches of the shore and had contact with the occasional white men.

"The folk in the out beyond do not know how to cure heads," old Ngurn explained, as he drew forth from the filthy matting and placed in Bassett's hands an indubitable white man's head.

Ancient it was beyond question; white it was as the blond hair attested. He could have sworn it once belonged to an Englishman, and to an Englishman of long before by token of the heavy gold circlets still threaded in the withered ear-lobes.

"Now your head..." the devil-devil doctor began on his favourite topic.

"I'll tell you what," Bassett interrupted, struck by a new idea. "When I die I'll let you have my head to cure, if, first, you take me to look upon the Red One."

"I will have your head anyway when you are dead," Ngurn rejected the proposition. He added, with the brutal frankness of the savage: "Besides, you have not long to live. You are almost a dead man now. You will grow less strong. In not many months I shall have you here turning and turning in the smoke. It is pleasant, through the long afternoons, to turn the head of one you have known as well as I know you. And I shall talk to you and tell you the many secrets you want to know. Which will not matter, for you will be dead."

"Ngurn," Bassett threatened in sudden anger. "You know the Baby Thunder in the Iron that is mine." (This was in reference to his all-potent and all-awful shotgun.) "I can kill you any time, and then you will not get my head."

"Just the same, will Vngngn, or some one else of my folk get it," Ngurn complacently assured him. "And just the same will it turn here in the and turn devil-devil house in the smoke. The quicker you slay me with your Baby Thunder, the quicker will your head turn in the smoke."

And Bassett knew he was beaten in the discussion.

What was the Red One?—Bassett asked himself a thousand times in the succeeding week, while he seemed to grow stronger. What was the source of the wonderful sound? What was this Sun Singer, this Star-Born One, this mysterious deity, as bestial-conducted as the black and kinky-headed and monkey-like human beasts who worshipped it, and whose silver-sweet, bull-mouthed singing and commanding he had heard at the taboo distance for so long?

Ngurn had he failed to bribe with the inevitable curing of his head when he was dead. Vngngn, imbecile and chief that he was, was too imbecilic, too much under the sway of Ngurn, to be considered. Remained Balatta, who, from the time she found him and poked his blue eyes open to recrudescence of her grotesque female hideousness, had continued his adorer. Woman she was, and he had long known that the only way to win from her treason of her tribe was through the woman's heart of her.

Bassett was a fastidious man. He had never recovered from the initial horror caused by Balatta's female awfulness. Back in England, even at best the charm of woman, to him, had never been robust. Yet now, resolutely, as only a man can do who is capable of martyring himself for the cause of science, he proceeded to violate all the fineness and delicacy of his nature by making love to the unthinkably disgusting bushwoman.

He shuddered, but with averted face hid his grimaces and swallowed his gorge as he put his arm around her dirt-crusted shoulders and felt the contact of her rancidoily and kinky hair with his neck and chin. But he nearly screamed when she succumbed to that caress so at the very first of the courtship and mowed and gibbered and squealed little, queer, pig-like gurgly noises of delight. It was too much. And the next he did in the singular courtship was to take her down to the stream and give her a vigorous scrubbing.

From then on he devoted himself to her like a true swain as frequently and for as long at a time as his will could override his repugnance. But marriage, which she ardently suggested, with due observance of tribal custom, he balked at. Fortunately, taboo rule was strong in the tribe. Thus, Ngurn could never touch bone, or flesh, or hide of crocodile. This had been ordained at his birth. Vngngn was denied ever the touch of woman. Such pollution, did it chance to occur, could be purged only by the death of the offending female. It had happened once, since Bassett's arrival, when a girl of nine, running in play, stumbled and fell against the sacred chief. And the girl-child was seen no more. In whispers, Balatta told Bassett that she had been three days and nights in dying before the Red One. As for Balatta, the breadfruit was taboo to her. For which Bassett was thankful. The taboo might have been water.

For himself, he fabricated a special taboo. Only could he marry, he explained, when the Southern Cross rode highest in the sky. Knowing his astronomy, he thus gained a reprieve of nearly nine months; and he was confident that within that time he would either be dead or escaped to the coast with full knowledge of the Red One and of the source of the Red One's wonderful voice. At first he had fancied the Red One to be some colossal statue, like Memnon, rendered vocal under certain temperature conditions of sunlight. But when, after a war raid, a batch of prisoners was brought in and the sacrifice made at night, in the midst of rain, when the sun could play no part, the Red One had been more vocal than usual, Bassett discarded that hypothesis.

In company with Balatta, sometimes with men and parties of women, the freedom of the jungle was his for three quadrants of the compass. But the fourth quadrant, which contained the Red One's abiding place, was taboo. He made more thorough love to Balatta—also saw to it that she scrubbed herself more frequently. Eternal female she was, capable of any treason for the sake of love. And, though the sight of her was provocative of nausea and the contact of her provocative of despair, although he could not escape her awfulness in his dream-haunted nightmares of her, he nevertheless was aware of the cosmic verity of sex that animated her and that made her own life of less value than the happiness of her lover with whom she hoped to mate. Juliet or Balatta? Where was the intrinsic difference? The soft and tender product of ultra—civilization, or her bestial prototype of a hundred thousand years before her?—there was no difference.

Bassett was a scientist first, a humanist afterward. In the jungle-heart of Guadalcanal he put the affair to the test, as in the laboratory he would have put to the test any chemical reaction. He increased his feigned ardour for the bushwoman, at the same time increasing the imperiousness of his will of desire over her to be led to look upon the Red One face to face. It was the old story, he recognized, that the woman must pay, and it occurred when the two of them, one day, were catching the unclassified and unnamed little black fish, an inch long, half-eel and half-scaled, rotund with salmon-golden roe, that frequented the fresh water, and that were esteemed, raw and whole, fresh or putrid, a perfect delicacy. Prone in the muck of the decaying jungle-floor, Balatta threw herself, clutching his ankles with her hands kissing his feet and making slubbery noises that chilled his backbone up and down again. She begged him to kill her rather than exact this ultimate love—payment. She told him of the penalty of breaking the taboo of the Red One—a week of torture, living, the details of which she yammered out from her face in the mire until he realized that he was yet a tyro in knowledge of the frightfulness the human was capable of wreaking on the human.

Yet did Bassett insist on having his man's will satisfied, at the woman's risk, that he might solve the mystery of the Red One's singing, though she should die long and horribly and screaming. And Balatta, being mere woman, yielded. She led him into the forbidden quadrant. An abrupt mountain, shouldering in from the north to meet a similar intrusion from the south, tormented the stream in which they had fished into a deep and gloomy gorge. After a mile along the gorge, the way plunged sharply upward until they crossed a saddle of raw limestone which attracted his geologist's eye. Still climbing, although he paused often from sheer physical weakness, they scaled forest-clad heights until they emerged on a naked mesa or tableland. Bassett recognized the stuff of its composition as black volcanic sand, and knew that a pocket magnet could have captured a full load of the sharply angular grains he trod upon.

And then holding Balatta by the hand and leading her onward, he came to it—a tremendous pit, obviously artificial, in the heart of the plateau. Old history, the South Seas Sailing Directions, scores of remembered data and connotations swift and furious, surged through his brain. It was Mendana who had discovered the islands and named them Solomon's, believing that he had found that monarch's fabled mines. They had laughed at the old navigator's child-like credulity; and yet here stood himself, Bassett, on the rim of an excavation for all the world like the diamond pits of South Africa.

But no diamond this that he gazed down upon. Rather was it a pearl, with the depth of iridescence of a pearl; but of a size all pearls of earth and time, welded into one, could not have totalled; and of a colour undreamed of in any pearl, or of anything else, for that matter, for it was the colour of the Red One. And the Red One himself Bassett knew it to be on the instant. A perfect sphere, full two hundred feet in diameter, the top of it was a hundred feet below the level of the rim. He likened the colour quality of it to lacquer. Indeed, he took it to be some sort of lacquer, applied by man, but a lacquer too marvellously clever to have been manufactured by the bush-folk. Brighter than bright cherry-red, its richness of colour was as if it were red builded upon red. It glowed and iridesced in the sunlight as if gleaming up from underlay under underlay of red.

In vain Balatta strove to dissuade him from descending. She threw herself in the dirt; but, when he continued down the trail that spiralled the pit-wall, she followed, cringing and whimpering her terror. That the red sphere had been dug out as a precious thing, was patent. Considering the paucity of members of the federated twelve villages and their primitive tools and methods, Bassett knew that the toil of a myriad generations could scarcely have made that enormous excavation.

He found the pit bottom carpeted with human bones, among which, battered and defaced, lay village gods of wood and stone. Some, covered with obscene totemic figures and designs, were carved from solid tree trunks forty or fifty feet in length. He noted the absence of the shark and turtle gods, so common among the shore villages, and was amazed at the constant recurrence of the helmet motive. What did these jungle savages of the dark heart of Guadalcanal know of helmets? Had Mendana's men-at-arms worn helmets and penetrated here centuries before? And if not, then whence had the bush-folk caught the motive?

Advancing over the litter of gods and bones, Balatta whimpering at his heels, Bassett entered the shadow of the Red One and passed on under its gigantic overhang until he touched it with his finger-tips. No lacquer that. Nor was the surface smooth as it should have been in the case of lacquer. On the contrary, it was corrugated and pitted, with here and there patches that showed signs of heat and fusing. Also, the substance of it was metal, though unlike any metal, or combination of metals, he had ever known. As for the colour itself, he decided it to be no application. It was the intrinsic colour of the metal itself.

He moved his finger-tips, which up to that had merely rested, along the surface, and felt the whole gigantic sphere quicken and live and respond. It was incredible! So light a touch on so vast a mass! Yet did it quiver under the finger-tip caress in rhythmic vibrations that became whisperings and rustlings and mutterings of sound—but of sound so different; so elusively thin that it was shimmeringly sibilant; so mellow that it was maddening sweet, piping like an elfin horn, which last was just what Bassett decided would be like a peal from some bell of the gods reaching earthward from across space.

He looked at Balatta with swift questioning; but the voice of the Red One he had evoked had flung her face downward and moaning among the bones. He returned to contemplation of the prodigy. Hollow it was, and of no metal known on earth, was his conclusion. It was right-named by the ones of old-time as the Star-Born. Only from the stars could it have come, and no thing of chance was it. It was a creation of artifice and mind. Such perfection of form, such hollowness that it certainly possessed, could not be the result of mere fortuitousness. A child of intelligences, remote and unguessable, working corporally in metals, it indubitably was. He stared at it in amaze, his brain a racing wild-fire of hypotheses to account for this far-journeyer who had adventured the night of space, threaded the stars, and now rose before him and above him, exhumed by patient anthropophagi, pitted and lacquered by its fiery bath in two atmospheres.

But was the colour a lacquer of heat upon some familiar metal? Or was it an intrinsic quality of the metal itself? He thrust in the blue-point of his pocket-knife to test the constitution of the stuff. Instantly the entire sphere burst into a mighty whispering, sharp with protest, almost twanging goldenly, if a whisper could possibly be considered to twang, rising higher, sinking deeper, the two extremes of the registry of sound threatening to complete the circle and coalesce into the bull-mouthed thundering he had so often heard beyond the taboo distance.

Forgetful of safety, of his own life itself, entranced by the wonder of the unthinkable and unguessable thing, he raised his knife to strike heavily from a long stroke, but was prevented by Balatta. She upreared on her own knees in an agony of terror, clasping his knees and supplicating him to desist. In the intensity of her desire to impress him, she put her forearm between her teeth and sank them to the bone.

He scarcely observed her act, although he yielded automatically to his gentler instincts and withheld the knife-hack. To him, human life had dwarfed to microscopic proportions before this colossal portent of higher life from within the distances of the sidereal universe. As had she been a dog, he kicked the ugly little bushwoman to her feet and compelled her to start with him on an encirclement of the base. Part way around, he encountered horrors. Even, among the others, did he recognize the sun-shrivelled remnant of the nine-years girl who had accidentally broken Chief Vngngn's personality taboo. And, among what was left of these that had passed, he encountered what was left of one who had not yet passed. Truly had the bush-folk named themselves into the name of the Red One, seeing in him their own image which they strove to placate and please with such red offerings.

Farther around, always treading the bones and images of humans and gods that constituted the floor of this ancient charnel-house of sacrifice, he came upon the device by which the Red One was made to send his call singing thunderingly across the jungle-belts and grass-lands to the far beach of Ringmanu. Simple and primitive was it as was the Red One's consummate artifice. A great king-post, half a hundred feet in length, seasoned by centuries of superstitious care, carven into dynasties of gods, each superimposed, each helmeted, each seated in the open mouth of a crocodile, was slung by ropes, twisted of climbing vegetable parasites, from the apex of a tripod of three great forest trunks, themselves carved into grinning and grotesque adumbrations of man's modern concepts of art and god. From the striker king-post, were suspended ropes of climbers to which men could apply their strength and direction. Like a battering ram, this king-post could be driven end-onward against the mighty red-iridescent sphere.

Here was where Ngurn officiated and functioned religiously for himself and the twelve tribes under him. Bassett laughed aloud, almost with madness, at the thought of this wonderful messenger, winged with intelligence across space, to fall into a bushman stronghold and be worshipped by ape-like, man-eating and head—hunting savages. It was as if God's World had fallen into the muck mire of the abyss underlying the bottom of hell; as if Jehovah's Commandments had been presented on carved stone to the monkeys of the monkey cage at the Zoo; as if the Sermon on the Mount had been preached in a roaring bedlam of lunatics.

The slow weeks passed. The nights, by election, Bassett spent on the ashen floor of the devil-devil house, beneath the ever—swinging, slow-curing heads. His reason for this was that it was taboo to the lesser sex of woman, and therefore, a refuge for him from Balatta, who grew more persecutingly and perilously lovely as the Southern Cross rode higher in the sky and marked the imminence of her nuptials. His days Bassett spent in a hammock swung under the shade of the great breadfruit tree before the devil-devil house. There were breaks in this programme, when, in the comas of his devastating fever-attacks, he lay for days and nights in the house of heads. Ever he struggled to combat the fever, to live, to continue to live, to grow strong and stronger against the day when he would be strong enough to dare the grass-lands and the belted jungle beyond, and win to the beach, and to some labour-recruiting, black-birding ketch or schooner, and on to civilization and the men of civilization, to whom he could give news of the message from other worlds that lay, darkly worshipped by beastmen, in the black heart of Guadalcanal's midmost centre.

On the other nights, lying late under the breadfruit tree, Bassett spent long hours watching the slow setting of the western stars beyond the black wall of jungle where it had been thrust back by the clearing for the village. Possessed of more than a cursory knowledge of astronomy, he took a sick man's pleasure in speculating as to the dwellers on the unseen worlds of those incredibly remote suns, to haunt whose houses of light, life came forth, a shy visitant, from the rayless crypts of matter. He could no more apprehend limits to time than bounds to space. No subversive radium speculations had shaken his steady scientific faith in the conservation of energy and the indestructibility of matter. Always and forever must there have been stars. And surely, in that cosmic ferment, all must be comparatively alike, comparatively of the same substance, or substances, save for the freaks of the ferment. All must obey, or compose, the same laws that ran without infraction through the entire experience of man. Therefore, he argued and agreed, must worlds and life be appanages to all the suns as they were appanages to the particular of his own solar system.

Even as he lay here, under the breadfruit tree, an intelligence that stared across the starry gulfs, so must all the universe be exposed to the ceaseless scrutiny of innumerable eyes, like his, though grantedly different, with behind them, by the same token, intelligences that questioned and sought the meaning and the construction of the whole. So reasoning, he felt his soul go forth in kinship with that august company, that multitude whose gaze was forever upon the arras of infinity.

Who were they, what were they, those far distant and superior ones who had bridged the sky with their gigantic, red-iridescent, heaven-singing message? Surely, and long since, had they, too, trod the path on which man had so recently, by the calendar of the cosmos, set his feet. And to be able to send a message across the pit of space, surely they had reached those heights to which man, in tears and travail and bloody sweat, in darkness and confusion of many counsels, was so slowly struggling. And what were they on their heights? Had they won Brotherhood? Or had they learned that the law of love imposed the penalty of weakness and decay? Was strife, life? Was the rule of all the universe the pitiless rule of natural selection? And, and most immediately and poignantly, were their far conclusions, their long-won wisdoms, shut even then in the huge, metallic heart of the Red One, waiting for the first earth-man to read? Of one thing he was certain: No drop of red dew shaken from the lion-mane of some sun in torment, was the sounding sphere. It was of design, not chance, and it contained the speech and wisdom of the stars.

What engines and elements and mastered forces, what lore and mysteries and destiny-controls, might be there! Undoubtedly, since so much could be enclosed in so little a thing as the foundation stone of a public building, this enormous sphere should contain vast histories, profounds of research achieved beyond man's wildest guesses, laws and formulae that, easily mastered, would make man's life on earth, individual and collective, spring up from its present mire to inconceivable heights of purity and power. It was Time's greatest gift to blindfold, insatiable, and sky-aspiring man. And to him, Bassett, had been vouchsafed the lordly fortune to be the first to receive this message from man's interstellar kin!

No white man, much less no outland man of the other bush-tribes, had gazed upon the Red One and lived. Such the law expounded by Ngurn to Bassett. There was such a thing as blood brotherhood. Bassett, in return, had often argued in the past. But Ngurn had stated solemnly no. Even the blood brotherhood was outside the favour of the Red One. Only a man born within the tribe could look upon the Red One and live. But now, his guilty secret known only to Balatta, whose fear of immolation before the Red One fast-sealed her lips, the situation was different. What he had to do was to recover from the abominable fevers that weakened him, and gain to civilization. Then would he lead an expedition back, and, although the entire population of Guadalcanal he destroyed, extract from the heart of the Red One the message of the world from other worlds.

But Bassett's relapses grew more frequent, his brief convalescences less and less vigorous, his periods of coma longer, until he came to know, beyond the last promptings of the optimism inherent in so tremendous a constitution as his own, that he would never live to cross the grass lands, perforate the perilous coast jungle, and reach the sea. He faded as the Southern Cross rose higher in the sky, till even Balatta knew that he would be dead ere the nuptial date determined by his taboo. Ngurn made pilgrimage personally and gathered the smoke materials for the curing of Bassett's head, and to him made proud announcement and exhibition of the artistic perfectness of his intention when Bassett should be dead. As for himself, Bassett was not shocked. Too long and too deeply had life ebbed down in him to bite him with fear of its impending extinction. He continued to persist, alternating periods of unconsciousness with periods of semi-consciousness, dreamy and unreal, in which he idly wondered whether he had ever truly beheld the Red One or whether it was a nightmare fancy of delirium.

Came the day when all mists and cob-webs dissolved, when he found his brain clear as a bell, and took just appraisement of his body's weakness. Neither hand nor foot could he lift. So little control of his body did he have, that he was scarcely aware of possessing one. Lightly indeed his flesh sat upon his soul, and his soul, in its briefness of clarity, knew by its very clarity that the black of cessation was near. He knew the end was close; knew that in all truth he had with his eyes beheld the Red One, the messenger between the worlds; knew that he would never live to carry that message to the world—that message, for aught to the contrary, which might already have waited man's hearing in the heart of Guadalcanal for ten thousand years. And Bassett stirred with resolve, calling Ngurn to him, out under the shade of the breadfruit tree, and with the old devil-devil doctor discussing the terms and arrangements of his last life effort, his final adventure in the quick of the flesh.

"I know the law, O Ngurn," he concluded the matter. "Whoso is not of the folk may not look upon the Red One and live. I shall not live anyway. Your young men shall carry me before the face of the Red One, and I shall look upon him, and hear his voice, and thereupon die, under your hand, O Ngurn. Thus will the three things be satisfied: the law, my desire, and your quicker possession of my head for which all your preparations wait."

To which Ngurn consented, adding:

"It is better so. A sick man who cannot get well is foolish to live on for so little a while. Also is it better for the living that he should go. You have been much in the way of late. Not but what it was good for me to talk to such a wise one. But for moons of days we have held little talk. Instead, you have taken up room in the house of heads, making noises like a dying pig, or talking much and loudly in your own language which I do not understand. This has been a confusion to me, for I like to think on the great things of the light and dark as I turn the heads in the smoke. Your much noise has thus been a disturbance to the long-learning and hatching of the final wisdom that will be mine before I die. As for you, upon whom the dark has already brooded, it is well that you die now. And I promise you, in the long days to come when I turn your head in the smoke, no man of the tribe shall come in to disturb us. And I will tell you many secrets, for I am an old man and very wise, and I shall be adding wisdom to wisdom as I turn your head in the smoke."

So a litter was made, and, borne on the shoulders of half a dozen of the men, Bassett departed on the last little adventure that was to cap the total adventure, for him, of living. With a body of which he was scarcely aware, for even the pain had been exhausted out of it, and with a bright clear brain that accommodated him to a quiet ecstasy of sheer lucidness of thought, he lay back on the lurching litter and watched the fading of the passing world, beholding for the last time the breadfruit tree before the devil—devil house, the dim day beneath the matted jungle roof, the gloomy gorge between the shouldering mountains, the saddle of raw limestone, and the mesa of black volcanic sand.

Down the spiral path of the pit they bore him, encircling the sheening, glowing Red One that seemed ever imminent to iridesce from colour and light into sweet singing and thunder. And over bones and logs of immolated men and gods they bore him, past the horrors of other immolated ones that yet lived, to the three-king—post tripod and the huge king-post striker.

Here Bassett, helped by Ngurn and Balatta, weakly sat up, swaying weakly from the hips, and with clear, unfaltering, all-seeing eyes gazed upon the Red One.

"Once, O Ngurn," he said, not taking his eyes from the sheening, vibrating surface whereon and wherein all the shades of cherry-red played unceasingly, ever a-quiver to change into sound, to become silken rustlings, silvery whisperings, golden thrummings of cords, velvet pipings of elfland, mellow distances of thunderings.

"I wait," Ngurn prompted after a long pause, the long-handled tomahawk unassumingly ready in his hand.

"Once, O Ngurn," Bassett repeated, "let the Red One speak so that I may see it speak as well as hear it. Then strike, thus, when I raise my hand; for, when I raise my hand, I shall drop my head forward and make place for the stroke at the base of my neck. But, O Ngurn, I, who am about to pass out of the light of day for ever, would like to pass with the wonder-voice of the Red One singing greatly in my ears."

"And I promise you that never will a head be so well cured as yours," Ngurn assured him, at the same time signalling the tribesmen to man the propelling ropes suspended from the king-post striker. "Your head shall be my greatest piece of work in the curing of heads."

Bassett smiled quietly to the old one's conceit, as the great carved log, drawn back through two-score feet of space, was released. The next moment he was lost in ecstasy at the abrupt and thunderous liberation of sound. But such thunder! Mellow it was with preciousness of all sounding metals. Archangels spoke in it; it was magnificently beautiful before all other sounds; it was invested with the intelligence of supermen of planets of other suns; it was the voice of God, seducing and commanding to be heard. And—the everlasting miracle of that interstellar metal! Bassett, with his own eyes, saw colour and colours transform into sound till the whole visible surface of the vast sphere was a-crawl and titillant and vaporous with what he could not tell was colour or was sound. In that moment the interstices of matter were his, and the interfusings and intermating transfusings of matter and force.

Time passed. At the last Bassett was brought back from his ecstasy by an impatient movement of Ngurn. He had quite forgotten the old devil-devil one. A quick flash of fancy brought a husky chuckle into Bassett's throat. His shot-gun lay beside him in the litter. All he had to do, muzzle to head, was to press the trigger and blow his head into nothingness.

But why cheat him? was Bassett's next thought. Head-hunting, cannibal beast of a human that was as much ape as human, nevertheless Old Ngurn had, according to his lights, played squarer than square. Ngurn was in himself a forerunner of ethics and contract, of consideration, and gentleness in man. No, Bassett decided; it would be a ghastly pity and an act of dishonour to cheat the old fellow at the last. His head was Ngurn's, and Ngurn's head to cure it would be.

And Bassett, raising his hand in signal, bending forward his head as agreed so as to expose cleanly the articulation to his taut spinal cord, forgot Balatta, who was merely a woman, a woman merely and only and undesired. He knew, without seeing, when the razor—edged hatchet rose in the air behind him. And for that instant, ere the end, there fell upon Bassett the shadows of the Unknown, a sense of impending marvel of the rending of walls before the imaginable. Almost, when he knew the blow had started and just ere the edge of steel bit the flesh and nerves it seemed that he gazed upon the serene face of the Medusa, Truth—And, simultaneous with the bite of the steel on the onrush of the dark, in a flashing instant of fancy, he saw the vision of his head turning slowly, always turning, in the devil-devil house beside the breadfruit tree.

◆❖◆

FRIEND ISLAND

Francis Stevens

GERTRUDE BARROWS BENNET (1884-1948) who wrote under the pseudonym of Francis Stevens, is generally considered the first major female writer in science fiction and fantasy. Stevens wrote mostly what we'd now call dark fantasy. She wrote several successful novels, short stories and novellas, with "Friend Island" being her most famous. Her fiction is generally believed to give rise to the kind of fantasy that H.P. Lovecraft and A. Merritt would write for Weird Tales. She stopped writing in 1925 for personal reasons and soon became forgotten. "Friend Island", rediscovered and reprinted in 1970 by science fiction critic Sam Moskowitz, means that Stevens now is getting the attention she deserves.

IT was upon the waterfront that I first met her, in one of the shabby little tea shops frequented by able sailoresses of the poorer type. The uptown, glittering resorts of the Lady Aviators' Union were not for such as she.

Stern of feature, bronzed by wind and sun, her age could only be guessed, but I surmised at once that in her I beheld a survivor of the age of turbines and oil engines—a true sea-woman of that elder time when woman's superiority to man had not been so long recognized. When, to emphasize their victory, women in all ranks were sterner than today's need demands.

The spruce, smiling young maidens—engine-women and stokers of the great aluminum rollers, but despite their profession, very neat in gold-braided blue knickers and boleros—these looked askance at the hard-faced relic of a harsher day, as they passed in and out of the shop.

I, however, brazenly ignoring similar glances at myself, a mere male intruding on the haunts of the world's ruling sex, drew a chair up beside the veteran. I ordered a full pot of tea, two cups and a plate of macaroons, and put on my most ingratiating air. Possibly my unconcealed admiration and interest were wiles not exercised in vain. Or the macaroons and tea, both excellent, may have loosened the old sea-woman's tongue. At any rate, under cautious questioning, she had soon launched upon a series of reminiscences well beyond my hopes for color and variety.

"When I was a lass," quoth the sea-woman, after a time, "there was none of this high-flying, gilt-edged, leather-stocking luxury about the sea. We sailed by the power of our oil and gasoline. If they failed on us, like as not 'twas the rubber ring and the rolling wave for ours."

She referred to the archaic practice of placing a pneumatic affair called a life-preserver beneath the arms, in case of that dreaded disaster, now so unheard of, shipwreck.

"In them days there was still many a man bold enough to join our crews. And I've knowed cases," she added condescendingly, "where just by the muscle and brawn of such men some poor sailor lass has reached shore alive that would have fed the sharks without 'em. Oh, I ain't so down on men as you might think. It's the spoiling of them that I don't hold with. There's too much preached nowadays that man is fit for nothing but to fetch and carry and do nurse-work in big child-homes. To my mind, a man who hasn't the nerve of a woman ain't fitted to father children, let alone raise 'em. But that's not here nor there. My time's past, and I know it, or I wouldn't be setting here gossipin' to you, my lad, over an empty teapot."

I took the hint, and with our cups replenished, she bit thoughtfully into her fourteenth macaroon and continued.

"There's one voyage I'm not likely to forget, though I live to be as old as Cap'n Mary Barnacle, of the Shouter. 'Twas aboard the old Shouter that this here voyage occurred, and it was her last and likewise Cap'n Mary's. Cap'n Mary, she was then that decrepit, it seemed a mercy that she should go to her rest, and in good salt water at that.

"I remember the voyage for Cap'n Mary's sake, but most I remember it because 'twas then that I come the nighest in my life to committin' matrimony. For a man, the man had nerve; he was nearer bein' companionable than any other man I ever seed; and if it hadn't been for just one little event that showed up the—the mannishness of him, in a way I couldn't abide, I reckon he'd be keepin' house for me this minute."

"We cleared from Frisco with a cargo of silkateen petticoats for Brisbane. Cap'n Mary was always strong on petticoats. Leather breeches or even half-skirts would ha' paid far better, they being more in demand like, but Cap'n Mary was three-quarters owner, and says she, land women should buy petticoats, and if they didn't it wouldn't be the Lord's fault nor hers for not providing 'em.

"We cleared on a fine day, which is an all sign—or was, then when the weather and the seas o' God still counted in the trafficking of the humankind. Not two days out we met a whirling, mucking bouncer of a gale that well nigh threw the old Shouter a full point off her course in the first wallop. She was a stout craft, though. None of your featherweight, gas-lightened, paper-thin alloy shells, but toughened aluminum from stern to stern. Her turbine drove her through the combers at a forty-five knot clip, which named her a speedy craft for a freighter in them days.

"But this night, as we tore along through the creaming green billows, something unknown went 'way wrong down below.

"I was forward under the shelter of her long over-sloop, looking for a hairpin I'd dropped somewheres about that afternoon. It was a gold hairpin, and gold still being mighty scarce when I was a girl, a course I valued it. But suddenly I felt the old Shouter give a jump under my feet like a plane struck by a shell in full flight. Then she trembled all over for a full second, frightened like. Then, with the crash of doomsday ringing in my ears, I felt myself sailing through the air right into the teeth o' the shrieking gale, as near as I could judge. Down I come in the hollow of a monstrous big wave, and as my ears doused under I thought I heard a splash close by. Coming up, sure enough, there close by me was floating a new, patent, hermetic, thermo-ice-chest. Being as it was empty, and being as it was shut up air-tight, that ice-chest made as sweet a life-preserver as a woman could wish in such an hour. About ten foot by twelve, it floated high in the raging sea. Out on its top I scrambled, and hanging on by a handle I looked expectant for some of my poor fellow-women to come floating by. Which they never did, for the good reason that the Shouter had blowed up and went below, petticoats, Cap'n Mary and all."

"What caused the explosion?" I inquired.

"The Lord and Cap'n Mary Barnacle can explain," she answered piously. "Besides the oil for her turbines, she carried a power of gasoline for her alternative engines, and likely 'twas the cause of her ending so sudden like. Anyways, all I ever seen of her again was the empty ice-chest that Providence had well-nigh hove upon my head. On that I sat and floated, and floated and sat some more, till by-and-by the storm sort of blowed itself out, the sun come shining—this was next morning—and I could dry my hair and look about me. I was a young lass, then, and not bad to look upon. I didn't want to die, any more than you that's sitting there this minute. So I up and prays for land. Sure enough toward evening a speck heaves up low down on the horizon. At first I took it for a gas liner, but later found it was just a little island, all alone by itself in the great Pacific Ocean.

"Come, now, here's luck, thinks I, and with that I deserts the ice-chest, which being empty, and me having no ice to put in it, not likely to have in them latitudes, is of no further use to me. Striking out I swum a mile or so and set foot on dry land for the first time in nigh three days.

"Pretty land it were, too, though bare of human life as an iceberg in the Arctic.

"I had landed on a shining white beach that run up to a grove of lovely, waving palm trees. Above them I could see the slopes of a hill so high and green it reminded me of my own old home, up near Couquomgomoc Lake in Maine. The whole place just seemed to smile and smile at me. The palms waved and bowed in the sweet breeze, like they wanted to say, 'Just set right down and make yourself to home. We've been waiting a long time for you to come.' I cried, I was that happy to be made welcome. I was a young lass then, and sensitive-like to how folks treated me. You're laughing now, but wait and see if or not there was sense to the way I felt.

"So I up and dries my clothes and my long, soft hair again, which was well worth drying, for I had far more of it than now. After that I walked along a piece, until there was a sweet little path meandering away into the wild woods.

"Here, thinks I, this looks like inhabitants. Be they civil or wild, I wonder? But after traveling the path a piece, lo and behold it ended sudden like in a wide circle of green grass, with a little spring of clear water. And the first thing I noticed was a slab of white board nailed to a palm tree close to the spring. Right off I took a long drink, for you better believe I was thirsty, and then I went to look at this board. It had evidently been tore off the side of a wooden packing box, and the letters was roughly printed in lead pencil.

"'Heaven help whoever you be,' I read. 'This island ain't just right. I'm going to swim for it. You better too. Good-by. Nelson Smith.'

That's what it said, but the spellin' was simply awful. It all looked quite new and recent, as if Nelson Smith hadn't more than a few hours before he wrote and nailed it there.

"Well, after reading that queer warning I begun to shake all over like in a chill. Yes, I shook like I had the ague, though the hot tropic sun was burning down right on me and that alarming board. What had scared Nelson Smith so much that he had swum to get away? I looked all around real cautious and careful, but not a single frightening thing could I behold. And the palms and the green grass and the flowers still smiled that peaceful and friendly like. 'Just make yourself to home,' was wrote all over the place in plainer letters than those sprawly lead pencil ones on the board.

"Pretty soon, what with the quiet and all, the chill left me. Then I thought, 'Well, to be sure, this Smith person was just an ordinary man, I reckon, and likely he got nervous of being so alone. Likely he just fancied things which was really not. It's a pity he drowned himself before I come, though likely I'd have found him poor company. By his record I judge him a man of but common education.'

"So I decided to make the most of my welcome, and that I did for weeks to come. Right near the spring was a cave, dry as a biscuit box, with a nice floor of white sand. Nelson had lived there too, for there was a litter of stuff—tin cans—empty—scraps of newspapers and the like. I got to calling him Nelson in my mind, and then Nelly, and wondering if he was dark or fair, and how he come to be cast away there all alone, and what was the strange events that drove him to his end. I cleaned out the cave, though. He had devoured all his tin-canned provisions, however he come by them, but this I didn't mind. That there island was a generous body. Green milk-coconuts, sweet berries, turtle eggs and the like was my daily fare.

"For about three weeks the sun shone every day, the birds sang and the monkeys chattered. We was all one big, happy family, and the more I explored that island the better I liked the company I was keeping. The land was about ten miles from beach to beach, and never a foot of it that wasn't sweet and clean as a private park.

"From the top of the hill I could see the ocean, miles and miles of blue water, with never a sign of a gas liner, or even a little government running-boat. Them running-boats used to go most everywhere to keep the seaways clean of derelicts and the like. But I knowed that if this island was no more than a hundred miles off the regular courses of navigation, it might be many a long day before I'd be rescued. The top of the hill, as I found when first I climbed up there, was a wore-out crater. So I knowed that the island was one of them volcanic ones you run across so many of in the seas between Capricorn and Cancer.

"Here and there on the slopes and down through the jungly tree-growth, I would come on great lumps of rock, and these must have came up out of that crater long ago. If there was lava it was so old it had been covered up entire with green growing stuff. You couldn't have found it without a spade, which I didn't have nor want."

"Well, at first I was happy as the hours was long. I wandered and clambered and waded and swum, and combed my long hair on the beach, having fortunately not lost my side-combs nor the rest of my gold hairpins. But by-and-by it begun to get just a bit lonesome. Funny thing, that's a feeling that, once it starts, it gets worse and worser so quick it's perfectly surprising. And right then was when the days begun to get gloomy. We had a long, sickly hot spell, like I never seen before on an ocean island. There was dull clouds across the sun from morn to night. Even the little monkeys and parrakeets, that had seemed so gay, moped and drowsed like they was sick. All one day I cried, and let the rain soak me through and through—that was the first rain we had—and I didn't get thorough dried even during the night, though I slept in my cave. Next morning I got up mad as thunder at myself and all the world.

"When I looked out the black clouds was billowing across the sky. I could hear nothing but great breakers roaring in on the beaches, and the wild wind raving through the lashing palms.

"As I stood there a nasty little wet monkey dropped from a branch almost on my head. I grabbed a pebble and slung it at him real vicious. 'Get away, you dirty little brute!' I shrieks, and with that there come a awful blinding flare of light. There was a long, crackling noise like a bunch of Chinese fireworks, and then a sound as if a whole fleet of Shouters had all went up together.

"When I come to, I found myself 'way in the back of my cave, trying to dig further into the rock with my finger nails. Upon taking thought, it come to me that what had occurred was just a lightning-clap, and going to look, sure enough there lay a big palm tree right across the glade. It was all busted and split open by the lightning, and the little monkey was under it, for I could see his tail and his hind legs sticking out.

"Now, when I set eyes on that poor, crushed little beast I'd been so mean to, I was terrible ashamed. I sat down on the smashed tree and considered and considered. How thankful I had ought to have been. Here I had a lovely, plenteous island, with food and water to my taste, when it might have been a barren, starvation rock that was my lot. And so, thinking, a sort of gradual peaceful feeling stole over me. I got cheerfuller and cheerfuller, till I could have sang and danced for joy.

"Pretty soon I realized that the sun was shining bright for the first time that week. The wind had stopped hollering, and the waves had died to just a singing murmur on the beach. It seemed kind o' strange, this sudden peace, like the cheer in my own heart after its rage and storm. I rose up, feeling sort of queer, and went to look if the little monkey had came alive again, though that was a fool thing, seeing he was laying all crushed up and very dead. I buried him under a tree root, and as I did it a conviction come to me.

"I didn't hardly question that conviction at all. Somehow, living there alone so long, perhaps my natural womanly intuition was stronger than ever before or since, and so I knowed. Then I went and pulled poor Nelson Smith's board off from the tree and tossed it away for the tide to carry off. That there board was an insult to my island!"

The sea-woman paused, and her eyes had a far-away look. It seemed as if I and perhaps even the macaroons and tea were quite forgotten.

"Why did you think that?" I asked, to bring her back. "How could an island be insulted?"

She started, passed her hand across her eyes, and hastily poured another cup of tea.

"Because," she said at last, poising a macaroon in mid-air, "because that island—that particular island that I had landed on—had a heart!

"When I was gay, it was bright and cheerful. It was glad when I come, and it treated me right until I got that grouchy it had to mope from sympathy. It loved me like a friend. When I flung a rock at that poor little drenched monkey critter, it backed up my act with an anger like the wrath o' God, and killed its own child to please me! But it got right cheery the minute I seen the wrongness of my ways. Nelson Smith had no business to say, 'This island ain't just right,' for it was a righter place than ever I seen elsewhere. When I cast away that lying board, all the birds begun to sing like mad. The green milk-coconuts fell right and left. Only the monkeys seemed kind o' sad like still, and no wonder. You see, their own mother, the island, had rounded on one o' them for my sake!

"After that I was right careful and considerate. I named the island Anita, not knowing her right name, or if she had any. Anita was a pretty name, and it sounded kind of South Sea like. Anita and me got along real well together from that day on. It was some strain to be always gay and singing around like a dear duck of a canary bird, but I done my best. Still, for all the love and gratitude I bore Anita, the company of an island, however sympathetic, ain't quite enough for a human being. I still got lonesome, and there was even days when I couldn't keep the clouds clear out of the sky, though I will say we had no more tornadoes.

"I think the island understood and tried to help me with all the bounty and good cheer the poor thing possessed. None the less my heart give a wonderful big leap when one day I seen a blot on the horizon. It drawed nearer and nearer, until at last I could make out its nature."

"A ship, of course," said I, "and were you rescued?"

"'Tweren't a ship, neither," denied the sea-woman somewhat impatiently. "Can't you let me spin this yarn without no more remarks and fool questions? This thing what was bearing down so fast with the incoming tide was neither more nor less than another island!

"You may well look startled. I was startled myself. Much more so than you, likely. I didn't know then what you, with your book-learning, very likely know now—that islands sometimes float. Their underparts being a tangled-up mess of roots and old vines that new stuff's growed over, they sometimes break away from the mainland in a brisk gale and go off for a voyage, calm as a old-fashioned, eight-funnel steamer. This one was uncommon large, being as much as two miles, maybe, from shore to shore. It had its palm trees and its live things, just like my own Anita, and I've sometimes wondered if this drifting piece hadn't really been a part of my island once—just its daughter like, as you might say.

"Be that, however, as it might be, no sooner did the floating piece get within hailing distance than I hears a human holler and there was a man dancing up and down on the shore like he was plumb crazy. Next minute he had plunged into the narrow strip of water between us and in a few minutes had swum to where I stood.

"Yes, of course it was none other than Nelson Smith!

"I knowed that the minute I set eyes on him. He had the very look of not having no better sense than the man what wrote that board and then nearly committed suicide trying to get away from the best island in all the oceans. Glad enough he was to get back, though, for the coconuts was running very short on the floater what had rescued him, and the turtle eggs wasn't worth mentioning. Being short of grub is the surest way I know to cure a man's fear of the unknown."

"Well, to make a long story short, Nelson Smith told me he was a aeronauter. In them days to be an aeronauter was not the same as to be an aviatress is now. There was dangers in the air, and dangers in the sea, and he had met with both. His gas tank had leaked and he had dropped into the water close by Anita. A case or two of provisions was all he could save from the total wreck.

"Now, as you might guess, I was crazy enough to find out what had scared this Nelson Smith into trying to swim the Pacific. He told me a story that seemed to fit pretty well with mine, only when it come to the scary part he shut up like a clam, that aggravating way some men have. I give it up at last for just man-foolishness, and we begun to scheme to get away.

"Anita moped some while we talked it over. I realized how she must be feeling, so I explained to her that it was right needful for us to get with our kind again. If we stayed with her we should probably quarrel like cats, and maybe even kill each other out of pure human cussedness.

She cheered up considerable after that, and even, I thought, got a little anxious to have us leave. At any rate, when we begun to provision up the little floater, which we had anchored to the big island by a cable of twisted bark, the green nuts fell all over the ground, and Nelson found more turtle nests in a day than I had in weeks.

"During them days I really got fond of Nelson Smith. He was a companionable body, and brave, or he wouldn't have been a professional aeronauter, a job that was rightly thought tough enough for a woman, let alone a man. Though he was not so well educated as me, at least he was quiet and modest about what he did know, not like some men, boasting most where there is least to brag of.

"Indeed, I misdoubt if Nelson and me would not have quit the sea and the air together and set up housekeeping in some quiet little town up in New England, maybe, after we had got away, if it had not been for what happened when we went. I never, let me say, was so deceived in any man before nor since. The thing taught me a lesson and I never was fooled again.

"We was all ready to go, and then one morning, like a parting gift from Anita, come a soft and favoring wind. Nelson and I run down the beach together, for we didn't want our floater to blow off and leave us. As we was running, our arms full of coconuts, Nelson Smith, stubbed his bare toe on a sharp rock, and down he went. I hadn't noticed, and was going on.

"But sudden the ground begun to shake under my feet, and the air was full of a queer, grinding, groaning sound, like the very earth was in pain.

"I turned around sharp. There sat Nelson, holding his bleeding toe in both fists and giving vent to such awful words as no decent seagoing lady would ever speak nor hear to!

"'Stop it, stop it!' I shrieked at him, but 'twas too late.

"Island or no island, Anita was a lady, too! She had a gentle heart, but she knowed how to behave when she was insulted.

"With one terrible, great roar a spout of smoke and flame belched up out o' the heart of Anita's crater hill a full mile into the air!

"I guess Nelson stopped swearing. He couldn't have heard himself, anyways. Anita was talking now with tongues of flame and such roars as would have bespoke the raging protest of a continent.

"I grabbed that fool man by the hand and run him down to the water. We had to swim good and hard to catch up with our only hope, the floater. No bark rope could hold her against the stiff breeze that was now blowing, and she had broke her cable. By the time we scrambled aboard great rocks was falling right and left. We couldn't see each other for a while for the clouds of fine gray ash.

"It seemed like Anita was that mad she was flinging stones after us, and truly I believe that such was her intention. I didn't blame her, neither!

"Lucky for us the wind was strong and we was soon out of range.

"'So!' says I to Nelson, after I'd got most of the ashes out of my mouth, and shook my hair clear of cinders. 'So, that was the reason you up and left sudden when you was there before! You aggravated that island till the poor thing druv you out!'

"'Well,' says he, and not so meek as I'd have admired to see him, 'how could I know the darn island was a lady?'

"'Actions speak louder than words,' says I. 'You should have knowed it by her ladylike behavior!'

"'Is volcanoes and slingin' hot rocks ladylike?' he says. 'Is snakes ladylike? T'other time I cut my thumb on a tin can, I cussed a little bit. Say—just a li'l' bit! An' what comes at me out o' all the caves, and out o' every crack in the rocks, and out o' the very spring o' water where I'd been drinkin'? Why snakes! Snakes, if you please, big, little, green, red and sky-blue-scarlet! What'd I do? Jumped in the water, of course. Why wouldn't I? I'd ruther swim and drown than be stung or swallowed to death. But how was I t' know the snakes come outta the rocks because I cussed?'

"'You, couldn't,' I agrees, sarcastic. 'Some folks never knows a lady till she up and whangs 'em over the head with a brick. A real, gentle, kind-like warning, them snakes were, which you would not heed! Take shame to yourself, Nelly,' says I, right stern, 'that a decent little island like Anita can't associate with you peaceable, but you must hurt her sacredest feelings with language no lady would stand by to hear!'

"I never did see Anita again. She may have blew herself right out of the ocean in her just wrath at the vulgar, disgustin' language of Nelson Smith. I don't know. We was took off the floater at last, and I lost track of Nelson just as quick as I could when we was landed at Frisco.

"He had taught me a lesson. A man is just full of mannishness, and the best of 'em ain't good enough for a lady to sacrifice her sensibilities to put up with.

"Nelson Smith, he seemed to feel real bad when he learned I was not for him, and then he apologized. But apologies weren't no use to me. I could never abide him, after the way he went and talked right in the presence of me and my poor, sweet lady friend, Anita!"

Now I am well versed in the lore of the sea in all ages. Through mists of time I have enviously eyed wild voyagings of sea rovers who roved and spun their yarns before the stronger sex came into its own, and ousted man from his heroic pedestal. I have followed—across the printed page—the wanderings of Odysseus. Before Gulliver I have burned the incense of tranced attention; and with reverent awe considered the history of one Munchausen, a baron. But alas, these were only men!

In what field is not woman our subtle superior?

Meekly I bowed my head, and when my eyes dared lift again, the ancient mariness had departed, leaving me to sorrow for my surpassed and outdone idols. Also with a bill for macaroons and tea of such incredible proportions that in comparison therewith I found it easy to believe her story!

DAGON

H. P. Lovecraft

HOWARD PHILIPS LOVECRAFT (1890-1937), a recluse his entire life, became one of the greatest writers of horror fiction in American letters. He wrote extensively for Weird Tales, eventually devising his own mythos, centering around a creature called Cthulhu. He was fascinated with ancient cultures as well as cultures that might have come and gone long before civilization came into being. He had a "circle" of friends who became writers of note themselves: Robert E. Howard, Clarke Ashton Smith, August Derleth, Robert Bloch, Henry Kuttner, and E. Hoffman Price. Stephen King called Lovecraft his greatest influence.

I am writing this under an appreciable mental strain, since by tonight I shall be no more. Penniless, and at the end of my supply of the drug which alone, makes life endurable, I can bear the torture no longer; and shall cast myself from this garret window into the squalid street below. Do not think from my slavery to morphine that I am a weakling or a degenerate. When you have read these hastily scrawled pages you may guess, though never fully realise, why it is that I must have forgetfulness or death.

It was in one of the most open and least frequented parts of the broad Pacific that the packet of which I was supercargo fell a victim to the German sea-raider. The great war was then at its very beginning, and the ocean forces of the Hun had not completely sunk to their later degradation; so that our vessel was made legitimate prize, whilst we of her crew were treated with all the fairness and consideration due us as naval prisoners. So liberal, indeed, was the discipline of our captors, that five days after we were taken I managed to escape alone in a small boat with water and provisions for a good length of time.

When I finally found myself adrift and free, I had but little idea of my surroundings. Never a competent navigator, I could only guess vaguely by the sun and stars that I was somewhat south of the equator. Of the longitude I knew nothing, and no island or coast-line was in sight. The weather kept fair, and for uncounted days I drifted aimlessly beneath the scorching sun; waiting either for some passing ship, or to be cast on the shores of some habitable land. But neither ship nor land appeared, and I began to despair in my solitude upon the heaving vastnesses of unbroken blue.

The change happened whilst I slept. Its details I shall never know; for my slumber, though troubled and dream-infested, was continuous.

When at last I awaked, it was to discover myself half sucked into a slimy expanse of hellish black mire which extended about me in monotonous undulations as far as I could see, and in which my boat lay grounded some distance away.

Though one might well imagine that my first sensation would be of wonder at so prodigious and unexpected a transformation of scenery, I was in reality more horrified than astonished; for there was in the air and in the rotting soil a sinister quality which chilled me to the very core. The region was putrid with the carcasses of decaying fish, and of other less describable things which I saw protruding from the nasty mud of the unending plain. Perhaps I should not hope to convey in mere words the unutterable hideousness that can dwell in absolute silence and barren immensity. There was nothing within hearing, and nothing in sight save a vast reach of black slime; yet the very completeness of the stillness and homogeneity of the landscape oppressed me with a nauseating fear.

The sun was blazing down from a sky which seemed to me almost black in its cloudless cruelty; as though reflecting the inky marsh beneath my feet. As I crawled into the stranded boat I realised that only one theory could explain my position. Through some unprecedented volcanic upheaval, a portion of the ocean floor must have been thrown to the surface, exposing regions which for innumerable millions of years had lain hidden under unfathomable watery depths. So great was the extent of the new land which had risen beneath me, that I could not detect the faintest noise of the surging ocean, strain my ears as I might. Nor were there any sea-fowl to prey upon the dead things.

For several hours I sat thinking or brooding in the boat, which lay upon its side and afforded a slight shade as the sun moved across the heavens. As the day progressed, the ground lost some of its stickiness, and seemed likely to dry sufficiently for travelling purposes in a short time. That night I slept but little, and the next day I made for myself a pack containing food and water, preparatory to an overland journey in search of the vanished sea and possible rescue.

On the third morning I found the soil dry enough to walk upon with ease. The odour of the fish was maddening; but I was too much concerned with graver things to mind so slight an evil, and set out boldly for an unknown goal. All day I forged steadily westward, guided by a far-away hummock which rose higher than any other elevation on the rolling desert. That night I encamped, and on the following day still travelled toward the hummock, though that object seemed scarcely nearer than when I had first espied it. By the fourth evening I attained the base of the mound which turned out to be much higher than it had appeared from a distance, an intervening valley setting it out in sharper relief from the general surface. Too weary to ascend, I slept in the shadow of the hill.

I know not why my dreams were so wild that night; but ere the waning and fantastically gibbous moon had risen far above the eastern plain, I was awake in a cold perspiration, determined to sleep no more. Such visions as I had experienced were too much for me to endure again. And in the glow of the moon I saw how unwise I had been to travel by day. Without the glare of the parching sun, my journey would have cost me less energy; indeed, I now felt quite able to perform the ascent which had deterred me at sunset. Picking up my pack, I started for the crest of the eminence.

I have said that the unbroken monotony of the rolling plain was a source of vague horror to me; but I think my horror was greater when I gained the summit of the mound and looked down the other side into an immeasurable pit or canyon, whose black recesses the moon had not yet soared high enough to illuminate. I felt myself on the edge of the world; peering over the rim into a fathomless chaos of eternal night. Through my terror ran curious reminiscences of Paradise Lost, and of Satan's hideous climb through the unfashioned realms of darkness.

As the moon climbed higher in the sky, I began to see that the slopes of the valley were not quite so perpendicular as I had imagined. Ledges and outcroppings of rock afforded fairly easy foot-holds for a descent, whilst after a drop of a few hundred feet, the declivity became very gradual. Urged on by an impulse which I cannot definitely analyse, I scrambled with difficulty down the rocks and stood on the gentler slope beneath, gazing into the Stygian deeps where no light had yet penetrated.

All at once my attention was captured by a vast and singular object on the opposite slope, which rose steeply about a hundred yards ahead of me; an object that gleamed whitely in the newly bestowed rays of the ascending moon. That it was merely a gigantic piece of stone, I soon assured myself; but I was conscious of a distinct impression that its contour and position were not altogether the work of Nature. A closer scrutiny filled me with sensations I cannot express; for despite its enormous magnitude, and its position in an abyss which had yawned at the bottom of the sea since the world was young, I perceived beyond a doubt that the strange object was a well-shaped monolith whose massive bulk had known the workmanship and perhaps the worship of living and thinking creatures.

Dazed and frightened, yet not without a certain thrill of the scientist's or archaeologist's delight, I examined my surroundings more closely. The moon, now near the zenith, shone weirdly and vividly above the towering steeps that hemmed in the chasm, and revealed the fact that a far-flung body of water flowed at the bottom, winding out of sight in both directions, and almost lapping my feet as I stood on the slope. Across the chasm, the wavelets washed the base of the Cyclopean monolith; on whose surface I could now trace both inscriptions and crude sculptures. The writing was in a system of hieroglyphics unknown to me, and unlike anything I had ever seen in books; consisting for the most part of conventionalised aquatic symbols such as fishes, eels, octopi, crustaceans, molluscs, whales, and the like. Several characters obviously represented marine things which are unknown to the modern world, but whose decomposing forms I had observed on the ocean-risen plain.

It was the pictorial carving, however, that did most to hold me spellbound. Plainly visible across the intervening water on account of their enormous size, were an array of bas-reliefs whose subjects would have excited the envy of Doré. I think that these things were supposed to depict men—at least, a certain sort of men; though the creatures were shewn disporting like fishes in waters of some marine grotto, or paying homage at some monolithic shrine which appeared to be under the waves as well. Of their faces and forms I dare not speak in detail; for the mere remembrance makes me grow faint. Grotesque beyond the imagination of a Poe or a Bulwer, they were damnably human in general outline despite webbed hands and feet, shockingly wide and flabby lips, glassy, bulging eyes, and other features less pleasant to recall. Curiously enough, they seemed to have been chiselled badly out of proportion with their scenic background; for one of the creatures was shewn in the act of killing a whale represented as but little larger than himself. I remarked, as I say, their grotesqueness and strange size, but in a moment decided that they were merely the imaginary gods of some primitive fishing or seafaring tribe; some tribe whose last descendant had perished eras before the first ancestor of the Piltdown or Neanderthal Man was born. Awestruck at this unexpected glimpse into a past beyond the conception of the most daring anthropologist, I stood musing whilst the moon cast queer reflections on the silent channel before me.

Then suddenly I saw it. With only a slight churning to mark its rise to the surface, the thing slid into view above the dark waters. Vast, Polyphemus-like, and loathsome, it darted like a stupendous monster of nightmares to the monolith, about which it flung its gigantic scaly arms, the while it bowed its hideous head and gave vent to certain measured sounds. I think I went mad then.

Of my frantic ascent of the slope and cliff, and of my delirious journey back to the stranded boat, I remember little. I believe I sang a great deal, and laughed oddly when I was unable to sing. I have indistinct recollections of a great storm some time after I reached the boat; at any rate, I know that I heard peals of thunder and other tones which Nature utters only in her wildest moods.

When I came out of the shadows I was in a San Francisco hospital; brought thither by the captain of the American ship which had picked up my boat in mid-ocean. In my delirium I had said much, but found that my words had been given scant attention. Of any land upheaval in the Pacific, my rescuers knew nothing; nor did I deem it necessary to insist upon a thing which I knew they could not believe. Once I sought out a celebrated enthnologist, and amused him with peculiar questions regarding the ancient Philistine legend of Dagon, the Fish-God; but soon perceiving that he was hopelessly conventional, I did not press my inquiries.

It is at night, especially when the moon is gibbous and waning, that I see the thing. I tried morphine; but the drug has given only transient surcease, and has drawn me into its clutches as a hopeless slave. So now I am to end it all, having written a full account for the information or the contemptuous amusement of my fellow-men. Often I ask myself if it could not all have been a pure phantasm—a mere freak of fever as I lay sun-stricken and raving in the open boat after my escape from the German man-of-war. This I ask myself, but ever does there come before me a hideously vivid vision in reply. I cannot think of the deep sea without shuddering at the nameless things that may at this very moment be crawling and floundering on its slimy bed, worshipping their ancient stone idols and carving their own detestable likenesses on the submarine obelisks of water-soaked granite. I dream of a day when they may rise above the billows to drag down in their reeking talons the remnants of puny, war-exhausted mankind—of a day when the land shall sink, and the dark ocean floor shall ascend amidst universal pandemonium.

The end is near. I hear a noise at the door, as of some immense slippery body lumbering against it. It shall find me. God, that hand! The window! The window!

FESSENDEN'S WORLDS

Edmond Hamilton

EDMOND HAMILTON (1904-1977) began his science fiction career in the late 1920s, publishing first in Weird Tales then branching out to appear in just about every science fiction pulp magazine on the market. He is credited with helping define the "space opera" subgenre along with such writers as E. E. "Doc" Smith, Murray Leinster, and a young John W. Campbell, Jr. "Fessenden's Worlds" appeared in Weird Tales in 1937 and became an instant classic. Its central conceit has been used variously in episodes of *The Twilight Zone*, *The Simpsons*, and *South Park*.

I wish now that I'd never seen Fessenden's damnable experiment! I wish my cursed curiosity had never taken me into his laboratory that night, to witness the thing that destroyed my peace of mind forever and made me for the rest of my life a somber and soul-sick man.

Arnold Fessenden was the greatest scientist this planet ever produced—and the evilest. I *know!* I'd have told about it before, but I knew that I wouldn't be believed. He assured me of that himself, grinning with sardonic mirth at me, that night he showed me what I'd like to forget.

It was a dark, wet, windy night in late October when I climbed the porch of Fessenden's big stone house near the campus, and rang the bell. He lived there quite alone now, I knew. Even his housekeeper had finally declared that she couldn't stand his queer ways any longer.

He came to the door himself. His big, powerful figure bulking against the dimly lit hall inside, he stared out at me and said, "Oh, it's you, Bradley. What do you want?"

I told him, "That's a poor way to receive guests. I just came over to gab a little—haven't seen you around the campus lately."

He hesitated a moment, then said, "I'm sorry, Bradley—I haven't had many guests of late. Come on in."

I went in and sat down in the slovenly-looking living-room. Fessenden sat in a chair and looked across at me with a queer mocking light in his piercing black eyes, and a sardonic smile on his flat, strong face.

I said, "Fessenden, why haven't you shown up at any of the faculty meetings lately? They tell me you've been letting a substitute take care of all your lecture courses, too."

Fessenden looked at me with that mocking smile and said, "What I like about you, Bradley, is that you're so transparent. You've heard everyone around the campus saying that I've got a little crazy, so you've come over to see for yourself."

"No, that's not so," I protested. "It's true that a good many people have been ridiculing those radical astrophysical theories you propounded, and that some of them think you're more than a little eccentric. But that means nothing to me. I know very well that whenever a man proposes something new, everyone at first thinks he's a little crazy."

I continued earnestly, "You know I'm only a foot soldier in the ranks of science myself—a poor devil of an instructor. Nevertheless, I've always recognized you as a great pioneer. I've been wondering a lot just what you've been working on here so intensively, and I'm honestly hoping you'll tell me something about it. But whether you do or not, you have my admiration and sympathy."

Fessenden's smile deepened. He told me, "Bradley, if you expect me to be grateful for your sympathy, you're wrong. I'm not. I have been called cold and unfeeling, and that is just what I want to be. The gabbling of the fools who have been ridiculing me does not disturb me, and means no more to me than does your sympathy."

My face must have fallen a little. Fessenden laughed.

"I'm glad that is clear to you," he said. "But now that it is, let me tell you that I have decided that I *will* show you what I am doing, after all. I'll show you the greatest experiment which any scientist on Earth has ever conducted."

I said, in surprise, "If you feel no more friendliness for me than you say, I don't see why you should."

He shrugged mockingly. "Because, unfortunately, I am still an ordinary human being at bottom, Bradley. As such, I have a certain ineradicable amount of exhibitionism in me which, deplore it as I may, persists and makes me want to show at least somebody what I have done." He laughed. "Just like any small boy who has built his first kite and wants somebody to see it. I recognize the folly of this, I am amused by it, but I can't wholly eliminate it from my make-up."

"Well, why not indulge this irrational desire for applause by demonstrating to you what I've done? You do not have enough intelligence to comprehend it all, of course. Still, you will be an auditor, an audience, and I shall satisfy this itch of mine to let someone know what I've accomplished."

I said quickly, "I promise that I'll keep everything you tell me absolutely confidential."

Fessenden roared with laughter. "You needn't promise that. For all I care, you can go out and tell the whole world what you see here. Only, if you do, they'll call you a madman and very likely confine you in an institution. By all means go ahead and tell them, if you want to."

He was still chuckling as he rose to his feet. "It's back in my laboratory, Bradley."

"But what is it, anyway?" I asked doubtfully. "What have you done?"

"I've created a universe," Fessenden told me.

I said impatiently, "That's a grandiose metaphor, but just what does it mean?"

"It's not a metaphor at all," Fessenden said blandly. "I mean literally that I have created a universe in my laboratory, a universe that has millions of suns, tens of millions of worlds."

I was silent. I was trying to avoid his eyes, to hide my disappointment from him.

Fessenden chuckled. "A minute ago," he said, "you were condemning the rest of the university for thinking me insane. Now you're thinking exactly the same thing, aren't you?—wondering how you can get out of this crazy Fessenden's house with good grace?"

He added, grinning sardonically, "Come along to the laboratory, Bradley, and see for yourself."

I followed his tall, powerful figure along the corridor. I did think now that his isolation and the ridicule his radical theories had evoked must have touched his mind. But still he must have something to show me, and I was eager to see what it was.

The laboratory was a long, stone-walled room whose walls were crowded with shelves of chemical and physical apparatus, and whose corners held great electrical mechanisms. Much of the equipment I saw was strange to my eyes. Then my gaze fastened on the thing at the center of the laboratory.

It consisted of two twelve-foot metal disks with grid-like surfaces, one on the floor and one on the ceiling directly over the other. They were connected by cables to the electrical machinery, and their grid-like surfaces shone faintly with wan blue light or force.

Between the two disks, floating unsupported in the air, hung a cloud of tiny sparks of light. It looked like a swarm of minute golden bees, countless in number, and the swarm was lenticular in shape. Mounted near this weird thing were several instruments that looked a little like telescopes, though unfamiliar in design. They seemed to be trained upon that thick little cloud of shining sparks.

Fessenden walked over to the thing and motioned calmly toward the blue-glowing disks in floor and ceiling. "These disks, Bradley, neutralize all the ordinary gravitational forces of Earth in the space between them."

"What?" I cried, astonished. I stepped forward, was about to thrust my hand between the two disks to test the assertion. But Fessenden held me back.

"Don't try that," he warned. "The human body is accustomed to Earth's gravitation, and is inwardly braced against it. If you were to step between those disks, out of Earth's gravitation, your body would explode from its own inward pressure, just as a deep-sea fish will explode when it is suddenly brought up from the tremendous pressures of its usual depths to the surface."

Fessenden added, gesturing to the floating swarm of sparks between the disks, "It was necessary that this should be outside Earth's gravitational influences. For this is the universe I have created."

I stared from him to the shining swarm, and then back again to his dark, amused face. "Those little flecks of light—a universe?"

"Just that," he assured me. "Look closer at them, Bradley."

I looked closer, and I felt a weird chill creeping over me. Those points of light were so infinitesimal that I could barely distinguish them one from another, and I knew there must be millions of them in this thick swarm. Yet there were some oddly familiar features about them.

Some of the tiny sparks were blazing white in color, others smoky red, others golden yellow. The colors of suns in our own universe! Some of them were in double or triple groups, and here and there were clusters of them that contained thousands. And here and there, too, were little glowing patches that looked like tiny nebula, and crawling sparks with tails of light like Lilliputian comets, just as the floating sparks looked like tiny suns.

Those sparks were tiny suns! I knew it, beyond doubt, even while my brain fought against the knowledge and called it impossible. I knew that I was looking at a miniature universe, one on a scale many billions of times smaller than our own universe, yet one that was comparatively as large in extent as our own. A little microcosm, floating here in Fessenden's laboratory.

Fessenden's eyes had been following my stupefied change of expression. He said calmly, "Yes, Bradley, it is true. That is a tiny, self-sustaining universe, with its own suns, nebulae and worlds. Everything in it, down to the atoms which compose it, is infinitely smaller in scale than our own. But it is a real universe, like our own."

"And you say you created this?" I gasped.

Fessenden nodded. "Yes, I did. After many failures, I succeeded in bringing that universe into being only a few weeks ago. I have been experimenting with it ever since."

His black eyes flashed a little. "Didn't I tell you that it was the greatest experiment any scientist had ever conducted? Think of what I am able to do—I can conduct my astrophysical and other experiments on a *cosmic* scale. I can change or destroy suns and nebulae at will, with the instruments I devised, can observe the minutest details of that tiny universe through my super-magnifying telescopes. I can make observations with a universe itself as my subject."

I said in amazement, "But how did you make it—start it?"

Fessenden shrugged. "How did our own universe start, Bradley? As a vast cloud of glowing gas that filled all space. The mutual attraction of the cloud's particles drew them together, so that the cloud condensed into huge nebulae. The nebulae further condensed into suns, which by tidal attraction and occasional collision, threw off matter that formed into circling worlds.

"Well, I started this tiny universe just like that. I filled the non-gravitational space between these disks with a cloud of glowing gas, whose atoms were infinitely tinier than our atoms because I had contracted their electronic orbits. Then all I had to do was watch while the same inevitable natural process that eons ago formed our universe, formed this little microcosm.

"I watched as the gas condensed into tiny nebulae. I saw those little nebulae condense further into miniature suns, just as in our own cosmos long ago. And I saw those suns, as their random wanderings brought them close to one another, throw off worlds.

"Millions on millions of tiny worlds, here in this little microcosm, Bradley! Worlds that I can change and tamper with and destroy at will, worlds with every conceivable kind of conditions, worlds whose life I can develop or wither as I wish. That is my experiment, Bradley!"

"'Whose *life*,' you say?" I repeated in a whisper. "On the tiny planets of this microcosm—life?"

"Of course," said Fessenden. "Life always develops automatically on worlds where conditions are favorable, and usually in very much the same forms." He reached toward one of the bulky, unfamiliar telescopic instruments. "Wait, and I shall find such a world for you, Bradley. I shall let you watch its life develop, for yourself."

He applied his eye to one of the lenses of the bulky telescope-instrument, focusing it upon the shining cloud of sparks; turning knobs, twisting, searching—until at last he straightened.

"Now look, Bradley."

I put my eye to one of the lenses, looked into that cloud of floating sparks. There leaped into my vision, dazzling and gigantic, a huge white sun booming majestically through the darkness of space. Just one of those tiny sparks, seen through the super-magnifying instrument!

Fessenden was beside me, gazing through the other lens of the instrument. His fingers were touching the focus knobs and he said calmly, "Keep watching. You'll see the changes of ages in a few minutes of our time. For, of course, the time of this microcosm runs at an infinitely swifter rate than the time of our vaster universe."

As he shifted the focus of the instrument, my gaze seemed to leap toward that great sun. I made out two planets that circled it, at tremendous speed. A year of their time no more than a moment of ours!

One of these planets was still partly molten, but the other was cooling, its vapor-envelope condensing. My vision leaped forward, in the telescope, until I seemed almost standing on that cooling world. It was a wild, rocky planet, rain falling heavily on its surface from the cloudy sky, water collecting with unbelievable swiftness in seas.

Green life came into being on the world, first along the shores of the warm, shallow seas, then creeping out and advancing over the land. Swiftly vegetation mantled the globe. And now crawling animal life made its appearance as the ages ticked swiftly by.

The animal life developed quickly. So rapid were the changes that my gaze could hardly follow them. Warring species of unhuman monsters passed and vanished. Tiny hordes of man-like animals began to throng here and there, to multiply with each passing moment.

I saw rude villages of huts spring up on that world. The villages quickly became cities as that people developed in intelligence, age after microcosmic age. The cities towered higher each moment, great ships sailed upon the seas, ages of progress and development were run through before my eyes in tiny moments.

I was shaking as I recoiled from the telescope. I cried, "This is all impossible—it can't be real—"

Fessenden smiled. "Your expressions of stupefaction satisfy my egotistic desire for applause, Bradley. But I assure you that that tiny race and their world are quite real." He chuckled. "No doubt that little folk think that they have reached such a pinnacle of power and knowledge that nothing can threaten them. We shall see now whether or not they are able to face a real danger."

He turned to a curious needle-like instrument and carefully trained it upon that part of the microcosm which held the tiny white spark that was the great sun of the world I had been watching.

There was a tiny comet crawling through the swarm, some distance from that white sun. Fessenden touched a knob, and from the needle-like instrument a thin, almost invisible filament of force crept into the microcosmic swarm of sparks and touched the little crawling comet. It seemed to veer a tiny bit aside.

"Now watch," said Fessenden with amused interest, "and we shall see just how great is the power of that little people."

I did not understand, but I looked again with him through the telescope at the tiny world. By now, so swift its development in terms of our time, its cities had become even vaster and were roofed with glass-like shields. Huge aircraft flashed above them.

All seemed peace and progress on that world. Generation after generation ticked by as we watched. Then came a mad stir of movement, a wild scurrying about of the little folk, a swift change in the tempo of their life. A faint green light was now falling upon their planet, the baleful glow of a monster comet that was coming headlong toward it.

I knew then that it was the tiny microcosmic comet whose course Fessenden had slightly altered. But in the telescope it was colossal, a huge orb dripping green light across the heavens as it rushed toward that world. Remorselessly it came on.

Then that comet struck the planet, and I saw the doom of the little folk's cities. The meteors that were the comet's only solid substance shattered the glass-roofed cities to ruin. The poisonous gases that made up the rest of the comet veiled that whole world in a toxic cloud.

The comet passed on as we watched, but its deadly gases had wiped away all life from that planet. It was still and brown and dead, now, a lifeless world circling its sun. The ruined cities melted swiftly down into decay and disappeared as we watched.

Fessenden's laugh rang in my ears as I stared in stunned horror. "You see—their knowledge was not enough to save them from the mere slight shifting of the comet's course."

"You killed them—killed every soul on that world!" My voice throbbed with the horror that I felt.

"Nonsense! It was just an experiment," Fessenden said. "It's no more murder than when a bacteriologist casually destroys germs he experiments with. Those little folk were millions of times smaller than any germ. But they and others like them on the countless worlds of this microcosm provide me with a subject for experimentation which no scientist has ever had before. Look at another world—here are two that interest me."

My vision in the telescope leaped to another sun, for Fessenden had shifted the focus. It was a yellow sun with four planets circling it. Two of them were airless worlds, but the other two bore different forms of life, one of them quite man-like, the other verging on the reptilian, each supreme on its own world. Both races had a certain amount of civilization, as was evident from the queer cities on their worlds. There was no contact or communication between them, for the two planets were widely separated from each other.

"Now I wonder," Fessenden was saying interestedly, "just what the result would be if those two races were to come into contact with each other. Well, we'll soon see," he mused aloud, and reached again toward the needle-like instrument.

Again a ghostly little thread of force stole into the microcosm. I saw its effects, through the telescope. One of those planets, beneath the impetus, began to change its orbit. It moved closer and closer toward the other inhabited world. Soon the two were so close together that they had formed an Earth-moon system, revolving around a common center of gravity as they circled their sun.

Soon, very soon, ships began to fly from one world to the other across the narrowed gulf. Communication had been established. And almost at once came war between the two worlds, a conflict of the man-like and reptilian races. Cities were destroyed by flashes of fire in that war, great throngs went to death in battles of incredible ferocity. The tide turned in favor of the reptilian race. Their invading hordes destroyed the last members of the man-like folk. Then it was all over. The reptilian race reigned supreme over both worlds.

"I'm a little surprised—I thought the human race would have won out," Fessenden said interestedly. "Apparently they didn't have the adaptability of the reptilian race."

I cried, "That little human people would have lived for generations in peace and happiness if you hadn't brought that other world into contact with their own! Why didn't you let them alone?"

He said impatiently, "Don't be a fool, Bradley. This is just a scientific experiment—those ephemeral little races and their tiny worlds are merely a subject for study." And he added, "Why, for days I've been observing and changing and tampering with these microcosmic worlds, just to see the reactions of their peoples to different stimuli and dangers. I've learned things from them that you'd never dream. Watch—I'll show you others."

In a stupefied trance I watched as Fessenden went on, taking my vision to world after world, prodding and changing, observing the fall of empires and the crash of planets with keen, amused detachment. I saw worlds of beauty incredible and worlds of horror unthinkable—planet after planet, race after race, and all of them merely the playthings of the experimenting scientist beside me.

Fessenden showed me a planet in the microcosm that was covered with wild forests in which dwelt little communities of hunting folk who chased the beasts of the forest. Generation after generation flashed by without change in their rude society—they were content to hunt and eat and love and die, without developing any higher civilization.

Then Fessenden turned upon that little world a tiny ray that altered its chemical stability. Beneath the influence of chemical changes, the plant life of that world began to unfold in weird hypertrophy, began to develop mobility, to change into great, rootless plant-things that soon fell upon and killed the animals. The communities of hunters battled valiantly for a few generations against the moving plant hordes, but in the end they all succumbed, and that world was covered only with restlessly moving plant life.

And Fessenden brought into our observation another world, planet of a sun out near the microcosm's edge. It was a watery world, covered with oceans over all of its surface. And teeming life had developed in that planetary sea, into intelligent, seal-like people who had reared in the sea great submarine cities whose spires lifted here and there above the waters.

Fessenden's filaments of force played upon that world, and the seas began to dwindle, the water molecules to fly off into space. And as the seas rapidly shrank, for generation after generation, more and more of that world became dry land and the seal-people had to desert many of their cities and retreat back with the waters.

Very soon, as we watched, there was but one shallow sea remaining on that little world. And here were crowded the last of the seal-folk, and here they fought blindly with all manner of scientific devices to prevent the evaporation of this last refuge. But the remorseless process that Fessenden had started went on, and that last sea dried and disappeared also, and there was only a desert planet with the ruined wrecks of the dead seal-folk's cities standing here and there as memorials of the vanished race.

World after world my dazed eyes watched. I saw an icy planet that swung far out from its parent sun, and upon which was strange life adapted to the cold, bloodless little folk who had reared also a mighty civilization. Their weird palaces and cities rose amid the awful chasms of eternal ice, and it was evident that they were far advanced in scientific power.

Fessenden reached and touched their sun with a tiny thread of force. And that sun blazed suddenly hotter and brighter, casting forth a quadrupled radiance. Its increased heat began to melt the ice-sheath of that far-swinging little world, and its people began to perish from the unaccustomed warmth.

We saw them frantically laboring for the next generation at a great work upon the side of their little world. Then its purpose became clear to us, for from that spot there projected a plume of fire and force whose rocket-like push moved their little planet suddenly outward. They were moving their world farther from their sun to escape the increased warmth, and at a suitable distance they let it settle into a new orbit where it was as cold as before. And Fessenden laughed and applauded their ingenuity.

And there was a world whose crowded peoples were ruled by an oligarchy of living brains. Time after time, each generation that passed, we saw the enslaved people revolt against the tyranny of the brains, and each time the weapons of their unhuman masters subdued them.

Fessenden's probing threads of force reached deep into the bowels of that little planet, and it rocked with terrific quakes that threw up vast masses of radioactive material from the interior. And a strange glowing plague seized the bodies of the people and also seized the brains, so that they began to rot and die.

Swiftly the people were annihilated by that glowing rot, but the brains managed to contrive for themselves an antidote against the deadly infections, so that most of the brains survived. For a few generations the brains clung to existence, served now by machines of their own devising. But they must have made their mechanical servants too intelligent, for in time the machines rose against the brains and destroyed them. And later still, without any directing intelligence, the machines themselves came to wreck and vanished from that world.

Dazed with horror, I watched as we viewed world after world of the microcosm, as Fessenden probed and changed and destroyed. And then there came into my view a world whose aching beauty brought tears to my eyes, a green and blossoming world whose people were human, but of a fineness and beauty far beyond our own humanity.

Not upon their world were any towering cities or huge machines or swarming vehicles. Their civilization had reached a plane above crude material progress, and their planet was like a green and surpassingly lovely park. Here and there amid the flowering trees shimmered exquisite buildings, and through flowers and forests went white-robed noble men and beautiful women. And their knowledge had almost conquered death, since for many microcosmic generations they remained unchanged.

I watched that world through the telescope with my heart struck at the vision, and in the peace and loveliness of that planet and its people I seemed to catch a glimpse of what humanity might aspire to in some unthinkably far future. And then I suddenly woke to the fact that Fessenden, beside me, was reaching again toward the needle-like instrument that loosed his tampering forces upon the microcosmic worlds.

I broke then from my trance and cried out, horrified, "Fessenden, you can't do anything to endanger *that* world!"

He smiled sardonically. "Of course I'm going to do something. I want to see whether that people have not become decadent in their peace and plenty—whether the science that brought them up to that level can save them now when real danger threatens."

He chuckled as he sighted the needle-like thing. "A mere tiny thread of force—but it will cause their little sun to spin so fast that it will break up. Will that people have the resourcefulness to save themselves by flight to another sun? We shall soon see."

But I tore him away from the deadly instrument and sent him staggering back across the laboratory with a wild thrust.

"No!" I cried. "These worlds and peoples that you experiment with and endanger and destroy—they're real! As real as ours, even though infinitely smaller. I'll not let you calmly vivisect and torment any more of them, out of your damnable scientific curiosity."

Fessenden's black brows drew together in a cold fury and he rasped, "I see now how foolish it was to show my experiment to an unreasoning sentimentalist like you. But that microcosm is *my* experiment, *my* property, and I'll experiment with and destroy every world in it, if I please. Get away from that instrument."

"I won't do it!" I shouted. "You've wreaked horror enough on those tiny planets with your inhuman experiments, subjecting those little races to agony and toil and death just to gratify your unholy curiosity. You're not going to do it now with this little world!"

Fessenden sprang straight at me, rage burning in his black eyes. His heavy fist descended on me and knocked me away from the instrument I held.

I reeled back from that blow. And at that moment I heard a hoarse cry. Fessenden had tripped on one of the cables in his wild spring, and was toppling into the space between the two disks.

His toppling body struck the microcosm squarely and it crashed around him in a broken shower of sparks. A universe wrecked in a second. At the same time, Fessenden's body exploded—it exploded into a bloated, torn thing of flesh, just as he had warned me any human body would do if it entered the area between the disks where there was no gravitation.

The cable he had tripped over had jerked loose—and there was a flash of fire across the lower disk. In an instant, destroying blue electrical flames enveloped the disks and Fessenden's body, and danced around the electrical machinery in the laboratory with a sputtering, increasing roar.

I turned and stumbled crazily out of the laboratory, out of the house into the wet and windy night. I heard a crackling roar behind me and the flickering light of the now flaming house shot past me as I staggered on, but I did not look back....

So ended Fessenden and his great experiment. No one doubted but that the eccentric scientist had somehow set fire to the house and had perished in the blaze, and I said nothing to change that opinion. And very soon his end was no longer remembered, and Fessenden is now forgotten by everyone. By everyone, except me.

I wish that I could forget too! But I can't forget Fessenden and his microcosmic worlds, and because I can't, my soul is sick and I have a shuddering, fearful wonder in me that will endure until I die, a black question to which I'll never get an answer, and which torments me every time I look up at the night stars.

And the question that quakes in my soul whenever I look up into the starry sky is this—is our own great universe nothing but a tiny microcosm, on some vaster scale? And in that vaster cosmos, is there a super-experimenter who regards our universe as nothing but an interesting experiment, and who smites us with disasters just to study our reactions for his own amusement? Is there a Fessenden up *there?*

THE BLUE GIRAFFE

L. Sprague de Camp

LYON SPRAGUE DE CAMP (1907-2000) was one of the cadre of writers nurtured by John W. Campbell Jr. when Campbell took over Astounding Science Fiction in late 1937 and helped bring science fiction into the modern age with accurate science and stories written in a recognizably American idiom. De Camp's fiction is often whimsical yet it possesses a dark edge, as in the story, "The Blue Giraffe," which was written when atomic power and the terrors of mutations were just becoming known to science.

ATHELSTAN Cuff was, to put it very mildly, astonished that his son should be crying. It wasn't that he had exaggerated ideas about Peter's stoicism, but the fact was that Peter never cried. He was, for a twelve-year-old boy, self-possessed to the point of grimness. And now he was undeniably sniffling. It must be something jolly well awful.

Cuff pushed aside the pile of manuscript he had been reading. He was the editor of *Biological Review*; a stoutish Englishman with prematurely white hair, prominent blue eyes, and a complexion that could have been used for painting box cars. He looked a little like a lobster who had been boiled once and was determined not to repeat the experience.

"What's wrong, old man?" he asked.

Peter wiped his eyes and looked at his father calculatingly.

Cuff sometimes wished that Peter wasn't so damned rational.

A spot of boyish unreasonableness would be welcome at times.

"Come on, old fella, out with it. What's the good of having a father if you can't tell him things?"

Peter finally got it out. "Some of the guys—" He stopped to blow his nose. Cuff winced slightly at the "guys." His one regret about coming to America was the language his son picked up. As he didn't believe in pestering Peter all the time, he had to suffer in silence.

"Some of the guys say you aren't really my father."

It had come, thought Cuff, as it was bound to sooner or later. He shouldn't have put off telling the boy for so long.

"What do you mean, old man?" he stalled.

"They say," *sniff,* "I'm just a 'dopted boy."

Cuff forced out, "So what?" The despised Americanism seemed to be the only thing that covered the situation.

"What do you mean, 'so what'?"

"I mean just that. What of it? It doesn't make a particle of difference to your mother or me, I assure you. So why should it to you?"

Peter thought. "Could you send me away some time, on account of I was only 'dopted?"

"Oh, so that's what's worrying you? The answer is no. Legally you're just as much our son as if…as anyone is anybody's son. But whatever gave you the idea we'd ever send you away? I'd like to see that chap who could get you away from us."

"Oh, I just wondered."

"Well, you can stop wondering. We don't want to, and we couldn't if we did. It's perfectly all right, I tell you. Lots of people start out as adopted children, and it doesn't make any difference to anybody. You wouldn't get upset if somebody tried to make fun of you because you had two eyes and a nose, would you?"

Peter had recovered his composure. "How did it happen?"

"It's quite a story. I'll tell you, if you like."

Peter only nodded.

"I've told you," said Athelstan Cuff, "about how before I came to America I worked for some years in South Africa. I've told you about how I used to work with elephants and lions and things, and about how I transplanted some white rhino from Swaziland to the Kruger Park. But I've never told you about the blue giraffe—"

In the 1940's the various South African governments were considering the problem of a park that would be not merely a game preserve available to tourists, but a completely wild area in which no people other than scientists and wardens would be allowed. They finally agreed on the Okvango River Delta in Ngamiland, as the only area that was sufficiently large and at the same time thinly populated.

The reasons for its sparse population were simple enough: nobody likes to settle down in a place when he is likely to find his house and farm under three feet of water some fine morning. And it is irritating to set out to fish in a well-known lake only to find that the lake has turned into a grassy plain, around the edges of which the mopane trees are already springing up.

So the Batawana, in whose reserve the Delta lay, were mostly willing to leave this capricious stretch of swamp and jumble to the elephant and the lion. The few Batawana who did live in and around the Delta were bought out and moved. The Crown Office of the Bechuanaland Protectorate got around its own rules against alienation of tribal lands by taking a perpetual lease on the Delta and surrounding territory from the Batawana, and named the whole area Jan Smuts Park.

When Athelstan Cuff got off the train at Francistown in September of 1976, a pelting spring rain was making the platform smoke. A tall black in khaki loomed out of the grayness, and said: "You are Mr. Cuff, from Cape Town? I'm George Mtengeni, the warden at Smuts. Mr. Opdyck wrote me you were coming. The Park's car is out this way."

Cuff followed. He'd heard of George Mtengeni. The man wasn't a Chwana at all, but a Zulu from near Durban. When the Park had been set up, the Batawana had thought that the warden ought to be a Tawana. But the Makoba, feeling chesty about their independence from their former masters, the Batawana, had insisted on his being one of their nation. Finally the Crown Office in disgust had hired an outsider. Mtengeni had the dark skin and narrow nose found in so many of the Kafiir Bantu. Cuff guessed that he probably had a low opinion of the Chwana people in general and the Batawana in particular.

They got into the car. Mtengeni said: "I hope you don't mind coming way out here like this. It's too bad that you couldn't come before the rains started; the pans they are all full by now."

"So?" said Cuff. "What's the Mababe this year?" He referred to the depression known variously as Mababe Lake, Swamp, or Pan, depending on whether at a given time it contained much, little, or no water.

"The Mababe, it is a lake, a fine lake full of drowned trees and hippo. I think the Okavango is shifting north again. That means Lake Ngami it will dry up again."

"So it will. But look here, what's all this business about a blue giraffe? Your letter was dashed uninformative."

Mtengeni showed his white teeth. "It appeared on the edge of the Mopane Forest seventeen months ago. That was just the beginning. There have been other things since. If I'd told you more, you would have written the Crown Office saying that their warden was having a nervous breakdown. Me, I'm sorry to drag you into this, but the Crown Office keeps saying they can't spare a man to investigate."

"Oh, quite all right, quite," answered Cuff. "I was glad to get away from Cape Town anyway. And we haven't had a mystery since old Hickey disappeared."

"Since who disappeared? You know me, I can't keep up with things out in the wilds."

"Oh, that was many years ago. Before your time, or mine for that matter. Hickey was a scientist who set out into the Kalahari with a truck and a Xosa assistant, and disappeared. Men flew all over the Kalahari looking for him, but never found a trace, and the sand had blown over his tire tracks. Jolly odd, it was."

The rain poured down steadily as they wallowed along the dirt road. Ahead, beyond the gray curtain, lay the vast plains of northern Bechuanaland with their great pans. And beyond the plains were, allegedly, a blue giraffe, and other things.

The spidery steelwork of the tower hummed as they climbed. At the top, Mtengeni said: "You can look over that way...west...to the other side of the forest. That's about twenty miles."

Cuff screwed up his eyes at the eyepieces. "Jolly good 'scope you've got here. But it's too hazy beyond the forest to see anything."

"It always is, unless we have a high wind: That's the edge of the swamps."

"Dashed if I see how you can patrol such a big area all by yourself."

"Oh, these Bechuana they don't give much trouble. They are honest. Even I have to admit that they have some good qualities. Anyway, you can't get far into the Delta without getting lost in the swamps. There are ways, but then, I only know them. I'll show them to you, but please don't tell these Bechuana about them. Look, Mr. Cuff, there's our blue giraffe."

Cuff started. Mtengeni was evidently the kind of man who would announce an earthquake as casually as the morning mail.

Several hundred yards from the tower half a dozen giraffes were moving slowly through the brush, feeding on the tops of the scrubby trees. Cuff swung the telescope on them. In the middle of the herd was the blue one. Cuff blinked and looked again. There was no doubt about it; the animal was as brilliant a blue as if somebody had gone over it with paint. Athelstan Cuff suspected that that was what somebody had done. He said as much to Mtengeni.

The warden shrugged. "That, it would be a peculiar kind of amusement. Not to say risky. Do you see anything funny about the others?"

Cuff looked again. "Yes…by Jove, one of 'em's got a beard like a goat; only it must be six feet long, at least, now look here, George, what's all this leading up to?"

"I don't know myself. Tomorrow, if you like, I'll show you one of those ways into the Delta. But that, it's quite a walk, so we'd better take supplies for two or three days."

As they drove toward the Tamalakane, they passed four Batawana, sad-looking reddish-brown men in a mixture of native and European clothes. Mtengeni slowed the car and looked at them suspiciously as they passed, but there was no evidence that they had been poaching.

He said: "Ever since their Makoba slaves were freed, they've been going on a…decline, I suppose you would call it. They are too dignified to work."

They got out at the river. "We can't drive across the ford this time of year," explained the warden, locking the car. "But there's a rapid a little way down, where we can wade."

They walked down the trail, adjusting their packs. There wasn't much to see. The view was shut off by the tall soft-bodied swamp plants. The only sound was the hum of insects.

The air was hot and steamy already, though the sun had been up only half an hour. The flies drew blood when they bit, but the men were used to that. They simply slapped and waited for the next bite.

Ahead there was a deep gurgling noise, like a foghorn with water in its works. Cuff said: "How are your hippo doing this year?"

"Pretty good. There are some in particular that I want you to see. Ah, here we are."

They had come in sight of a stretch of calm water. In the foreground a hippopotamus repeated its foghorn bellow. Cuff saw others, of which only the eyes, ears, and nostrils were visible. One of them was moving; Cuff could make out the little V-shaped wakes pointing back from its nearly submerged head. It reached the shallows and lumbered out, dripping noisily.

Cuff blinked. "Must be something wrong with my eyes."

"No," said Mtengeni. "That hippo she is one of those I wanted you to see."

The hippopotamus was green with pink spots.

She spied the men, grunted suspiciously, and slid back into the water.

"I still don't believe it," said Cuff. "Dash it, man, that's impossible."

"You will see many more things," said Mtengeni. "Shall we go on?"

They found the rapid and struggled across; then walked along what might, by some stretch of the imagination, be called a trail. There was little sound other than their sucking footfalls, the hum of insects, and the occasional screech of a bird or the crashing of a buck through the reeds.

They walked for some hours. Then Mtengeni said: "Be careful. There is a rhino near."

Cuff wondered how the devil the Zulu knew, but he was careful. Presently they came on a clear space in which the rhinoceros was browsing.

The animal couldn't see them at that distance, and there was no wind to carry their smell. It must have heard them, though, for it left off its feeding and snorted, once, like a locomotive. It had two heads.

It trotted toward them sniffing.

The men got out their rifles. "My God!" said Athelstan Cuff. "Hope we don't have to shoot him. My God!"

"I don't think so," said the warden. "That's Tweedle. I know him. If he gets too close, give him one at the base of the horn and he…he will run."

"Tweedie?"

"Yes. The right head is Tweedledum and the left is Tweedledee," said Mtengeni solemnly. "The whole rhino I call Tweedle."

The rhinoceros kept coming. Mtengeni said: "Watch this."

He waved his hat and shouted: "Go away! *Footsack*!"

Tweedle stopped and snorted again. Then he began to circle like a waltzing mouse. Round and round he spun.

"We might as well go on," said Mtengeni. "He will keep that up for hours. You see Tweedledum is fierce, but Tweedledee, he is peaceful, even cowardly. So when I yell at Tweedle, Tweedledum wants to charge us, but Tweedledee he wants to run away. So the right legs go forward and the left legs go back, and Tweedle, he goes in circles. It takes him some time to agree on a policy."

"*Whew!*" said Athelstan Cuff. "I say, have you got any more things like this in your zoo?"

"Oh, yes, lots. That's what I hope you'll do something about."

Do something about this! Cuff wondered whether this was touching evidence of the native's faith in the white omniscience, or whether Mtengeni had gotten him there for the cynical amusement of watching him run in useless circles. Mtengeni himself gave no sign of what he was thinking.

Cuff said: "I can't understand, George, why somebody hasn't looked into this before."

Mtengeni shrugged. "Me, I've tried to get somebody to, but the government won't send anybody, and the scientific expeditions, there haven't been any of them for years. I don't know why."

"I can guess," said Cuff. "In the old days people even in the so-called civilized countries expected travel to be a jolly rugged proposition, so they didn't mind putting up with a few extra hardships on trek. But now that you can ride or fly almost anywhere on soft cushions, people won't put themselves out to get to a really uncomfortable and out-of-the-way place like Ngamiland."

Over the swampy smell came another, of carrion. Mtengeni pointed to the carcass of a waterbuck fawn, which the scavengers had apparently not discovered yet.

"That's why I want you to stop this whatever-it-is," he said. There was real concern in his voice.

"What do you mean, George?"

"Do you see its legs?"

Cuff looked. The forelegs were only half as long as the hind ones.

"That buck," said the Zulu. "It naturally couldn't live long. All over the Park, freaks like this they are being born. Most of them don't live.

In ten years more, maybe twenty, all my animals will have died out because of this. Then my job, where is it?"

They stopped at sunset. Cuff was glad to. It had been some time since he'd done fifteen miles in one day, and he dreaded the morrow's stiffness. He looked at his map and tried to figure out where he was. But the cartographers had never seriously tried to keep track of the changes in the Okavango's multifarious branches, and had simply plastered the whole Delta with little blue dashes with tufts of blue lines sticking up from them, meaning simply "swamp." In all directions the country was a monotonous alternation of land and water. The two elements were inextricably mixed.

The Zulu was looking for a dry spot free of snakes. Cuff heard him suddenly shout "*Footsack*!" and throw a clod at a log. The log opened a pair of jaws, hissed angrily, and slid into the water.

"We'll have to have a good fire," said Mtengeni, hunting for dry wood. "We don't want a croc or hippo wandering into our tent by mistake."

After supper they set the automatic bug sprayer going, inflated their mattresses, and tried to sleep. A lion roared somewhere in the west. That sound no African, native or Africander, likes to hear when he is on foot at night. But the men were not worried; lions avoided the swampy areas. The mosquitoes presented a more immediate problem.

Many hours later, Athelstan Cuff heard Mtengeni getting up.

The warden said: "just remembered a high spot half a mile from here, where there's plenty of firewood. Me, I'm going out to get some."

Cuff listened to Mtengeni's retreating steps in the soft ground; then to his own breathing. Then he listened to something else. It sounded like a human yell.

He got up and pulled on his boots quickly. He fumbled around for the flashlight, but Mtengeni had taken it with him.

The yell came again.

Cuff found his rifle and cartridge belt in the dark and went out. There was enough starlight to walk by if you were careful. The fire was nearly out. The yells seemed to come from a direction opposite to that in which Mtengeni had gone. They were high-pitched, like a woman's screams.

He walked in their direction, stumbling over irregularities in the ground and now and then stepping up to his calves in unexpected water. The yells were plainer now. They weren't in English. Something was also snorting.

He found the place. There was a small tree, in the branches of which somebody was perched. Below the tree a noisy bulk moved around. Cuff caught the outline of a sweeping horn, and knew he had to deal with a buffalo.

He hated to shoot. For a Park official to kill one of his charges simply wasn't done. Besides, he couldn't see to aim for a vital spot, and he didn't care to try to dodge a wounded buffalo in the dark. They could move with race-horse speed through the heaviest growth.

On the other hand, he couldn't leave even a poor fool of a native woman treed. The buffalo, if it was really angry, would wait for days until its victim weakened and fell. Or it would butt the tree until the victim was shaken out. Or it would rear up and try to hook the victim out with its horns.

Athelstan Cuff shot the buffalo. The buffalo staggered about a bit and collapsed.

The victim climbed down swiftly, pouring out a flood of thanks in Xosa. It was very bad Xosa, even worse than the Englishman's. Cuff wondered what she was doing here, nearly a thousand miles from where the Maxosa lived. He assumed that she was a native, though it was too dark to see. He asked her if she spoke English, but she didn't seem to understand the question, so he made-shift with the Bantu dialect.

"*Uveli phi na*?" he asked sternly. "Where do you come from? Don't you know that nobody is allowed in the Park without special permission?"

"*Izwe kamafene wabantu*," she replied.

"What? Never heard of the place. Land of the baboon people, indeed! What are you?"

"*Ingwamza*."

"You're a white stork? Are you trying to be funny?"

"I didn't say I was a white stork. Ingwamza's my name."

"I don't care about your name. I want to know what you are."

"*Umfene umfazi.*"

Cuff controlled his exasperation. "All right, all right, you're a baboon woman. I don't care what clan you belong to. What's your tribe? Batawana, Bamangwato, Bangwaketse, Barolong, Herero, or what? Don't try to tell me you're a Xosa; no Xosa ever used an accent like that."

"*Amafene abantu.*"

"What the devil are the baboon people?"

"People who live in the Park."

Cuff resisted the impulse to pull out two handfuls of hair by the roots. "But I tell you nobody lives in the Park! It isn't allowed! Come now, where do you really come from and what's your native language and why are you trying to talk Xosa?"

"I told you, I live in the Park. And I speak Xosa because all we *amafene abantu* speak it. That's the language Mqhavi taught us."

"Who is Mqhavi?"

"The man who taught us to speak Xosa."

Cuff gave up. "Come along, you're going to see the warden. Perhaps he can make some sense out of your gabble. And you'd better have a good reason for trespassing, my good woman, or it'll go hard with you. Especially as it resulted in the killing of a good buffalo." He started off toward the camp, making sure that Ingwamza followed him closely.

The first thing he discovered was that he couldn't see the light of any fire to guide him back. Either he'd come farther than he thought, or the fire had died altogether while Mtengeni was getting wood. He kept on for a quarter of an hour in what he thought was the right direction. Then he stopped.

He had, he realized, not the vaguest idea of where he was.

He turned. "*Sibaphi na?*" he snapped. "Where are we?"

"In the Park."

Cuff began to wonder whether he'd ever succeed in delivering this native woman to Mtengeni before he strangled her with his bare hands. "I know we're in the Park," he snarled. "But where in the Park?"

"I don't know exactly. Somewhere near my people's land."

"That doesn't do me any good. Look: I left the warden's camp when I heard you yell. I want to get back to it. Now how do I do it?"

"Where is the warden's camp?" don't know, stupid. If I did I'd go there."

"If you don't know where it is, how do you expect me to guide you thither? I don't know either."

Cuff made strangled noises in his throat. Inwardly he had to admit that she had him there, which only made him madder. Finally he said: "Never mind, suppose you take me to your people. Maybe they have somebody with some sense."

"Very well," said the native woman, and she set off at a rapid pace, Cuff stumbling after her vague outline. He began to wonder if maybe she wasn't right about living in the Park. She seemed to know where she was going.

"Wait," he said. He ought to write a note to Mtengeni, explaining what he was up to, and stick it on a tree for the warden to find. But there was no pencil or paper in his pockets. He didn't even have a match safe or a cigarette lighter. He'd taken all those things out of his pockets when he'd Iain down.

They went on a way, Cuff pondering on how to get in touch with Mtengeni. He didn't want himself and the warden to spend a week chasing each other around the Delta. Perhaps it would be better to stay where they were and build a fire—but again, he had no matches, and didn't see much prospect of making a fire by rubbing sticks in this damned damp country.

Ingwamza said: "Stop. There are buffalo ahead."

Cuff listened and heard faintly the sound of snapping grass stems as the animals fed.

She continued: "We'll have to wait until it gets light. Then maybe they'll go away. If they don't, we can circle around them, but I couldn't find the way around in the dark."

They found the highest point they could and settled down to wait. Something with legs had crawled inside Cuffs shirt. He mashed it with a slap.

He strained his eyes into the dark. It was impossible to tell how far away the buffalo were. Overhead a nightjar brought its wings together with a single startling clap. Cuff told his nerves to behave themselves. He wished he had a smoke.

The sky began to lighten. Gradually Cuff was able to make out the black bulks moving among the reeds. They were at least two hundred yards away. He'd have preferred that they were at twice the distance, but it was better than stumbling right on them.

It became lighter and lighter. Cuff never took his eyes off the buffalo. There was something queer about the nearest one. It had six legs.

Cuff turned to Ingwamza and started to whisper: "What kind of buffalo do you call—" Then he gave a yell of pure horror and jumped back. His rifle went off, tearing a hole in his boot.

He had just gotten his first good look at the native woman in the rapidly waxing dawn. Ingwamza's head was that of an overgrown chacma baboon.

The buffalo stampeded through the feathery papyrus. Cuff and Ingwamza stood looking at each other. Then Cuff looked at his right foot. Blood was running out of the jagged hole in the leather.

"What's the matter? Why did you shoot yourself?" asked Ingwamza.

Cuff couldn't think of an answer to that one. He sat down and took off his boot. The foot felt numb, but there seemed to be no harm done aside from a piece of skin the size of a sixpence gouged out of the margin. Still, you never knew what sort of horrible infection might result from a trifling wound in these swamps. He tied his foot up with his handkerchief and put his boot back on.

"Just an accident," he said. "Keep going, Ingwamza."

Ingwamza went, Cuff limping behind. The sun would rise any minute now. It was light enough to make out colors. Cuff saw that Ingwamza, in describing herself as a baboon-woman, had been quite literal, despite the size, general proportions, and posture of a human being. Her body, but for the greenish-yellow hair and the short tail, might have passed for that of a human being, if you weren't too particular. But the astonishing head with its long bluish muzzle gave her the appearance of an Egyptian animal-headed god. Cuff wondered vaguely if the *'fene abantu* were a race of man-monkey hybrids. That was impossible, of course. But he'd seen so many impossible things in the last couple of days.

She looked back at him. "We shall arrive in an hour or two. I'm sleepy." She yawned. Cuff repressed a shudder at the sight of four canine teeth big enough for a leopard. Ingwamza could tear the throat out of a man with those fangs as easily as biting the end off a banana. And he'd been using his most hectoring colonial-administrator tone on her in the dark!

He made a resolve never to speak harshly to anybody he couldn't see.

Ingwamza pointed to a carroty baobab against the sky. "*Clzew kamagene wabantu.*" They had to wade a little stream to get there. A six-foot monitor lizard walked across their path, saw them, and disappeared with a scuttle.

The *'fene abantu* lived in a village much like that of any Bantu people, but the circular thatched huts were smaller and cruder. Baboon people ran out to peer at Cuff and to feel his clothes. He gripped his rifle tightly. They didn't act hostile, but it gave you a dashed funny feeling. The males were larger than the females, with even longer muzzles and bigger tusks.

In the center of the village sat a big *umfene umntu* scratching himself in front of the biggest hut. Ingwamza said, "That is my father, the chief. His name is Indlovu." To the baboon-man she told of her rescue.

The chief was the only *umfene umntu* that Cuff had seen who wore anything. What he wore was a necktie. The necktie had been a gaudy thing once.

The chief got up and made a speech, the gist of which was that Cuff had done a great thing, and that Cuff would be their guest until his wound healed. Cuff had a chance to observe the difficulties that the *'fene abantu* had with the Xosa tongue. The clicks were blurred, and they stumbled badly over the lipsmack. With those mouths, he could see how they might.

But he was only mildly interested. His foot was hurting like the very devil. He was glad when they led him into a hut so he could take off his boot. The hut was practically unfurnished. Cuff asked the *'fene abantu* if he might have some of the straw used for thatching. They seemed puzzled by his request, but complied, and he made himself a bed of sorts. He hated sleeping on the ground, especially on ground infested with arthropodal life. He hated vermin, and knew he was in for an intimate acquaintance with them.

He had nothing to bandage his foot with, except the one handkerchief, which was now thoroughly blood-soaked. He'd have to wash and dry it before it would be fit to use again. And where in the Okavango Delta could he find water fit to wash the handkerchief in? Of course he could boil the water. In what? He was relieved and amazed when his questions brought forth the fact that there was a large iron pot in the village, obtained from God knew where.

The wound had clotted satisfactorily, and he dislodged the handkerchief with infinite care from the scab. While his water was boiling, the chief, Indlovu, came in and talked to him. The pain in his foot had subsided for the moment, and he was able to realize what an extraordinary thing he had come across, and to give Indlovu his full attention. He plied Indlovu with questions.

The chief explained what he knew about himself and his people. It seemed that he was the first of the race; all the others were his descendants. Not only Ingwamza but all the other *amafene abafazi* were his daughters. Ingwamza was merely the last. He was old now. He was hazy about dates, but Cuff got the impression that these beings had a shorter life span than human beings, and matured much more quickly. If they were in fact baboons, that was natural enough.

Indlovu didn't remember having had any parents. The earliest he remembered was being led around by Mqhavi. Stanley H. Mqhavi had been a black man, and worked for the machine man, who had been a pink man like Cuff. He had had a machine up on the edge of the Chobe Swamp. His name had been Heeky.

Of course, Hickey! thought Cuff. Now he was getting somewhere. Hickey had disappeared by simply running his truck up to Ngamiland without bothering to tell anybody where he was going. That had been before the Park had been established; before Cuff had come out from England. Mqhair must have been his Xosa assistant. His thoughts raced ahead of Indlovu's words.

Indlovu went on to tell about how Heeky had died, and how Mqhavi, not knowing how to run the machine, had taken him, Indlovu, and his now numerous progeny in an attempt to find his way back to civilization. He had gotten lost in the Delta. Then he had cut his foot somehow, and gotten sick, very sick. Cuff had come out from England. Mqhavi must have Mqhavi, had gotten well he had been very weak. So he had settled down with Indlovu and his family. They already walked upright and spoke Xosa, which Mqhavi had taught them. Cuff got the idea that the early family relationships among the *'fene abantu* had of necessity involved close inbreeding. Mqhavi had taught them all he knew, and then died, after warning them not to go within a mile of the machine, which, as far as they knew, was still up at the Chobe Swamp.

Cuff thought, that blasted machine is an electronic tube of some sort, built to throw short waves of the length to affect animal genes. Probably Indlovu represented one of Hickey'S early experiments. Then Hickey had died, and—left the thing going. He didn't know how it got power; some solar system, perhaps.

Suppose Hickey had died while the thing was turned on. Mqhavi might have dragged his body out and left the door open. He might have been afraid to try to turn it off, or he might not have thought of it. So every animal that passed that doorway got a dose of the rays, and begat monstrous offspring. These super-baboons were one example; whether an accidental or a controlled mutation, might never be known.

For every useful mutation there were bound to be scores of useless or harmful ones. Mtengeni had been right: it had to be stopped while there was still normal stock left in the Park. He wondered again how to get in touch with the warden. He'd be damned if anything short of the threat of death would get him to walk on that foot, for a few days anyhow.

Ingwamza entered with a wooden dish full of a mess of some sort. Athelstan Cuff decided resignedly that he was expected to eat it. He couldn't tell by looking whether it was animal or vegetable in nature. After the first mouthful he was sure it was neither. Nothing in the animal and vegetable worlds could taste as awful as that. It was too bad Mqhavi hadn't been a Bamangwato; he'd have really known how to cook, and could have taught these monkeys. Still, he had to eat something to support life. He fell to with the wooden spoon they gave him, suppressing an occasional gag and watching the smaller solid particles closely. Sure enough, he had to smack two of them with the spoon to keep them from crawling out.

"How it is?" asked Ingwamza. Indlovu had gone out.

"Fine," lied Cuff. He was chasing a slimy piece of what he suspected was waterbuck tripe around the dish.

"I am glad. We'll feed you a lot of that. Do you like scorpions?"

"You mean to eat?"

"Of course. What else are they good for?"

He gulped. "No."

"I won't give you any then. You see I'm glad to know what my future husband likes."

"What?" He thought he had misunderstood her.

"I said, I am glad to know what you like, so I can please you after you are my husband."

Athelstan Cuff said nothing for sixty seconds. His naturally prominent eyes bulged even more as her words sank in. Finally he spoke.

"*Gluk*," he said.

"What's that?"

"*Gug. Gah.* My God. Let me out of here!" His voice jumped two octaves, and he tried to get up. Ingwamza caught his shoulders and pushed him gently, but firmly, back on his pallet. He struggled, but without visibly exerting herself the *'fene umfazi* held him as in a vise.

"You can't go," she said. "If you try to walk on that foot you will get sick."

His ruddy face was turning purple! "Let me up! Let me up, I say! I can't stand this!"

"Will you promise not to try to go out if I do? Father would be furious if I let you do anything unwise."

He promised, getting a grip on himself again. He already felt a bit foolish about his panic. He was in a nasty jam, certainly, but an official of His Majesty didn't act like a frightened schoolgirl at every crisis.

"What," he asked, "is this all about?"

"Father is so grateful to you for saving my life that he intends to bestow me on you in marriage, without even asking a bride price."

"But...but...I'm married already," he lied.

"What of it? I'm not afraid of your other wives. If they got fresh, I'd tear them in pieces like this." She bared her teeth and went through the motions of tearing several Mistresses Cuff in pieces. Athelstan Cuff shut his eyes at the horrid sight.

"Among my people," he said, "you're allowed only one wife."

"That's too bad," said Ingwamza. "That means that you couldn't go back to your people after you married me, doesn't it?"

Cuff sighed. These *'fene abantu* combined the mental outlook of uneducated Maxosa with physical equipment that would make a lion think twice before attacking one. He'd probably have to shoot his way out. He looked around the hut craftily. His rifle wasn't in sight. He didn't dare ask about it for fear of arousing suspicion.

"Is your father set on this plan?" he asked.

"Oh, yes, very. Father is a good umntu, but he gets set on ideas like this and nothing will make him change them. And he has a terrible temper. If you cross him when he has his heart set on something, he will tear you in pieces. Small pieces." She seemed to relish the phrase.

"How do you feel about it, Ingwamza?"

"Oh, I do everything father says. He knows more than any of us."

"Yes, but I mean you personally. Forget about your father for the moment."

She didn't quite catch on for a moment, but after further explanation she said: "1 wouldn't mind. It would be a great thing for my people if one of us was married to a man." Cuff silently thought that that went double for him.

Indlovu came in with two other *amafene abantu*. "Run along, Ingwamza," he said. The three baboon-men squatted around Athelstan Cuff and began questioning him about men and the world outside the Delta.

When Cuff stumbled over a phrase, one of the questioners, a scarred fellow named Sondlo, asked why he had difficulty. Cuff explained that Xosa wasn't his native language.

"Men do speak other languages?" asked Indlovu, "I remember now, the great Mqhavi once told me something to that effect. But he never taught me any other languages. Perhaps he and Heeky spoke one of these other languages, but I was too young when Heeky died to remember."

Cuff explained something about linguistics. He was immediately pressed to "say something in English." Then they wanted to learn English, right then, that afternoon.

Cuff finished his evening meal and looked without enthusiasm at his pallet. No artificial light, so these people rose and set with the sun. He stretched out. The straw rustled. He jumped up, bringing his injured foot down hard. He yelped, swore, and felt the bandage. Yes, he'd started it bleeding again. Oh, to hell with it. He attacked the straw, chasing out a mouse, six cockroaches, and uncounted smaller bugs. Then he stretched out again. Looking, up, he felt his scalp prickle. A ten-inch centipede was methodically hunting its prey over the underside of the roof. If it missed its footing when it was right over him—He unbuttoned his shirt and pulled it up over his face. Then the mosquitoes attacked his midriff. His foot throbbed.

A step brought him up; it was Ingwamza.

"What is it now?" he asked.

"*Ndiya kuhlaha apha*," she answered.

"Oh no, you're not going to stay here. We're not well, anyway, it simply isn't done among my people."

"But Esselten, somebody must watch you in case you get sick. My father—"

"No, I'm sorry, but that's final. If you're going to marry me you'll have to learn how to behave among men. And we're beginning right now."

To his surprise and relief, she went without further objection, albeit sulkily. He'd never have dared to try to put her out by force.

When she had gone, he crawled over to the door of the hut. The sun had just set, and the moon would follow it in a couple of hours. Most of the *'fene abantu* had retired. But a couple of them squatted outside their huts, in sight of his place, watchfully.

Heigh ho, he thought, they aren't taking any chances. Perhaps the old boy is grateful and all that rot. But I think my fiancée let the cat out when she said that about the desirability of hitching one of the tribe to a human being. Of course the poor things don't know that it wouldn't have any legal standing at all. But that fact wouldn't save me from a jolly unpleasant experience in the meantime. Suppose I haven't escaped by the time of the ceremony. Would I go through with it? *Br-r-r!* Of course not. I'm an Englishman and an officer of the Crown. But if it meant my life...I don't know. I'm dashed if I do. Perhaps I can talk them out of it...being careful not to get them angry in the process—

He was tied to the straw, and enormous centipedes were dropping off the ceiling onto his face. Then he was running through the swamp, with Ingwamza and her irate pa after him. His feet stuck in the mud so he couldn't move, and there was a light in his face. Mtengeni—good old George—was riding a two headed rhino. But instead of rescuing him, the warden said: "Mr. Cuff, you must do, something about these Bechuana. Them, they are catching all my animals and painting them red with green stripes." Then he woke up.

It took him a second to realize that the light was from the setting moon, not the rising sun, and that he therefore had been asleep less than two hours. It took him another second to realize what had wakened him. The straw of the hut wall had been wedged apart, and through the gap a *'fene umntu* was crawling. While Cuff was still wondering why one of his hosts, or captors, should use this peculiar method of getting in, the baboon-man stood up. He looked enormous in the faint light.

"What is it?" asked Cuff.

"If you make a noise," said the stranger, "I will kill you."

"What? What's the idea? Why should you want to kill me?"

"You have stolen my Ingwamza."

"But...but—" Cuff was at a loss. Here the gal's old man would tear him in pieces—small pieces—if he didn't marry her, and a rival or something would kill him if he did, "Let's talk it over first," he said, in what he hoped was a normal voice. "Who are you, by the way?"

"My name is Cukata. I was to have married Ingwamza next month. And then you came."

"What...what—"

"I won't kill you. Not if you make no noise. I will just fix you so you won't marry Ingwamza." He moved toward the pile of straw.

Cuff didn't waste time inquiring into the horrid details. "Wait a minute," he said, cold sweat bedewing not merely his brow, but his whole torso. "My dear fellow, this marriage wasn't my idea. It was Indlovu's, entirely. I don't want to steal your girl. They just informed me that I was going to marry her, without asking me about it at all. I don't want to marry her. In fact there's nothing I want to do less."

The *'fene umntu* stood still for a moment, thinking. Then he said softly: "You wouldn't marry my Ingwamza if you had the chance? You think she is ugly?"

"Well—"

"By u-Qamata, that's an insult! Nobody shall think such thoughts of my Ingwamza! Now I will kill you for sure!"

"Wait, wait!" Cuff's voice, normally a pleasant low baritone, became a squeak. "That isn't it at all! She's beautiful, intelligent, industrious, all that a *'ntu* could want. But I can never marry her." Inspiration! Cuff went on rapidly. Never had he spoken Xosa so fluently. "You know that if lion mates with leopard, there are no offspring." Cuff wasn't sure that was so, but he took a chance. "It is that way with my people and yours. We are too different. There would be no issue to our marriage. And Indlovu would not have grandchildren by us to gladden his old age."

Cukata, after some thought, saw, or thought he did. "But," he said, "how can I prevent this marriage without killing you?"

"You could help me escape."

"So. Now that's an idea. Where do you want to go?"

"Do you know where the Hickey machine is?"

"Yes, though I have never been close to it. That is forbidden. About fifteen miles north of here, on the edge of the Chobe Swamp, is a rock. By the rock are three baobab trees, close together. Between the trees and the swamp are two houses. The machine is in one of those houses."

He was silent again. "You can't travel fast with that wounded foot. They would overtake you. Perhaps Indlovu would tear you in pieces, or perhaps he would bring you back. If he brought you back, we should fail. If he tore you in pieces, I should be sorry, for I like you, even if you are a feeble little *isi-pham-pham*." Cuff wished that the simian brain would get around to the point. "I have it. In ten minutes I shall whistle. You will then crawl out through this hole in the wall, making no noise. You understand?"

When Athelstan Cuff crawled out, he found Cukata in the alley between two rows of huts. There was a strong reptilian stench in the air.

Behind the baboon-man was something large and black. It walked with a swaying motion. It brushed against Cuff, and he almost cried out at the touch of cold, leathery hide.

"This is the largest," said Cukata. "We hope some day to have a whole herd of them. They are fine for traveling across the swamps, because they can swim as well as run. And they grow much faster than the ordinary crocodile."

The thing was a crocodile but such a crocodile! Though not much over fifteen feet in length, it had long, powerful legs that raised its body a good four feet off the ground, giving it a dinosaurian look. It rubbed against Cuff, and the thought occurred to him that it had taken an astonishing mutation indeed to give a brainless and voracious reptile an affection for human beings.

Cukata handed Cuff a knobkerry, and explained: "Whistle, loudly, when you want him to come. To start him, hit him on the tail with this. To stop him, hit him on the nose. To make him go to the left, hit him on the right side of the neck, not too hard. To make him go to the right, hit him—"

"On the left side of the neck, but not too hard," finished Cuff. "What does he eat?"

"Anything that is meat. But you needn't feed him for two or three days; he has been fed recently."

"Don't you use a saddle?"

"Saddle? What's that?"

"Never mind." Cuff climbed aboard, wincing as he settled onto the sharp dorsal ridges of the animal's hide.

"Wait," said Cukata. "The moon will be completely gone in a moment. Remember, I shall say that I know nothing about your escape, but that you go out and stole him yourself. His name Soga."

There were the baobab trees, and there were the houses. There were also a dozen elephants, facing the rider and his bizarre mount and spreading their immense ears. Athelstan Cuff was getting so blasé about freaks that he hardly noticed that two of the elephants had two trunks apiece; that another of them was colored a fair imitation of a Scotch tartan; that another of them had short legs like a hippopotamus, so that it looked like something out of a dachshund breeder's nightmare.

The elephants, for their part, seemed undecided whether to run or to attack, and finally compromised by doing nothing. Cuff realized when he was already past them that he had done a wickedly reckless thing in going so close to them unarmed except for the useless kerry. But somehow he couldn't get excited about mere elephants. His whole life for the past forty-eight hours had had a dreamlike quality. Maybe he was dreaming. Or maybe he had a charmed life. Or something. Though there was nothing dreamlike about the throb in his foot, or the acute soreness in his gluteus maximus.

Soga, being a crocodile, bowed his whole body at every stride. First the head and tail went to the right and the body to the left; then the process was reversed. Which was most unpleasant for his rider.

Cuff was willing to swear that he'd ridden at least fifty miles instead of the fifteen Cukata had mentioned. Actually he had done about thirty, not having been able to follow a straight line and having to steer by stars and, when it rose, the sun. A fair portion of the thirty had been hugging Soga's barrel while the croc's great tail drove them through the water like a racing shell. No hippo or other crocs had bothered them; evidently they knew when they were well off.

Athelstan Cuff slid—almost fell—off, and hobbled up to the entrance of one of the houses. His practiced eye took in the roof cistern, the solar boiler, the steam-electric plant, the batteries, and finally the tube inside. He went in. Yes, by Jove, the tube was in operation after all these years. Hickey must have had something jolly unusual. Cuff found the main switch easily enough and pulled it. All that happened was that the little orange glow in the tube died.

The house was so silent it made Cuff uncomfortable, except for the faint hum of the solar power plant. As he moved about, using the kerry for a crutch, he stirred up the dust which lay six inches deep on the floor. Maybe there were notebooks or something which ought to be collected. There had been, he soon discovered, but the termites had eaten every scrap of paper, and even the imitation-leather covers, leaving only the metal binding rings and their frames. It was the same with the books.

Something white caught his eye. It was paper. lying on a little metal-legged stand that the termites evidently hadn't thought well enough of to climb. He limped toward it eagerly. But it was only a newspaper, *Umlindi we Nyanga*—"The Monthly Watchman"—published in East London. Evidently, Stanley H. Mqhavi had subscribed to it. It crumbled at Cuff's touch.

Oh, well, he thought, can't expect much. We'll run along, and some of the bio-physicist chappies can come in and gather up the scientific apparatus.

He went out, called Soga, and started east. He figured that he could strike the old wagon road somewhere north of the Mababe, and get down to Mtengeni's main station that way.

Were those human voices? Cuff shifted uneasily on his Indian fakir's seat. He had gone about four miles after leaving Hickey's scientific station.

They were voices, but not human ones. They belonged to a dozen *'fene abantu*, who came loping through the grass with old Indlovu at their head.

Cuff reached back and thumped Soga's tail. If he could get the croc going all out, he might be able to run away from his late hosts. Soga wasn't as fast as a horse, but he could trot right along. Cuff was relieved to see that they hadn't brought his rifle along. They were armed with kerries and spears, like any of the more savage *abantu*. Perhaps the fear of injuring their pet would make them hesitate to throw things at him. At least he hoped so.

A familiar voice caught up with him in a piercing yell of "Soga!" The croc slackened his pace and tried to turn his head. Cuff whacked him unmercifully. Indlovu's yell came again, followed by a whistle. The croc was now definitely off his stride. Cuff's efforts to keep him headed away from his proper masters resulted in his zigzagging erratically. The contrary directions confused and irritated him. He opened his jaws and hissed. The baboon-men were gaining rapidly.

So, thought Cuff, this is the end. I hate like hell to go out before I've had a chance to write my report. But mustn't show it. Not an Englishman and an officer of the Crown. Wonder what poor Mtengeni'll think.

Something went *whick* past him; a fraction of a second later, the crash of an elephant rifle reached him. A big puff of dust ballooned up in front of the baboon-men. They skittered away from it as if the dust and not the bullet that made it were something deadly. George Mtengeni appeared from behind the nearest patch of thorn scrub, and yelled, "Hold still there, or me, I'll blow your heads off." If the *'fene abantu* couldn't understand his English, they got his tone.

Cuff thought vaguely, good old George, he could shoot their ears off at that distance. but he has more sense then to kill any of them before he finds out. Cuff slid off Soga and almost fell in a heap.

The warden came up. "What…what in the heavens has been happening to you, Mr. Cuff? What are these?" He indicated the baboon-men.

"Joke," giggled Cuff. "Good joke on you, George. Been living in your dashed Park for years, and you never knew—Wait, I've got to explain something to these chaps. I say, Indlovu…hell, he doesn't know English. Got to use Xosa. You know Xosa, don't you George?' He giggled again.

"Why, me, I…I can follow it. It's much like Zulu. But my God, what happened to the seat of your pants?"

Cuff pointed a wavering finger at Soga's sawtoothed back. "Good old Soga. Should have had a saddle. Dashed outrage, not providing a saddle for His Majesty's representative."

"But you look as if you'd been skinned! Me, I've got to get you to a hospital…and what about your foot?"

"T'hell with the foot. 'Nother joke, Can't stand up, can't sit down. Jolly, what? Have to sleep on my stomach. But, Indlovu! I'm sorry I had to run away. I couldn't marry Ingwamza. Really. Because…because—" Athelstan Cuff swayed and collapsed in a small, ragged pile.

Peter Cuff's eyes were round. He asked the inevitable small-boy question: "What happened then?"

Athelstan Cuff was stuffing his pipe. "Oh, about what you'd expect. Indlovu was jolly vexed, I can tell you, but he didn't dare do anything with George standing there with the gun. He calmed down later after he understood what I had been driving at, and we became good friends. When he died, Cukata was elected chief in his place. I still get Christmas cards from him."

"Christmas cards from a baboon?"

"Certainly. If I get one next Christmas, I'll show it to you. It's the same card every year. He's an economical fella, and he bought a hundred cards of the same pattern because he could get them at a discount."

"Were you all right?"

"Yes, after a month in the hospital. I still don't know why I didn't get sixteen kinds of blood poisoning. Fool's luck, I suppose."

"But what's that got to do with me being a 'dopted boy?"

"Peter!" Cuff gave the clicks represented in the Bantu languages by *x* and in English by *tsk*. "Isn't it obvious? That tube of Hickey's was on when I approached his house. So I got a full dose of the radiations. Their effect was to produce violent mutations in the germ-plasm. You know what that is, don't you? Well, I never dared have any children of my own after that, for fear they'd turn out to be some sort of monster. That didn't occur to me until afterward. It fair bowled me over, I can tell you, when I did think of it. I went to pieces, rather, and lost my job in South Africa. But now that I have you and your mother, I realize that it wasn't so important after all."

"Father—" Peter hesitated.

"Go on, old man."

"If you'd thought of the rays before you went to the house, would you have been brave enough to go ahead anyway?"

Cuff lit his pipe and looked off at nothing. "I've often wondered about that myself. I'm dashed if I know. I wonder...just what would have happened—"

THEY

Robert A. Heinlein

ROBERT ANSON HEINLEIN (1907-1988) emerged early on in the pages of John W. Campbell Jr.'s Astounding Science Fiction as a major star in the field. He wrote in a punchy, conversational style that belied his controversial ideas about religion, government, the individual, and freedom. Less the technocrat, Heinlein was a libertarian but believed in governments composed of self-reliant individuals who earn their citizenship (see *Starship Troopers*). "They" is a classic statement of the sovereignty of the individual who is at war with the world and perhaps even himself, a theme Philip K. Dick would explore in the Fifties and Sixties.

THEY would not let him alone.

They never would let him alone. He realized that that was part of the plot against him—never to leave him in peace, never to give him a chance to mull over the lies they had told him, time enough to pick out the flaws, and to figure out the truth for himself.

That damned attendant this morning! He had come busting in with his breakfast tray, waking him, and causing him to forget his dream. If only he could remember that dream

Someone was unlocking the door. He ignored it.

"Howdy, old boy. They tell me you refused your breakfast?" Dr. Hayward's professionally kindly mask hung over his bed.

"I wasn't hungry."

"But we can't have that. You'll get weak, and then I won't be able to get you well completely. Now get up and get your clothes on and I'll order an eggnog for you. Come on, that's a good fellow!"

Unwilling, but still less willing at that moment to enter into any conflict of wills, he got out of bed and slipped on his bathrobe. "That's better," Hayward approved. "Have a cigarette?"

"No, thank you."

The doctor shook his head in a puzzled fashion. "Darned if I can figure you out. Loss of interest in physical pleasures does not fit your type of case."

"What is my type of case?" he inquired in flat tones.

"Tut! Tut!" Hayward tried to appear roguish. "If medicos told their professional secrets, they might have to work for a living."

"What is my type of case?"

"Well—the label doesn't matter, does it? Suppose you tell me. I really know nothing about your case as yet. Don't you think it is about time you talked?"

"I'll play chess with you."

"All right, all right." Hayward made a gesture of impatient concession. "We've played chess every day for a week. If you will talk, I'll play chess."

What could it matter? If he was right, they already understood perfectly that he had discovered their plot; there was nothing to be gained by concealing the obvious. Let them try to argue him out of it. Let the tail go with the hide! To hell with it!

He got out the chessmen and commenced setting them up. "What do you know of my case so far?"

"Very little. Physical examination, negative. Past history, negative. High intelligence, as shown by your record in school and your success in your profession. Occasional fits of moodiness, but nothing exceptional. The only positive information was the incident that caused you to come here for treatment."

"To be brought here, you mean. Why should it cause comment?"

"Well, good gracious, man—if you barricade yourself in your room and insist that your wife is plotting against you, don't you expect people to notice?"

"But she *was* plotting against me—and so are you. White, or black?"

"Black—it's your turn to attack. Why do you think we are plotting against you'?"

"It's an involved story, and goes way back into my early childhood. There was an immediate incident, however—" He opened by advancing the white king's knight to KB3. Hayward's eyebrows raised.

"You make a piano attack?"

"Why not? You know that it is not safe for me to risk a gambit with you."

The doctor shrugged his shoulders and answered the opening. "Suppose we start with your early childhood. It may shed more light than more recent incidents. Did you feel that you were persecuted as a child?"

"No!" He half rose from his chair. "When I was a child I was sure of myself. I knew then. I tell you; I knew! Life was worth while, and I knew it. I was at peace with myself and my surroundings. Life was good and I was good, and I assumed that the creatures around me were like myself."

"And weren't they?"

"Not at all! Particularly the children. I didn't know what viciousness was until I was turned loose with other 'children.' The little devils! And I was expected to be like them and play with them."

The doctor nodded. "I know. The herd compulsion. Children can be pretty savage at times."

"You've missed the point. This wasn't any healthy roughness; these creatures were *different*—not like myself at all. They *looked* like me, but they were not like me. If I tried to say anything to one of them about anything that mattered to me, all I could get was a stare and a scornful laugh. Then they would find some way to punish me for having said it."

Hayward nodded. "I see what you mean. How about grownups?"

"That is something different. Adults don't matter to children at first—or rather, they did not matter to me. They were too big, and they did not bother me, and they were busy with things that did not enter into my considerations. It was only when I noticed that my presence affected them that I began to wonder about them."

"How do you mean?"

"Well, they never did the things when I was around that they did when I was not around."

Hayward looked at him carefully. "Won't that statement take quite a lot of justifying? How do you know what they did when you weren't around?"

He acknowledged the point. "But I used to catch them just stopping. If I came into a room, the conversation would stop suddenly, and then it would pick up about the weather or something equally inane. Then I took to hiding and listening and looking. Adults did not behave the same way in my presence as out of it."

"Your move, I believe. But see here, old man—that was when you were a child. Every child passes through that phase. Now that you are a man, you must see the adult point of view. Children are strange creatures and have to be protected—at least, we do protect them—from many adult interests. There is a whole code of conventions in the matter that—"

"Yes, yes," he interrupted impatiently, "I know all that. Nevertheless, I noticed enough and remembered enough that was never clear to me later. And it put me on my guard to notice the next thing."

"Which was?" He noticed that the doctor's eyes were averted as he adjusted a castle's position.

"The things I saw people doing and heard them talking about were never of any importance. They must be doing something else."

"I don't follow you."

"You don't choose to follow me. I'm telling this to you in exchange for a game of chess."

"Why do you like to play chess so well?"

"Because it is the only thing in the world where I can see all the factors and understand all the rules. Never mind—I saw all around me this enormous plant, cities, farms, factories, churches, schools, homes, railroads, luggage, roller coasters, trees, saxophones, libraries, people and animals. People that looked like me and who should have felt very much like me, if what I was told was the truth. But what did they appear to be doing? They went to work to earn the money to buy the food to get the strength to go to work to get the strength to buy the food to earn the money to go to—until they fell over dead. Any slight variation in the basic pattern did not matter, for they always fell over dead. And everybody tried to tell me that I should be doing the same thing. I knew better!"

The doctor gave him a look apparently intended to denote helpless surrender and laughed. "I can't argue with you. Life does look like that, and maybe it is just that futile. But it is the only life we have. Why not make up your mind to enjoy it as much as possible?"

"Oh, no!" He looked both sulky and stubborn. "You can't peddle nonsense to me by claiming to be fresh out of sense. How do I know? Because all this complex stage setting, all these swarms of actors, could not have been put here just to make idiot noises at each other. Some other explanation but not that one. An insanity as enormous, as complex, as the one around me had to be planned. I've found the plan!"

"Which is?"

He noticed that the doctor's eyes were again averted.

"It is a play intended to divert me, to occupy my mind and confuse me, to keep me so busy with details that I will not have time to think about the meaning. You are all in it, every one of you." He shook his finger in the doctor's face. "Most of them may be helpless automatons, but you're not. You are one of the conspirators. You've been sent in as a troubleshooter to try to force me to go back to playing the role assigned to me!"

He saw that the doctor was waiting for him to quiet down. "Take it easy," Hayward finally managed to say. "Maybe it is all a conspiracy, but why do you think that you have been singled out for special attention? Maybe it is a joke on all of us. Why couldn't I be one of the victims as well as yourself?"

"Got you!" He pointed a long finger at Hayward. "That is the essence of the plot. All of these creatures have been set up to look like me in order to prevent me from realizing that I was the center of the arrangements. But I have noticed the key fact, the mathematically inescapable fact, that I am unique. Here am I, sitting on the inside. The world extends outward from me. I am the center—"

"Easy, man, easy! Don't you realize that the world looks that way to me, too? We are each the center of the universe—"

"Not so! That is what you have tried to make me believe, that I am just one of millions more just like me. Wrong! If they were like me, then I could get into communication with them. I can't. I have tried and tried and I can't. I've sent out my inner thoughts, seeking some one other being who has them, too. What have I gotten back? Wrong answers, jarring incongruities, meaningless obscenity. I've tried, I tell you. God!—how I've tried! But there is nothing out there to speak to me—nothing but emptiness and otherness!"

"Wait a minute. Do you mean to say that you think there is nobody home at my end of the line? Don't you believe that I am alive and conscious?"

He regarded the doctor soberly. "Yes, I think you are probably alive, but you are one of the others—my antagonists. But you have set thousands of others around me whose faces are blank, not lived in, and whose speech is a meaningless reflex of noise."

"Well, then, if you concede that I am an ego, why do you insist that I am so very different from yourself?"

"Why? Wait!" He pushed back from the chess table and strode over to the wardrobe, from which he took out a violin case.

While he was playing, the lines of suffering smoothed out of his face and his expression took on a relaxed beatitude. For a while he recaptured the emotions, but not the knowledge, which he had possessed in dreams. The melody proceeded easily from proposition to proposition with inescapable, unforced logic. He finished with a triumphant statement of the/ essential thesis and turned to the doctor. "Well?"

"Hm-m-m." He seemed to detect an even greater degree of caution in the doctor's manner. "It's an odd bit, but remarkable. 'S pity you didn't take up the violin seriously. You could have made quite a reputation. You could even now. Why don't you do it? You could afford to, I believe."

He stood and stared at the doctor for a long moment, then shook his head as if trying to clear it. "It's no use," he said slowly, "no use at all. There is no possibility of communication. I am alone." He replaced the instrument in its case and returned to the chess table. "My move, I believe?"

"Yes. Guard your queen."

He studied the board. "Not necessary. I no longer need my queen. Check."

The doctor interposed a pawn to parry the attack.

He nodded. "You use your pawns well, but I have learned to anticipate your play. Check again—and mate, I think."

The doctor examined the new situation. "No," he decided, "no—not quite." He retreated from the square under attack. "Not checkmate—stalemate at the worst. Yes, another stalemate."

He was upset by the doctor's visit. He couldn't be wrong, basically, yet the doctor had certainly pointed out logical holes in his position. From a logical standpoint the whole world might be a fraud perpetrated on everybody. But logic means nothing—logic itself was a fraud, starting with unproved assumptions and capable of proving anything. The world is what it is!—and carries its own evidence of trickery.

But does it? What did he have to go on? Could he lay down a line between known facts and everything else and then make a reasonable interpretation of the world, based on facts alone—an interpretation free from complexities of logic and no hidden assumptions of points not certain? Very well—

First fact, himself. He knew himself directly. He existed.

Second facts, the evidence of his "five senses," everything that he himself saw and heard and smelled and tasted with his physical senses. Subject to their limitations, he must believe his senses. Without them he was entirely solitary, shut up in a locker of bone, blind, deaf, cut off, the only being in the world.

And that was not the case. He knew that he did not invent the information brought to him by his senses. There had to be something else out there. Some otherness that produced the things his senses recorded. All philosophies that claimed that the physical world around him did not exist except in his imagination were sheer nonsense.

But beyond that, what? Were there any third facts on which he could rely? No, not at this point. He could not afford to believe anything that he was told, or that he read, or that was implicitly assumed to be true about the world around him. No, he could not believe any of it, for the sum total of what he had been told and read and been taught in school was contradictory, so senseless, so wildly insane that none of it could be believed unless he personally confirmed it.

Wait a minute—The very telling of these lies, these senseless contradictions, was a fact in itself, known to him directly. To that extent they were data, probably very important data.

The world as it had been shown to him was a piece of unreason, an idiot's dream. Yet it was on too mammoth a scale to be without some reason. He came wearily back to his original point: Since the world could not be as crazy as it appeared to be, it must necessarily have been arranged to appear crazy in order to deceive him as to the truth.

Why had they done it to him? And what was the truth behind the sham? There must be some clue in the deception itself. What thread ran through it all? Well, in the first place he had been given a superabundance of explanations of the world around him, philosophies, religions, "common sense" explanations. Most of them were so clumsy, so obviously inadequate, or meaningless, that they could hardly have expected him to take them seriously. They must have intended them simply as misdirection.

But there were certain basic assumptions running through all the hundreds of explanations of the craziness around him. It must be these basic assumptions that he was expected to believe. For example, there was the deep-seated assumption that he was a "human being," essentially like millions of others around him and billions more in the past and the future.

That was nonsense! He had never once managed to get into real communication with all those things that looked so much like him but were so different. In the agony of his loneliness, he had deceived himself that Alice understood him and was a being like him. He knew now that he had suppressed and refused to examine thousands of little discrepancies because he could not bear the thought of returning to complete loneliness. He had needed to believe that his wife was a living, breathing being of his own kind who understood his inner thoughts. He had refused to consider the possibility that she was simply a mirror, an echo—or something unthinkably worse.

He had found a mate, and the world was tolerable, even though dull, stupid, and full of petty annoyance. He was moderately happy and had put away his suspicions. He had accepted, quite docilely, the treadmill he was expected to use, until a slight mischance had momentarily cut through the fraud—then his suspicions had returned with impounded force; the bitter knowledge of his childhood had been confirmed.

He supposed that he had been a fool to make a fuss about it. If he had kept his mouth shut they would not have locked him up. He should have been as subtle and as shrewd as they, kept his eyes and ears open and learned the details of and the reasons for the plot against him. He might have learned how to circumvent it.

But what if they had locked him up—the whole world was an asylum and all of them his keepers.

A key scraped in the lock, and he looked up to see an attendant entering with a tray. "Here's your dinner, sir."

"Thanks, Joe," he said gently. "Just put it down."

"Movies tonight, sir," the attendant went on. "Wouldn't you like to go? Dr. Hayward said you could—"

"No, thank you. I prefer not to."

"I wish you would, sir." He noticed with amusement the persuasive intentness of the attendant's manner. "I think the doctor wants you to. It's a good movie. There's a Mickey Mouse cartoon—

"You almost persuade me, Joe," he answered with passive agreeableness. "Mickey's trouble is the same as mine, essentially. However, I'm not going. They need not bother to hold movies tonight."

"Oh, there will be movies in any case, sir. Lots of our other guests will attend."

"Really? Is that an example of thoroughness, or are you simply keeping up the pretense in talking to me? It isn't necessary, Joe, if it's any strain on you. I know the game. If I don't attend, there is no point in holding movies."

He liked the grin with which the attendant answered this thrust. Was it possible that this being was created just as he appeared to be—big muscles, phlegmatic disposition, tolerant, dog-like? Or was there nothing going on behind those kind eyes, nothing but robot reflex? No, it was more likely that he was one of them, since he was so closely in attendance on him.

The attendant left and he busied himself at his supper tray, scooping up the already-cut bits of meat with a spoon, the only implement provided. He smiled again at their caution and thoroughness. No danger of that—he would not destroy this body as long as it served him in investigating the truth of the matter. There were still many different avenues of research available before taking that possibly irrevocable step.

After supper he decided to put his thoughts in better order by writing them; he obtained paper. He should start with a general statement of some underlying postulates of the credos that had been drummed into him all his "life." Life? Yes, that was a good one. He wrote:

> "I am told that I was born a certain number of years ago and that I will die a similar number of years hence. Various clumsy stories have been offered me to explain to me where I was before birth and what becomes of me after death, but they are rough lies, not intended to deceive, except as misdirection. In every other possible way the world around me assures me that I am mortal, here but a few years, and a few years hence gone completely—non-existent.
>
> "WRONG—I am immortal. I transcend this little time axis; a seventy-year span on it is but a casual phase in my experience. Second only to the prime datum of my own existence is the emotionally convincing certainty of

my own continuity. I may be a closed curve, but closed or open, I neither have a beginning nor an end. Self-awareness is not relational; it is absolute, and cannot be reached to be destroyed, or created. Memory, however, being a relational aspect of consciousness, may be tampered with and possibly destroyed.

"It is true that most religions which have been offered me teach immortality, but note the fashion in which they teach it. The surest way to lie convincingly is to tell the truth unconvincingly. They did not wish me to believe.

"Caution: Why have they tried so hard to convince me that I am going to 'die' in a few years? There must be a very important reason. I infer that they are preparing me for some sort of a major change. It may be crucially important for me to figure out their intentions about this—probably I have several years in which to reach a decision. Note: Avoid using the types of reasoning they have taught me."

The attendant was back. "Your wife is here, sir."

"Tell her to go away."

"Please, sir—Dr. Hayward is most anxious that you should see her."

"Tell Dr. Hayward that I said that he is an excellent chess player."

"Yes, sir." The attendant waited for a moment. "Then you won't see her, sir?"

"No, I won't see her."

He wandered around the room for some minutes after the attendant had left, too distrait to return to his recapitulation. By and large, they had played very decently with him since they had brought him here. He was glad that they had allowed him to have a room alone, and he certainly had more time free for contemplation than had ever been possible on the outside. To be sure, continuous effort to keep him busy and to distract him was made, but, by being stubborn, he was able to circumvent the rules and gain some hours each day for introspection.

But, damnation!—he did wish they would not persist in using Alice in their attempts to divert his thoughts. Although the intense terror and revulsion which she had inspired in him when he had first rediscovered the truth had now aged into a simple feeling of repugnance and distaste for her company, nevertheless it was emotionally upsetting to be reminded of her, to be forced into making decisions about her.

After all, she *had* been his wife for many years. Wife? What was a wife? Another soul like one's own, a complement, the other necessary pole to the couple, a sanctuary of understanding and sympathy in the boundless depths of aloneness. *That* was what he thought, what he had needed to believe and had believed fiercely for years. The yearning need for companionship of his own kind had caused him to see himself reflected in those beautiful eyes and had made him quite uncritical of occasional incongruities in her responses.

He sighed. He felt that he had sloughed off most of the typed emotional reactions which they had taught him by precept and example, but Alice had gotten under his skin, way under, and it still hurt. He had been happy—what if it had been a dope dream? They had given him an excellent, a beautiful mirror to play with—the more fool he to have looked behind it!

Wearily he turned back to his summing up.

> "The world is explained in either one of two ways: the common-sense way which says that the world is pretty much as it appears to be and that ordinary human conduct and motivations are reasonable, and the religio-mystic solution which states that the world is dream stuff, unreal, insubstantial, with reality somewhere beyond.
>
> "WRONG—both of them. The common-sense scheme has no sense to it of any sort. 'Life is short and full of trouble. Man born of woman is born to trouble as the sparks fly upward. His days are few and they are numbered. All is vanity and vexation.' Those quotations may be jumbled and incorrect, but that is a fair statement of the common-sense world-is-as-it-seems in its only possible evaluation. In such a world, human striving is about as rational as the blind dartings of a moth against a light bulb. The 'common-sense

> world' is a blind insanity, out of nowhere, going nowhere, to no purpose.
>
> "As for the other solution, it appears more rational on the surface, in that it rejects the utterly irrational world of common sense. But it is not a rational solution, it is simply a flight from reality of any sort, for it refuses to believe the results of the only available direct communication between the ego and the Outside. Certainly the 'five senses' are poor enough channels of communication, but they are the only channels."

He crumpled up the paper and flung himself from the chair. Order and logic were no good—his answer was right because it smelled right. But he still did not know all the answers. Why the grand scale of the deception, countless creatures, whole continents, an enormously involved and minutely detailed matrix of insane history, insane tradition, insane culture? Why bother with more than a cell and a strait jacket?

It must be, it had to be, because it was supremely important to deceive him completely, because a lesser deception would not do. Could it be that they dare not let him suspect his real identity no matter how difficult and involved the fraud?

He had to know. In some fashion he must get behind the deception and see what went on when he was not looking. He had had one glimpse; this time he must see the actual workings, catch the puppet masters in their manipulations.

Obviously the first step must be to escape from this asylum, but to do it so craftily they would never see him, never catch up with him, not have a chance to set the stage before him. That would be hard to do. He must excel them in shrewdness and subtlety.

Once decided, he spent the rest of the evening in considering the means by which he might accomplish his purpose. It seemed almost impossible—he must get away without once being seen and remain in strict hiding. They must lose track of him completely in order that they would not know where to center their deceptions. That would mean going without food for several days. Very well—

he could do it. He must not give them any warning by unusual action or manner.

The lights blinked twice. Docilely he got up and commenced preparations for bed. When the attendant looked through the peephole he was already in bed, with his face turned to the wall.

Gladness! Gladness everywhere! It was good to be with his own kind, to hear the music swelling out of every living thing, as it always had and always would—good to know that everything was living and aware of him, participating in him, as he participated in them. It was good to be, good to know the unity of many and the diversity of one. There had been one bad thought—the details escaped him—but it was gone—it had never been; there was no place for it.

The early-morning sounds from the adjacent ward penetrated the sleep-laden body which served him here and gradually recalled him to awareness of the hospital room. The transition was so gentle that he carried over full recollection of what he had been doing and why. He lay still, a gentle smile on his face, and savored the uncouth, but not unpleasant, languor of the body he wore. Strange that he had ever forgotten despite their tricks and stratagems. Well, now that he had recalled the key, he would quickly set things right in this odd place. He would call them in at once and announce the new order. It would be amusing to see old Glaroon's expression when he realized that the cycle had ended—

The click of the peephole and the rasp of the door being unlocked guillotined his line of thought. The morning attendant pushed briskly in with the breakfast tray and placed it on the tip table. "Morning, sir. Nice, bright day—want it in bed, or will you get up?"

Don't answer! Don't listen! Suppress this distraction! This is part of their plan—But it was too late, too late. He felt himself slipping, falling, wrenched from reality back into the fraud world in which they had kept him. It was gone, gone completely, with no single association around him to which to anchor memory. There was nothing left but the sense of heartbreaking loss and the acute ache of unsatisfied catharsis.

"Leave it where it is. I'll take care of it."

"Okey-doke." The attendant bustled out, slamming the door, and noisily locked it.

He lay quite still for a long time, every nerve end in his body screaming for relief.

At last he got out of bed, still miserably unhappy, and attempted to concentrate on his plans for escape. But the psychic wrench he had received in being recalled so suddenly from his plane of reality had left him bruised and emotionally disturbed. His mind insisted on rechewing its doubts, rather than engage in constructive thought. Was it possible that the doctor was right, that he was not alone in his miserable dilemma? Was he really simply suffering from paranoia, delusions of self-importance?

Could it be that each unit in this yeasty swarm around him was the prison of another lonely ego—helpless, blind, and speechless, condemned to an eternity of miserable loneliness? Was the look of suffering which he had brought to Alice's face a true reflection of inner torment and not simply a piece of play-acting intended to maneuver him into compliance with their plans?

A knock sounded at the door. He said, "Come in," without looking up. Their comings and goings did not matter to

"Dearest—" A well-known voice spoke slowly and hesitantly.

"Alice!" He was on his feet at once, and facing her. "Who let you in here?"

"Please, dear, please—I had to see you."

"It isn't fair. It isn't fair." He spoke more to himself than to her. Then: "Why did you come?"

She stood up to him with a dignity he had hardly expected. The beauty of her childlike face had been marred by line and shadow, but it shone with an unexpected courage. "I love you," she answered quietly. "You can tell me to go away, but you can't make me stop loving you and trying to help you."

He turned away from her in an agony of indecision. Could it be possible that he had misjudged her? Was there, behind that barrier of flesh and sound symbols, a spirit that truly yearned toward his? Lovers whispering in the dark—"You *do* understand, don't you?"

"Yes, dear heart, I understand."

"Then nothing that happens to us can matter, as long as we are together and understand—" Words, words, rebounding hollowly from an unbroken wall—

No, he *couldn't* be wrong! Test her again—"Why did you keep me on that job in Omaha?"

"But I didn't make you keep that job. I simply pointed out that we should think twice before—"

"Never mind. Never mind." Soft hands and a sweet face preventing him with mild stubbornness from ever doing the thing that his heart told him to do. Always with the best of intentions, the best of intentions, but always so that he had never quite managed to do the silly, unreasonable things, that he knew were worth while. Hurry, hurry, hurry, and strive, with an angel-faced jockey to see that you don't stop long enough to think for yourself—

"Why did you try to stop me from going back upstairs that day?"

She managed to smile although her eyes were already spilling over with tears. "I didn't know it really mattered to you. I didn't want us to miss the train."

It had been a small thing, an unimportant thing. For some reason not clear even to him he had insisted on going back upstairs to his study when they were about to leave the house for a short vacation. It was raining, and she had pointed out that there was barely enough time to get to the station. He had surprised himself and her, too, by insisting on his own way in circumstances in which he had never been known to be stubborn.

He had actually pushed her to one side and forced his way up the stairs. Even then nothing might have come of it had he not—quite unnecessarily—raised the shade of the window that faced toward the rear of the house.

It was a very small matter. It had been raining, hard, out in front. From this window the weather was clear and sunny, with no sign of rain.

He had stood there quite a long while, gazing out at the impossible sunshine and rearranging his cosmos in his mind. He re-examined long-suppressed doubts in the light of this small but totally unexplained discrepancy. Then he had turned and had found that she was standing behind him.

He had been trying ever since to forget the expression that he had surprised on her face.

"What about the rain?"

"The rain?" she repeated in a small, puzzled voice. "Why, it was raining, of course. What about it?"

"But it was not raining out my study window."

"What? But of course it was. I did notice the sun break through the clouds for a moment, but that was all."

"Nonsense!"

"But darling, what has the weather to do with you and me? What difference does it make whether it rains or not—to us?" She approached him timidly and slid a small hand between his arm and side. "Am I responsible for the weather?"

"I think you are. Now please go."

She withdrew from him, brushed blindly at her eyes, gulped once, then said in a voice held steady: "All right, I'll go. But remember—you can come home if you want to. And I'll be there if you want me." She waited a moment, then added hesitantly: "Would you...would you kiss me goodbye?"

He made no answer of any sort, neither with voice nor eyes. She looked at him, then turned, fumbled blindly for the door, and rushed through it.

The creature he knew as Alice went to the place of assembly without stopping to change form. "It is necessary to adjourn this sequence. I am no longer able to influence his decisions."

They had expected it, nevertheless they stirred with dismay.

The Glaroon addressed the First for Manipulation. "Prepare to graft the selected memory track at once."

Then, turning to the First for Operations, the Glaroon said: "The extrapolation shows that he will tend to escape within two of his days. This sequence degenerated primarily through your failure to extend that rainfall all around him.

Be advised."

"It would be simpler if we understood his motives."

"In my capacity as Dr. Hayward, I have often thought so," commented the Glaroon acidly, "but if we understood his motives, we would be part of *him*. Bear in mind the Treaty! He almost remembered."

The creature known as Alice spoke up. "Could he not have the Taj Mahal next sequence? For some reason he values it."

"You are becoming assimilated!"

"Perhaps. I am not in fear. Will he receive it?"

"It will be considered."

The Glaroon continued with orders: "Leave structures standing until adjournment. New York City and Harvard University are now dismantled. Divert him from those sectors. Move!"

AFTERWORD

The First Science Fictions

Paul Cook

SCIENCE FICTION, as we now recognize it, appeared on the literary scene when Mary Shelley published Frankenstein is 1819. There had been stories in literature for centuries that had elements of the fantastic or the speculative. Some were satires, some were merely fanciful. We have Cyrano de Bergerac's high-flying dreams of travel to the moon in 1657. We have utopias such as Plato's Republic, Thomas Moore's Utopia and The New Atlantis by Francis Bacon. But Frankenstein was written in an intellectual climate already absorbed with the wonders of the Industrial Revolution, especially the new experiments in electricity, particularly those of Alessandro Volta (1745-1827). Even though no laboratory is in evidence in Frankenstein and no bolts of electricity are shown channeling into the monster's skull (all famous tropes from the dozens of movies that have since been made of Frankenstein), readers in Mary Shelley's time knew all too well that such a monster could be created by science.

Mary Shelley, who had written the novel as a challenge by her friends one stormy night to write a "ghost story", was herself a child of the future. She was alive at a time when the Dutch empire (the then reigning world-class economy) had begun to lose its influence and England was beginning to feel its oats. Already railroads were changing the face of the countryside with the influx of materials to build factories and mills. Steamships were replacing wind-driven ships and the British Empire was beginning to expand around the globe in ways the Dutch could not. But so quickly was change entering into the consciousness of the average person in England that it was easy for the young Shelley to tap into the angst that the new technologies were creating. In the late 1960s Alvin Toffler in the United States would call this unease "future shock" and define it as an unsettling (and perhaps inarticulate) anxiousness one feels over the influx, on a personal level, of new technology. Anyone who has had to learn computers from scratch or learn a new technology-based skill has felt future shock. Though we in the twenty-first century are used to such rapid change, men and women of Mary Shelley's time were not. Yet the idea, in her era, that a man of protean genius could reanimate a person from dead body parts through the application of electricity seemed to be something that could be done, because people had recognized that electricity moved human muscle. (Any student in high school biology class could duplicate Volta's experiments with animating the legs of a dead frog.) A true sense of the future was slowly creeping into the Zeitgeist of England and it seemed that there were to be no limits on what humans could now do.

Parallel with the development of the Industrial Revolution in the 18th century was the widespread habit of reading among the lower classes. This time particularly saw the origin of the novel itself, especially the gothic novel. While long, serial narratives had been pieced together before the 1730s and made into books (such as Lady Murasaki's Tale of Genji in Japan in 1021 and Miguel De Cervantes's Don Quixote in 1605), the novel as a cohesive, self-contained narrative where character develops as the plot progresses did not come into existence until Daniel Defoe and Samuel Richardson began writing in the early 1700s. These novels often appeared as diaries or journals (Robinson Crusoe and Moll Flanders) because the British public had an aversion to stories that they (or their vicar) perceived were merely frivolous or salacious. Later Samuel Richardson would construct his books as a "collection" of letters, or epistles, from various characters. The epistolary novel was one such strategy to give the appearance of truthfulness (or verisimilitude) so that the reader would no feel he or she was wasting their time with cheap thrills and suffer the possibility of going to hell.

What these authors were trying to avoid were "romances". We use this word differently today, but three centuries ago the term "romance" referred to any manner of adventure or exaggeration of the truth to human or historical affairs. (This would clearly define any of today's identifiable publishing genres: the western, war stories, adventure, romance, detective, spy thrillers, science fiction, fantasy, and horror. All are exaggerated adventures of one kind or another.) Why would some authors want to avoid publishing romances? It turns out that the Protestant Reformation, begun in 1517, was making powerful inroads in the Church of England by the early 18th century. England had kicked out the Puritans in 1620 who had tried to "purify" the Church of England which was then not at all like German Protestantism. But given another century, the Church of England drifted farther and farther from its Roman Catholic affectations and more toward the austere mannerisms of Protestant Christianity. When the Industrial Revolution created the need for workers to read manuals and books in order to run their machines, England in turn passed laws requiring children to go to school in order to read. Still, the prevailing morality suggested that one should not spend one's reading time delving into books that polluted the mind or debased the spirit. One should stay away from romances. (This is why, even in this day and age, science fiction is still not considered to be literature at most universities.) So authors began telling their tales disguised as the reports, the journals, the diaries of supposedly real people. Only when Jane Austen and Mary Shelley began writing did this prejudice began to fade. Ever since, it's practically vanished.

Nevertheless, not only is Frankenstein written in this mode of verisimilitude in order to make the experience of the novel seem plausible to the reader (in the form of letters, journal entries, diary excerpts, etc.), the novel gains much of its effect from its "romance" (or gothic) roots. The gothic tale itself goes back hundreds of years, but officially the first novel published in this genre was Horace Walpole's The Castle of Otranto, published in 1765. The "gothic" in the gothic tale is often hard to characterized, beyond elements embracing the supernatural, the mysterious, the occult ("veiled") sciences such as witchcraft and sorcery. Sometimes it can involve the merely strange. The word itself harks back to the Goths who settled the Balkan countries and built wonderful castles that, over time, fell into ruins and left behind stories in local folklore of craven families, debauched patriarchs, and hints of the other-worldly. This "other-worldly" aspect of the gothic is very important to science fiction. Indeed, science fiction currently can be described as:

> ...an expression in literature of an author's sense of dread based on perceived or imagined changes in society brought about by science and technology since the time of the Industrial Revolution.

This sense of "dread" comes from that slight, perhaps inexpressible sense of unease brought on by some approaching catastrophe that has been let loose because of science or technology.

Mary Shelley taps into this with Frankenstein, capturing that sense of dread in the creation of a monster that now wants to breed and be like his creator. The dread also comes from the mere suggestion that science, coupled with humankind's innate curiosity, might now be able to create all sorts of things we might regret. Hers is a novel of consequences rather than character. Those consequences are wrought with fear and dread and terror—things we can't see and only barely can imagine.

Advances in printing and publishing were also products of the Industrial Revolution and these were crucial to the success of Frankenstein. Better papers were being invented, better inks and dyes. Better presses were able to print daily newspapers in the tens of thousands without breaking down. Distribution by railroad and steamship brought reading materials to a waiting public faster than ever. Into this same climate, in America, appeared Edgar Allan Poe (1806-1849) who invented the short story. There had always been short narratives: anecdotes, fables, jokes, tales, and the like, but the short story as we now understand it hadn't appeared until Poe came along. To Poe a short story was a self-contained narrative that could be read in one sitting and have a conclusion that resolved some sort of conflict. Like Shelley, Poe wanted a format within which authors could explore the inner life as well as the outer life of a character, but he wanted it self-contained. And he had no qualms about verisimilitude. In fact, most Americans did not.

As the century progressed, most science fiction tended to appear in it's most recognizable format, the novel. The very best of those short stories, some reaching into the 20th century, are contained in this anthology. But the reader might want to read these in conjunction with the great science fiction novels of the 19th century to see how they all fit together. Here are just a few such novels to consider:

Frankenstein, Mary Shelley, 1818

The Last Man, Mary Shelley, 1826

Journey to the Center of the Earth, Jules Verne, 1864

From the Earth to the Moon, Jules Verne, 1865

Twenty-Thousand Leagues Under the Sea, Jules Verne, 1870

The Begum's Fortune, Jules Verne, 1879

Across the Zodiac, Percy Gregg, 1880

The Strange Case of Dr. Jekyll and Mr. Hyde, Robert Louis Stevenson, 1886

Robur the Conqueror, Jules Verne, 1886

She, H. Ryder Haggard, 1887

Looking Backwards, Edward Bellamy, 1888

Urania, Camille Flammarion, 1888

Carpathian Castle, Jules Verne, 1882

The Time Machine, H. G. Wells, 1895

The Island of Dr. Moreau, H.G. Wells, 1896

The Invisible Man, H.G. Wells, 1896
The War of the Worlds, H.G. Wells, 1897
When the Sleeper Wakes, H.G. Wells, 1898

This new genre would not receive a name until Hugo Gernsback would call it "science fiction" in 1929 in the pages of the first magazine to devote itself to all science fiction stories, Amazing Stories. Critics have often blamed Gernsback for ghettoizing science fiction by making it strictly "pulp" fiction—a kind of adventure fiction for teen-aged boys—but in an earlier century many authors dabbled the tropes and conceits common to this new genre all in the service of literature. These included authors such as James Fenimore Cooper, Johann Wolfgang von Goethe, Honoré de Balzac, John Keats, Edward Bulwer-Lytton, Benjamin Disraeli, Samuel Butler, Guy de Maupassant, and Thomas Hardy to name just a few. In the 20th century, mainstream writers such as Sinclair Lewis, George Orwell, Aldous Huxley, John Updike, Doris Lessing, E. L. Doctorow and Margaret Atwood had all had a hand at writing novels that were clearly science fiction. Some will argue that it's still adventure fiction for teen-aged boys. Others will contend that science fiction is a whole lot more than that. You get to decide.

The Arc Manor Book of Classic Science Fiction is a collection of stories taken from across the 19th century and into the early 20th that shows many of the concerns of a wide range of authors. Some are horror stories; some are satires; some are just strange. As you will see, science fiction today hasn't veered too far from the concerns of these early writers. It's been a vibrant and alive genre from the very beginning.

PAUL COOK is a Lecturer in the English Department at Arizona State University in Tempe, Arizona and the author of seven science fiction novels. His website can be found at **www.paulcook-sci-fi.com.**

CPSIA information can be obtained
at www.ICGtesting.com
Printed in the USA
LVOW08*0336200317
527785LV00004B/46/P

9 781612 423012